Farzana Moon

I0562474

The Moghul Exile

Editions Dedicaces

THE MOGHUL EXILE

Published by:
    Editions Dedicaces LLC
    12759 NE Whitaker Way, Suite D833
    Portland, Oregon, 97230
    www.dedicaces.us

Library of Congress Cataloging-in-Publication Data
    Moon, Farzana
        The Moghul Exiler / by Farzana Moon.
        p. cm.
        ISBN-13: 978-1-77076-483-5 (alk. paper)
        ISBN-10: 1-77076-483-6 (alk. paper)

Farzana Moon

The
Moghul Exile

Dedicated to Ozair. My computer guru,
eeping my blog alive with live links.

Table of Contents

Chapter One - Carpet of Mirth 7
Chapter Two - Prince Hindal's wedding..21
Chapter Three - Din Panah—The Asylum of Faith 37
Chapter Four - Fortress of Chitor...49
Chapter Five - People of the Elephant 59
Chapter Six - Portuguese from Goa 73
Chapter Seven - Battlefield at Chausa..87
Chapter Eight - Grief consecrated 105
Chapter Nine - Prophecy of Exile 119
Chapter Ten - Emperor's Dream-Bride..131
Chapter Eleven - The Birth of an Heir 147
Chapter Twelve - From Helmand to Persia 163
Chapter Thirteen - Gift of Kohinoor to Persian King 185
Chapter Fourteen - Persian Nauroz 197
Chapter Fifteen - Kabul Conquered 211
Chapter Sixteen - Feast of Circumcision...229
Chapter Seventeen - Emperor's Soul Bride 239
Chapter Eighteen - Celebration of Riwaj 251
Chapter Nineteen - Buddha's Blessings...271
Chapter Twenty - Death of Prince Hindal..285
Chapter Twenty-one - Back to Delhi of the Moghuls 301
Chapter Twenty-two - Exiled from the World 317

Bibliography...329

Chapter One
Carpet of Mirth

The justice of Muhammed Humayun Ghazi, Sultan of the Great Illustrious, may God bless his territory and Sultanate.

One gold ashrafi with this *inscription* was floating in Humayun's head and before his sight. Humayun, the second Moghul emperor of Hindustan, was looking down from his royal barge at the glittering waters of Jamna below. He had dropped one ashrafi into the holy waters of Jamna, watching it vanish into its bottomless deeps, where his thoughts alone could arrest the slumbering, ever-scheming fates. His features were lit up by the amber gleam in his eyes, revealing a wealth of youth and energy. A smile, both boyish and whimsical, was curling on his thick, red lips. Though, he was standing there aloof and majestic, in utter isolation inside the confines of his solitude. His handsome features were proud and mysterious, as if concealing the secret of his might and power within the lone recesses of his mind. A whiff of certainty was entering the chamber of his mind, rather the breeze of perfect knowledge that no one would dare impinge on his solitude, not even the Begums, until he himself desired such contact or diversion.

This particular evening, Humayun was donned in green silks, the color of planet Venus. His apparel was in conformity with his mood, brimming with the sense of joy, harmony and kindness. His moods were capricious though, vacillating between gaiety and melancholia. True to its color, his mood was mingling with the serenity of the Jamna. And yet, gathering also the sad, poetic shades of melancholy. This veil of dusk, violet and gossamer, and mating with the quicksilver waves, was teasing his aesthetic senses. Inside him were the hungers of the soul famished and of the soul gluttonous. He could literally feel the rills of silence inside his soul, as he stood there inert and contemplative. Though master of his solitude, he could not pretend that he was alone. The soft murmurs of gaiety, mingling with song and music, were reaching his awareness. These familiar sounds were drowning the laughter of the lapping waves down below, and rising above the surface of his awareness like sweet intruders.

He was awakening from his reveries and absorbing all railleries, so tempting, so irresistible and so frolicsome! Some wild impulse was pressing upon his heart this brand of a need, that he should join the festivities and abandon himself completely to the seduction of merrymaking. But his solitude was stern and forbidding, offering him the wine of serenity, and keeping him imprisoned inside its own walls of ether and oblivion. His gaze was feasting on the canvas of peace and beauty, so vividly etched on the blue bowl of a sky with strokes bold and artistic. He could not tear his gaze away from the ochre and vermilion handiwork of nature, the jewel-bright streaks quivering and diving deep to explore the treasures of immortality.

Little did the young emperor know that this sense of peace, within and without, would not last long? Much like his moods, ephemeral and fleeting, it would be effaced by the hands of time? His thoughts could not divine, right this moment, that he would hunger and thirst for such peace and beauty till eternity. And, that if he ever again witnessed such miracles of nature he would be closer to the beauty in death than fleeing away from pain and ugliness in life. Perhaps, he knew, but was not willing to accept this edict of fate.

Nothing seemed to move Humayun out of the spell of this perfect immobility. He kept standing on the deck of his exquisitely carved boat, as if he knew no other world, but the world of his caprice and ingenuity. He had designed this boat himself, the invention of his fantastic imagination. Swathed in crimson silks and partitioned into vast pavilions, this boat was the dream of an architect. It was furnished with a large canopy of gold and silver, and embellished with Zodiac signs of all hue and color. This was earthly heaven, bringing closer the remote luminaries. It seemed that heaven and earth were united. One could see the fates laughing, and the planets tossing hopes in a mist of divinations. All stars were clad in the armor of oracles, spilling the wine of betrayals, or scattering the seeds of fortunes. The eyes of these starry heavens were keen and piercing, foretelling even the destiny of those men who were doomed to exile, knowing neither peace, nor consolation.

The jests celestial!

Humayun was thinking, but his thoughts were returning to the stars of his own invention. This boat, along with other three, was for the sole pleasure of his royal whims, Humayun could hear his thoughts murmuring and protesting. More so, to consecrate the holy waters of Jamna with the gifts of Moghul opulence and splendor, his thoughts were craving praise and approval. All these four boats of the emperor were vast palaces on water, boasting gilded chambers, and colonnades spruced with Persian carpets. There were lush, fragrant gardens too, hosting colorful bazaars and entertainments. These boat palaces were three storeys high with grand staircases leading up to the royal bedrooms for imperial use alone. The most ingenious appurtenances to these boats were the movable iron bridges, reserved for use in case of naval wars. At such times, they could be attached to the pleasure boats to convert them into galleons. All boats could be joined together with the aid of these iron bridges, so that the troops could move easily from one boat to the other without the fear of drowning, while constrained to swim under the burden of fatigue and distance. This way, the need to communicate with all posts at all hours, was satisfied efficiently, reducing the chances of disorder and recklessness.

A thin smile touched the curves of Humayun's lips as he stood there demurring. His thoughts seemed to be wading through the ripples of burnished gold in lapping waves, and absorbing the shores of Jamna. But he was not thinking, only gazing, his thoughts quiet and suspended. Below his deck was the colorful bazaar, half concealed under rich canopies, and half sprawling over the dining hall below. The emperor was oblivious to all, even to the glory of this efflorescent garden which was lending him the perfume of beauty and solitude. A cluster of pink roses on white trellis were wafting their scent, rather teasing his senses, but his gaze was riveted to the sheet of gold-dusk on Jamna. The waves were gilded, the violet and crimson glow from the heliotrope west bleeding through their veins in tinsel-like brilliance.

A jingle of mirth from one of his wives reached Humayun's awareness, and it stayed arrested in his head. With a slight toss of his head, he banished this mirth aside, his plumed turban in green silks with ropes of pearls settling with a shudder. It was lending his six feet stature a few more inches, and almost making him six year younger than his twenty-seven springs of youth. He was in the spring of his youth, indeed! *The purity of soul his armor and yet this very virtue a challenge to his youth and vulnerability!* His fair features hosting a brown mustache and trimmed beard were rather melancholy. And so were his eyes, revealing the sad, happy years of royal duties and burdens. Though, melancholy of disposition, his heart this moment was bubbling with joy and laughter.

The emperor was thinking about his *Basati-Nishat*, the carpet of mirth, all silk-wool of Persian design in blue and ivory. This carpet was gracing the third tier of the boat, waiting for his august presence to preside over the makeshift court of viziers and grandees. He was to announce new changes concerning his nascent reign, but his thoughts were wandering beyond duties and burdens. They were drifting toward the royal chambers on his boat, where ladies of the harem sat whiling away their hours with song and music.

His thoughts were abandoning this vision too, and journeying inward to commune with his soul. Within its depths were mirrored tides upon tides of actions both noble and corrupt, and his thoughts were watching all, bewildered and fascinated. Silent and unashamed, they were peering deep into the lucid tides of his peace-loving soul. Catching a few ripples of passions sweet and terrible, and foundering deeper. Aghast and stunned, his thoughts were retreating, for they had seen the mating of evil with good, and the seduction of purity by corruption. A beam of white, dazzling light was following his thoughts, thundering down commands and challenges.

The abyss impenetrable! The imponderables unconquerable!

Humayun's thoughts were exploring the reeds of his passions, where desires were suckled by the need for lust, not ever sated, always hungering. His first wife of youth was Bega Jan, whom he had ceased to love. Their first son, Prince Alaman, had died young, and that precious loss was forgotten. Their second daughter, Princess Aqiqa was still his favorite, spoiled and cosseted by him. The emperor's second bride was Gulbarg Birlas, gaining his love only on the night of her wedding, and then banished from his mind and heart. Much like his previous marriage, this new bride had fed the hunger of his body, but not of the soul. And he was filled with remorse at the knowledge within him that he would never make love to her again. Such was the paradox of his lusts, needs, hungers and passions, that to divorce love from his heart, he needed no reasons or justifications, guided by his whim and caprice both. His third bride,

10

Aqiq Khanum had been fortunate as compared to the last two, for keeping the emperor's love alive for a couple of months. The fourth bride, Chand Bibi, was more fortunate than the rest, till the emperor had wedded Gunwar Bibi. The dark and celestial, as Humayun called her, but he was already wearied of her too.

Gunwar Bibi! Humayun could hear one frolic of a curiosity in his thoughts, his hands stroking his beard.

Humayun also called Gunwar Bibi, the nameless one, for the ladies of the harem with their love for gossip, were still unsure of the identity of this bride. They all thought her to be the widow of Bikermajit, the Rani of Gwalior. Unsure and vacillating, they wanted to believe that she was the same Rani of Gwalior, with whom Humayun had fallen in love during the conquest of Hind by his father Babur. Humayun could still remember those princely, careless days of wars and conquests. He was nineteen then, loving only the cities of Kabul and Badakhshan, deeming both these cities his love and spouse in one. Humayun had to leave that spouse behind when Babur had conquered Hind at the battle of Kanahwa, commanding him to march to Agra and to guard the treasures of the slain foe, Raja Bikermajit. That was when he had met the widow of Raja Bikermajit, the Rani of Gwalior. She had presented to him the diamond Kohinoor, but he had lost his heart to that *jewel of beauty* with dark, mysterious eyes. Alone and forlorn, unable to possess the love of Rani, he had returned to Badakhshan. He had not only lost his heart, but his soul. His soul searching always the *mystery of the mysterious*! That spark of love unforgotten and unforgettable! So after his accession to the Throne of Hind, when he had wedded Gunwar Bibi in all haste and secrecy, the rumors were flown from Agra to Kabul to Badakhshan that the emperor had wedded his Rani of Gwalior. The nameless one was named? *The mysterious one wedded to lies!*

Could I but snatch her from the fabric of time, I would keep her with me till the end of time! If time was not my foe, permitting me to find my beautiful Jewel— Humayun's heart was aching all of a sudden. His thoughts were fluttering from continent to continent in search of Rani of Gwalior, but they were returning empty handed, defeated by the gluttony of time. Gunwar Bibi was not the mysterious bride, but a misalliance concocted by his mother, Mahim Begum. The dowager queen, fearing the wrath of the mullahs had procured this Hindu bride for his son in utmost secrecy, hoping that she would beget sons, as heirs to the throne.

My heart and soul hungering and thirsting always! What for? Humayun could hear one rumble of a challenge in his quiet contemplations. *Sarvaqad, her voice alone fills me with bliss and peace. The chaste betroth of Munim Khan, is she really chaste? The sorceress! Has she cast a spell on me? Am I in love again? Could I dispatch Munim Khan on some grueling campaign? Death comes easy on the battlefield. But then, would I not banish Sarvaqad from my heart, as I did the whole horde of them whom I professed to love? The only blessed one, isn't she the one, whom I dare not possess? Thirsting only for the sweet wine in her voice and suffering the agonies of passion sublime and exquisite. Am I not drugged with agony, loving this pain of separation? Such longings dear, would they not be divorced if I was wedded once again? The bride of my soul! Where is she? Where will I find her?* His passionate heart was throbbing all of a sudden. Searching not for the bride of his soul, but exploring the graves of his loved ones!

Mamma, where is she now? Is she with the emperor, Padishah? And my innocent son. Are they all together? Humayun's thoughts were stirring the cinders of grief. Though the lips of his heart were uttering the name of his mother, his thoughts were kneeling at the sick-bed of his father, the late emperor, Babur, Padishah.

Do naught against thy brothers, even if they may deserve it— This last injunction from the lips of his dying father was coming alive in Humayun's mind.

Can any man on this planet of greed and ambition love his brothers as dearly as I do my own? No harm shall ever come to them. Humayun could see the faces of his brothers reflected in the mirror of his mind. *Prince Kamran, the vivacious. More of a poet and a cavalier than the king of Kabul and Kandahar. Prince Askeri, the gentle one, ruling his small kingdom of Shambal. Prince Hindal, my youngest and most adorable of brothers! Is he not the master of Kalpi, Alwar, Benares, Gwalior, Dholpur, Kalinjar? Have I not bestowed rich kingdoms on all my half-brothers?* His thoughts were shuffling back and forth into the colonnades of past and present.

The staircase to the present was garlanded with the blooms of joy and hope. Prince Hindal was to be wedded one week from now, the propitious date set for his wedding, the next Sunday. All the brothers were already here to honor the wedding celebrations.

Inside the tunnel of the past were the waters of mourning, where his mother sat on the throne of grief at her husband's death with grace and dignity. She had appointed her brother Asas Ali to honor the rites of death and burial. Sixty mullahs were summoned to recite verses of Quran at the grave of the emperor, for all forty days of mourning. The dowager queen had also ordered the distribution of cooked food to the poor, twice daily, in great quantities. Each day, one ox, two sheep and five goats were required to fix such meals for the entire period of mourning, in addition to a ton of rice.

As soon as the mourning period was over, the queen mother had shifted all her attention to honor the succession of her son, Prince Humayun, with great rejoicings. She was not willing to tarnish the gold of her son's accession to the Throne of Hind with the rust of her grief, and had issued a Farman that all the houses in Agra be decorated for the coronation of emperor Humayun. The court at Agra too was decked like a bride, with candles and garlands. Gold broidered robes, totaling twelve thousand in number, were beautifully stitched and wrapped, to be bestowed upon the courtiers and grandees. On the day of his coronation, Humayun had mounted his jeweled throne to preside over the sea of feasting and rejoicing. The emperor's throne was smothered with maroon velvets, shaded by royal umbrella of golden silk from Gujrat. The pavilions attached to his throne were of shimmering brocades from Europe, and of fine silks from Portugal. His mother had showered gold on his head with her blessed hands, even filling his boat, Kashtizar, with gold coins, to be distributed amongst the poor.

Eat, for wealth is the wealth of God, and life is the life of God, and Qambar Diwana is the cook of God. Humayun was abandoning his solitude at the voice of his merry cook, who was permitted the liberty of announcing the time for serving dinner.

No more a prisoner of his solitude, emperor Humayun was seated on his velvet throne under the crimson sails of his royal boat, enjoying the bazaar of song and feasting. Right below his throne was his famous carpet, Basati-Nishat, the center of mirth and gaiety, its floral motifs dancing and giggling, it seemed. Lamps were lit on all storeys of the boat, since dusk was swallowed by darkness. Though, the sky was studded with a cluster of stars, white and throbbing. And a luminous moon was suspended up high, pale and waxen. More than a thousand guests sat below the throne, drinking and feasting, while the emperor sated with food and drink, was feeding his soul with the light and beauty of Sarvaqad. He seemed oblivious to the presence of his young brides, all perfumed and bejeweled, much like the scented blooms in his boat-garden which he had designed himself.

This particular evening, even the star-studded sky didn't lure him to its celestial mysteries, his love for astronomy and astrology obscured and forgotten. Indeed, nothing could divert his attention from beautiful Sarvaqad, who alone had stolen all stars from the sky, gathering them in her eyes as brilliant as the diamond-blue heavens. Her small face with fair features was bathed in light from the diamonds in her hair and around her throat. She was all light and sparkle, her silks too stitched with diamonds. Only the fire of red, red rubies on her lips, evoking the sweetest of songs, was melting the emperor's heart to tears of ecstasy.

A medley of tunes on the strings of sitar was filling the night air with sadness. Though, this sadness was donning the mantle of cheerfulness at the sudden explosion of loud beat from the tablas. Humayun, drugged with joy, more by the wine in Sarvaqad's eyes than by the cups of wine mixed with opium, was heeding the jests of his wives, along with flatteries from his aunts and brothers. They were extolling his genius in creating this wonder-boat, the size of a great city. The emperor was absorbing all jests or flatteries, but his soul for some vague reason, was reflecting unrest and vacuity. Rather, isolated in its orb of silence, it was venturing on a journey to lift the veils of illusion and ignorance. His heart was longing for some bride chaste and eternal. Apparently, the center of wit and parlance, Humayun could see illusion reflected from the flames of candles in gold candelabras, to the flagons of gold swollen with the sweetness of wines rare and exquisite. He had just washed his hands in rose-water from the gold ewer offered by his ewer-bearer, his gaze sweeping over the sea of his courtiers where they sat laughing and feasting. A sea of color it was, all turbans jeweled and sparkling spilling some aura of mirth and grandeur.

Humayun himself had chosen those colors for different sets of turbans, so that he could distinguish the ranks of his courtiers at a mere glance, without getting deep into the rituals of etiquette and presentation. The color of superstition was in the emperor's head when he had selected those turbans, but now that was faded to the hue of caprice and insignificance. Purple turbans were bestowed on

14

the nobles and the grandees, besides being the legacy of the royal princes and of the high-ranking officers as the imperialists. The poets, mullahs, writers, attorneys and philosophers were assigned the color saffron. Green turbans were the sole right of the singers, painters, musicians and architects, in addition to the patrons of art and literature. Suddenly, the color of superstition in Humayun's head was alive and vivified, evoking different names and nuances which had made him the architect of this varied scheme in hue and distinction. Color purple had adopted the name, *Ahl-i-Daulat*, meaning, prosperity. *Ahl-i-Saadat* signified color saffron, denoting success. And bright green by the fantastic name of *Ahl-i-Murad* had no other connotation, but desire.

Colors most sweet with connotations exquisite! Not just colorless words? What wordless fortunes? Humayun was losing interest in colors.

Sarvaqad was spilling the libations of wine in songs from her lovely lips, adorably and mysteriously. Humayun was drinking from her eyes alone, his gaze alighting on Munim Khan, and kindling the flames of jealousy and bitterness. Longings nameless and implacable were rippling inside him with a sudden violence, his heart throbbing and shuddering. It was hungry for the ambrosia of love, dying to unveil the bride of his soul. His gaze was bright and blazing, searching the faces of his brides, and then sweeping over to the ladies of the harem with a quicksilver awakening. Princess Gulbadan, the emperor's lovely bloom of a youngest sister, was the first one to graze his awareness. Seated next to her was his aunt, Khazanda Begum. Bibi Mubaraka Begum, the beloved wife of his late father, had her own circle of companions, Dildar Begum and Gulrukh Begum, two other wives of the late emperor, including two concubines, Gulnar Agacha and Nurgul Agacha. Humayun's gaze was restless and wandering, returning feverishly to Sarvaqad. His heart was pierced by the sting of *need and longing*. Each splintered throb within him blistering forth to efface the whole horde of humanity from the face of this earth. With the exception of Sarvaqad, of course, the *Venus of his soul*! The emperor's gaze was frolicking again, arresting Biram Khan in its wake, where he sat inspecting the gold arrows with utmost absorption. These gold arrows were Humayun's invention too, inscribed with numbers in conformity with the ranks of his viziers.

"Come, Biram, bring those arrows here. The emperor needs to shoot commands through them, if not fill the coffers of his court with the gold in wisdom?" Humayun shot an abrupt command. His eyes were lit up with amber brilliance.

All other voices were dwindled to whispering at the sound of the emperor's command, only the night breeze defiant and groaning. Biram Khan was stumbling to his feet with an arm-load of gold arrows, and hastening toward the throne. Even Sarvaqad had stopped singing in rapport with the pervading hush and silence.

"Please do not deprive us of the sweet wine of music in your voice, Sarvaqad Begum." Humayun requested softly, his attention shifting back to Biram Khan.

"Your Majesty." Biram Khan offered perfect curtsy as introduced by Humayun. The emperor had named this curtsy taslim, the art of bowing low with a great flourish. "Thirteen gold arrows in all, Your Majesty. I thought you ordered twelve?" He held out the neat bundle.

"Thirteen in all, that's what the emperor wanted. Even if one arrow was less, someone would be accused of royal theft!" Humayun sipped his wine thoughtfully. "The one with number thirteen the emperor ordered for Shah Tahmasp of Persia. That will be sent to him when his kingdom is as large as the empire of Hindustan?" He snatched one arrow out of the bundle, his gaze sweeping over all with a somber intensity. "This first arrow the emperor claims for himself. This would be my talisman to rule and protect my vast empire. And this second one I present to my dear brother." He held out the arrow engraved with number two to Prince Kamran, his younger half-brother. "May you nurture the seeds of unity and harmony amongst all brothers for the prosperity for our empire?" He smiled.

"Your Majesty." Prince Kamran offered impeccable taslim, his poetic genius spilling forth one impromptu couplet.

"To Kamran, thy love and kindness are gold
To Your Majesty's fortunes, this poor prince is sold."
His lips were professing love, though his heart was concealing deceit and corruption.

"Poor princes barter love for gold, Kamran, their hearts seduced by the glitter of greed, I have heard." Humayun's eyes were lit up with a smile both wistful and enigmatic. "The emperor hopes, dear Kamran, that you will exchange not your kingly robes

16

with the rags of slavery. You are the king of Kabul and Kandahar, with riches boundless, and you must guard these treasures with wisdom and perspicacity."

Prince Kamran bowed low in silence. The lamps of Lucifer-charm in his hazel eyes were kindling bright stars, as he retreated to his seat, smiling winsomely.

"Prince Kamran, Your Majesty, has twice the riches in wives than in kingdoms." Prince Askeri claimed the emperor's attention, his look half mocking, half inebriated. "While, I the lonesome prince have only one kingdom to rule. Shambal and that too home for the exiles."

"You have taken a vow to celibacy, if the emperor is not mistaken. How are you going to win the kingdom of houris, if you shun marriage?" Humayun tossed a gentle reprimand at his drunken half-brother, seven year younger than Prince Kamran. "If Shambal is home for the exiles, then many kings covet that prize, don't you know? You believe in canards, I fear. Besides, you are distracting the emperor from his duties." He claimed another arrow from the bundle, returning his attention to his courtiers. "This arrow is the emblem of wisdom and knowledge. I bestow this upon Maulana Bekasi. You are assigned the duties of nurturing and promoting art and literature, as well as theology and philosophy.

"Your Majesty." Maulana Bekasi staggered to his feet. He was overwhelmed by this honor, for he was expecting Maulana Ferghali to be entrusted with this duty, since he was the chief theologian. "I am honored beyond—" He couldn't speak, numb with pride and exultation. Claiming the gold arrow, he retreated amidst his succession of curtsies.

"Terdi Beg, fortunes are yours to claim and retain under the grace of this arrow." Humayun was quick to retrieve the next arrow, his eyes shining with impatience. "All the imperialists will be under your command, including the viziers and grandees. You will perform your duties with honesty and diligence."

"Your Majesty." Terdi Beg bowed low. Unskilled in offering taslim, he stumbled before returning to his seat.

"This fifth arrow is for Ali Kuli, giving him authority to preside over the councils." Humayun began exigently. "The sixth one goes to Haji Muhammed, who will be responsible for scheduling the council meetings. Khan Birlas and Abdal Hai are to receive the seventh and eighth, entrusted with the task of recording the minutes of all council meetings." He was commanding his royal attendant to present these arrows to the men just named.

"Your Majesty, Your Majesty—" All four recipients were singing a chorus of thanks and curtsying.

"Jouhar, the emperor's cup-bearer, gets the ninth one, burdened with the task of looking to the needs of all the royal ladies in my harem." Humayun was losing interest in assigning duties.

"Your Majesty!" Jouher's eyes were lit up with joy and pride. His taslim was lengthy, as he almost prostrated himself at the foot of the throne.

"Muhrdar will guard and protect the imperial treasury under the seal of arrow number ten. Number eleventh is assigned to Khwaja Ibrahim, vested with the power to bestow gifts of crown lands on the men of valor and distinction. Biram Khan, of course, gets the twelfth one, acting as the master of generosity, bestowing robes and honors on men of talents with great inspirations." Humayun's eyes were lit up with the stars of caprice and mischief all of a sudden. "Shah Tahmasp will be the recipient of this last one when he can make his lean kingdom of Persia grow fat with lands and riches." He let this last arrow fly toward Prince Askeri, who in an act of catching it spilled his drink. "Drink from the carpet of mirth, my happy Prince." A volley of mirth escaped Humayun's lips. "Persia is really a dot on the map of the world as compared to the Moghul Empire. Our empire stretching northeast from the river Oxus to Balkh, Kunduz and Badakhshan, then to Delhi, Kabul, Ghazni and Kandahar! South western dominions are ours too! Punjab, Abohar, Sirsa, Hissar, Multan, Ganeshgarh, Hanumangarh, and the kingdoms of Sindh, just to name a few." He tossed one pellet of opium into his mouth from the gold bowl beside him.

The emperor was laughing, but his heart was rigged with longing and loneliness. Sarvaqad was painted in there somewhere within wounds deep, throbbing with lusts and desires. The serpent of jealousy was uncurling its lips inside the pit of his stomach. The serpent of agony too, leaping out of his soul, was challenging the serpent of jealousy. Some strange, terrible emotions were simmering and exploding inside the very rivers of his psyche, his gaze sweeping over his aunts, wives, princess', all dear and beloved.

"My dear, beloved all. Though the emperor is besieged by warring factions and rebellions, his thoughts always turn to the ladies of his harem, their safety and protection foremost, always." Humayun began dreamily and reluctantly. "Hindustan, unlike Kabul, is not the place where royal ladies can indulge in the pleasures of riding and hunting. This is the land of passions and prejudices where one must guard one's virtue at the cost of freedom. All ladies of the imperial household, from now on, are requested to stay within the walls of the harem. We will have gardens, bazaars and entertainments inside the very gates of our palace, and much more if anything is missing. The emperor will issue a Farman concerning this change, after the wedding of Prince Hindal." His thoughts were licking clean the flames of agony and jealousy.

"Your Majesty, will you permit me to speak as Padishah did, though I am not that young anymore?" Princess Gulbadan ventured a protest. Only a bloom of eleven summers, she looked much older in her velvet gown, with a matching cap strewn with rubies and diamonds.

"Only because you were much loved by Padishah, my sweet Rose." Humayun could not help borrowing this endearment from the lips of the late emperor. "To honor the sweet memory of our father, how could I deny you your request? If you don't protest too much, you may proceed." He smiled indulgently.

"Mahim Begum, Your Majesty, didn't she sit on the throne with Padishah, in open court, in Kabul?" Princess Gulbadan began diffidently. Taking advantage of her privileged position as being the youngest sister of the emperor. "Even I sat with Padishah in his court at Kabul, remember, Your Majesty? I can't stay inside the harem, Your Majesty, please. I like to ride. Riding, if not hunting" She couldn't continue, overwhelmed by the stars of amusement in the emperor's eyes.

"*My sweet rebel!* Borrowing this endearment from Padishah, if I may?" Humayun's eyes were lit up with the songs of mirth and mischief. "Mahim Begum, may God rest her soul in peace. She was not only my mamma, but a great mother to all my brothers and sisters, and you want to use her name as a bait to tempt the emperor to change his mind? Did she not tell you that you are a little philosopher, and would rob all scholars of their wisdom? Well, sweet Princess, Padishah of Kabul became the emperor of Hindustan. And I am sure of one thing at least that honoring the customs of Hindustan he didn't want royal ladies to go riding. If he was alive, he would not be able to retain the former etiquettes of his court in Kabul. So, be content, my dear. Those vivid stars of poetry in your eyes! One day, you would write the history of the Moghul court, the emperor can tell." His gaze was shifted to one bloom of a young princess beside his sister, whom he had not noticed before. "Come, dear Rose, sit with the emperor." His attention was already turning to his aunt, Khazanda Begum. "My dearest Aunt, who is that lovely bloom seated next to my sister?" He murmured, since Khazanda Begum was honored with a seat next to him.

"Maya Jan, the orphaned princess from Badakhshan, Your Majesty." Khazanda Begum breathed low. Her opulent coronet studded with diamonds was accentuating her pallor.

"She will be my bride, even before Prince Hindal's wedding, I am sure." Humayun murmured back. He was watching the jeweled cap on his sister's head, as she posted herself at his feet in one velvet heap. Remembering suddenly, the different connotations attached to a cap and the coronet. *Unmarried princesses wore the caps, while the married ones adorned their hair with coronets.* "Order a precious coronet for that white rose from Badakhshan, dear Aunt. She won't be wearing that small cap anymore." He intoned whimsically.

"Your Majesty! She is so young." Khazanda Begum's protest died on her lips by the sudden kindling of fire in the emperor's eyes.

"Her youth itself lends her the privilege of becoming the emperor's bride." Humayun smiled, getting to his feet in a spurt of impatience and restlessness. "Basati-Nishat needs rest, and so does the emperor." He held out his arms, receiving Princess Gulbadan in one eager embrace. "Lull my Rose Princess to sleep, dear Aunt, and the emperor himself will retire to his lonely bed, not courting the pleasure of his happy brides," He linked his arm with his aunt's, holding close Princess Gulbadan with the other. He was dismounting his throne, dreamy and sightless.

Chapter Two
Prince Hindal's wedding

Prince Hindal is my spear, my strength, the light of my eyes, the sight of my arm. The desired, the beloved! Humayun replaced the pen in jade ink-stand, resting his head against the velvety back on his gilt chair.

The emperor was seated at his rosewood desk in his royal library called, House of Good Fortune. Donned in purple silks with jewels blazing from his turban down to his cummerbund, he seemed to be the master of fortunes indeed. But his thoughts were commencing a journey most strange and perilous. Seeking dewdrop visions inside the eyes of the starry nights, and avoiding the abysmal deeps where treason and corruption stood raw and throbbing. The faint ripples of music and laughter from the hall down below were reaching his awareness, and splintering his thoughts. This hall named, Mystic House, was brimming with guests and musicians this very evening, in celebration of Prince Hindal's wedding. The emperor's own wedding with Maya Jan was celebrated a couple of days ago, with song and feasting.

The emperor's wedding, evoking no songs of bliss or rapture—only carnal pleasure. The weight of poetic melancholy in Humayun's heart was pressing his thoughts to explore the unslaked hungers of his body and soul. *So many brides and not even one of them staying in the emperor's heart! Strange, that one loves, and loves not? Bega Jan, Gulbarg Birlas, Aqiq Khanum, Chand Bibi, Gunwar Bibi, Maya Jan, don't I love them all? Loving all, as I love beauty in nature! Jewels and feasts too, and music and pageantry, all my loves. One love. Astronomy the greatest of my loves. And yet, my soul, dark and loveless. Searching. For what? For a perfect bride! Will I ever find her?* He was not writing these thoughts, only contemplating.

The journal was abandoned, along with his royal mood, shifting from one of deep concentration to frolic and levity. Paradoxically, he was trying to avoid the strange, disturbing thoughts which were concealed inside the dark chambers of his mind like the little troopers, equipped with secrets they could not contain. He was surrendering himself to their sudden assault, and becoming a victim of his honed perspicacity. Had he been less perceptive, he would not have discovered the rivers of greed and corruption inside the hearts of his brothers, but as it were, those rivers were a shining mirage in his psyche. This mirage was no illusion, but a shimmering reality, which he didn't wish to touch, for his kind and loving heart couldn't endure the sight of ugliness and wickedness as far as his brothers were concerned.

Prince Hindal has a heart of gold, though vulnerable to intrigue, if left without guidance. Humayun's thoughts were rising in defense against his youngest brother, before embarking on an expedition to peer into the souls of the others. *Prince Askeri, intrepid and scheming. Prince Kamran, devious and wicked! Whipped by ambition? And yet, why do I love them, condoning their faults? Loving them, always*—His thoughts were chasing his royal cousins instead. *Wretches ingrate! Inveterate rebels, the whole horde of them. Zaman Mirza, didn't I bestow the jagir of Behar on him? Sultan Mirza, didn't I make him the lord over Qunauj? And Khutb Wali, whom I loved and trusted? Shah Mirza and Ulugh Mirza too, all turned rebels, betraying the trust of the emperor, joining hands with most hated of my foes, Behader Shah, that Afghan Rat! Intrigue and rebellion, twice over, and forgiven each time! How unfortunate that they couldn't desist from rebelling again, meeting just punishment, blinded with fire-pencils.* His heart was fluttering all of a sudden.

The rills of contemplations in Humayun's head were splitting and crackling. The threats of looming wars were spinning before his mind's sight, curling above and beyond into the plumes of ruin and devastation. Rebellions were fermenting in clouds distant and menacing. The bolts of seditions were raining down their hungry flames to kindle the fires of greed and ambition.

Shah Tahmasp of Persia! Flaunting his standards of Fish over Herat and Khorasan. Marching power-mad to subjugate the Osmanli Turks in Azerbaijan. Ah, that Persian reptile, rendered impotent by the rebellion of Alom and Takhy, who were wise to seek alliance with the Osmanli Turks! What a cauldron of intrigues? Shah Tahmasp defeating Obeid Khan in Herat, then marching onward to conquer Ghurjistan. And where is Obeid Khan now? Finding refuge in Bokhara, I guess? And now, Sulaiman The Magnificent, plotting to lay Iraq under siege? Humayun's thoughts were tumbling over a mound of chaos and confusion. *Rajas, Afghans, Rajputs, they too violating the peace of our empire, slitting open the womb of Hindustan with daggers sharp and poisonous! Behader Shah stirring revolt in Chitor. The city of Churan simmering in revolt by the genius of Sher Shah? Sultan Ibrahim baring his fangs to devour the kingdom of Juanpur! Isn't he goaded and supported by the very villains of Hind, Baban and Bayezid? While the emperor sits in his palace at Delhi, celebrating the wedding of his dear brother with feasting and entertainment?* A veil of silence was lowered over his thoughts, dark and impenetrable.

The emperor was stirring to his feet, slowly and thoughtlessly. Listening to the mirth of scorn within him against the warring maggots that were not powerful enough to challenge the might of the Moghul Empire. This music of inner mirth was dear to emperor's mystic temperament, as he snatched a pellet of opium from the gold bowl on his desk, and tossed it into his mouth. He stood there demurring, heeding not the voice of his psyche that all those maggots, along with his dear brothers, would prove to be the bane of his love and generosity. His soul was lamenting some tragedy unforeseen. One shadow of a premonition was crossing over his gentle features, and his psyche murmuring that the very foundations of the Moghul Empire were crumbling. The low murmur of a warning, holding open the book of fate, was eluding him. And yet, he had caught a glimpse most astounding, as if he had lost all and was wandering homeless. Chased and hounded by enemies from the very shores of Oxus to the borders of Persia, his great spirit crushed and bleeding.

Leering fates, most false and cunning! What sense is there to dig the splinters of future sorrows, when joys and fortunes are visiting my palace? Humayun sailed past his desk, his gaze sweeping over the layers of books on polished shelves with a devouring intensity. *Out of chaos comes peace. Conformity and renunciation too! And the renewal of joy.* He thought aloud, turning to his heels. His intention to leave the library was stalled by the breezy appearance of Maya Jan.

"Your Majesty." Maya Jan dipped her head in a brief curtsy, her gold-brown eyes sparkling brighter than the opals and diamonds in her hair. "Your brother's wedding, Your Majesty, and you are shutting yourself up in the library. Prince Hindal is longing to see you and wondering when you would come down?"

"My Beauty." Humayun caught her in one eager embrace, kissing her with the sudden fever and hunger of a famished lover. "Tell the impatient bridegroom that the emperor would join him in a month." He released her laughingly.

Maya Jan had fled all flustered and blushing. Laughing to himself under the spell of capricious mirth, Humayun emerged from the library with the intention of following his wife, but his feet were leading him toward the House of Pleasure. This grand chamber, all gilded and adorned with tapestries, was selected by his wives as their haven for pleasure and entertainment. But right now it was abandoned in favor of the wedding celebrations downstairs, and left in a glittering disarray, revealing the neglect and carelessness of the royal occupants. Mirth had left Humayun, his eyes dazzled by the clutter of jewels and dresses on the bedstead where his wives had discarded them in their haste to adorn themselves for the wedding with something more precious than the ones left behind. Involuntarily, Humayun snatched one necklace of rubies and diamonds from the blaze of jewels on the bedstead, his gaze admiring the sparkle of ice and fire on the palm of his hand.

Leo wedded to Aries in this work of art. Humayun's thoughts were exploring the heart of astronomy in this glitter of gold and jewels. *This could be a perfect gift for the bride of my soul? Alas, that the emperor lives under the sign of Pisces, and rubies would never serve as harlots to the lust of bloodstones in their fixed orbits. Will I ever find the bride of my soul? Where is she?* His heart was hammering all of a sudden. Laughter was not far behind, an imperceptible shudder crawling down his back like the hiss of a serpent. He turned abruptly, confronting two royal blooms as his wives, mirth trilling on their lips.

"Your Majesty, Your Majesty." Both Bega Jan and Gulbarg Birlas curtsied.

"More emissaries from the bridegroom, if the emperor may be permitted to toss a wild guess!" Humayun joined them in their mirth.

"A brilliant guess, Your Majesty! Sure as daylight, Prince Hindal is longing for your company." Bega Jan teased, her cheeks flushed.

"And Khazanda Begum, Your Majesty, is willing all her thoughts to lure you to your jeweled throne, which is installed in the middle of the Mystic House, and waiting for your pleasure." Gulbarg Birlas chanted mirthfully.

24

"Sad and pitiful, that my wives don't want me down in the Mystic House, only my aunt and my brother!" Humayun declared. "And yet, the emperor is willing to join the festivities right this minute if you fetch all his wives to persuade him?" He challenged, recalling their secret schemes.

"Aqiq Begum, Your Majesty, can't come. She has changed her mind this third time, and still can't decide which jewels match which dress?" Gulbarg Begum was quick to whip up this bright excuse.

"Chand Begum, Your Majesty, has banished us all from the feasting hall. Commanding us not to speak to her till all the arrangements for the wedding feast are in perfect order. And Gunwar Begum can't possibly leave, being assigned the honor of sitting with the bride." Bega Jan concocted this jumble of lies, smiling winsomely.

"Mystic House needs not the emperor then! Not right away, as is obvious." Humayun stood guarding the secret of his wives inside his heart. "Besides, the emperor must court the bride of his solitude a little longer before wooing his brides in the Mystic House." He gathered both his wives into his arms, hugging. "Now, leave the emperor. And let him whet his appetite on silence, so that he could feast on song and music with much pleasure, later, later." He released them laughingly.

Humayun stood curling his mustache after his happy wives had left, leaving behind a trail of mirth and perfume. His fair features were glowing with the inner warmth of knowledge and gloating that the pre-planned rebellion of his wives was no secret to him. He had caught each word of their planning the night before when they sat talking and giggling, not even knowing that the emperor had returned to the adjoining chamber earlier than anticipated. All those missiles of rebellion were now surfacing in Humayun's mind as he stood twirling his mustache.

All of us imprisoned inside the harem! Who put this idea into the emperor's head anyway? Didn't we play polo in Badakhshan? Went riding and hunting? How could we stay confined in our harem, if this notion takes firm root in the emperor's head? Won't we feel stifled? We would surely die! Do you know what I am going to do? Just to show my displeasure, I am going to dress like a man on the very day of Prince Hindal's wedding. Not like a prince, but like a peasant. That would drive the truth home, making the emperor think and relent. Aqiq Begum had been the first one to kindle the sparks of rebellion.

Maulana Bekasi must have put this idea into the emperor's head, who else? Bega Jan had commenced in a fever of rage and protest. *Imagine, how dull and funereal the court life would be without the presence of us bright and beautiful wives? The courts would be invaded by the mullahs. No wit, no song, no music and no laughter. All those fools and bigots! Where does it say in the Quran that women should stay inside their homes? How these mullahs have distorted each word out of proportion, don't you see? The streets of Hind are witness to their edicts false and shameful. Isn't it a shame that Muslim women fall victim to such grand lies through the lips of the men with false piety? Veiled, as if in mourning? Or, walking like ghosts on the streets under the billowing weight of rough cotton, more useful for burial shrouds, than for mockery in living and believing—* More protests, wild and feverish, had snipped short the spool of her thoughts.

*We should all be dressed like men, and follow Aqiq Begum's brilliant plan—*A chorus of protests, similar in context, had caught tides upon tides of mirth.

No, only Aqiq Begum and me should dress like men, since she shared this plan with me first! Chand Begum's suggestion had fluttered above the din of mirth. *The emperor might get angry? Oh, Prince Hindal's wedding, let's not—* Chand Begum's fears had been drowned in another volley of mirth.

Humayun could not recall any more, laughter bubbling in his eyes and heart. The emperor was abandoning his bower of reveries, and sailing out of the House of Pleasure. Scuttling past his library, he was tempted into the sanctuary of another chamber named, House of Dominion. Involuntarily, his feet had come to a sudden halt before the nine military appurtenances, affixed so grandly on the east wall of this sumptuous chamber. Cluttering this grand display were quivers, broad daggers, curved daggers and jeweled scimitars. A jewel-like armor too was gracing this wall, radiating its aura of sparkle and color. He was standing there in utter immobility, his thoughts stealing the quivers of lies, and shooting the arrows of *reason.* Reason was just an insignificant accomplice in his thoughts, usurping the throne of his heart, where hungers of the soul reigned supreme.

What would Sarvaqad say, if I were to issue this Farman? Humayun's thoughts were heeding the protests of his wives. *Is the emperor jealous? Isn't jealousy the root of all evil?* The cinders of his loneliness were blinking ignorance. *Yes, my sweet rebels are right! Bigotry and intolerance in Islam! The wounds of zeal from ages past, bleeding through the flesh of lies raw and countless. The Lodis, the Sheikhs and the Sikanders. Bigots and tyrants all. The soot of dogma, and the rust of false piety, always clinging.* His thoughts were seeking the pavilions of Din Panah.

Din Panah, meaning literally, *asylum of faith*, was the sole sanctuary of Humayun, designed by him to fulfill his need for *unity and peace*. This grand edifice was erected on a small hill overlooking the waters of Jamna, and only five miles away from his palace at Delhi. The emperor had chosen this site for its aesthetic value, learning much later of its significance other than its charm and beauty. Before Din Panah could lift its head in grand style, a host of facts were unearthed from the mouth of this dainty site, joined by a succession of rugged hills. Those hills hosted the tomb of saint Nizamuddin, making that spot holy for the Muslims. Polishing it further with the gold of holiness, for the Pandavas in the Holy Book of Mahabharata had graced this place with their presence. Sacred to the Hindus, this same site by the name of Indraprashta was to become the cradle of faith as Din Panah.

The unfolding of such facts was elixir to Humayun's need for a holy place, and he had doubled his attentions in molding his dream of Din Panah into the architecture of reality. Most of the building materials were imported from the old ruins of Sikri, Kilugarhi and Firuzabad. The emperor himself had laid the first brick as the foundation of Din Panah, and within a few months a whole new city had begun to sprawl in its wake to honor the asylum of faith. And yet, Din Panah was the first one to emerge forth chaste and noble, its low ramparts with curved bastions housing the walls of chiseled stone quite possessively, much like the Arvalli hills in the west, standing guard as the mighty fortifications. Its gilded gates were flaunting one gold inscription, *Shahr-i-Padishah-i-Din-Panah*. In the back of this architectural wonder, was erected one citadel all complete with grille fortifications as a landmark for the construction of palaces and gardens. A mosque with white gleaming minarets, and marble floor in turquoise, was another dream-miracle in the emperor's head, to be incorporated into this grand plan. And a vast library overlooking the flotilla of lagoons on the very shores of Jamna!

And fruit orchards stretching far and wide. Humayun's thoughts were leaving his palace through the Red Gate called Lal Darwaza.

This swift journey in the emperor's head was taking a brief pause at the Lal Darwaza to admire the life-size lions and elephants carved into stone palisades. Journeying through time and space, his thoughts were circling over the vast hall with painted rotunda in Din Panah, where a grand meeting of the minds was conducted last week with great feasting and celebration. The poets and the Sufis, along with the astrologers and astronomers, were invited to share their talents. A host of pundits and mullahs, well versed in religion and philosophy, were welcomed to discuss their faiths in open discussions.

Who were the ones voicing condemnation against the Safavid in that jungle of discussions? And a fire of disapproval for the Ottomans for their acts of tyranny and religious persecution! Humayun thought aloud, recalling one snippet of the discussion. *Sunnis adhered to the first four Khalifas. While Shias, regarding Ali, the cousin and son-in-law of the Prophet, as his lawful heir, considered the first three Khalifas as usurpers. They cursed those three Khalifas in the mosques, openly and fiercely, not sparing them even in their private orisons, and pronouncing them as traitors—* His recollections were splintered by the sudden rustle of silks behind him.

"Your Majesty." Gunwar Begum dipped her silks in one breezy curtsy. "Prince Hindal is craving your pardon, but wishing that you would join him now." Her dark, mysterious eyes were lit up by the profusion of diamonds in her hair.

"My Devi! The emperor is obedient to your command." Humayun linked his arm in hers, sweeping her along with him down the marble staircase.

The vast, octagonal Mystic House, garlanded with vines and flowers, was the hearth of wedding celebrations where Humayun sat on his jeweled throne with Khazanda Begum to his right. A myriad of candles from gold and silver candelabras were casting fantastic shadows over the octagonal cistern in the middle of the room, brimming with lotus ponds and bubbling fountains. A bevy of singers and dancers were entertaining the guests while they sat feasting and gormandizing with a carefree abandon. The wine-bearers too, with gold flagons tucked under their arms, were letting the ruby nectar flow smoothly into the goblets most precious. A legion of royal servants in gold turbans was fluttering around to replenish the banquet tables with viands aromatic and delectable. The mutton dishes roasted brown and pheasants whole in golden sauce, garnished with nuts and fruits. Shami kabobs and nargasi koftas. Cornish hens stuffed with raisins and almonds. Ducks carved in shapes of lotuses, resting on the exotic heaps of rice pilaf. Many varieties of fish doused in dark wines with aspic and honey. And trays upon trays of colorful sweets with beaten thin layers of gold and silver. Humayun's dainty appetite was sated with a few of his favorite dishes, and now he sat indulging in the sole pleasure of wine and opium.

Drugged with both wine and opium, the emperor was feeling light and exhilarated. Besides, appareled in purple silks the color of Jupiter, he could not help but feel beamish and generous. His heart was glittering like the chalice of gold, much like the gold coffer beside him, form which he was bestowing the pearls of generosity in real gold and jewels on friends and family alike. Ruled by the sign of Jupiter, his thoughts were sailing high on the wings of rapture and reveries. His body and soul too, were soaring and expanding, more by the sweet wine of songs from the lips and eyes of Sarvaqad than by the ruby nectar in his jeweled goblet. Now and then, his gaze would drift toward the gilded davenport where Prince Hindal sat with his bride, Sultanum Begum, almost drowned in tides upon tides of gifts and felicitations. Right now, his gaze was arrested to one young princess seated beside the bridal couple. She was wearing a blue velvet dress with a matching cap, studded with diamonds and sapphires. Her soft, white face was radiant, and her large blue eyes attaining the gleam of the velvets and diamonds as she smiled.

"Could she be the bride of my soul? What's her name? I have seen her before? No. In dreams, perhaps?" Humayun's thoughts were chortling inanities.

The emperor could not tear his gaze away from that bloom of loveliness, snatched out of his very dreams! But an abrupt crescendo of music on tablas and tambourines, leaping high in one orchestral explosion was diverting the emperor's attention from his dream-vision to the houris of dancers with gilded studs in their noses and bright tilaks on their foreheads. Amidst this fervor of music and dancing, Humayun could espy Aqiq Begum and Chand Begum dressed as cavaliers, their plumed turbans bobbing up and down as they joined the dancers. Mad as whirling dervishes, they were pirouetting toward the gilded davenport, then kneeling beside the bride, and bathing her hands with kisses wild and passionate.

"Leave the happy bride with her bridegroom, my sweet rebels!" Humayun's command rang out loud and clear. Mirth-rebuke shining in his eyes. "Come, woo the emperor. He might find you comely brides, if you must be wedded to passions rude and perverse." He laughed. "Since you are disguised as princes bold and gallant, the emperor commands you to present these gifts to the bride." He selected a pearl necklace from the heap of gifts beside him. Adding one dress also, of pure silk and glittering with jewel-rosettes of topaz, emerald and turquoise.

Aqiq Begum and Chand Begum trooped toward the emperor with smiles bright and mischievous. Offering sweeping curtsies in the manner of the courtiers, they were quick to claim the gifts, mutely and obediently. And without voicing their concealed protests and grievances, they were happy to carry the gifts to the bride. The bride in white dress stitched with pearls and a coronet of diamonds blazing on her head, was receiving gifts from the happy brides of the emperor with joy and laughter in her eyes. Prince Hindal's gaze was reaching out to the emperor, his jeweled turban with red plume bathing his fair features with rose and sparkle. Humayun's gaze, following his rebel-brides, was alighting on Prince Hindal, and kindling the lamps of affection.

"To you, my happy Prince, the emperor bestows the gift of his love, besides other gifts too numerous to name." Humayun intoned wistfully. "Gold and jewels, and exquisite pieces of furniture, all yours to claim and possess. And slaves from Turkey, Russia, Abyssinia and Circassia are your wedding gifts too. They will keep your kingdom of Alwar healthy and prosperous." He caught the pewter gleam of joy in his brother's eyes, and continued rather boastfully. "Four Chupatak horses, all bedizened and caparisoned, are your wedding gifts too. Including two elephants with gilded howdahs, and furnished with trained mahouts."

"Thank you, Your Majesty, thank you." Prince Hindal exclaimed joyfully, his agate eyes shining with love and gratitude. "Your gifts are as bounteous as your love, and your love I will

30

cherish more than all these precious gifts." The lamps of gratitude in his eyes were bright, stealing the glitter of gold from his brocaded vest.

"Love in its purest form is a rarity indeed, my Prince! Remember that! Against love's purity, all riches in gold and jewels become pebbles, quite insignificant." Humayun's gaze was shifting to Prince Askeri. "Come, my celibate Prince, claim your own gift of love from the emperor. This robe of Chinese silk all woven in gold." His very eyes were commanding half inebriated Prince to the decorum of celebration.

"Your Majesty." Prince Askeri stumbled in his act of taslim, all awkward and flustered. "Your prince, Your Majesty, is wedded to freedom, not to celibacy."

"Freedom, my handsome Prince, has its own fetters of gold, which permit not the victim to seek joys and privileges in life." Humayun was abandoning the task of bestowing gifts into the hands of Khazanda Begum.

Khazanda Begum had attracted a flock of princes and princess', all eager to receive gifts. While Humayun sat sipping his wine, and suggesting a few gifts now and then, to the favored guests and courtiers. Vessels of gold and silver were bestowed on the poets and the artists, and nobles and grandees had received velvet pouches brimming with gold coins and precious jewels. Even the royal servants were pocketing fifty gold ashrafis each, with exclamations of joy and gratitude. But the emperor was losing interest in bestowal of gifts, his gaze skipping and frolicking over the sea of guests, and absorbing colors and nuances. All ladies were a billowing ocean of silks, velvets and brocades, jewels glittering on them in the color of the rainbows. This glitter and sparkle was blinding the emperor's sight, his thoughts accosting the inner sanctuary of peace and silence. Yet, no peace was to be found in there, only longing and restlessness. His gaze too was lured toward the *nameless one*, laughter trilling on her lips and inside the blue oceans of her eyes.

"She is a dream incarnate! Some moon-goddess from mists white and ethereal!" The pools of longings in Humayun's heart were reciting poetry. "The whisper of wind in the pine-valleys from her very throat!" The voice of poetry within him was dying all of a sudden. His soul was expanding with the familiar pain of a quest holy and unforgotten. *It was longing to find its bride lost and*

31

peerless. Though, moon-goddess was knocking at the portals of his sight and sanity. "Must I seek the approval and confidence of aunt Khazanda to wed this young bloom? Will Dear Lady favor the emperor with indulgence and kindness once more? Who will name the nameless one? Biram Khan, perhaps? Where is he?" His gaze wandering in search of Biram Khan was arrested to Prince Kamran. Prince Kamran was wearing a look of suppliant in his eyes, pleading special boons, if not gifts precious.

"The emperor has not forgotten you, my beloved Prince." Humayun caught and held the stark naked appeal in his brother's eyes into his own. He was not deceived by the Lucifer-charm of his brother, but continued genially. "You are the wealthy lord of kingdoms fair and bountiful, my king of Kabul and Kandahar! To you, the emperor holds out choices rich and tempting. Choose what you will? Two Arabian horses of finest breed. Or, perhaps, you would like a pair of Kirman rugs of silk and wool? Maybe, a large chest with koftgari design hosting a treasure of rubies?" The mystic gleam in his eyes was searching the soul of his brother.

"Your Majesty." Prince Kamran swept his arm in one gallant curtsy, raising his goblet in the other hand in the act of proposing a toast. "Your empire may grow and prosper under the shadow of your love and generosity." He made one histrionic gesture, as if concealing the daggers of jealousy inside the folds of his crimson robe. "Your love, Your Majesty, is more precious than all the gifts rich and exquisite. If permitted, I would choose that above all! Then there would be no dearth of jewels or kingdoms. And horses of finest breed would graze happily on the foothills of Kabul. My palaces too, would be adorned with rugs precious and beautiful." The hazel pools in his eyes were ringed with mirth and flattery.

"You would choose unwisely, my fair Prince, and risk losing all the other gifts." A shadow of regret clouded Humayun's eyes as if he had seen the face of evil and greed inside the hearts of his brothers. "The emperor's love is given freely to all his brothers, regardless of time or occasion. How could it be otherwise, holding sacred the injunction of my father on his death-bed. *Do naught against thy brothers, even if they may deserve it.* These words alone are my talisman to keep on loving all my brothers. It appears to me, dear Kamran, that you would rather have gifts than choices, so they are all yours." He smiled, requesting Khazanda Begum to dole out the gifts of jewels to Prince Kamran.

The emperor's gaze was wandering again, restless and searching. It was lingering on Monaim Khan, then shifting to Khwaja Kilan, the trusted friend and advisor of the late emperor. Next, the bridal couple was luring his attention and the nameless one, but his gaze was sprinting toward the bevy of younger princess' where Princess Gulbadan sat talking and laughing. At the sight of his youngest sister, Humayun's thoughts were somersaulting back to his former decision in announcing the betrothal of Princess Gulbadan to Khwaja Khizr. His gaze as well his thoughts were searching Khwaja Khizr in this sea of gaiety and feasting. Soon, he had espied this young beau caught inside his circle of song and revelry. The emperor's own thoughts were suspended in a circle, pacing and demanding release. He was about to summon Khwaja Khizr to his presence, when his attention was diverted to Mehdi Khwaja, the husband of Khazanda Begum, who was landing upon the laughter of the younger princes with a roar of his own. All thoughts were taking a brief pause in Humayun's head and then pacing wildly, as he returned his gaze to Khazanda Begum.

"Dear aunt, how you have neglected your husband! Did the emperor not choose the costliest of robes to be bestowed upon him?" Humayun murmured. Caprice and bewilderment were stinging his thoughts as he heard himself command abruptly, borrowing the familiar endearment as used by his late father. "My Rose Princess, take a seat beside the new bride. Khwaja Khizr, you sit by Prince Hindal. This auspicious day, the emperor announces the betrothal of Rose Princess to Khwaja Khizr." He commanded, puzzled by his haste and impatience.

Princess Gulbadan, all flushed and ecstatic, was finding refuge on the gilded davenport. Khwaja Khizr too, rapt and bemused was sleepwalking toward the garlanded stage where the bridal couple sat greeting and applauding. A flurry of applause in a chorus of felicitations was rising above the melodies of wedding songs. Aunts and Begums were flocking around the newly betroth, and splintering the sweet tunes of music with their cries of joy and blessing. Dildar Begum was the first one to crush her daughter, the Rose Princess, in one loving embrace, tears of joy glistening in her bright eyes. The Mystic House was filled afresh with song and music, the singers vying with the dancers in costumes bright and glittering. Humayun's heart was brimming with love and laughter, especially, when he could behold his nameless one suffused with the light of purity and innocence. She was laughing, her face lifted up to Biram Khan in the likeness of a holy child with all the eagerness of absorbing each word from the lips of a seer or saint.

"Biram Khan, come and sit by the emperor. He needs your advice, if not the kernels of your wisdom and judgment." Humayun commanded above the din of music and felicitations.

"Your Majesty." Biram Khan was startled to his feet. "Your servant at your command, Your Majesty." He curtsied before approaching the throne.

"Who is that flower in blue velvets with eyes the color of stars and diamonds?" Humayun shot his poetic query to the very face of his bewildered vizier, adding. "Could such a rare bloom be branded with an earthly name?"

"That rare bloom is my sister, Your Majesty. Her earthly name is Mah Chuchak." Biram Khan breathed low.

"She is to be the emperor's bride." Humayun declared arbitrarily.

"A child, Your Majesty! She is too young." The icy gleam in Biram Khan's eyes blazed in a silent protest.

"Tender age, my prudent lord, heralds maturity quite miraculously when young girls find themselves wedded before their time." Humayun's eyes were gathering the stars of impatience and challenge. "Besides, young blooms are eager to unfold their longings to the promise of joy and love, nurturing their youth and beauty till ripe age."

"Youth lasts but one brief season, Your Majesty." Biram Khan intoned as if reciting profundities. "Much like an autumn leaf, it succumbs to the dictates of time in a flash, becoming old and wrinkled. The scars ugly and cankerous which we detect in ripe age are but the manifestations of life inside the hideous valleys of time. Youth tainted with age, and beauty marred by longing, before—" He was succumbing to silence by the imperious wave of the emperor's arm.

"The emperor must not wait too long then, my wise mentor." Humayun got to his feet, commanding the musicians to play the tunes for bhangra dance. "My Dear Lady." He turned abruptly to Khazanda Begum. "You will make the emperor happy in becoming his partner for this dance." He linked his arm into hers, leading her down the throne most gallantly.

34

The orchestral medley from tablas and harmonium was carving its way toward the explosion of bhangra tunes, echoing the notes of *dandia* a Gujrati dance. Heaps upon heaps of bhutans were procured by the royal servants, all wrapped in silks and brocades, and shimmering like the candy canes in swirling colors. Humayun was already a part of the large circle, facing Khazanda Begum. His gaze was chasing Aqiq Begum and Chand Begum who were longing to be whirled into this dance by the gallantry of the young princes. An amused smile was alighting on the emperor's lips at this scene, and his voice was carried across the circle to his giddy wives.

"Since you are dressed as princes, my lovely rebels, you can't be led into this dance by the male partners." Humayun's very eyes were flashing rebukes. "You may choose Bega Jan or Gulbarg Begum as your partners." He mocked. "The seeds of rebellion in my harem must taste the fruits of royal etiquettes. Be grateful, my sweet flowers, that the emperor doesn't command you to wear beards, as colorful as your turbans." A volley of laughter escaped his lip.

The bhangra dancers were a billowing sea of color in silks and brocades. Jewels sparkling, and plumed turbans creating their own rhythmic dance, were caught in a whirlwind of music and frenzy. The partners twirling their bhutans seemed to be floating and shifting amidst ripples of thunder and lightning. Prince Hindal and Sultanum Begum, carried on the wings of song and music, were swept into the middle of the circle, their jeweled bhutans a blaze of wonder and fireworks. The wild notes of the music were now lowering their sails, the tals on tablas wooing the gentle notes of the harmonium. A few tides of music were renewing their feverish strain, exploding forth in one final crescendo before the shuddering strain could claim silence. The emperor was whirled into the vortex of dreamland, finding himself paired with the dream-girl called Mah Chuchak.

"You shall be the emperor's bride, my beautiful flower." Humayun gazed into her radiant eyes, spellbound.

The emperor was transported into some world magical and enchanting, as if hypnotized by this beauty in all its perfection. He was lost in the blue pools of those lovely eyes, rather stunned by the vision of truth, so vivid and unashamed. In those sparkling cups, he could see the miracle of youth and innocence with all its awe and fear. Love and adoration too, and the mingling of hate and challenge! Something mysterious and astonishing were unfolding inside the emperor's heart. He was listening to the voice of silence within. *One stark naked spool of time was spooling his life of love and loss into knots of memories.*

Yes, here's the bride of my soul, my lost one! Bolts upon bolts of lightning were flashing in Humayun's head. *I have found her! Must claim her back, body and soul, inside my own soul? I must have her, or I would go stark mad. Must conquer all, love and hate, agony and challenge too, or I will perish for sure?* He was laughing like a child.

"Your Majesty." Mah Chuchak's voice and curtsy were suspended before the emperor's sight. His eyes stinging with tears of mirth.

"You know, sweet child, the time itself shall wait for you till the end of time." Humayun breathed hoarsely. "And so would the emperor." He whirled on his feet, waving farewell to the guests.

Chapter Three
Din Panah—The Asylum of Faith

The soft hands of dusk had washed the Arvalli hills in purple glow. The waters of Jamna down below too were painted gold and mauve by the brushstrokes of this early sunset. Din Panah itself was the jewel of all sunsets, cradled by the island of Indraprashta most adoringly and possessively. It was hosting the poets and the musicians, the viziers and the grandees, the scholars and the theologians. Humayun was their patron kind and generous, seated amongst them like the emperor of the world, as if oblivious to the throes of his empire on the verge of crumbling right under his feet. But deep down inside him were chaos and storm, as if the earth was shaking the very foundations of Hind where all kingdoms lay slain and bleeding. Guided by his moods, not by the sheer virtue of his will, he had learned to deal with all adversities in the scale of action and contemplation, the latter preceding the first.

Donned in Piscean-gray this evening, Humayun's mood was boding inner suffering and deep compassion. His silent thoughts were on the verge of riot and rebellion though, matching the red plume in his turban and the clusters of bloodstones on his cummerbund. There were wounds in his heart and inside the hearts of the seasons, splintered with the daggers of wars and betrayals. Betrayals were countless, threatening still, to devour his empire, garnished with the condiments of carnage, intrigue and sedition. The emperor was trying not to think about war and devastation. Fairly obedient, his thoughts were escorting Mah Chuchak on her journey to Kabul, away from the den of intrigue and rebellion in Hindustan. The bride of his soul was accompanied by Sarvaqad, his bride of the spirit.

Both the brides were leaving Humayun's thoughts, stealthy and sure-footed. Wars were surfacing in his head, scooping blisters of the past in a handful of spring and half the summer. The time itself was lost into the wrinkled face of timelessness before the emperor could return to Agra to snatch a few moments of respite and ideation. Kalinjar was the first south-eastern territory on the border of Bundenkhand, to nurture rebellion. Fortunately, as soon as the emperor had reached there to quell the rebellion, the rebel Raja had sued for peace. A peace treaty was signed, and the Raja had delivered several bales of silver as a token of his fidelity and peace offering. Marching back from Kalinjar, the emperor was informed that Sultan Ibrahim was inciting all the Afghans to rebel against the Moghuls. A large contingent of the imperialists was sent to Dadrah against the chief foes, Baban and Bayezid. Both these foes were killed, and their horde of rebels routed and dispersed.

No reprieve was granted the imperialists in wars, the boon of victories being replaced with more wars and peace treaties. The next expedition was toward Bihar, where Sher Khan was laying siege over the great fortress of Chunar. Wars sprouting like the locusts, Humayun was constrained to sign a peace treaty with the most formidable of his foes, no other than Sher Khan himself. Sher Khan and his son Jalal Khan were permitted to keep the fortress under the banner of Moghul suzerainty, with five hundred Afghans posted there as retainers. Sher Khan's younger son, Kutb Khan was drafted into the imperial army in conformity with the rules of the peace treaty. Then the imperialists had marched headlong to fight Behader Shah, who was gathering his forces on the very borders of Delhi.

While the emperor was embroiled in quelling rebellions in the east of Ganges and south-east of Benares, Prince Kamran was marching toward Lahore with the intention of war and conquest. His intentions were concealed in the shining armor of pretense that he was journeying posthaste to congratulate the emperor on his recent victories in Dadrah and Kalinjar. His pretense was torn to rags, when reaching Lahore he had arrested the emperor's governor, Yunis Ali. Commanding his release swiftly as soon as he had learned that the emperor was returning to Agra sooner than he had anticipated! Skilled in the art of stealth, Prince Kamran was now guilty of conspiring with Behader Shah. On the surface though, he was professing love and fidelity to the emperor. Sher Khan, on the other hand, was violating the rules of the peace treaty, and employing devious means to become the sole claimant of the Chunar fortress. His son, Kutb Khan, had abandoned his duties, contriving a successful escape. Meanwhile, Zaman Mirza had succeeded in escaping the prison of Gwalior, along with Sultan Mirza and his two sons, Shah Mirza and Ulugh Mirza. All these royal rebels had now formed a coalition with Kutb Khan to breed unrest and sedition.

Such were the gossamer mists in Humayun's head, parading wars and intrigues, as he sat on his jeweled throne, feasting on the morsels of wisdom from the lips of the Sufis and the poets. The Zodiac signs painted bold on the inverted bowl of a rotunda above him, were whispering to him in tongues quiet and strange. *He was not the master of fates as he had thought himself to be, and his thoughts were the simmering bubbles of regret and bitterness.* The white mists in his head were longing for love and sweetness inside the comfort of his harem, and effacing the signs of wars and betrayals from the map of his memory. Wine and opium was his dearest of friends, lending him warmth and solace, but his heart was empty and lonely. He was missing the songs of mirth and raillery from the lips of his wives in this monastic-like sanctuary, his own beloved Din Panah. No Farman was yet issued by him as to the seclusion of his harem ladies, but amidst the onslaught of wars and intrigues, he had had no time to conduct courts after his return to Agra. This particular evening, he had literally ripped out time from the scrolls of his royal duties, to indulge in the luxury of scholarly discussions. Wisdom and knowledge were turned loose inside the gilded portals of Din Panah, and time itself was perched high on the throne of forgiveness, for the emperor had decided to play along with the pretense of Prince Kamran. Forgiving, if not condoning his acts of treason and betrayal!

Empty and lonesome, the emperor's heart was reaching out to the bride of his soul. Sarvaqad, the bride of his spirit, was singing to him, songs sad and mysterious. The Kingdom of love inside him was one large abysmal rent, silent and throbbing. His soul was fluttering, as if torn out of his body to embrace the very heavens. Searching for something? Something nameless and unforgotten! Something unattainable and inconceivable. An avalanche of thoughts was crashing against the bridge of his perseverance, making it lurch and sway. The loss of kingdoms was nothing to him, since he was not whipped by the gusts of greed and ambition. But the loss of lives, blanketed with grief and agony, were torments supreme inside his heart and mind. His thoughts were pounding deep into his psyche, melting treason with compassion. Compassion was flooding in his gaze too, as he noticed prince Kamran doubling under the assault of mirth uncontrollable.

"Your mirth, my Prince, is wafting such boundless joy, that the emperor wonders if you have added more kingdoms to your kingship of Kabul and Kandahar?" Humayun flashed his half-brother a warm, yet piercing smile.

"Your Majesty." Prince Kamran curtsied with a slight bow of his head, in conformity with the etiquettes observed outside the regular court sessions. "I have extended the kingdom of my poetry by adding one fresh ghazal! In honor of you, Your Majesty. And I would not barter this ghazal, even for the kingdom of Punjab. No more kingdoms do I covet, but the wine of your pleasure."

"Yes, my handsome Poet, you would covet kingdoms, if permitted? You would, you know that?" Humayun commented without regret or bitterness. "Even for one strip of land worthless, you would sell your poems and inspiration all. Why should you covet Punjab, since the emperor has bestowed on you this kingdom rich with gardens and architecture. Guard it well, for it is the heart of our empire, boasting its wealth in industry and agriculture. Punjab feeds the whole of Hind, and can still spare tons of grain to feed the world. Without the rich bounties of Punjab, we would all go hungry? But right now the emperor is hungering for the morsels of wisdom and poetry. Recite your ghazal quickly, before the emperor decides to exact ransom for his gift of Punjab." The amber stars in his eyes were kindling their own commands.

"Your obedient slave, Your Majesty." The hazel pools in Prince Kamran's eyes were gilded with a poetic gleam.

"May thy beauty grow each moment
And thy destiny be happy and glorious
The dust that rises on thy path
Illumines the eyes of this afflicted
The dust that rises on Laila's path
Its rightful place is Majnun's eyes
He who did not turn around thee like
The outer leg of a pair of compass
Is outside this circle
Kamran, so long as this world lasts
Let the monarch of the Age be Humayun."

He smiled winsomely, his heart a volcano of envy.

"For this ghazal alone, my poet Prince, the emperor bestows on you the kingdom of Hisar Firuza!" Humayun declared. He was genuinely moved by this half enchanting,

40

half flattering verse. "Take care, Kamran. Desist from writing more couplets lest the emperor loses his whole empire in this fiddle of a bargain." He laughed, catching the rills of greed in the eyes of his brother.

"Your Majesty. An Empire for a dirhem I will sell it back to you!" Was Prince Kamran's elated response, his heart ecstatic at this unexpected boon.

"Great God, the emperor of Hindustan is crying for a dirhem!" The poet Kabir sang abruptly, his dark eyes fixed to Prince Kamran.

"Your madness will lead you to the gallows." Humayun flashed a singeing rebuke at the mad poet. "Or, would you prefer death under the feet of a raging elephant?" His eyes were gathering flints of rage.

"Your Majesty." Kabir doubled low under the weight of his chagrin. "I was mimicking the prophecy of a dervish, Your Majesty. A mad dervish who flattered Sher Khan's father once. I heard this story from my father when I was a child."

"Poets are no fools though victims of divine madness at times, my unhappy Poet." Quicksilver gentleness was returning to Humayun's gaze with the caprice of lightning. "You should recite couplets, not canards. Couplets are rewarded with gold, while canards fetch the penalty of death. And yet, the emperor offers you one dirhem for your story. You will be saved from being trampled under the feet of my favorite elephant too, if you are quick to tell this story as told to you by your father."

"Your Majesty." Kabir murmured relief. He continued hastily, noticing the daggers of impatience in the emperor's eyes. "Sher Khan was only four when his father took him to the bazaar. Passing by the sweet shop, he began to fuss, demanding one dirhem from his father to buy sweets. One holy dervish was watching as the father refused to give in to his son's demands. Suddenly, the dervish cried, *Great God, the emperor of Hindustan is crying for a dirhem.* The superstitious father interpreted this cry as some divine prophecy, and bought his son as many sweets as he wanted. Also, he gave one dirhem to his son to keep, and gave two to the dervish. From then on, never in his lifetime he failed to tell his son that he would be the emperor of Hindustan one day."

"Ah, Sher Khan! That intriguing lout! He aspires to become the emperor of Hindustan?" Humayun demurred aloud. "The son of a horse dealer! Doesn't he reek of dung? No kingly garb would ever purge the odor of deceit and wickedness in that low born wretch." His heart was throbbing ominously, but his eyes were gathering mirth and contempt. "A mannerless cur as far as I can recall! One evening, at a royal feast in my father's court, he proceeded to cut his venison with a dagger, and began eating his meal with a spoon. My father watching him remarked amusedly. *This Afghan is a man of sense and spirit.* Taking this remark as some sort of prelude to punishment, he finished his food quickly, and literally fled." He paused, the reminiscent stars in his eyes kindling more lamps of recollections. "No man is yet born to match the foul designs within his heart in intrigue and corruption. He came to Agra as a common soldier, even taking part in expedition to Chanderi, and professing loyalty to the imperialists. Right in the thick of the campaign, he defected most treacherously, and sought alliance with Sultan Mahmud at Patna." His gaze was alighting on the Hindu saints, and it was arrested there. "Unseal the temples in your hearts, my revered saints, and delight the emperor with the wealth of jewels from Holy Gita or Mahabharata. Yet, the tongues of wisdom must wait, tell the emperor of some mad, wild canards which whip Sher Khan with the rods of prophecy and superstition."

"Many canards are settled on the dust of Hind, Your Majesty, but they dare not rise until the emperor commands." Saint Ramanand bobbed his head in curtsy, the saffron plume in his turban protesting. "Sher Khan patronizes all mendicants, especially the one who told him that he would be the king of kings. He frequents bazaars quite often too, searching for omens and divinations. They seem to fall his way too. One day he was walking on foot, when a fakir exclaimed, *Behold, the king of Delhi is walking on foot.* Another canard, Your Majesty, not fit for your royal ears. You wouldn't like it?" He added ruminatively.

"The emperor commands, my beloved Saint. Proceed." Humayun smiled, his eyes attaining the pewter gleam of agog and intensity.

"Hind is the belly of wars and intrigues, Your Majesty, if I may say so." Saint Ramanand began discreetly. "Where ambition fails, greed conquers. Where greed stops, superstition begins. And Sher Khan is climbing the ladder of superstition, posing himself as the holy child of Hind. He himself and his followers are letting this rumor grow and spread that he is the issue of a virgin birth. Before his mother conceived, she dreamt that the moon in its full brightness descended from heaven and entered her womb. And that after he was born the divine light of the moon flowed from her womb into his body."

"From her womb into the tomb of evil and corruption within him! A malefic genius he is, the emperor agrees!" Humayun breathed fire and disdain. "A chameleon of a foe that the emperor must vanquish by guile, for he understands not the virtues of valor and honor in wars." His eyes were flashing, his thoughts digging the tunnels of knowledge sacred or profane. "Virgin Birth, indeed! And this holy child! The tales snatched from the tombs of irreverent pagans and unblessed heathens! Mithra, the archetypal holy child born of Virgin Earth! Egyptian Horus, the Son of Virgin Isis. Greek Dionysus from the womb of Virgin Persephone. Zeus approached Persephone in the form of a snake? Buddha descended from heaven to his mother's womb in the shape of a milk-white elephant? God, the Holy Ghost, in the form of a dove approached Virgin Mary?" His gaze as well as his thoughts was getting wearied. "The emperor can't afford to court the kernels of wisdom this evening, it seems. He must discover means to thwart the ambition of his foes." His gaze was arrested to Prince Askeri. "What do you say, my valorous Prince? Which foe the emperor should vanquish first? Sher Khan or Behader Shah?"

"Both these foes are suing for peace, Your Majesty, or pretending to do so?" Prince Askeri began cautiously, lowering his head in a charming curtsy. "Sher Khan, playing the part of a happy bridegroom, has divorced all thoughts of rebellion, I hear. And Behader Shah, Your Majesty, replied to your command most humbly as you know, *to hear is to obey.* In my opinion, Your Majesty, whoever dares stir revolt first, should be the one dealt with just punishment."

"By the law and virtue of your cunning, my Prince, you are a politician, if not a philosopher!" An abrupt volley of mirth escaped Humayun's lips. "Behader Shah obeys no one. Not even God! Obedient only to the dictates of his mind, he commits the most heinous of crimes. After the death of his father, he murdered all his brothers for the petty kingship of Gujrat. The daggers of cruelty and bigotry are concealed inside his heart, but the emperor knows his designs. One of his own servants, escaping the blows of this tyrant has confessed as much, that he is preparing to deface and destroy all the Hindu shrines in Hindustan." His look was wistful all of a sudden, as he continued. "Ah, those shrines holy and beautiful! Why would anyone wish to efface beauty and holiness? One enchanting temple in Bundenkhand perched high on a hilltop, reminiscent of song and poetry in Mahabharata! The emperor must visit it again. And the Shiva-Purana, with Shiva's name engraved in gold. Below it, the inscription reads, *he who causes time to grow old.* Such exquisite temples to cherish and preserve! Shiva lingas and Jaina statues. Caves inside caves, and temples within temples! Yes, the emperor must not let these treasures succumb to ruin by the sheer insanity of one man, cruel and bigoted. He must vanquish Behader Shah first. Sher Khan will be next, that ingrate wretch, cowering, waiting and plotting."

"Your Majesty." Biram Khan stepped forward, curtsying and seeking the emperor's attention. "Sher Khan is the most dangerous of foes, Your Majesty. Time is his mighty weapon. If left free with time on his hands, he would mold time into bullets and cannons." A string of words were pouring forth on his lips with the violence of a hailstorm. "His mind is cold and calculating. Watchful like a hawk, he waits and plots. Your Majesty knows too well, how he subjugated Bihar with deceit and cold-blooded audacity. Now that he is married to Lad Malikah, he considers Chunar as her dowry, and his possession! He is turning this fortress of Chunar into the pillar of his might and strength. He has even employed one astrologer, who flatters him that he would be the king of Bengal, and that on the first day of his kingship, Ganges will be fordable for one hour. The most formidable of foes is Sher Khan, Your Majesty, and he should be vanquished first."

"Lad Malikah." Humayun rolled this name on his tongue, as if tasting its sweetness. He seemed heedless to Biram Khan's gloom and apprehension. "She is both wise and beautiful, I have heard! The fortunate widow of the unfortunate Taj Khan, isn't that true? Didn't her step-son attempt to kill her, Taj Khan intervening, and being killed himself? Such tireless fates, spooling and un-spooling the webs of shame and murder! Had the emperor seen her first, she might have ruled the emperor and the empire." His thoughts were becoming giddy and restless. "Have no fear, Biram, as far as Sher Khan is concerned, consider him as an insect in the hour-glass of time, and the emperor will deal with him when he dares come out of his cocoon. Behader Shah must be crushed first and foremost! Has he not incited my vizier, Alam Khan, to sedition? That vile traitor, besieging the fortress of Chitor after signing a peace treaty with the Raja! And after accepting the celebrated crown, a jeweled belt and a chest-full of gold ashrafis from the very hands of the Raja?" A shadow of sadness crossed his brow, as he announced abruptly. "Two weeks at the most, and we march back to Kapli and Gwalior. We would capture the fortress of Chitor, the kind Raja must be liberated from the bloody claws of Behader Shah. Look to the preparations of this expedition, Biram, and make sure there is no dearth of comforts for the ladies of my harem." He waved his arm in dismissal. "Sweet mystics and scholars, fill the emperor's heart with the wine of poetry before it journeys forth toward the sun-baked roads on campaigns long and grueling." He closed his eyes.

"Your Majesty, these words of wisdom would drive the warring thoughts out of your head." Prince Hindal snatched this opportunity to recite Rumi. *Every moment drink wine sweeter than life in exchange for every bitterness you have quaffed for our sake.*" He drank deep out of his goblet.

"Your Majesty. The Moghuls have adopted Rumi as their patron god, it seems?" Prince Askeri couldn't help quoting his beloved Rumi.

"Each atom doth invisibly enshrine
The deep-veiled beauty of the soul divine."

"Rumi is the god of poetry, Your Majesty, as we all agree on this point." Prince Kamran could not be left behind, reciting one snippet from Rumi's ode.

"Had Plato seen the beauty and loveliness of that moon
He would have become even madder and more distressed than I."

He watched the emperor open his eyes, reciting another couplet of Rumi.

"Eternity is the mirror of the temporal. The temporal the mirror of pre-eternity. In that mirror, those two are twisted together like His tresses."

"Poetry divine from the pure oceans of the Quran, Your Majesty." Maulana Ferghali began hastily, as if fearing the onslaught of the poets and the Sufis.

"Allah is the light of the heavens and the earth
The similitude of His Light is as a lustrous niche
Wherein is the lamp

This lamp is in a glass
The glass as it were a glittering star
This lamp is lit by a Blessed Tree
An olive, neither of the East nor of the West
Whose oil will well-nigh glow forth
Though fire toucheth it not
Light upon Light
Allah guides to His Light whomsoever He wills.
And Allah sets forth parables to men
And Allah knows all things full well"

"Verse divine and music sublime!" Humayun eased himself up slowly. "The emperor must say farewell to the god of poetry, and to the Prophet of the Quran. He is wearied." He waved his arm in a gesture of dismissal.

The brief journey from Din Panah to royal palace under the dark firmament of starless sky, had added more gloom and loneliness to the emperor's heart. His heart was aching for love and peace, not for wars and campaigns. Abandoning his gilded howdah and a retinue of somber viziers, he had sought refuge inside the sanctuary of his harem. Gunwar Bibi was his chosen bride of the night, and he had satisfied the hungers of his flesh before falling prey to the hungers of his soul. Sleep was continents away from his eyes and thoughts, as he lay awake, suffering the pangs of envy at the sleeping beauty beside him. This surge of envy was splintered by the pangs of agony too, that his passion and violence which had blessed her with sleep, had robbed him of his own, keeping alive only remorse and unsurfeit.

Reason is a chain. Heart a cheat. Body a delusion. Soul a veil. The way is hidden from all these heavinesses, my son. Humayun was seeking the aid of Rumi to summon sleep, but the dark voids in wakefulness were leering at his feeble attempt.

The emperor was flinging open the gates of his soul, where silence with glittering eyes was glaring back at his face. Chaos and storm in sliced chunks of reality were there too, white and gleaming. The ether of awareness was deep and abysmal, looking into the tiny mirrors of time and timelessness. The bride of his soul was there, draped in the pine-valleys of Kabul as her bridal gown. Sarvaqad, riding on the livid chariot of cloud, was singing. The hills and the valleys were intoxicated by the music in her voice, swollen and swaying. A sudden whiff of gusts in thunder and

46

lightning were obliterating all. Mists and storms were playing harlot with each other. Fear was cowering against the robe of longing, and longing was courting presage. Fear and yearning were the slaves of his psyche, he knew them too well, but presage? Yes, presage. He had yet to discover its existence. It was rising within him like a deformity shapeless. Its ugly lips were parting in one terrible grin, and murmuring.

You would lose your great empire. Never again would you return to your palaces, gardens, Din Panah— Those lips were dripping blood at the very altar of love in Humayun's soul.

This altar of love was licking the dewdrop tears in blood, painting a face dear and beloved. It was Rani of Gwalior. His *devi*, lost to him. Devoured by the galaxies of time! Tossed into some oceans deep! One cold, white star was throbbing above her head. A blaze of *illusion*! What was it? This *great illusion* was holding the bride of his soul prisoner. She was melting, reduced to one bubble of a dewdrop. His soul was mourning, pale as the virgin dawn, searching for something in ages past and seasons lost. Fatigue and hopelessness were entering the heart of his mournful soul. All three huddled together. The light of bliss was filtering. Slowly, slowly, very slowly.

Humayun's soul and psyche were closing the portals of illusion, and pounding at the gates of reality. Dreams in droves were slithering by to block the passage of perception and understanding. He was standing outside one mosque with gleaming minarets, inside the beautiful temple of his soul, oblivious to the duality of his flesh and *thought*. All knowledge was laid bare before his sight. He could see and hear the night-songs dancing on the strings of wisdom. Yet, he was alienated from them all. The light of bliss was fading. The temple in his soul was dark and menacing. The mosque was effaced. Cold and shivering, he was pleading asylum inside his heart. *Warm, loving heart was embracing him.* It had all what he needed, the noble mosque, the sacred temple, the *great spirit*. They were all one, twined in one knot, awful and sublime, terrible and mysterious. And yet again, he was outside them all. Alone and forlorn! Shunned by wisdom. Mocked by understanding!

The emperor was whirled into the emptiness of a church. The floor under him gaping open, hurling him toward doors of a synagogue. He was forbidden to enter this sanctuary. Noticing one girl perched at the flagstone steps, weeping.

Come here, little girl. The emperor would guide you down from the end of time to the beginning of timelessness. Humayun's soul was speaking, his psyche aghast. *No more rungs to climb, no more heights to scale. We would turn ourselves into spiders, weaving beautiful webs, all the way from heavens to the very deeps in earth. Leaving future behind. Sailing on the wings of present and returning to the eye of the past. Remember this, my child, now is never, and forever will be ever after.* He was lifted up against the throne of knowledge. Contemplating the stars.

Venus, the harpist, was leading a heavenly choir. Aquarius was sniffing the night air, swollen with the water of pride. Virgo was lowering pewter kisses from its virgin lips. The Sun in Aries was locked in one amorous embrace with the Moon in Virgo. The great Canopus was courting the slender peaks in Yemen.

The emperor was blinking away dreams under the canopy of his own Zodiac signs, which adorned not only his tents, but his boats and royal palaces too. And yet he was suspended between heaven and earth in his sleep. The eyes of the stars were glittering, and singing lullabies to him. Red Ram was caught inside the mouth of Aries. The blue Bull was teasing the coppery mountains in Taurus. The yellow Twins were laughing inside the heart of Gemini. The purple crabs were suckling at the breasts of Cancer. The gold Lion was roaring at the mouth of Leo. The Virgin in saffron silks was kneeling at the feet of Virgo. The scarlet scorpion was resting on the bosom of Scorpio. The Archer in purple robes was piercing the heart of Sagittarius. The green sea-goat was entering the womb of Capricorn. The Water-carrier was draining the citron belly of Aquarius. The gray Fishes were kissing the lips of Pisces.

There is no beginning, no middle, no end, but the continual spool of illusion. Humayun had entered the valley of sleep, exiled? In perpetual exile! Fighting and fleeing. Conquering and abandoning. Wandering from continent to continent! *Nothingness comes out of nothingness, dissolving into nothingness. That's the essence of life, pulsating in nothingness. Aspiring, failing, succeeding, not ever dying and living in nothingness. A throb of negation, false and supreme!* He was finally drifting into sleep, as the god of light, embracing his goddess of darkness.

Chapter Four
Fortress of Chitor

The silken city of tents was a colorful bivouac on the plains of Mandasor. Humayun was seated in his Zodiac tent with his nabobs, viziers and courtiers. The emperor was discussing the strategies in sieges and campaigns, though his thoughts were suing for peace. On the surface, this encampment looked peaceful. The guns were silent after the whole three months of siege, since Behader Shah had decided to adopt the measures of defense in favor of challenging the imperialists to open combat. Not far from this city of tents, down below the ghat were horses and war elephants, also breathing respite from the noise of the cannon and musketry. *Especially, the emperor's favorite elephants, Sharzah and Pastinger, groomed and painted by the order of the emperor's mood and caprice.* Right now, the emperor's mood was one of contemplation, abandoning the rungs of strategies, and retreating into the alleys of times trying and times incongruous. The viziers and grandees were left foundering in their pools of discussions and maneuvers, while the emperor sat hugging his favorite guns, Laila and Majnun, in his thoughts and contemplations.

For the past year and a half, the Moghul Empire was smoldering in flames of intrigues and rebellions. Greeds and betrayals were sprouting everywhere, and the warfare of power and ambition kindling a wildfire. The highways were getting unsafe and dangerous, teeming with robbers and cut-throats. Rajas and kings were not the only ones embroiled in contentions to rule and subjugate, but the foreign intruders too, pillaging and plundering in hope of gaining ascendancy over the local despots. Months without respite the imperial troops had marched from city to city, quelling rebellions and enforcing peace and order. But of no avail, for no sooner did the troops disappear into the next states, that peace and quiet in the cities left behind would rekindle fresh sparks of revolt. The chief foes were Sher Khan and Behader Shah, inciting the lesser lords to sedition and contention. Though, Sher Khan, his territories extending from Barh to river Kiul, was still professing his loyalty to the emperor. Behader Shah too, plotting to conquer Agra and Delhi, was affecting his devotion and fidelity to the emperor. He had sent his vizier Sadr Khan with gifts to the emperor, a copy of the Quran, all lacquered and illumined.

With this gift as his oath of friendship, Behader Shah had continued his siege over the fortress of Chitor in Gwalior. Discovering this act of treachery on the part of this scheming foe, Humayun had marched toward Gwalior with a large contingent of troops. Half way to Gwalior, the emperor was informed that Behader Shah had dispatched his son, Tartar Shah, at the head of forty thousand soldiers to capture Agra. Humayun was then constrained to march back, learning on the way that Tartar Shah had taken possession of Biana, marching posthaste toward the very gates of Agra. Speeding hastily toward Agra, the emperor had then sent quick commands to Delhi, urging Prince Hindal and Prince Askeri to fight and vanquish the traitor before he could reach the gates of Agra.

Both the princes at the head of eighteen thousand imperialists had boldly attacked Tartar Shah, his army routed and slaughtered on the very banks of Jamna. Tartar Shah himself had succumbed to death in this fierce battle on the field of Mandreal. When the emperor had arrived in Biana, this city too was recovered without having the need to fire a single shot. No sooner had he recovered this city, when he had learned that Behader Shah's vizier, Sadr Khan, urged by the ever-scheming foe, had joined his forces with the arch rebel, Alam Shah. And that they were on their way to subjugate Delhi. The emperor along with his royal brothers had then shifted his attention to Delhi. At the approach of the imperialists, the foes were scattered pell-mell, fleeing and disheartened. Sadr Khan and Alam Shah were taken prisoners, and brought back to Agra. Sadr Khan was forgiven by the virtue of his being loyal to his own master, Behader Shah. But Shah Alam was punished for his treason and disloyalty to the emperor. His deceit and defection had cost him one of his feet, which was cut off as a ransom to life.

Marking the end of those expeditions, Humayun had spent one whole year in vain celebrations of his victories, dividing his time between Agra and Delhi. Though aware of unrest and revolt in the territories of Bihar, Gujrat and Bengal, he had totally neglected to take action against intrigues and insurrections. So engrossed was he in his literary pursuits at Din Panah that he had convinced himself that to take notice of such petty seditions was a waste of time. Finally, when he had turned his attention to quell the rebellions, Behader Khan had emerged forth as the master-magician of all warfare, employing guerrilla tactics, and planting seeds of discord in every strip of land. While the emperor had indulged himself in the pleasures of astronomy and entertainment, Behader Shah had spent all his energies and resources toward gathering a fleet of hundred warships. After his failure in capturing Agra or Delhi, he had diverted his attention against the Portuguese at the port of Diu. The Portuguese were filtering into Hind via Cape of Good Hope from Ceylon to Red Sea, and he had decided to test his might with them before fighting the Moghuls. Failing in that enterprise too, he had resorted to the means of breeding contention in every city of the empire to weaken the power of the Moghuls.

Behader Shah's first choice was the state of Malwa, with the intention of lying waste the city of Ujjain on the banks of Sirppa. He had chosen this city for his deep-rooted hatred for the Hindus, so that he could destroy its awesome temple, Mahakali, which was sacred to the Hindus for its semi-mythical importance in the capitol of Vikramaditya. Fortunately, Humayun had learned about the intentions of this most inveterate of his foes beforehand, and had dispatched a large contingent of forces to thwart the designs of Behader Shah. The city of Ujjain was saved, but before beating a hasty retreat, Behader Shah had succeeded in pillaging and plundering the state of Malwa. When the emperor had reached Malwa with reinforcements, its fortifications were a desert of ruin through the hands of Rumi Khan, the master-gunner of Behader Shah. The cannon and artillery of Rumi Khan had caused such devastation, that Humayun upon passing through the crumbling gates of Malwa was moved to tears. Immediately, he had commanded masons to be summoned from Delhi to restore Malwa to its original state of glory and grandeur. Then he had hastened toward Mandasor where Behader Shah had fled after wreaking great havoc in Malwa.

Humayun's thoughts were returning to his tent painted with Zodiac signs, and trying to glean truth out of the secret missive of Rumi Khan who had revealed his wish to leave Behader Shah, and take an oath of allegiance to the emperor. Dressed in the pale gold of Saturn, the emperor's mood was one of fortitude and resilience. In conformity with this mood, his thoughts were escaping once again to the warring abode of Mandasor, and retreating back to Agra. Something vague and comical was teasing his senses. His mind was unearthing the tender protests of Bega Jan in opposition to his paying more attention to his aunts than to his wives.

Your Majesty. Are thorns strewn on the path to my chamber that you avoid visiting me? Your wives scarcely see you, while you visit your aunts without fail— Bega Jan had spilled forth a torrent of complaints.

Humayun's thoughts were justifying this complaint as he had done before, that his aunts had no husbands and were lonely, so more in need of his attention and companionship. His thoughts were leaving the harem, one rude splinter of a memory uncurling its own lips of shock and bewilderment. The seeds of cruelty and compassion inside him were the burning coals of awareness. *No waters of justification to quench the fires of dark cruelty inside him, even if they were swaddled in the bandages of his compassion.* That memory was linked with the attempted escape of Alam Shah and Sadr Khan, kindling the seeds of his cruelty to raging flames. So incensed was he at their vain attempts, that he had ordered their heads cut off. After this savage punishment was carried out, his heart was filled with remorse and compassion, but too late. That was the time he had discovered the dark side of his *self* where more vile deeds were yet to blossom.

The stars of contrition were throbbing inside Humayun's heart and in his eyes, as he sat listening to the babel of his viziers and grandees. Yet, he was trying his best to escape his *dark self* without getting embroiled into the knots of arguments wild and indecisive. Plunging deeper into the solitary rivers of his soul and psyche, he was getting closer to the rungs of truth, and drifting farther from the staircase of reality. The bride of his soul was lost to him, and the bride of his spirit singing some mournful hymns. His head was spinning amidst a whirlwind of tearful mists where a cluster of tragedies stood peering from behind the curtain of imponderables. The emperor was embroiled in wars, braving the hurricanes of defeats and wanderings. *The face of exile was etched on all four poles of his empire. Exile from home. Exile from the quest of knowledge. Banishment from the bride of his soul?* The emperor was trying to flee the ghosts of exile, and landing into the marshland of correspondence with Behader Shah since his journey from Agra to Gwalior.

God forbid, your promises be neglected
For I cannot afford to be forgotten by you

Behader Shah had sent this couplet in response to Humayun's command in sending the traitor Zaman Mirza into the custody of the Imperialists. Adding:

Your Majesty. I have given asylum to Prince Zaman Mirza, keeping in mind, that he is the husband of your beloved half sister, Masuma Begum. Command this slave with further instructions on this subject, Your Majesty, and I will comply with your wishes— Behader Shah had ignored all subjects of contention most discreetly. Posing himself as a helpless man with not a friend to console him in his plight.

A thousand friends are too few, and one enemy of too many. Humayun had laced his response with a verse written by Shah Ismail of Persia.

Plant the tree of amity, that it may bear fruit, namely
The fulfillment of the heart's desire
Uproot the sapling of hostility which yields countless ills
He had added his own quatrain at the end.

Who is the most helpless man in the world
He who has no friend
No, the most helpless man is he who had a
Friend, but has managed to lose him
Receiving this allegorical missive from the emperor, Behader Shah had written back with the pride and violence of a mountain lion.

Your Majesty. Five reasons that generally lead to war. Behader Shah had cited all five with the sting of a challenge.

The desire of creating a kingdom where none existed before.

The desire of protecting and safeguarding the territory that are possessed.

The zeal which prompted one to attack the unjust possessor of a kingdom with the sword of justice.

The desire of adding to the wealth that one already possessed.

An attempt to fill the earth with strife, out of a love and conquest and plunder, and out of arrogance toward the submissive.

None of these reasons, Your Majesty, have actuated me to the brink of this war! But Your Majesty's shower of accusations on the virtue of my loyalty. He had glossed his feigned loyalty with one of his favorite quotes.

In neither of the two worlds have I any ill-will against others. If someone else has any against me, let God's mercy be in abundance of him.

Humayun's reflections were halting at the arena of this snippet from his commands, hurled at Behader Shah during the missiles of combat in words.

We, who believe in unity and concord, could not imagine that you would transgress the Quranic verse—O ye, that believeth, abide by your agreements. Did you not press this Sura to your lips, and repeat an oath of fidelity to the emperor? Were you not reminded by our emissaries, Qasim Ali and Keracha Beg, that you should either return those traitor rebels to us, or to banish them elsewhere from the sanctuary of your protection? You had ignored the just demands of our emissaries, sending them back with this lame excuse— What harm if Zaman Mirza stays with me Is this the only reed of an argument you could cling to? You are commanded once again to hand over those traitors to us. In compliance, you could prove your allegiance to us, otherwise, your oaths of loyalty would continue to ring false and facetious. Humayun's thoughts were recalling this quatrain sent to Behader Shah.

O thou, that boasteth of a loving heart
Greetings to thee, if thy heart and tongue accord
This will suffice as advice, if only you listen to it
By sowing thorn, no jasmine can be reaped

The final exchange of quatrains between him and his foe were invading his thoughts.

Oh thou art Chitor's foe
How art thou occupied seizing the infidels
A king has arrived at thy head
And thou seated in hope of seizing Chitor

Humayun had written.

I that am foe to the city of Chitor
Am seizing the infidels by force
He who succors Chitor
Thou shalt see, how I seize him too

Behader Shah had emptied his own quiver of poetry.

The poet-mystic in Humayun, this particular moment, was rehearsing a quatrain in conformity with his tender mood. He would have liked to send it to Behader Shah as his last attempt at peace offering, if his heart was not turned bitter with a sense of rage and betrayal.

From grief every fold of my heart has turned into blood
To think that in spite of our oneness, duality is attributed to us
I never recollect you without weeping bitterly
Nay, I seldom recollect you for fear that I may have to weep much

Humayun buried this quatrain in his head before turning his attention to Biram Khan.

"Should we offer one last chance to our chameleon of a foe, Biram, before he must lick the tongue of our sword? What do you say, my prudent Vizier?" Humayun flashed him a smile, his eyes brimming with the gleam of poetry.

"Your Majesty. Behader Shah's tongue is more lethal than a sword, if I may be permitted to say?" Biram Khan muttered with a slight toss of his head. "It needs blunting, and a little bleeding could accomplish favorable results. The aim is to purge his tongue of all pride and poison. His arrogance alone marks him as the prime candidate to forfeit his life. That vile maggot, Your Majesty, if you remember the letter he sent you? He should be roasted alive, just for that!"

"Ah, that rude, audacious piece of a puzzle, dripping ignorance!" Humayun laughed. "That letter was the invention of Satan himself. Written by Behader Shah's evil scribe, Mulla Lari, since the chameleon-foe is illiterate. He composes poetry well, I must admit though. Another confession which I must voice is that Mulla Lari's quotation in that letter amused me immensely:

The ascetic asked for the wine of the Paradise and
Hafiz for the cup of wine

And if I was offended, all offense was melted by this postscript of a verse." He continued rather cheerfully. "You sound much like Behader Shah this evening, Biram, ready for war, and smoldering with rage? How is Behader Shah comporting himself against this siege? Are his soldiers restless and longing for war?"

"Behader Shah fears the might of the Moghuls, Your Majesty, and he is unwilling to capitulate until bombarded by bullets and cannon shots." Biram Khan snapped loose his thoughts. "He is contriving means of defense in the Turkish fashion. Ordering his troops to entrench themselves in the open field, guarded by cartloads of artillery and wagons full of ammunition. His men laboring day and night to dig trenches around the encampment are not only suffering fatigue, but famine. Almost three months since their supplies were cut off, no more grain for them or fodder for their horses. Faint with hunger, their horses are falling like the flies. Their soldiers too, for lack of nourishment, are losing heart, appealing to the tyrant Shah to sue for peace, but does he relent? Who knows? Such hunger and misery, even death, could be averted, Your Majesty, if we can put an end to the life of this tyrant?"

"Ah, to suffer the pain in living! Wouldn't death be a welcome reprieve to the ones who become the victims of hunger and deprivation?" Humayun's cheerfulness was drowning in a flood of mysticism. "Is it right to wage war without exhausting all means of gaining peace and understanding? If an object can be attained by gentleness, why have recourse to harsh measures?" His thoughts were a mockery of disbelief, concealing a dagger of cruelty under their arms, and peering into the heart of his cruel foe. "Is Behader Shah really thinking of fighting with the Portuguese once again, calling them infidels, *feringhis*? *Say unto the Christians, their God and my God are one.* Even if Prophet Muhammed was to recite this verse from the Quran to this heathen Shah, he would deny it with the rod of his own—"

Humayun's voice was swallowed by a sudden volcano of noise from cannon and artillery. He had leaped to his feet, snatching his gold helmet from the table beside him, and aiming to rush out into this thunderous fury of the sky and the earth. Rage and implacability were kindling his eyes to quicksilver awakening. His eyes were flashing mute commands at Biram Khan, but before he could unburden his rage, Rumi Khan stumbled into the tent, falling prostrate at the emperor's feet.

"Your Majesty. Behader Shah is fleeing—he has set fire to cannon and artillery. All our guns and cannon in smoke—"Rumi Khan's incoherent tones were swallowed by an abrupt thunder of a command from Humayun's lips, falling on Biram Khan, instead of on the dithering master-gunner.

"Biram Khan, order all the troops to their posts. Half of them would follow us to the gates of the fortress, and half to salvage cannon and artillery through that pit of ruin and devastation." Humayun was storming out of his tent, followed by Biram Khan and Rumi Khan.

The night air thick with acrid smoke and palls of black clouds was following imperial riders down the very slopes, where the fortress of Chitor stood looming in the distance. Left behind was the blaze of fire in its last throes of crackle and splutter, a few rude flames shooting here and there to lick the dying splinters of metal to silence. The soldiers left behind to extinguish the blazing enormity had doused the entire scene of devastation with buckets of sand and water. The horses and elephants close by were wounded and scorched by the shower of metal and gun-powder, their groans loud and maddening. Humayun, at the head of his chosen troops, had escaped this gruesome scene of misery and hopelessness. And yet he had encountered both these foes as misery and hopelessness face-to-face, as soon as he had entered the fortress of Chitor. The mashalchis—torch-bearers, holding bright diyas on long poles were lighting the way for the emperor, stunned to silence by the traces of plunder and violence on the very walls of this fortress.

Before fleeing, Behader Shah had made sure that he would strip naked this fortress, of all gold and treasure. The gilded walls were gouged and slashed, leaving gaping holes where gold sconces must have been, for a few were left smashed on the floor, as a rude reminder to the victors of their enemy's rage and contempt. The great hallway too, in mockery of dark smiles, was unfolding a succession of faded glory where large paintings were no more to tell their stories of ages past and countless. *Tapestries all torn and shredded, colors bleeding through their wounds in rags and yarn. Bolts of silks reduced to ashes, and caskets of jewels empty and disfigured.* Humayun was drifting along under the spell of daze and fatigue, his thoughts barely grazing the traces of greed and malice so vividly alive and throbbing. Rumi Khan and Biram Khan were following the emperor, and he was becoming aware of the loud gasps from the lips of the other soldiers who too were exploring the fortress. A dismal staircase was winding up through the foyer, luring Humayun toward the vaulted landing. The mashalchis had halted before one golden cage, gazing into the eyes of the parrot, whose very eyes seemed to be spitting rage and venom. Suddenly, the parrot started spewing out words, as if reciting a lesson.

"The scoundrel Rumi Khan—traitor Rumi Khan." The parrot seemed drugged by his words, as taught by Behader Shah, it was obvious.

"If any man had uttered these words, the emperor would have ordered his tongue to be cut off." Humayun murmured over his shoulders without looking at Rumi Khan. "But what could be done to this sweet bird, tutored by the malefic tongue of Behader Shah himself?" He retraced his steps, seeking the staircase. "Biram, find out the extent of our losses, and report to the emperor." He commanded.

The night sky lowering its beams of silvery sorrow was guiding Humayun toward the opulent tent of Behader Shah. Unlike the fortress, this great tent was left untouched, its pegs of gold and silver coming alive against the blaze of torches held high by the mashalchis. Jewels in large caskets and bolts upon bolts of silk were stored neatly in one corner of this sumptuous tent. Velvets and brocades were strewn in unkempt heaps in the middle of the tent, where Humayun stood brooding. Biram Khan had stolen behind him, but he was aware of his vizier's return, and queried.

"Don't hesitate, Biram, to tell the emperor of all the losses we have suffered so far by the treachery of Behader Shah?" Humayun turned slowly.

"Laila and Majnun, your guns, Your Majesty, are completely destroyed." Biram Khan admitted reluctantly.

"Ah, the children of my own volcanic intellect! Nurtured by the fire of my love?" Humayun lamented aloud, his eyes commanding him to continue.

"Your favorite elephants, Your Majesty. Sharzah and Patsinger, wounded, dying." Biram Khan murmured.

"Ah." Humayun's voice was choked, as he stood there overwhelmed with sudden grief. "Let the night roar with the drumbeat of war cries, Biram. We will chase Behader Shah and his horde of marauders to the very gates of perdition." He stormed out into the pale night. His gaze reaching out to the cold, glittering stars. "Delhi relies on its wheat and millet for revenue, while Gujrat counts upon its corals and pearls." A volley of hysterical mirth escaped his lips as if mocking the cold, heedless stars.

Chapter Five
People of the Elephant

Humayun, seated in one sumptuous hall inside the fort of Champanir, was indulging in the pleasure of feasting and entertainment along with his wives and ladies of the harem. This fortress recently conquered was a sprawling monument of ugliness on the very banks of Douriah, fortified by moats and towering bastions, but inside were chambers all gilded, flanked by spacious courtyards. The night-long feasting was nowhere close to lulling the royal occupants to sleep, for the emperor had no intention to retire as yet. Guided by the guardian planet of Mars, this particular Tuesday, he was dressed in red, challenging his inner foes equipped with the daggers of cruelty and vengeance to an open combat inside the rivers of wakefulness. Tuesday was no more, for the Chinese clock on the ornate mantel was chiming the hour past midnight, and the emperor was relieved that his cruel, vengeful foes within were vanquished for the night against his whimsical campaign in the head to befriend joy and kindness. His gaze alighting on the dancers and musicians was poetic and melancholy, straying over to the jeweled treasures as his wives, and resurrecting memories sweet and wistful.

Surfeit, carnality and feasting! A sudden wave of ache and longing in Humayun's soul was drowning his thoughts into the abyss of reveries. His heart was thirsting for the wine of songs from the lips of Sarvaqad, but his eyes were revealing their own parched hungers, searching for the bride of his soul. He could feel his heart and soul foundering inside the rivers of hungers and thirsts, his thoughts commanding escape, and hurling themselves down the alleys of time where all spiritual hungers were choked amidst the brambles of wars and intrigues. Behader Shah, though pursued by the imperialists, had proved to be a genius in escaping and wreaking havoc while fleeing from one city to the other with the agility and precision of a master-magician. Leaving behind false traces of his flight, he had repaired to Gujrat, collecting all his jewels and possessions, and finding refuge in Diu. Skilled in

59

deception and guerrilla-tactics, he had kept the imperialists at bay, even managing to seek alliance with the king of Constantinople, Sulaiman the Magnificent. He had sent the king Sulaiman a gift of six hundred thousand gold pieces, requesting military aid to fight the Moghuls. But since the king had declined to accept the gift or to offer aid, he had swallowed his pride, making alliance with the Portuguese, suppressing his deep-rooted hatred for the feringhis inside his heart. To win the favor of the Portuguese was no easy task, for Behader Shah had to surrender his kingdom of Bassein to them in exchange for their promise to fight the Moghuls.

Humayun's gaze was alighting on his daughter, Princess Aqiqa, a rare bloom of eight with dark eyes and pale face, but his thoughts were still entangled inside the labyrinth of Behader Shah's tricks and cruelties. *Unearthing in its wake, his own bouts of rages and tyrannies, even when he was not dressed in red under the sign of blistering Mars.* Right after Behader Shah's alliance with the Portuguese, they had helped him built an impregnable fortress close to the banks of Diu. This fortress was erected within forty days, affording him time to design more defenses before the imperialists could reach there to challenge his alliances and fortifications. Deeming himself the master of his fate, Behader Shah had become an absolute slave to the power of the Portuguese, obeying each reed of their advice or command like a man drowning inside the stormy waters of his confusion. The Portuguese had advised him to burn his fleet of hundred ships at the port of Cambay, lest the imperialists seize them to their benefit. And Behader Shah had realized but too late, that he had designed this string of fleet to fight the infidels, the feringhis themselves. Meanwhile, Humayun, at the head of a large force was marching closer, quelling rebellions on the way, and claiming conquests before reaching the port of Cambay.

A squall of his rage and tyranny at Cambay was enveloping Humayun's thoughts in a dust-cloud of memories, though apparently he sat talking and laughing. Before reaching the port of Cambay all rebellions were quelled, the warring lords pardoned and their oaths of fidelity accepted. Peace and order were restored in the cities of Gujrat, Mandu and Batwa, along with the territories of Surkhaj, Myhindri, Kankarya Tal and Muhammadad. At Cambay, the imperialists had suffered a night raid by the audacity of the Bhils and the Gowers. This horde of marauders was incited by two chiefs from the district of Kolwara. Ahmed Lad and Rakh Daud were the culprits who had dispatched this horde to plunder the royal encampment while their occupants lay resting and unsuspecting. Unsuspecting was true, but the Moghul guards were vigilant, despite the overpowering sense of fatigue. Humayun, upon learning this outrage, had ordered the whole town of Cambay to be torched.

The large ruby in Humayun's turban was suddenly ablaze, as if lit by the fire of rage and inexorability in his thoughts. But his thoughts were not raging, only sliding down the slippery isles of trials and travails. Leaving Cambay behind in ruin and ashes, the imperialists had then continued their march toward Champanir to win this impregnable fort, defended by Nar Singh and Ikhtiar Khan. Rage still smoldering in Humayun's heart at the audacity of the marauders at Cambay, he had commanded immediate attack on the fortress of Champanir. Watching the fortress looming high on one large hill, Humayun himself had designed a master-plan, employing his rare gift of ingenuity to vanquish his foes. Large, heavy spikes of iron, eighty in all, were driven into the jagged inclines for the escaladers to reach the fortress from the top, where it was least likely to be guarded. One hundred soldiers had ventured this steep incline, including the emperor himself, gaining entry into the fortress and taking the enemy by surprise. Suddenly, the trumpets and the kettledrums had begun to sound the victory for the Moghuls, while Ali Kuli and Rumi Khan at the foot of the hill had let their cannonade roar to check the flight of the garrison, caught in a whirlwind of chaos and confusion. Ikhtiar Khan, along with a few of his followers had succeeded in escaping through a narrow defile unguarded by the Moghuls.

Humayun's thoughts were gathering hush all of a sudden. Falling like the little troopers themselves. Stunned and impenitent! All the prisoners in this fortress were put to sword, and all the treasures confiscated. Jewels in gold and silver of exquisite design had fallen into the hands of the imperialists. And bales of silk from Rum, Khita, Ferang, Turkey, China and Europe. Velvets and brocades too, and paintings all gilded and engraved. Arms and armory in abundance. And quivers in all gilt, swollen with bows and arrows! Alam Khan had discovered more treasures, locked and concealed. Daggers with jade handles and swords studded with onyx, agate and carnelians. His joy was boundless, when he had found a cistern full of gold, boasting of his discovery to the emperor as soon as he had managed to drain it of all water.

These glittering treasures with the glitter of victories were leaving Humayun's thoughts. Instead, a parade of hunting and feasting was entering his mind's sight where the city of Champanir throbbed vast and alluring. The emperor had given himself entirely to such pleasures after his victory at Champanir, while the two most inveterate of his foes were splintering his empire with war and intrigue. Those splinters were now sprouting in his head like the daggers of nemesis. While Behader Shah was still allied with the Portuguese, Sher Khan had succeeded in capturing the cities of Bihar, Patna, Gour and Benares. In addition, by the sheer virtue of his deceit, he had gained victory over the strongest fort of the Rhotas. Humayun's thoughts were getting wearied of wars and intrigues, holding sacred only the reeds of his victories. Malwa was conquered and bestowed on Prince Hindal. The conquered city of Gujrat was under the rule of Prince Askeri. Prince Kamran was appointed the governor of Lahore. Khwaja Kilan was defending Kandahar? Victories too were standing pale and gaunt at the portals in Humayun's mind, watching the flight of Zaman Mirza to Lahore, who had contrived escape along with Shah Mirza and Ulugh Mirza. Humayun's gaze was returning to Princess Aqiqa once again, her expression rapt and avid, arresting his attention. The little princess was absorbing each detail of the story from the lips of her mother, Bega Jan.

"You would not ever want to visit the fortress of the Rhotas, my dear, it's ugly and monstrous." Bega Begum was expounding vehemently. "One could feel giddy, going up the winding road before reaching the table-land, where this fortress rises as big as the mountain itself. It belonged to Raja Hari Kishan, who said that it can't be conquered, even by the gods—Hindu gods, that is." Her very eyes were teaching her daughter the lessons in history, it seemed. "And now Sher Khan has conquered it, as I told you before. But that is not enough for your precious head, and you must know, how? Well, Sher Khan sent a message to the Raja requesting if he could store his treasures in Raja's fortress. Also, requesting him to let his ladies stay in the fortress since he is afraid of the war with Moghul troops. The Raja agreed, and Sher Khan put armed men disguised as women in the *dolis* to be sent to the fortress. At the gates when Raja demanded to look into the dolis, Sher Khan said that all his women were Muslims, strictly veiled, and would be offended if forced to show their faces to a stranger. A thousand dolis passed this way into the fortress, and what happened next, my sweet

Aqiqa, you are too young to know. Just remember this, all Raja's men and women died by the shameful trickery of Sher Khan."

"Your glittering tales, my love, will corrupt the innocence of our young princess." Humayun smiled, claiming his goblet of wine which he had neglected so far under the spell of his reveries. "Any other tales simmering in your pretty head, my beauty, which may enlighten the emperor of more worthy intrigues." He mocked.

"Your soldiers, Your Majesty, might be getting drunk in the garden of Halol, since you have sent them flagons of wine?" Bega Begum chimed prophetically.

"And the rivers of wine in your own eyes, my sweet, are feeding my thoughts with memories strange and astonishing." Humayun's eyes were gathering a whiff of nostalgia and tenderness. "Isn't it strange that of all the grueling times past and recent in wars, this tender recollection comes to my mind? The mosque in Ayodhya which I visited but twice. There is an inscription on its facade in honor of my father. *Babur, the Kelander is well known in the world as a king.* I guess, this comes to my mind in connection with the not too-distant arguments in Din Panah. This mosque is erected on the holy ground sacred to Hindus, as the birth-place of Lord Rama, the scholars argue and dispute. I have even heard that it was built during the reign of my father when he was fighting wars and quelling rebellions. Upon learning of this outrage as a violation to the sanctity of the Hindu gods, my father had commanded the mad zealots to be trampled under the feet of the elephants, the ones who were accused of committing this sacrilege. Now the Hindus are sending me petitions that this mosque should be demolished, to be replaced with a temple in honor of Lord Rama."

"You would not order that mosque demolished, Your Majesty, would you? That would be a desecration." Gunwar Begum opined aloud, aghast and frightened.

"No, my love. Muslims would cut the throat of the emperor before such a Farman could breathe on his lips." Humayun smiled. "Though, I have pacified the petitioners that a temple will be built right beside this mosque as soon as the warring lords in my empire afford me respite. None could desecrate the holy of holies, my love. Rama, Buddha, Jesus, Allah, Yahweh, they have their shrines inside the hearts of men, not in temples, mosques, churches or synagogues."

"Wish, you could issue a Farman to abolish suttee, Your Majesty!" Was Chand Begum's wistful challenge, as if to test the power of her emperor-husband.

"Have no fear, my love! No one would force you to jump into the funeral pyre if the emperor was to die tomorrow?" Humayun's eyes were beacons of mischief as he continued. "Besides, you could always dress like a man, as you did on Prince Hindal's wedding, and escape this raging fate of being burnt alive." He laughed. "Suttee is another shrine inside the hearts of the Hindu women, where they enact the ritual of living and dying for the sake of love and holiness. And no man, not even the emperor has the power to violate the sanctity of that shrine, only the hand of time. And that hand of time, gentle or severe, would replace this shrine with a holy temple, where love for living could be more sacred than the ritual of dying."

"For the sake of Gulbadan Begum alone, Your Majesty, if you could?" Aqiq Begum voiced her concern. "She is terrified by the mere name of suttee, and says—"

"My child Princess of a Rose, now a Begum!" Was Humayun's sudden exclamation. "Did the emperor hear it right? When was she married?"

"How you forget, Your Majesty? Didn't you announce the betrothal of Princess Gulbadan to Khwaja Khizr? After you left Agra, Your Majesty, Prince Hindal solemnized the marriage with all due rites and propriety. Didn't Prince Hindal write to you? I thought he did?" Aqiq Begum looked flustered.

"And don't you know, Your Majesty, that in your absence Prince Hindal acted like an emperor!" Bega Jan couldn't miss a chance to voice her fears and concerns. "Indulging in feasting and entertainment, and issuing Farmans? Young and heedless as he is, Your Majesty, he should be checked in his excesses. I know he is the most adored of your brothers, but prone to be influenced by ambitious Timuirids."

"He is too honest to be guided by guile or ambition, my lovely sibyl." Humayun chided amusedly. "Besides, he loves the emperor much too much." He laughed, ignoring the sudden kindling of rage and bitterness inside him. "Amongst my royal brothers, my sweet Bega, Prince Kamran is the one goaded by ambition. He should be the one strictly watched, if not chastised?"

His gaze was turning to the lovely dancers, but his heart was churning some violence most savage and nameless.

"Prince Kamran is content with his kingdom at Lahore, Your Majesty. Don't think, he is ambitious." Bega Begum murmured. "Prince Askeri, I am not sure. Such conflicting reports from Gujrat, as you know. Issuing Farmans openly, and seeking alliances covertly?" She was watching the emperor apprehensively.

"Then why is the capricious Prince Kamran, not driven mad by ambition as you think, turned traitor to the emperor?" Was Humayun's low comment.

"Those base, vile rumors, Your Majesty! They don't amount to anything?" Bega Begum was all for defending the wicked prince. "Prince Kamran's only fault is in boasting. Maybe, he just wants to encourage his troops when he tells them that they are more strong and powerful than the entire army of the emperor?"

"My sweet, royal brothers!" Humayun's gaze was straying toward the ebony doors with brass nails, as if nailing his inner torment to some sort of discipline. "All innocent, all plotting." He got to his feet restlessly. "What do you say, my loves! Should we invade the garden with song and poetry?" He let his gaze sweep over his lovely wives. "If my drunken horde of soldiers is still there, as you profess, the emperor will pack them off to their tents?" He beamed, his heart breeding sedition.

"What a delightful idea, Your Majesty! How we miss the garden parties of Agra and Delhi—" All the emperor's wives were ecstatic.

"How wonderful! We haven't done that since months—" Gulbarg Begum appeared to be swooning with joy.

"We will sing songs and recite couplets." Maya Begum chanted happily.

"To watch sunrise in the garden of Halol and to be out of the fort of Champanir! Who would have thought we could—" Bega Begum's sing-song voice was dissolved by Humayun's loud command to summon his Keeper of the Seal.

"Muhrdar, fetch the librarian, we need a bundle of books on prose and poetry." Humayun waved a command. "Also instruct the guards to make sure that no intruder is permitted in the garden while we are there." He turned, smiling whimsically.

A great flurry was let loose in this chamber of gilt and damask. The servants were whipped to action by the commands of the Begums to fetch Pashmina shawls and velvety cushions, as if they were going on a long excursion, not just walking out into the garden. Humayun himself had shot a few more commands for furnishing the garden with Persian rugs and colorful lamps. The musicians were scrambling their instruments, and the dancers were wild with anticipation to dance under the starlit sky. While the plans for outdoor activity were being executed, Humayun had begun to pace, amused by the rapt absorption of the Begums in striving toward making this garden of Halol an arena of festivity and entertainment.

Apparently calm and amused, his heart was revealing a volcano of fire he had not ever seen before. Some sort of chaos and violence within, fiery and sibilant. Something in his very psyche were crackling and splintering, throwing open the portals of his soul with one thunder of a warning. Kindness was posted at the door of cruelty like a guard weak and vacillating, just like his moods and vagaries. One sliver of a revelation was thundering in his psyche with a bolt of lightning. He could feel the tongue of this chaos inside him, could hear its edict and inevitability. Yes, he recognized this *tyrant*, it was his *mood*, he had cursed its *power* before, had feared its assault always. This mood was caught inside the hissing of a storm, foretelling calamity? His own powerless self, cruel and invulnerable. His feet were coming to a sudden halt, the mists of reveries in his eyes clearing to snatch the form of Muhrdar.

"Your Majesty. Saw Biram Khan out there—says, can't find the librarian. Guards are missing too—" Muhrdar's incoherent expression was truncated by the sudden blaze of anger in Humayun's eyes.

"Jolt the drunken louts to awakening then, you cowering wretch! Were they not supposed to keep watch in the garden? Drag them out of their silken tents, and hurl them out into the abyss of the night?" Humayun thundered.

"All empty, the tents, Your Majesty. Biram Khan says, they are all gone to—" Muhrdar lost his voice once more as Humayun exclaimed.

"Gone! Where? Are you gone mad, you simpering fool? Efface yourself and send Biram Khan—" Humayun's rage and impatience were now landing on his vizier, who had the misfortune of walking through the ebony doors. "Tell me, Biram, where are the guards, and is the librarian gone whoring?"

"Much worse, Your Majesty." Biram Khan offered reluctantly. "I have confirmed, Your Majesty, they have all gone to Deccan, including the librarian. And a handful of your loyal soldiers too, Your Majesty."

"Without the emperor's permission, how dare they leave this encampment?" Humayun's gaze was gathering flints of rage. "Tell the emperor, Biram, how this unplanned *hijra* came about escaping the notice of the emperor and his viziers?"

"If you would, Your Majesty, grant me a private audience?" Biram Khan pleaded, as if overwhelmed by the presence of the beautiful ladies. "The details, Your Majesty, quite bizarre, might offend the delicate senses of the ladies of your harem."

"The comedy of intrigues! Is that it, Biram?" One snort of a laughter escaped Humayun's lips, as he shifted his smoldering gaze to his wives. "No couplets under the stars this night, my loves. Some other propitious night perhaps when the emperor's fools could mend their wits by the stars of their fates?" He averted his gaze, gliding toward the ebony doors. "The emperor will hear the gruesome details out in the garden, Biram. The cool air might soothe the fires in my body and soul." He murmured over his shoulders, as if fleeing his fates.

The night air seething with the scent from champa flowers was lending Humayun's rage a subtle whiff of comfort so that he could absorb each word of Biram Khan patiently and attentively. Both the emperor and the vizier were strolling side by side in the majestic garden of Halol, its hush broken only by the low intonations of Biram Khan, squeezing the lengthy report into a handful of words. The livid moon up there was lowering its tinsel-beams, and tracing the cobbled paths in silvery lace from the leaves on champa trees. Their yellow blooms washed pale by the flood of moonlight were teasing Humayun's senses, but he was forcing his thoughts to stay in tune with the rhythm of betrayals, absurdities. He thought he could hear violet hills in the distance, even the low moans from the lake of Bara Talao down yonder, but they were only the steady downpour of intonations from the lips of Biram Khan.

"The soldiers flushed with drinking and feasting, Your Majesty, and half drugged with the wine of recklessness, were playing backgammon." Biram Khan was saying, as if reciting some tale long forgotten. "While playing, they began to boast of their skills in archery and warfare, and I am repeating what was reported to me. One of the guards who had been drinking religiously, came upon them, and started reciting one excerpt from Zafar Nama, where Tamerlane was depicted as a venerable lord, nurturing the seeds of unity amongst his soldiers. *Tamerlane, during one of his campaigns had taken two arrows each from his forty companions. Tying them in a bundle and challenging each one of them to break the bundle without removing one single arrow. That bundle could not be broken, though all forty of them had tried with all their might. Then he had returned each pair of arrows to his companions, commanding them to break, and they had no difficulty in doing so.* After hearing this excerpt, the soldiers had forgotten their game of backgammon, and were shouting to each other to join their hands and take an oath of unity. Unity for what, they were asking each other, and then deciding all of a sudden to march to Deccan to test the wisdom of Tamerlane. The royal librarian was royally drunk too, Your Majesty, and he joined the guards and the soldiers without a thought and off they went."

"Gone without the permission of the emperor!" Humayun echoed his thoughts aloud. "That is treason, Biram, if not folly insufferable and unpardonable? Oh, the ignorant, undisciplined horde! Where do they think they are going? Riding posthaste to Deccan, are they? What do you think is brewing in their empty heads? The emperor knows their minds. They are fighting the winds with the rods of false chivalry. Thinking of challenging the Muslim states, Bedar, Berar, Bijapur, Golconda, Ahmadnagar, one by one, on their mad spree? Have they not been talking about this, even when sober? If they succeed in executing this plan without a dint of provocation from our Muslim brethren, they would soil the honor of the entire battalions stationed here. We are in danger of losing Gujrat, even if they attack but one state?" He whirled around, retracing his steps. "Let the trumpets sound, Biram. Command a battalion of ten thousand to follow those vile desperadoes. Our faithful imperialists are to capture them, and bring them back bound hand and foot. Tomorrow is the judgment day for them, the emperor will see to that." He could feel the power of Mercury churning inside him as he retraced his steps toward the palace.

"Your Majesty." Biram Khan voiced a low protest.

"This is the emperor's Farman, Biram, the imperialists commence their march this very hour!" Humayun was drifting toward his palace, the shadow of blind rage his lone companion.

68

Biram Khan was left behind, sculpted alive on the blades of grass as if freshly impaled.

The night expedition unfolding itself into another dawn, noon and evening, had wreaked havoc in the emperor's soul and into the soul of the universe. All four hundred desperadoes were brought back, bound hand and foot, and before noon could breath life into the heart of the evening, their fates were sealed by the edict of the emperor. That edict, most savage and harrowing! The color emerald for Wednesdays which the emperor chose always with the intention of indulging in sport and pleasure was switched to red again this particular day, the color of Mars for his guardian planet of Tuesday. Arrayed thus in rage and splendor of the Mars, he had commanded the most brutal of punishments for his soldiers who had dared leave Champanir without his permission. The doomed victims were first stripped of all human dignity, their ears, noses and fingers hacked away, before they were trampled under the feet of the elephants. And if the wretched victims were left alive, writhing in agony, their bodies were torn from limb to limb, and their heads cut off from their shoulders by the unerring sabers of the executioners.

The emperor's heart was in the profoundest of despairs after the executioners' bloody deeds were done by his explicit command, but even now the billowing rage inside him was unquenched as he sat enthroned in the garden of Halol with his viziers and grandees. His gaze was fixed ruefully to the crimson sunset, splashed with ochre and vermilion, as if he could see the blood of his victims bleeding through the blue bowl of this sky. The sky itself was mournful, almost livid and violet, casting hush and fright into the hearts of his companions, who had witnessed the emperor's wrath before, but not to the extent of this brutal violation of sense and sanity. Paradoxically, Humayun himself was confounded by his acts of cruelty and violence! Falling victim to his moods of rage and implacability, when all he wanted to do was to be kind and forgiving. He had donned the color of Mars to defy and challenge his moods, and practice gentleness as was his wont with his brothers, no matter what their offense or treason, but had succeeded only in becoming the slave of his Zodiac master. The blood-streaked sky was pouring fear, even into the emperor's heart, his very soul wounded and inconsolable. The weight of his commands was sitting on his brow as the burden of sorrow, his thoughts searching realms quiet and painless. He could still feel the naked sword of his *cruel self* poised at his jugular vein, and he closed his eyes. Sarvaqad, one wound in his heart was throbbing and expanding. His lips were parched, thirsting for the wine of music, beauty, intercession divine.

Some sort of intercession was flapping its wings down from the minarets of a white mosque in the distance. The loud intonations of a muezzin, calling the faithful to prayer, were splintering the night hush with the poetry of praise and surrender to God. Humayun's head was lowering, the swath of rubies in his turban raging and glittering. Biram Khan seated next to the emperor, was aware only of the charged silence in the garden and inside the emperor's heart, it seemed, his own heart grief-stricken and bewildered. His eyes ringed with the fever of despair were fixed to the lute-player, Majnan, who was evoking the saddest of melodies in conformity with the hush and dolor of the evening. Biram Khan's grief was responding to this music, as if these sad notes were escaping the strings of his own heart.

Suddenly, Biram Khan's heart was leaping and missing a few beats, as if washed by the light of a revelation. His voice was circling over Majnan, whose songs could even lull the demons to sleep, he had heard. This gentle youth could melt the emperor's rage to waters of peace by the sheer sweetness in his voice, Biram Khan's thoughts were wading toward the shore of this revelation. Though, he was stricken dumb by the sudden flash of this revelation. Thinking, that he could have helped save many lives by making Majnan sing, for sweet songs had always proved to be an antidote to the emperor's fits of rage. With his honed perception, even now, he could feel the fever of rage lapping inside the emperor's heart, his feverish thoughts reaching out to Majnan for the sweet wine of songs. But before he could voice his request to Majnan he was distracted by the loud recitation of Maulana Ferghali.

In the name of Allah, the Gracious, the Merciful
Hast thou not seen how thy Lord dealt with the People of the Elephant
Did He not cause their plan to miscarry
And He sent against them swarms of birds
Which ate their carrion, striking them against stones of clay?
And thus made them like broken straw, eaten up

70

Maulana Ferghali blissfully ignorant of the meaning of this verse from the Quran didn't know that the emperor's heart was on fire by the connotation of such holy injunctions. To a learned theologian, this verse portrayed the destruction of the People of the Elephant. The prime victim was the Abyssinian king of Yemen, who had attempted impiously to destroy the temple at Mecca. The tyranny of the king was delineated explicitly, along with his followers, who had brought an elephant with them with the intention of destroying the very foundations of Kaaba. The Meccans were frightened by the large armies of the king, knowing not that they were going to witness a great miracle. That elephant upon reaching the sacred grounds of Mecca had fallen to its knees as if in prostration, refusing to move an inch though goaded by its mahout. Next, a flock of birds were seen hovering over Mecca. By the providence of God Himself, it was obvious, for they were raining down pebbles over the Abyssinians, causing their bodies to break forth in boils, large and grotesque.

"You, impious wretch!" Humayun thundered. "How dare you recite this sanctimonious allusion aimed directly at the emperor?" The bolt of lightning in his gaze was falling on his guard and vizier. "Haji Muhammed, seize this holy viper at this very instant, and hurl him under the feet of my elephant. Slit his throat with your sword if his breath leaves not the corruption of his body?"

In obedience to the emperor's command, Maulana Ferghali was dragged to his doom, stunned and un-protesting. Maulana Bekasi too was mute and stricken with grief, his intention of interceding on behalf of the victim dying on his lips, as he fell prostrate at the emperor's feet. Biram Khan, dazed and aghast, was commanding Majnan to sing a song. Suddenly, the mournful hush was swollen with divine music from the lips of Majnan, as if a choir of angels was playing sweet melodies on the strings of his heart. The emperor's own heart was fluttering on the wings of time, wounded and inconsolable. His rage was melting, but in its molten haze were ebbing forth storms wild and savage. His inner self dubbed as *cruel self* was whimpering and pleading for the life of his Imam, but he was drugged by the ripple of sweetness in Majnan's voice, his former command staying intact and irrevocable. An eternity had swept past with the fury of a hurricane before the sweetness of Majnan's voice was sucked back into silence, and at the same time the noose of fate had tightened around the neck of Maulana Ferghali.

The pious Imam was no more, trampled to death against the assault of time cruel and fate laughing.

"Our royal treasury is at your disposal, my devoted soldiers and grandees." Humayun leaped to his feet, as if escaping the fires of the Underworld within him. "Gold and jewels for you all. The emperor will retire to mourn the deaths of his friends! As fools they could have lived, but as traitors they became the victims of death. And yet, pray for the emperor as you must pray for the souls of the victims too. Pray that my heart may see the light of justice and understanding." His eyes were burning with the haze of torments indescribable.

Rage, you are to be shunned as a leper. One agonized shudder in Humayun's thoughts was whipping him away to the very gates of his fortress. *Sarvaqad! Tell me, sweetness, will the emperor ever find the bride of his soul?* Oblivious to the regiment of viziers at his heels and to the sound of kettledrums, his thoughts were silenced.

Chapter Six
Portuguese from Goa

Agra palace was the abode of the emperor this sultry afternoon. Humayun was seated at his rosewood desk in his library called, The House of Good Fortune. A subtle whiff of perfume from tuberoses in gold bowls, was reaching his awareness, but he seemed not aware of their scent or of the oppressive heat in this vast library. Only the fire of his thoughts sprinkled on papers was polishing the large sapphire in his turban, his robe of Chinese silk the color of a night sky. Actually, his thoughts were not original, but gleaning facts from the journal written by Gulbadan Begum. The emperor had requested her to write this daily journal, recording various events of the court and royal household. Later, his request had taken the form of a command, entrusting her with the task of writing Humayun-Nama, delineating the details of his reign as the second Moghul emperor of Hind. Absorbed in his narration of rewriting the history of his empire, he had almost forgotten about his wife, Maya Jan. She was seated by the marble lacework window, looking out into the garden down below, efflorescent with roses and cooled by the bubbling fountains. The book of Saadi was abandoned on her lap which she was reading earlier, her thoughts absorbing fresh air from the miracle of a garden in the courtyard, than the whiffs of stale air by the diligent efforts of Ghaffur in moving the brocaded monstrosity of a fan on the ceiling by constant pulling and releasing of the golden ropes.

Humayun sat tugging at the golden ropes in his head, and unknotting a thousand absurdities which words could never voice or portray. He had been sitting here almost all morning with the exception of appearing at the window called jharoka, for the sole satisfaction of his subjects, to insure that the emperor was in good health and available to listen to their grievances. *Justice*, Humayun's thoughts were exploring the reeds of his innovation, when he had introduced the system of beating drums at different hours of the day, not only for justice, but for the cultivation of peace and spirituality. The drum Saadat was sounded just before dawn in conformity with the call to prayers. A different drum named Daulat had its own tune to welcome each day at sunrise. The drum Murad was reserved for the evenings to herald peace and harmony for all. Naqassah-shadifanah was a special drum, sounded exclusively on the first and fourteenth night of each month, offering peace and goodwill to friends and foes alike. Yet, the most important of all drums was Tabli-adal, accessible to the ones who wished to seek justice from the emperor.

Hoping that no justice was required of the emperor this afternoon, Humayun sat sorting historic data in a plethora of deletions and annotations. He was not accomplishing much since the mystic streak in his head was alive and throbbing. Din Panah was his refuge and sanctuary from wars and betrayals, since he had returned to Agra. His quest for peace and truth was a gnawing hunger inside him, which knew no surfeit and could not be appeased. To feed his spiritual hungers, he had sought the platters of ancient wisdom from the tongues of the great Sufis. Rumi, Jami, Saadi, Al-Ghazali, Fariddin, the emperor had mixed their wisdom in one potpourri of a feast, but the flavor of perception was eluding him always. Paradoxically, his perception could behold the splinter-truth of cosmic reality more often than the banality of existence with all its illusions and absurdities. And yet the mystic vein in his head could not contain all that was within him, and that which came to him from without in allusive spurts of cognition and bewilderment. Right now, his head was turning to acknowledge the presence of his adorable wife, Maya Jan, whom he had favored to sit with him as his literary companion.

"How very tiresome for you, my dear, to keep the emperor company, while he sits there buried in his manuscripts without saying a word!" Humayun exclaimed suddenly, replacing the pen in his jade inkstand. "Selfish of me to keep you here for the pleasure of listening to your voice, for you recite the poetry of the old Masters with such passion. And that too, I haven't requested for the past two hours?" He got to his feet wearily. "You would rather be with the Begums than sit here with dull books as your only companions?" He laughed, his look warm and opiate.

"No, Your Majesty." Maya Jan Begum protested sweetly. "I would rather be here with you than any place else." Her gold-brown eyes were shining.

"Such sweet flattery, just to cheer the emperor's heart." Humayun's eyes were lit up with amusement. "Tell me, my lovely poet, do you like reading odes and couplets which have been buried for so long inside the wrinkled pages of time itself?"

"A wealth of music and beauty in them, Your Majesty, keeps me chained to them." Was Maya Jan Begum's flustered response. "Much is in there which I don't understand, yet I like the words and the rhythm—" She could not continue. Overwhelmed by this sudden longing to write couplets!

"The stars of poetry in your eyes, my love, are twinkling with the promise of inspiration." Humayun could see the light of intelligence in her eyes. "The emperor has decided to find a tutor for you, who could teach you the art of prosody and versification. Then you will discover much that is not only profound, but heart-warming." His gaze was wistful and enigmatic. "If I had the time, I would like to be a devout disciple of some Sufi or a Mystic. What mad longings breed in my soul at times? If I could only escape the burden of my royal duties, I would love to go wandering on the streets, or spin on my toes like a whirling dervish? Dancing in mad abandon to the dictates of my need for love, peace and harmony." He began to pace.

"Your Majesty!" One caution of a protest died on Maya Jan's lips. Her attempt to draw the emperor's attention to Ghaffur was left unheeded.

"I am wearing the color of the Sufis, my love, though they don't wear silk, but wool." Humayun seemed oblivious to his pacing. "The Sufis regard wool as the emblem of honor. The color blue is the color of mourning. But for the Sufis, it suggests love, sadness and enlightenment—" His feet came to a sudden halt, as if he was awakening from a dream. "Come, sweet, let me release you from the cage of this dull ideation." The act of holding out his arms was stalled, as his gaze fell on Ghaffur. "This warm air is not going to clear cobwebs in the emperor's head, Ghaffur! Better fetch the slippery waves of Ganges to cool this palace." He waved dismissal.

The golden rope slipped from Ghaffur's hand, and he seemed jolted out of his monotonous task by this sudden command from the emperor. After doubling low in one awkward curtsy, he was quick to flee the library. Maya Jan was heaving a sigh of relief at the flight of Ghaffur, for she did not wish him to hear the inmost longings of the emperor, which were sure to take wing on the shoulders of royal gossip.

"Love was the theme in my thoughts, not sadness." Humayun lifted Maya Jan to her feet, and held her close to him. "Fly away, my golden bird, and leave the emperor to his strange ruminations." He kissed her with the passion of a famished lover. "The emperor might be able to weave his thoughts into gold couplets after you leave? But do remind the Begums of our night-long excursion on the royal *safina*. And, yes, I have chosen Kashtizar as requested by them, so they don't need to come on the pretext of confirmation." He released her laughingly.

Humayun stood transfixed on one spot after his *golden bird* had fled, and was lost into the marble halls inside the palace. His mirth was replaced by a quiet hush from within and without. His thoughts too were dull and vacuous, unrolling a mindless tapestry where no golden couplets were to be found to weave beautiful patterns of inspiration. Will-lessly, he was drifting toward the polished shelves, his gaze sweeping over the books, all illumined and lacquered. The names of the authors in gilded letters were a mystic-dance before his sight, the loneliness within him reaching out for comfort and companionship. Faiz, Hafiz, Nizama, Omar Khayyam, Sheikh Saadi, Mulla Nusrudin, Jalaluddin Rumi, Fariduddin Attar, Al-Ghazali, Ibn-El-Arabi. His gaze was absorbing each name most dearly and intimately, as if the names themselves were his closest of friends. This was true in a sense, since all these books were a part of his royal entourage, whether he was engaged in campaigns, or journeying to distant retreats for pleasure and hunting.

Ah, the Bahristan of Jami! One low murmur in Humayun's thoughts was rapt. His hand was reaching out to feel this cherished book, but he was pulling out the one next to it. This book was by Fariduddin Attar, and he stood flitting through its pages until his gaze could command the obedience of his fingers, and he began to read.

The sea was asked why it was dressed in blue, the color of mourning. And why it became agitated as if fire made it boil? It answered that the blue robe spoke of the sadness of separation from the Beloved. That it was the fire of love which made it boil.

Humayun stood contemplating these words, but no spark of light was entering his vacant thoughts. His gaze was slipping over the next lines, as if he was trying to feel the pearls of wisdom which he himself did not possess.

Yellow is the color of gold, the alchemy of the Perfected Man, who is refined until he is in the sense, gold. The robe of initiation consists of the blue mantle of the Sufi with a hood and a yellow band. Together, these two colors, when mixed with green, represent the color of nature and initiation, and of truth and immortality.

The word *immortality* was carving a deep rent in Humayun's psyche, as if this word alone could unsheathe the scepter of truth in its ever-dying, ever-living essence of reality and illusion. Involuntarily, his feet were guiding him toward the marble lacework window where Maya Jan had occupied the gilded chair, but a few moments ago. He stood looking out at the glorious blooms in his garden down below. The gleaming swath of primula, gentian, and edelweiss were radiating their colors amidst the warble of fountains tall and cascading. His gaze was turning toward the gardeners, who, naked to their waists and absorbed in their labor of love, were pruning the bushes in shapes of swans and peacocks. Standing there inert and pensive, his thoughts were commencing a slow march down the alleys of time where the past two years were buried under the shrouds of tinsel-peace and Teflon-turmoil.

Inside Humayun's head, the word immortality was hacked to pieces by the scythe of time. Each piece suffering the pangs of early labor and breeding only the child of ignorance! *A weak and crippled child from the womb of light and darkness!* The bride of his soul was his lamp of sanity amidst the jungles of wars and betrayals, and he had lost sight of *her*, yet always searching for that lamp and light. Darkness was the shadow to his *light*, always pressing closer, carrying the naked sword of need for survival. Wars and betrayals were the legacy of the Moghuls, Humayun had confessed to himself, but this confession alone could not keep him away from the pleasure of cultivating knowledge or indulging in the cherished sports of polo and hunting. Since the past two years, his pleasures were numbered few, and betrayals piling high on the very hearth of sea and land.

Humayun's stay at Champanir, slashed by the arrows of cruelties and victories and girding the shield of penance, had its rewards and repercussions. The whole of Gujrat was subjugated, and Prince Askeri made its governor, in addition to his governorship of Ahmadnagar. To celebrate this victory, Humayun had abandoned himself to the pleasures of music and feasting, and arranging poetry sessions on his royal safina under the moonlit skies. Such romantic nights were not to last long, for soon the reports had reached him of

Prince Askeri's boasts and ambition. Prince Askeri, finding himself the lord of Gujrat, had given himself entirely to drink and dissipation. On one of his state banquets, he had begun to boast of his might and wealth. Declaring in the presence of all his viziers, that he is the shadow of God! A mighty king to rule and subjugate all the lords in Hind! Prince Askeri's cousin, Guznaffar, upon hearing this boast, had whispered to the vizier.

Yes. He is the king of the worlds, just now, because, he is very, very drunk.

This low comment from Guznaffar had resulted into a volley of mirth by the other viziers and grandees. Prince Askeri, after exploring the sea of this mirth, was so incensed that he had ordered Guznaffar to be thrown into prison. Guznaffar had contrived escape, conniving with three hundred of Prince Askeri's soldiers, and they all had fled to seek alliance with Behader Shah. Behader Shah was elated to find the imperial kin at his door, and encouraged by the defection of the imperialists from right under the nose of the imperial brother. Joined by these defectors, Behader Shah had stirred out of Diu with the intention of attacking Ahmadabad.

Humayun's thoughts were coming to a stalemate all of a sudden, and then ricocheting back to the follies of his dear brother, Prince Askeri. An imperceptible shudder passed through his tall frame, the large ruby in his turban catching a glint of sunshine and blazing, but he stood there inert and unseeing. Prince Askeri, unconcerned about the flight of Guznaffar, had fallen prey to the guidance of his vizier, Hindu Beg. Hindu Beg was one crust of an ambitious man, feeding the besotted prince with the morsels of ill-advice and flattery. He had succeeded in convincing Prince Askeri to march to Agra, and add this city to his kingdom of Gujrat. Hindu Beg had chalked out all the plans, that after the conquest, the coins would be struck in the name of Prince Askeri, and khutba read in his name in all the mosques in Agra. These raw and fantastic plans were shattered, when Prince Askeri had learned that Behader Shah was on his way to conquer Ahmadabad.

Stirring himself from the dreams of conquering Agra, Prince Askeri had then marched toward Ahmadabad to fight Behader Shah. Meanwhile, Humayun had marched from Champanir to thwart the designs of Behader Shah, but before he could confront him, this inveterate foe had succeeded in defeating Prince Askeri on the plains of Surkhaj. Prince Askeri had fled, reaching Champanir enroute

Mahi River, pleading with the emperor's vizier, Terdi Beg, for the loan of soldiers and provisions. But Terdi Beg had refused to lend the fugitive prince even a dirhem, knowing well, the incendiary plans of the prince to conquer Agra. Humayun, at this time marching in pursuit of Behader Shah, had found Prince Askeri at Chitor, where the fugitive prince was wandering destitute and homeless. Humayun, wearied of pursuing the chameleon foe, had pardoned his fool of a brother, and had returned to Agra.

The odor of death was assailing Humayun's thoughts, the death of Behader Shah with all its reek of deceit. But this reek was embedded deep inside the grave of wars, where the map of Hind could be seen smoldering in flames of unrest and sedition. Humayun had begun to pace, as if the smoldering anguish inside his heart was kindled to wildfire. Before the sword of death could conquer Behader Shah, he himself had conquered Malwa and Champanir. Terdi Beg had found refuge in Mandu. On the left bank of the Ganges, Sultan Mirza was forcing his way into Belgram. Guarding Qunauj on one side, he had sent his son Ulugh Mirza to besiege Juanpur. At the same time, Shah Mirza was reducing the territories of Karranmanikpur to ashes. Amidst this conflagration of rebellions, Humayun had sent Prince Hindal to secure peace and discipline. Prince Hindal had succeeded in re-conquering Qunauj and Belgram, and the traitors had fled to Kuch-Behar. Another rebel was Bhopal Rai, challenging not the imperialists but Behader Shah, and defeating him in Malwa. Encouraged by the success of Bhopal Rai, one more rebel by the name of Milu Khan had taken this opportunity in taking possession of Gujrat. Behader Shah had no choice left, but to flee back to Diu, hoping to secure the aid of the Portuguese. At this juncture, Humayun's thoughts as well as his pacing were trampling over the grave of Behader Shah, as if pounding bloody facts into dust with the mortar of reality.

Behader Shah had reached Diu distraught and disconsolate, imploring aid from Portuguese viceroys with the urgency of a suppliant. These viceroys were Nuno'd Acuna and Emenuel de Souza, who had just returned from Goa, bringing along with them a large fleet and trained men from the Portuguese army. Nuno'd Acuna, upon receiving this plea from Behader Shah, had feigned illness, though inviting him on his barge to discuss the terms of military aid. Behader Shah had accepted the invitation and was on his way to the barge in his boat, when he was assailed by a sudden foreboding that his life was in danger. Turning his boat around, he was about to shoot back to his safe refuge, when his intended flight was checked by E. de Souza. In a flash, E. de Souza had jammed his boat into Behader Shah's, intercepting his retreat. Without a word, both were locked in one fierce scuffle with the result that E. de Souza's foot had slipped and he had fallen into the river. A beehive of boats with Portuguese shouting outrage, were closing in on Behader Shah. In sheer panic, Behader Shah had jumped from his boat with the hope of contriving escape, but could not escape the sudden blow of halberd wielded by the angry hands of one Portuguese soldier. *Strange, that the bodies of these drowned victims, Behader Shah and E. de Souza were never found, and the Portuguese had maintained silence on this subject after all attempts in searching were proved fruitless.*

Humayun's thoughts were pacing to and fro, in conformity with his pacing, and searching the fruits of death and devastation, of revolt and ambition, where the stars of fate could lead all mortals to their dooms prophesied. The Portuguese had seized Behader Shah's palace with all its jewels and treasures. His arsenal too and the ships amounting to one hundred and twenty in all, were confiscated by the Portuguese. They had not neglected to send condolences to Behader Shah's mother, Makhduma Jehan, offering their support. Makhduma Jehan, after graciously declining the offer of support form the Portuguese, had embarked on her lonesome journey toward Ahmadabad. She was received kindly by Prince Asir in Ahmadabad, who had provided her with a team of escorts on her journey toward Gujrat.

On her way, she had met the fugitive prince, Zaman Mirza. Taking advantage of her recent grief, and with the armload of his base flatteries, Zaman Mirza had succeeded in convincing her to adopt him as her own son. No sooner had she reached Gujrat, that she had proclaimed Shah Mirza the Sultan of Gujrat. He was given command over a battalion of twelve thousand soldiers, and khutba was read in his name in Safa mosque. Zaman Mirza's rule was not to last long, for Imaddul Mulk had proclaimed another king of Gujrat, the son of Behader Shah's sister. He himself had dethroned Zaman Mirza, drafting his battalion of twelve thousand into his own body of troops. Zaman Mirza was fugitive once again, fleeing to Sindh, and then returning to Agra, seeking forgiveness from the emperor.

The curse of forgiveness! Why do I always forgive? Humayun's thoughts were wearied, longing for rest and release. But he could see them hovering over the trails of Bengal, where Sher Khan was rising like a vulture of the east. Sher Khan was swift and conniving, quick to lay waste Gorga and to plunder Benares. Wearing ambition on his shoulders, he had marched across Behar, adding Patna to his recent conquests. His sweeping victories had reached the limits of southern Behar, including Mongeir and the whole of Bengal itself. One forlorn thought in Humayun's head was watching the rapid rise of Sher Khan, but it was falling limp at the sudden beat of drums from down below, which he could neither silence, nor condone. Slowly and reluctantly, his feet were guiding him toward the marble lacework window. Expecting to hear the grievances of some lone suppliant, he was surprised to see Prince Kamran sounding the drum of Justice. Humayun stood watching his princely brother with an indulgent smile, while Prince Kamran exclaimed histrionically.

"Your Majesty. Pardon this intrusion, but your brother seeks justice in the manner of a common suppliant. The matter stands urgent, if I may gain your audience in the House of Dominion?" Prince Kamran waved his arms in one desperate appeal.

"Seek the love of the emperor, my rude Prince, and justice might follow!" Humayun let this rebuke escape the quiver of his indulgence. "The House of Dominion, it is then, and your pleas will receive due attention." He turned to his heels, abandoning this sanctuary in favor of the House of Dominion.

The emperor had landed into the House of Dominion unannounced, where he was wont to sit on his throne, dividing his time between family discussions and matters of the state. All were astir at the abrupt entrance of the emperor, the kettledrums blaring to announce his arrival, and the Begums shuffling to their feet in a flurry of curtsies. Amidst this sea of greetings, Humayun seemed to be wading through waves upon waves of color in silks and jewels. Espying Gulbadan Begum on the way, he halted abruptly, claiming her hand and kissing it reverently.

"My dear Rose! No more a princess, but a Begum. Last time I saw you, you were wearing a cap, and now this coronet studded with diamonds, proclaiming you a married woman? My adorable princess turned Begum! Can one arrest time in the bubble of timelessness?" He laughed.

Before Humayun could proceed further, his attention was caught by the trilling of mirth on Chand Bibi's lips. From the flowerbed of Humayun's six wives, only Chand Bibi was carrying his royal seed in her tender womb, and tenderness was alighting in his eyes at the sight of his giddy wife.

"My lovely Chand, are you feeding our royal babe with your mirth alone? You look pale, my love." Humayun hugged her. And as she just giggled in response, he sought the comfort of his throne.

Seated comfortably on his throne, Humayun let his gaze sweep over his royal brood with customary silence, before teasing the stream of royal gossip or royal parlance. His gaze was lingering on Zaman Mirza, who was sitting with his wife Masuma Begum most complacently, since he had gained full pardon from the emperor and was restored to his favor unconditionally. One spool of a revelation was unspooling in Humayun's head as to why he had pardoned this inveterate rebel. *For this one simple reason that he is married to my dear sister, unfortunate Masuma!* This revelation in Humayun's thoughts was one vague tremor, but that was not the only reason, he could hear more ripples of confessions. But his gaze was already shifting to Prince Askeri, and then alighting on Prince Kamran, where he stood wearing the mantle of a suppliant in his very eyes.

"You may come and sit with the emperor, my royal suppliant." Humayun waved his assent. "What caprice moved you to beat the drum of Justice, my audacious Prince? How long you are to test the emperor's love, which remains constant and boundless? As my brother, you would not ever be subject to the emperor's rage, but as a suppliant you might suffer a hundred lashes for your pain and grievance."

"Your Majesty." Prince Kamran bounced closer, offering an impeccable taslim. "Your love and kindness have made your brother bold, not impertinent, I hope?" He continued brightly, his hazel eyes twinkling mirth. "No caprice of mine, Your Majesty, which seeks your audience, but my love and devotion for you. Also, my need for the crumbs of your justice and wisdom. No need to recount the defections and disloyalties of the imperialists, Your Majesty, you know them too well. And yet the disloyalties of our kin cause me endless suffering." He stole a glance at Zaman Mirza before filling the quiver of his thoughts with complaints. "One little kingdom of Lahore is all I have to rule and defend, and yet it tends to slip away when I am commanded to defend the other kingdoms of your empire, Your Majesty. Kandahar, I saved from the tyranny of Shah Tahmasp's brother, Sam Mirza, and yet upon my return found Lahore smoldering in flames of insidious plots, even a bold attack from Shah Hussain. And who incited him to such sedition, you know that too." He flashed a quick glance at Shah Mirza, donning his Lucifer-charm while returning his gaze to emperor. "Right now the justice I seek, Your Majesty, is against the vile conduct of Khwaja Kilan, since the return of Shah Tahmasp to Khorasan. Favoring the route of Balkh, Shah Tahmasp has conquered Herat without much resistance. And now that he is planning to launch an attack on Kandahar, Khwaja Kilan has left his palace there at the disposal of Shah Tahmasp, instructing his guards to furnish the table with gold and silver plates to welcome the king. Khwaja Kilan has not only left all his possessions there, but a welcoming note as his farewell greeting to the king. *From want of warlike store, I have neither the means to defend Kandahar, nor to confront you on the battlefield, as I would have liked to do. The next most honorable cause I can pursue is to furnish my palace in good taste to welcome you as a royal guest, since I won't be there in person to entertain you.* Now this paragon of wisdom, as many deem Khwaja Kilan to be, is in Lahore, seeking my approval and audience, but I have forbidden him to set foot in my palace. The justice I seek, Your Majesty, is in terms of arms, horses, provisions, so that I may drive heretic pack of Shias, justly called rafizis for their heresy, out of Kandahar! And soldiers strong and valorous!"

"Men and provisions come not easy, when there is famine of peace in our empire." Humayun intoned thoughtfully, seeing through the thin veil of his brother's wickedness. "Khwaja is wise, the emperor has no doubt. I wish he would have stayed with me. I need his wisdom, if not his humor." He smiled wistfully. "His valor, fidelity and judgment are indisputable. There is something precious in the subtle wisdom of his little note and big action, the proof of refinement in a man which most of us sorely lack." A shadow of pain crossed his features, as he continued. "You have great forces at your command, while the imperialists are divided to be posted at all fronts to fight rebellions. We need to join our forces to defend our empire from the vulturine designs of Sher Khan! We must march to Chunar first—Kandahar is far, though it must be defended too?"

"Kandahar is of strategic importance, Your Majesty, that much is obvious." Prince Kamran began cautiously. "If I am to defend Kandahar, I must fly there without delay. And yet, such a campaign requires great expense. If you could spare some funds from your royal treasury, Your Majesty?" He requested.

"Rubies and diamonds fetch not victories, my wise Prince! And gold glitters, to deceive both the victor and the vanquished!" One Sufic epigram escaped Humayun's wearied thoughts. He got to his feet abruptly, his gaze profound and restless. "The emperor is wearied of wars and intrigues. How pleasant it would be to go riding at this hour of the day? Yes, you are welcome to accompany the emperor, and we might discuss wars, if not boons." He sauntered toward the gilded portals, Prince Kamran following him obediently.

The Chupatak horses, all caparisoned, were carrying royal riders through the maze of orchards into the dusty trails, edged with rice paddies and scattered huts. Both the prince and the emperor were absorbing the afternoon hush, their thoughts too arrested in quiet ruminations. Prince Kamran's pale silks were lending his features the sobriety of a wise schemer, while the blue silks on Humayun, in contrast to the red ruby in his turban, were enveloping his whole being in the sun-gold of fire and mystery. Behind them were a coterie of guards in crimson robes and plumes. But the prince and the emperor seemed oblivious to all, as if riding inside the wilderness of their own worlds, where no one could dare violate the sanctity of silence.

Humayun's thoughts might as well, could have been foundering amidst the waves of Ganges, where Sher Khan's treachery and assault had corrupted the holy waters on the verge of tempests wild and inclement. Emerging clear from the waters of unrest, Humayun's thoughts were following the blood-soaked terrains of wars, where Sher Khan had wreaked ruin and havoc. Gour Chausa, Benares, Qunauj, Sambhal, Juanpur, Bahraich, Surajpur. All these cities blackened by the soot of Sher Khan's greed, malice and cruelty were rising in Humayun's head like the sand-dunes of time, stark and shuddering. One black premonition was looming against all this kaleidoscope of intrigues and rebellions. The voice in his psyche was repeating the name, Chausa, as if the word itself was swollen with its helium of grief and despair. To escape this terrible voice of the psyche, his thoughts were hurling themselves into the soul of Prince Kamran to gauge the height of his brother's greed and ambition. And yet his inner being was welcoming sweet songs from the lips of Sarvaqad. This song itself was unfolding gulfs and voids, beyond which stood one bloom of a girl, the sister of Biram Khan. The bloom of Kabul, his thoughts were swooning, the bride of his soul! Drugged with desire he could hear his heart fluttering and expanding. Truth was smiling! Love shuddering! Anguish grinning! The pain in living was rising up to his throat to choke the reality of *dream* and *beloved*.

Prince Kamran's thoughts were choking too, but from under the burden of his vile plots in an attempt to usurp all power from the hands of the emperor, and to wear the crown of sovereignty till the end of his life. Knowing fully well the emperor's virtue or weakness as his love and kindness for all brothers, he was sure to get most of the funds and provisions he needed, and soldiers too, for his cherished campaign of Kandahar. He had great confidence in his warring skills, and was sure to gain victory, since he had done that twice before, emerging victorious both times. His estrangement with Khwaja Kilan had no deep roots. In fact, he had already forgiven him in his heart. And was gloating inwardly that he would be able to profess his obedience to the emperor! Expecting quite ingeniously and with the precision of a skilled diviner that the emperor would command him to restore his favor to Khwaja Kilan. As to Sher Khan's victories in Gujrat and Bengal, he had very little concern and that too for the reasons of his own safety and power. He had already sketched a plot in his head how he was to gain Sher Khan's alliance in order to weaken further the power of the emperor. Intrigue and betrayal were the shining bubbles in his head, as he could foresee the downfall of Sher Khan, and he alone installed on the *throne of power*. What would be the fate of the deposed emperor, he had not yet decided? These lofty plans were still bubbling in his head, when he became aware that they were riding through a wild stretch of land, cradling one cemetery the size of a polo field. His attention was arrested to the dog beside one tombstone. The dog was lifting his leg, shooting forth a jet of urine over the deserted grave.

"The man who lies buried there must be a rafizi!" Was Prince Kamran's abrupt comment, laughter spilling from his eyes.

"Yes. And that dog an orthodox brute!" Humayun retorted. Whirling his horse around and racing back toward his palace.

Chapter Seven
Battlefield at Chausa

The imperial city of tents was pitched right on the banks of Chupat, not far from Chausa, overlooking the dike where the river Son merges into the waters of the Ganges. Humayun, this wan evening, had left the silken comforts of his encampment, and was taking a quiet stroll on the sandy beach under some spell of gloom and ideation. Though fully appareled in chain mail and polished boots with gold helmet on his head and jeweled scimitar at his waist, he knew that there was no threat of assault from Sher Khan at this hour of the evening. Besides, he had sent Baighiz Muhammad with an offer of peace-treaty to this inveterate foe, and in conformity with the code of honor in wars, both sides would withhold their assaults as long as the negotiations were under way. He could see the waters of Ganges swollen, the citron evening polishing its surface to pewter-gleam. Incessant rains for the past one week had made the land and sea one slippery landscape, and he could smell the salt air with the looming threat of another stormy week. And yet, inclement storms were brewing in his head, more savage than the ones wrought by nature.

The sky was turning violet, a subtle hush within him dark and impenetrable. Some abysmal longing inside him was yawning and churning, as if his entire soul was flooded with torment. But this longing had nothing to do with his torment speechless, which was not from within, but from without. A flood of agony was pouring forth from the vessel of his psyche, though this agony too was twisted and gnarled by the ravages of time. *Time itself had ceased to heed the cries of wars and betrayal, where succession of months cared not if they gave birth to defeats or conquests. All were same in the measure of trials and tribulations.* Since his march from Agra to check the insurrections of Sher Khan in Gujrat and Bengal, Humayun had known but little peace amidst the jungles of gain and loss. Prince Kamran had left at the head of a grand army to defend Kandahar, appointing Haider Mirza as the governor of Lahore. Humayun too had entrusted his kingdoms into the hands of his able viziers before chasing his all-time foe, Sher Khan. Fakhr Ali was to guard and protect Delhi, and Agra to be safeguarded under the rule of Muhammed Bakhshi. Juanpur was assigned to Hindu Beg, while Yadgar Mirza was to watch Kalpi, and Nurreddin Mirza was to guard Qunauj. Prince Askeri, Prince Hindal and Zaman Mirza were included in the entourage of the emperor, along with Biram Khan and Sheikh Bahlul. The imperial cavalcade had then left Agra in the manner of palace-on-wheels, including the ladies of the harem and the entire selection of books from the royal library.

The imperial cavalcade had barely reached Behar when the imperialists were confronted with rebellion from the Afghans, probably incited by the covert designs of Sher Khan. After quelling this rebellion, they were on their way to Chunar to win back its great fortress, guarded by Sher Khan's son, Jalal Khan. Sher Khan had also appointed his brother, Ghazi Khan, to defend this impregnable fort in his absence. Upon reaching Chunar and laying siege for four months, the imperialists had failed to capture this fortress despite their persistent assaults. Only the guile of Rumi Khan had worked wonders. Rumi Khan, after subjecting one Abyssinian slave by the name of Kelafat to the punishment of mild flogging, had dressed his wounds to appear like deep lacerations. He had then dispatched Kelafat to the enemy's garrison with explicit instructions to act the part of a deserter, and to find about the strategies and weaknesses of the besieged. The quick-witted Kelafat had not only learned about the weak points of the enemy, but had returned unscathed, his wounds, rather chaffed skin already healed by the salve of his success and excitement. Fates were favoring Rumi Khan as he had directed his cannonade toward the exact position where walls were scalable, making a large enough breech for the Moghuls to attack and conquer. The victory was still hard-won as hundreds of men were perished on both sides.

Humayun, elated by this sudden victory, had pardoned the rebels, and had granted them the boon of freedom. Rumi Khan, on the other hand, drugged by his ingenuity and without the permission of the emperor, had cut off the hands of all three hundred prisoners he himself had captured. Humayun was so incensed after learning about this brutal massacre by Rumi Khan that he had ordered his death. A small dose of poison was swift in lending him freedom from pain in living and hating.

The weight of those unfortunate memories was heavy on Humayun's shoulders, as he kept strolling in utter oblivion to his spirit restless. After installing Beg Mirak as the guardian of Chunar fortress, Humayun had marched to Benares, claiming swift victory and coming face to face with Sher Khan. Sher Khan was not expecting this strange encounter, and was quick to feign ignorance on all charges of sedition on his part, or of inciting Afghans against the imperialists. Professing devotion to the emperor and exclaiming with the fervor of an aggrieved suppliant.

I am your slave, Your Majesty! Give me a fixed boundary in which I may establish myself.

This astonishing exclamation with all its incongruity of time and place was hovering above Humayun's contemplations like a cloud, dark and impenetrable. Sher Khan was commanded to sign a treaty with the imperialists, surrendering all the Afghan territories, upon which he had laid claim in Behar. Though, he was granted permission to retain Bengal as his conquered domain, paying annual tribute of ten lakhs to the emperor. This treaty was not yet ratified, when a sudden request from the king of Gour had reached the emperor with the urgency of seeking assistance from the imperialists in his dire plight. Mahmud Shah was the victim, besieged by Jalal Khan, who had driven the king into exile from his fortress of Gour, keeping his wife and children captive inside their own palace.

Humayun was so greatly moved by the plight of this king, that forgetting about his affairs in Gujrat, he had embarked on a hasty march to render aid to the king of Gour. This march was proving auspicious, since the imperialists were able to add Barh, Patna, Mongeir, Surajpur, Nawabganj and Bhagalpur to their conquests on their way to Gour. Unfortunately, as soon as they had entered the territory of Kahalagoan where the king was staying in exile, his exile from the world was announced. Mahmud Shah had died suddenly. At this juncture, Humayun's grief was so deep as if his own brother had passed away, and he had pressed forward toward Gour, carrying the body of the late king all embalmed and secured in a polished coffin. The fortress of Gour was captured without much resistance, but Jalal Khan had fled. Before leaving, the vile rebel had murdered the wives and the children of Mahmud Shah.

Humayun's gaze was exploring the silent waves of the Ganges, as if trying to bury all sorrows in their liquid peace. Peace was lapping its way inside his thoughts too, and flooding the city of Gour in its light of rest and reprieve. The emperor had rested in this city for whole nine months, naming it, Janatabad. Gour, meaning grave, was in stark contrast to the beauty of this city, so Humayun had chosen the name Janatabad, which means literally, the Paradise. This Paradise was unfolding its sweet charms in his head right now, as he turned abruptly, retreating his steps toward his encampment. Each monument in this city was etched in his mind like a piece of art, sculpted by angels and preserved by God. Adina mosque, a jewel pure and glowing, its slender minarets reaching to the very heights in heavens! The marble halls of Firuz Mina, sprinkling the light of white truth in silence and solitude! Tombs of the saints, Akhi Sirajuddin and Shah Nimatullah, wafting forth the scent of poetry and wisdom. One sliver of a thought was splintering the awesome journey in Humayun's head with its pebbles of reality smooth and mundane. Chand Bibi was pregnant this second time around! Pregnant in the real sense, for her last pregnancy had proven to be a false one.

Wasn't it in Agra that I had learned about her false pregnancy? How disappointed I was. Why? No mistaking now, her belly is swollen with child! Two more months, and the joy of holding a royal babe in my arms. The miracle of life. Humayun's thoughts were disputing this issue of joy and hope, and getting lost once again inside the garden of Janatabad.

The emperor was becoming aware of the hush and silence all around, from within and without, as if Ganges itself was holding its breath, the waves deep down contemplating a storm? He thought he was transported back into the wilderness of Janatabad where he had discovered three wells, rumored to be contaminated with poison. Arrested in that time-bubble of the past, he could see why he had had those wells drained of all water. Unlike heaven, Janatabad couldn't boast of rivers of wine, milk and honey, Humayun had commented while renaming Gour. But upon discovering the wells filled with poison, he couldn't endure the thought of such corruption inside the heart of his newly proclaimed Paradise, so after commanding the water to be drained, they were filled with rocks and pebbles. Then cypress and pomegranate trees were planted around these wells as the emblem of love and eternity. Sagradini and Piyasbari, Humayun was trying to remember the name of the third well, his gaze lifted up to the sky, and arrested there to the bright Venus above. The face of the moon was livid against the white purity of the Venus, and Humayun couldn't tear his gaze away, his feet coming to a slow halt involuntarily. Some mystic beams were escaping the eyes of the moon, uncurling the city of Jumhirpur with its crocodiles carved in stone, representing saints and disciples.

The map of the sky was changing, as if inviting a few glittering stars to mark new territories, but the map of memories in Humayun's head was stationed at Janatabad, and seeing only Gour. It was in Gour that the emperor had sent Prince Hindal to Tirhoot to guard and protect this city. At the same time, a reminder was sent to Nurreddin to let no rebellion disrupt the peace in Qunauj. Both were instructed to rule these respective cities and to safeguard them against the assaults of any power-hungry lord or miscreant. Those instructions had lasted them but a few months, for they had abandoned their posts and had gone back to Agra.

Knots of betrayals inside the tapestry of doom! Humayun's thoughts were too weak to leave the sanctuary of Janatabad.

The emperor's reprieve from wars, even in Janatabad, was short-lived. He had learned that Sher Khan had thrown off his mask of loyalty, and had killed Mir Fazli, the governor of Benares. After capturing this city, he had seized Qunauj and Tirhoot also, since they were abandoned by Prince Hindal and Nurreddin. Extending his conquests further between Kosi and Ganga, Sher Khan had become the master of North Hind. Fortunes were favoring Sher Khan, for Hindu Beg of Juanpur had died suddenly, succeeded by Baba Khan. Sher Khan had lost no time in attacking Juanpur, also raising blockades in Gujrat, so that no aid from the imperialists could reach Baba Khan. Successful in capturing Juanpur, he had then diverted his attention to the rebellious Afghans in Behar, and had soon subjugated this city from the cradle of the Himalayas to the bosom of wilderness in Gondwaras. Sher Khan's next move was to conquer the city of Mongeir, and Humayun freshly alarmed at these disastrous news, was able to send Biram Khan at the head of a large force to check the advance of this inveterate foe. Mongeir had succumbed to the power of Sher Khan, who had burnt its gates to cinders, and his governor Khwas Khan had imprisoned Biram Khan.

Isn't the emperor himself a prisoner of fate and calamities? One wound of a protest was throbbing in Humayun's head, his gaze reaching the far embankment.

The scene was bucolic and peaceful, the horses grazing in carefree abandon. Cannons large and gloomy were a wild contrast to this tranquil scenery in the distance, and neatly piled rows upon rows of artillery were mocking the hush and peace in the evening. Humayun's gaze as well as his thoughts was reluctant to enter the gates of Chausa where Sher Khan loomed large and menacing. He was approaching close to his own city of tents, overwhelmed by a sudden longing to commune with Moveiid Beg. Moveiid Beg, a great mystic and a scholar, was befriended by Humayun in Janatabad right after the news of Biram Khan's imprisonment, and since then he had become his most devoted of viziers and advisors. Humayun was not heeding the voice of his longing, only envisioning the comfort of his royal tent, painted bright with Zodiac signs. These signs were leading him back on the trail of his journey from Janatabad toward Agra. Agra was lost in the glare of those Zodiacal signs, for barely his cavalcade had left the Grand Trunk Road, when its advance was blocked at the very precincts of Chausa by the great blockades of Sher Khan.

Sher Khan was merely waiting, it seemed, and brewing some insidious plots, for he had shown no sign of engaging the imperialists in an open battle. Humayun had decided to stay on the defensive, meanwhile, sending a string of missives to Prince Hindal and Prince Kamran, commanding them to fetch their forces in a battle against this foe, turned bold and mighty. So far, he had received no response, but was hoping that they would join him in this just cause to save his empire from the blood-thirsty claws of Sher Khan. Lately, he had sent Sheikh Bahlul with urgent commands of reinforcements from Agra. The royal tent with gold and damask was greeting the emperor's return, but his attention was diverted by the liveried messengers at the far end of the encampment, who were alighting from their steeds.

News from Agra, perhaps? One soporific thought in Humayun's head attempted to kindle a spark of joy, but he was already seeking the comfort of his harem inside his luxuriant tent. The emperor was wearied of all news, his heart closing its shutters of hope and fear.

Under the canopy of Zodiac signs in his tent, Humayun sat in his gilded chair, sipping ruby-red wine from his goblet. The Persian carpet under his feet was blooming in colors vivid, and so were his wives in colorful silks and jewels. Brass tables, holding candelabras in gold and silver and illumined books, were adding warmth to this luxuriant abode. But the hearts of the royal occupants were dark and chilled, as was obvious from the drift of the conversation, somber and cheerless. Only Princess Aqiqa was carefree and sprightful, somersaulting on the carpet and landing into the lap of Bega Begum. Chand Begum was quiet, and all knew what she was thinking. More so the emperor, for he knew that she was wishing Baike Begum was with her on this journey fraught with dangers.

Baike Begum was the wife of Zahid Beg, Humayun's favored vizier. Chand Begum had befriended Baike Begum at the time when Humayun was engaged in quelling rebellions in Bengal. Their friendship was strengthened after Chand Begum had grown heavy with child. Baike Begum was expert in the realms of child bearing and she had become Chand Begum's advisor and confidant both. Unfortunately, their friendship was truncated at the turn of some events not congenial to the emperor's mood and temperament. Before embarking on another expedition, Humayun had offered the governorship of Bengal to Zahid Beg. Zahid Beg had readily accepted, but on the instigation of his wife, had returned to the emperor, complaining bitterly.

Your Majesty could find no better place but Bengal to make away with his royal subject?

Humayun was so incensed that he had dismissed this impudent wretch under a shower of harsh rebukes. Postponing all or any mode of punishment till his anger was abated. Before the emperor could reach a decision, the offended vizier with the help of Haji Koka had fled from Bengal. Soon after, Humayun had left Bengal, appointing Ali Kuli as the governor with a contingent of five thousand body and horse to defend this fractious kingdom. All these contingents of memories were floating in Humayun's head, his gaze sad and thoughtful. He wanted to say comforting words to his wives, but his lips were sealed, it seemed.

"Your Majesty, now that the rains have stopped and Ganges fordable, when are we going to start for Agra?" Bega Begum sang her wish abruptly and wistfully.

"As soon as the devil incarnate in the guise of Sher Khan heeds the voice of reason! If no peace treaty is signed, we would march back to Agra fighting our way through land and sea?" Humayun's lips were unsealed in one bitter response.

"I wish Baike Begum was—" Chand Begum's wish was silenced by Aqiq Begum's startled look, shooting her warnings.

"Don't you know, you are not to utter that name in the presence of the emperor." Aqiq Begum was whispering, her eyes flashing.

"We will be in Agra, my dear, when it's time for your baby to see the light of the world." Gunwar Begum was quick to comfort the frightened mother-to-be.

"Oh, how we all miss Agra!" Gulbarg Begum sighed to herself.

"Your Majesty, could we go back to Janatabad? We were so happy! No songs, no music, no poetry here." Maya Begum chirped.

"Janatabad is where my harem is!" Humayun quipped, the amber stars in his eyes bright and dancing. "The emperor is selfish. What need he has of the heavens when all the houris are right here with him? And all these poetry books! Yet, one doesn't need to read books to enjoy the sweetness of poetry and wisdom." A subtle whiff of pain and nostalgia was seething in his voice as he continued. "My mamma had committed the entire book of Shahnama to memory. She was fond of reciting the works of Saadi and Hafiz too. We could, if you all wish, feast on song and poetry this very—" His thoughts were left unuttered, as he noticed Zaman Mirza.

Zaman Mirza was standing at the door of the royal tent, seeking the emperor's permission to enter. After the royal consent, two envoys were announced. One was Baighiz Muhammad, the Moghul envoy, and the other Sheikh Khalil, an envoy from Sher Khan. Humayun, ignoring the protocol of curtsies, was commanding them to speak, his gaze bright and smoldering.

"Your Majesty." Baighiz Muhammad lowered his head, words escaping his lips reluctantly. "Sher Khan agrees to sign a peace treaty. If all the terms are agreeable to Your Majesty, then Sheikh Khalil will act as a witness in signing this contract." He unrolled the paper in his hand and began reading solemnly. *"Bengal and Behar are ceded to Sher Khan and he is to acknowledge Your Majesty as the sole sovereign of Hindustan. Khutba will be read in your name, Your Majesty, in all the mosques in Behar and Bengal. Chunar is to be restored to Sher Khan."* He held out the contract to the emperor.

"My revered Sheikh, as you are known to all who have met you." Humayun turned to Sheikh Khalil, after claiming the contract

94

absently. "You are a spiritual father of the pious and the believers, I have heard. Lend me your judgment, if you will. Even if the emperor signs this treaty, what proof he has that Sher Khan will not betray him once again?" The absent look in his eyes was replaced by a profound one.

"No proof, Your Majesty, but faith in the will of Allah." Sheikh Khalil's lips parted in one sliver of a smile. "And yet proof there is, if it can be ascertained as a noble action. Sher Khan's troops are already leaving Chausa with the intention of fighting the Chero Chief, who has been a long-time foe of Sher Khan. He is so confident that the emperor will sign the treaty, that he is concerned only in defeating the Chero Chief." His eyes alone were pleading with the emperor to sign this treaty.

"Since when the emperor has become so predictable in signing agreements without a dispute or discussion?" One wisp of a joyless laughter grazed Humayun's lips. "And yet, true it is that the emperor desires nothing but peace. Fetch me my pen, Zaman Mirza, and let the emperor seal the fates of all into a vacuum of words." He flashed a command at his brother-in-law, returning his gaze to Sheikh Khalil. "Yes, the will of Allah! Wars, betrayals, intrigues! We should leave all into the hands of God. Convey this message of the emperor to Sher Khan, my revered Sheikh, that kingdoms gained by the dust of deceit and betrayal have no solid foundation, crumbling between one's fingers before a monument of victory could be erected. And the emperor will return soon, to reclaim what he has lost." He signed the treaty with one violent stroke of his jeweled pen. "Now take this fateful, if not hateful piece of agreement to Sher Khan, and implore him to desist from further evil."

A sudden wave of fatigue and emptiness was overpowering Humayun's senses, and he closed his eyes. When he opened them, Sheikh Khalil had already left. His gaze sweeping over all was arrested to Zaman Mirza.

"You are to keep the night watch, Zaman Mirza, and be vigilant. Sher Khan is not to be trusted." Humayun's psyche itself was issuing this command.

"Yes, Your Majesty, your obedient slave." Zaman Mirza curtsied.

Humayun was dismissing his brother-in-law with a wave of his arm, when he espied Moveiid Beg at the unguarded entrance, waiting to be announced. The emperor's weariness was replaced by an abrupt surge of joy and warmth, as if he had been waiting for this friend since eons. A garden of song and poetry was unfolding in his eyes, wafting forth the scent of love and friendliness.

"Welcome, my valorous Beg, welcome." Humayun greeted cheerfully. "Begums desire entertainment this evening. You have arrived at an opportune moment, for the task of arranging mushaira, or poetry recital as you prefer to call it, falls on your shoulders. We would recite couplets all night! And at dawn, we journey back to Agra." He chanted with the dream-languor of a mystic.

"The couplets have to wait, Your Majesty. To be recited at Agra, I hope." Was Moveiid Beg's solemn appeal. "Your messenger, Nur Beg, whom you sent earlier to Agra, is back. He has brought a quiver of news, which he wishes to share with you, and craves your audience, Your Majesty. Urgent news, he says?"

"Ah, the delights of poetry must wait, says the prudent poet himself!" Humayun laughed, his gaze cradling all his lovely wives in one eager embrace. "You must find comfort in sleep, and dream of song and poetry. Agra awaits us, and we will be there before you awaken?" He teased, getting to his feet abruptly. "My messenger from Agra, bent double under the weight of grievous news, my heart tells me. This burden heaped upon his shoulders by the kindness of my dear, dear brothers? Is Sheikh Bahlul on his way to Chausa too, carrying the ammunition of excuses from the bales of ingratitude from my brothers? Come, Beg, the emperor is a glutton to suffering, and let him satisfy his appetite this night in the privacy of a tent, so wretchedly named, Audience Hall." He dashed toward the door.

A small tent, furnished with Kirman rugs and gilt chairs, was serving as an audience hall to Humayun's need for privacy and decorum. The emperor had taken his helmet off, and it lay abandoned on the ivory table beside him. His pallor was bleeding through even from the silk of his small beard and thin mustache, as he sat receiving the missiles of reports from the lips of Nur Beg. The molten hush of the candles in gold and silver candelabras was absorbing the color of greed and deceit of the royal brothers, it seemed, which was reflected in the dream-mists of the emperor's gaze. Moveiid Beg had abandoned himself to silence, admiring the emperor's stoic reserve, and honing his own weapons of Sufic restraint. Humayun's stoicism was splitting like a rag, soiled and frayed, and he could hear the agony of his soul, its lips twisted with pain! And its anguish shriveling inside like the old, gnarled branches of a tree, which had suffered blight after blight from the very hands of nature.

"Your messengers had reached Agra alright, Your Majesty." Nur Beg was saying. "They were received by Prince Hindal and Prince Kamran. But since both of your brothers were always disputing and challenging each other, they couldn't reach a decision to send any aid as commanded by you, Your Majesty. Prince Hindal was guided by Nurreddin, who was advising him to proclaim himself as the emperor, and to command that Khutba be read in his name in all the mosques at Agra. Then the fugitive lords from Bengal, Zahid Beg, Khusrau Beg and Haji Beg had come to Agra, supporting Nurreddin in his cause to win kingship for Prince Hindal. That was when Sheikh Bahlul reached Agra, Your Majesty, but Nurreddin was absent on some secret mission. Free from the influence of Nurreddin, Prince Hindal had promised Sheikh Bahlul all the aid commanded by you. All the troops and armaments were gathered, but it took five whole days. By that time, Nurreddin was back in Agra, and noticing the supplies of artillery and cannon to be sent to you, Your Majesty, he was seized with rage. Finding the culprit of this mission, no other than Sheikh Bahlul, he had ordered him imprisoned. Then he himself had dragged him to the very banks of Jamna, beheading him with his halberd and exclaiming. *His treason has cost him his head, since he is caught conspiring with the Afghans against us.*" He paused, but the daggers of impatience in Humayun's eyes were goading him to continue.

"Nurreddin then proclaimed Prince Hindal the emperor of Hindustan, Your Majesty." Nur Beg gasped for breath, and then continued hastily. "Prayers were recited in the name of the new emperor and coins struck in his name. The courtiers at the courts of Delhi and Agra were appalled at these strange turn of events. The ladies of the harem were aghast at first, then raising loud laments they were heard pleading with Prince Hindal to abandon this charade of power and to come to his senses, but of no avail. Muhammed Bakhshi, your spiritual leader, Your Majesty, had stayed in utter shock after the murder of Sheikh Bahlul, but upon learning of Prince Hindal as the emperor, had ran to him like a madman, crying. *You have slain the Sheikh. Now kill me, the sinner in your eyes!* Prince Hindal's only response was. *Enough blood has already been shed—away.* Prince Hindal's mother, Dildar Begum,

Your Majesty, went to the court one day dressed in the color of mourning. Prince Hindal was seated on the throne and observed. *Dear Mamma, why are you dressed in deep mourning? My accession to the throne calls only for joy and festivity?* Dildar Begum replied. *I am mourning for you, my unfortunate son! Already mourning over your bier, I feel. You are young, and on account of the instigation of the sedition-mongers, you have lost the true way. You have girded your loins for your own destruction. To your guilt, you have added the stain of innocent blood. You have murdered the holy Sheikh. Do not ever come to me for blessings. And do not ever defile my palace with your sinful presence, till you come to your senses. Till the rightful emperor returns."*

"Do not hesitate, my good messenger. Pour it all, till no drop of poison is left to corrupt the peace of this silent night." The rills of anguished commands in Humayun's eyes were scalding the very air in this silken tent.

"After gaining the throne of Agra, Your Majesty, Prince Hindal was planning a siege over Delhi to add it to his crown. At the head of a large force, he had left Agra, but as soon as he had reached Hamidpur, he had learned of the strong opposition of Yadgar Mirza and Fakhr Ali, who had won a contingent of the imperialists on their side to thwart the designs of Prince Hindal, and to safeguard this kingdom for you, Your Majesty. Since Prince Kamran had returned to Lahore after his successful campaign in Kandahar, adding Hisar Firuza, Zemindawer and Badakhshan to his conquests, Yadgar Mirza had sought his assistance too, against Prince Hindal. Prince Kamran had lost no time in starting from Lahore at the head of twelve thousand troops, not as an ally to Yadgar Mirza, but to seize the throne of Delhi for himself. Yadgar Mirza had learned of these evil plans, and had acted most wisely to check the advance of Prince Kamran. Prince Hindal too was informed of Prince Kamran's hasty approach, and had abandoned his plan of siege, returning to Agra peacefully. As soon as Prince Kamran had reached Sombat on the borders of Panipat, Fakhr Ali had hastened to welcome him, advising him to follow Prince Hindal, and secure his submission. Prince Kamran, his hopes thwarted, had agreed. Reaching Agra, he had forced Prince Hindal to submit to his sole authority in renouncing the throne. Fakhr Ali had stayed with the princes, persuading them to send you aid, Your Majesty, as commanded by you. They had complied, professing to dispatch a large contingent, while Fakhr Ali had gone back to Delhi. Learning later, that they had no intention of sending any aid. As the matters stand, Your Majesty, Prince Kamran is in league with Sher Khan, covertly. He hopes that you would not come back, and fears that you would. That is all, Your Majesty." He concluded painfully.

After this woeful account, a profound hush followed, inside the hearts of the emperor, the vizier and the messenger too. None dared say a word, lest the tongues of grief kindle wildfire on the very waters of Ganges. Moveiid Beg had not moved a muscle, either during this painful account, or after its conclusion. Seated there mute and waxen, he seemed to represent a portrait of sorrow. The emperor too had fallen into a trance, beyond shock, beyond grief. Only the wheels of despair churning inside him, were hurling him further into the abyss of oblivion. Time was standing still, it seemed, jolting the vizier and the messenger to awareness, but not the emperor. Both in unison had tried to engage the emperor in conversation, but of no avail. His responses had been occasional smiles, thin or rueful, or a few laconic expressions heavy with anguish and bitterness. Moveiid Beg had even recited poetry, and Nur Beg had fetched fruits and sweets, but Humayun had feasted only on wine and opium. Silent and pensive, the emperor seemed to be glued to his chair, only a low command escaping his blanched lips, like a whisper in the wind.

Moveiid Beg, obedient to the emperor's command, had gone out to check personally the preparations of journey to Agra in the morning. The soldiers at the royal encampment were diligently engaged in packing the baggage, and a flotilla of boats was gathered near the bridge which was quite skillfully thrown over the karmanassa in Ganges for a safe passage toward Agra. Some were reloading the galleons with armaments, and the others busy packing their personal belongings. Satisfied with these preparations, Moveiid Beg had returned to the emperor's tent, finding him still alert and taciturn. Nur Beg too had made several rounds around the encampment, and after settling down finally had closed his eyes in a state of fatigue and wakefulness. The emperor had begun to pace, neither speaking, nor showing any intention of retiring to his comfortable abode.

A sea of agony was simmering and churning in Humayun's heart as he kept pacing. His thoughts were wooing the harlot of deceit and treachery inside the hearts of his brothers, but the prostitution of grief with despair was the only reality, fluttering its wings to consume him body and soul. The murder of Sheikh Bahlul was a raw wound carved in his own breast, stinging and throbbing, gnawing and cutting, but more savage than this searing pain was the pulse of a foreboding. He could feel it coiling around in the pit of his stomach like a serpent. *The sibilant sounds in there were the blades of threat, violence and inevitability. Some child of inevitability was rising inside him. Faceless.* And what he couldn't see was too truly happening right across from his royal encampment.

Sher Khan, gloating over his genius in throwing the imperialists off-guard, was plotting more acts of treachery other than the simple act of signing a peace treaty. His scheme of a surprise attack was working magnificently. As soon as the darkness had descended on the waters of the Ganges, he had recalled his troops back, who had moved away earlier with the pretense of fighting the Chero Chief. Commanding his soldiers to their assigned posts, he was further elated by fresh reports that the imperialists were preparing for departure, not in the least suspicious of any assault. The gulf between the night and morning was shrinking by the hour, and the imperialists under the burden of fatigue and anticipation had fallen asleep. The moment of treachery on Sher Khan's part was drawing nigh, and he was informed by his spies that even the royal night-guard, Zaman Mirza, was snoring peacefully. Girding the shield of his spirit vengeful and malicious, Sher Khan was ready to pound the imperialists into a handful of dust.

The dust of presage in Humayun's psyche at this very precise moment was rising like a billowing storm, but his thoughts were still clutching at the wound in his breast, and lamenting the demise of Sheikh Bahlul. He was still pacing, as if drugged with agony and despair. His heart was breaking it seemed, writhing in pain and convulsion. He could feel his soul groaning, a loud, terrible laceration in his very thoughts oozing forth shock and disbelief.

"Sheikh Bahlul murdered! By my own brothers? The cankers of the Moghul Empire." Humayun's feet came to an abrupt halt before his friend and vizier. "Is Sher Khan really gone to fight the Chero Chief?" The voice in his psyche, not his lips, was uttering this query.

"Yes, Your Majesty. I myself saw the troops moving out" Moveiid Beg's voice was drowned against the thunder of cannon-shots.

100

"Look to the safety of the Begums." Humayun shot one frenzied command. Snatching his helmet from the table, he dashed out into the very volcano of war.

The *eye of dawn* was startled open by this treacherous assault of Sher Khan. The enemy was landing upon the unsuspecting imperialists like carrion, and they in turn were jolted out of their sleep, drugged with stupor and fatigue. Sher Khan had hemmed in the imperial troops on all three sides. Granting them retreat, if possible, into the merciless waters of the Ganges itself. His son Jalal Khan was commanding the right wing. The left wing was under the command of his vizier, Khwas Khan, equipped with orders to capture the emperor alive or dead. Sher Khan himself was riding in the center, with mighty elephants in the rear. This ugly dream was unfolding swiftly, staining the battlefield at Chausa with blight and bloodshed. The bridge thrown across karmanassa was destroyed by artillery and cannon. Smoke from the flotilla of the imperial boats, torched by Sher Khan, could be seen rising to veil the kingly face of the sun. Chaos and pandemonium were in the air, the spears whistling, the clanging of swords, and the thunder of cannons. The cries of the wounded and the dying could not be heard against the roar of the cannons, but bodies were piling up high with their throats slit or limbs dismembered. The best of the Humayun's troops, the valorous Tartars, were choking in their own streams of blood, lost and bewildered. Some were jumping into the bottomless abyss of the Ganges, clinging to the rafters, or snatching planks from the demolished galleons to float to safety.

Humayun was fighting like the one possessed. Defying the edicts of sanity! Challenging death. Welcoming the agony of defeat, as if pressed by an insane will to disfigure the very face of fate and ugliness! Oblivious to the daggers of death poised before his very eyes, he was hacking his way to the front. Spurring his horse at full speed, he could be seen weaving his spear right and left, and dealing death-blows to the ones who dared challenge his prowess. In his blind struggle to cut the enemy to pieces, he was urging his horse onward, when he found his path blocked by an elephant. Seething with rage and impatience, he thrust his spear into the skull of the beast. Feeling the thrust of madness in his feverish thoughts, he was trying with all his might to retrieve his spear, but could not pull it out no matter how hard he tried. In his mad struggle, Humayun had failed to notice the mahout concealed inside the howdah who was armed with a crossbow aimed at him with the precision of a skillful archer. Just when the emperor had managed to loosen his spear, a sharp arrow pierced his arm. Blinded by pain, he could see one half of his spear dangling in his hand, the other half still stuck in the skull of the elephant. The emperor was falling down from his white steed, the agony of his soul more terrible than the agony of his flesh.

The wounded and unarmed emperor was hauled onto the back of a horse by one of his loyal soldiers, whose one and only thought was to save the emperor. With the speed of lightning, this devoted rider with the royal load on his mount was heading straight to the liquid sanctuary of the Ganges. Plunging headlong into the waters of the Ganges, the horse and the riders were carried upstream. Suddenly, a wild current, with the fury of a foaming giant unhorsed the soldier and the emperor, and both were drifted apart, foundering deeper and deeper into the horrors of death and silence. Death was seen everywhere, riding on the quicksilver waves of the Ganges, and grinning at the wavelets of lives, all torn and shredded. Some were sinking into oblivion, and some holding on to the reeds of hopes. Some were swimming frantically, and others clinging to the rafters in stupor of misery and hopelessness.

Amidst this flood of misery and hopelessness, Humayun had surrendered himself to the will of the fates. Though an expert swimmer, each stroke of his arms and legs were causing him the most excruciating of pains. More savage than this pain was the agony in his soul, and he was letting go of himself. Somewhere out there, on the dry strip of a land, the light of truth was shining. He had seen it, but he had no wish to carry it into the gaping void of surcease. Rocked by waves, he didn't know that one water-carrier floating on his water-gourd, was trying to reach closer to save his life. Suddenly, a great tide, foaming at the mouth, was carrying the water-carrier to the very abode of his longing to rescue the emperor. Almost losing his water-gourd, the water-carrier was quick to regain his balance and to pull the emperor to his side, forcing his arms around the water-gourd for support.

Humayun was snatched out of the jaws of death into the fetters of life eternal and inviolate. The hungry, parched lips of truth, now reflected in his psyche, were muttering inanities. An eternity of pain in living! Some mad, leering thoughts from the very voids in ether were crowning his head with stars. *The harsh, piercing light of freedom! Such blinding glare. This maddening will to live and suffer!* Humayun's head was spinning like the orbit of earth, circling around the Sun.

"What is your name?" One bubble of an inquiry was bursting forth on Humayun's lips. His thoughts were floating outside his head, though he could feel himself perched on the water-gourd, drifting along so very lightly.

"Nizam Aulia, Your Majesty." The water-carrier murmured. His heart sinking under the weight of fright and delight. Fright, at being close to the emperor. And delight at the sparkling certainty of his perception that they would land safely on the opposite bank of the Ganges.

"If the emperor sees Agra one more time in his life, Nizam, he will grant you the boon of sitting on his throne for one whole day." Humayun was closing his eyes, the ghosts of his tragedy pounding at the doors of his awareness.

Somewhere down the profound, glittering deeps of the Ganges, his harem and kingdoms were perishing. The river swollen and bloated was sealing the fate of Hind with the dike of defeat. He was whisked into the jungles of exile, chasing the legacy of his dreams, and forgetting the face of truth. The dreams were slippery and molten. Imploring him to knock at the gates of reality! Goading him to ride on the currents of victories. Fever and delirium were escorting him to lands unknown. Peace in death was white and silent. The scepter of truth had retreated with a groan. The agony of awareness was standing guard. Come back, come back! To the pain in living!

Chapter Eight
Grief consecrated

The great soul of nature in Zar Afshan garden was brimming with colors against the haze of dusk, all heliotrope. Humayun and Gunwar Bibi were strolling side-by-side in utter silence, their souls suffused with hush and sadness, feeling only the color of death and tragedy. The emperor was donned in blue silks, the clusters of pearls and sapphires in his turban accentuating his pallor to the smooth glow of ivory in sunset. Gunwar Bibi was appareled in all white, her pure silks stitched with carnelians, and her tiara of diamonds and emeralds lending her the semblance of a fairy queen, arrested under some spell of magic and enchantment. The blooms of enchantment were in the background though, where an open court was set, furnished with a jeweled throne and succession of carpets. Humayun had just left his viziers and grandees behind under the marquee in gold and crimson, after expressing his wish to take a stroll, and requesting his lovely wife to accompany him. The sound of fountains murmuring in the distance, mingling with music from the open court, was evoking the saddest of memories in Humayun's mind, his thoughts fluttering and tearing open the wings of time and tragedies.

Four agonized months, sliced thin by the knife of loss and grief, had succumbed to quiet despair since the emperor's return to Agra after his defeat at Chausa and his miraculous escape. Another miracle was that after drinking the potions of countless griefs and agonies, he had survived. Perhaps, finding the soma of perseverance as an antidote, or vying with the patience of Job, he himself didn't know. One whole month of fever and delirium had lent him the bliss-comfort of sanity, which no sane person could ever claim in the face of tragedies insane and heart-rending. Within this month his wound in the arm had healed, and in his heart too, yet shattered again and again by blows violent and merciless. Princess Aqiqa, Aqiq Begum, Maya Begum, Chand Begum, Gulbarg Begum, all was perished into the holy waters of the Ganges. The blister-wounds in Humayun's heart at such news were snapped open, falling into such an ocean of grief, that he didn't know if there was enough balm in this world to heal the roaring madness in one's heart and soul. And yet, the same wounds had grown numb with agony and were paralyzed by grief. Whatever pain was left inside him was transformed into a jungle of mourning, quiet and menacing in its stealth and silence.

This stealth and silence were in Humayun's soul, and from the colonnades of its mourning, was rising forth one sand-dune of a memory. His pace was slackening, the enchantress queen beside him with dark eyes and olive complexion, evoking in him the sense of tenderness and awareness. But his thoughts were stealing into the ruins of the past four months, where his first wife of youth, Bega Jan, was held captive by Sher Khan. Pain and loneliness were grazing the lips of silent wounds within him, but he was restraining their assault with the reminder that Sher Khan had promised her safe return to Agra. Another face was surfacing from the sand-dune of his memory, and that was of Zaman Mirza, swallowed by the raging currents of the Ganges, leaving behind the emperor's sister Masuma Begum, a widow, disconsolate and grief-stricken. More faces were breaking forth from the grains of sand, and those were rather the faceless bodies of the soldiers, Moghuls, Tartars, Rajputs, all slain or drowned. All effaced from the mindless map of existence.

The familiar odor of agony and retching was rising in Humayun's head, but he was pouring it into the bottle of his stoic restraint, before it could knock him senseless into the sanctuary of his former oblivion. *Inertia and oblivion which had made him numb and weak to such a degree that his viziers were afraid even to utter the name of Sher Khan in his presence, save alone recount his fresh exploits.* It was only recently that he had demanded reports concerning the latest maneuvers of Sher Khan, impressing upon his befuddled viziers that the betrayal of his own brothers was much more agonizing to him than the deceit of Sher Khan. Adding further that all his sorrows and torments had lost their sting. *After this confession, the gates of hell were flung open, and through those had marched forth the saplings of Sher Khan's new conquests.* This wicked foe, who had acted most dishonorably at Chausa, had now conquered Bengal. He had become the undisputed master of Behar. Across from the Ganges, he had seized Juanpur as far east as Qunauj. His youngest son, Doab, was sent on a campaign to besiege Etwa and Kalpi.

106

Humayun's thoughts, as the little troopers of defense, were trying to find a few crumbs of purity inside the heart of his deceitful foe. Yes, he could see inside the corruption in Sher Khan's heart one dewdrop of goodness, trembling and foundering. This dewdrop was holding tight the honor of Bega Jan's safety, since Sher Khan had promised her return with all due courtesy to the emperor of Hind. *Emperor of Hind!* One ripple of mockery in Humayun's thoughts was loud and bitter, his gaze following the kingfisher in its carefree flight.

Hind is dying! Slowly and pugnaciously dying, and the emperor no more—in name alone. The mockery in Humayun's thoughts was turning bitter, and mournful.

The empire of Hind was crumbling right under his feet. The kingdoms were reduced to dust, and their grandeur effaced. The emperor had lost his will to rule, and the joy in living was fading from his heart and soul. Chill and loneliness were his companions, yet inside the pulse of silence within, he could see one large rent of a longing. His longing to know truth, a glimpse of which he had caught while on the verge of death in Ganges, but now that truth was no more, only haze and bewilderment. His longing was for the wine of poetry from Sarvaqad's lips too, some dream illusive and ineffable.

The eyes of his heart, though aching with constant weeping, were always thirsting for the beauty of Kabul and Badakhshan. One little sprig of a longing which could never leave him alone was the quest for the bride of his soul. His unwedded bride, yet betrothed to him by the holiness in time immemorial. He was overwhelmed by this longing at times, when he wished to abandon all wars, kingdoms and treasures, and wander from continent to continent in search of that bride to the very deeps in the beginning of timelessness. His love for pageantry was gone, and his spiritual hungers famished, begging for crumbs holy from the almshouse of Din Panah. But he had had no time to set foot into the sanctuary of Din Panah against the storms of wars, deaths and betrayals. And the seeds of spirituality inside him, along with his blooms of astrology and astronomy, were dry and shriveled, too weak to beg for sustenance.

I am mourning only the death of love inside me. Where is love gone? Hungers carnal and spiritual! Thirsts base and noble! Humayun could inhale the scent of tuberoses, his senses coming alive to the beauty of garden around him. *And yet what kind of love*

107

this is that I love my brothers still? Why don't I throw them in dungeons dark and terrible? Feeding this love with the morsels of vengeance? His thoughts were feeding on chaos, and seeking solace in the injunction from the lips of his father on his death-bed. *Do naught against thy brothers, even if they may deserve it.* His thoughts were whirling him back to the rungs of reality.

The emperor was becoming aware of Gunwar Bibi beside him, but his thoughts capricious as ever were racing after Nizam inside the gilded halls of his palace. This particular day, as promised by the emperor earlier, Nizam Aulia was granted permission to sit on the emperor's throne. Taking full advantage of this high position as his just reward for saving the life of the emperor, Nizam Aulia had been sitting on the throne since morning, issuing Farmans and exercising his scepter of power with despotic tenacity. He had accomplished much already, securing posts for his friends and relatives with the imperial household. He had ordered his water-gourd to be cut into several pieces, the size and shape of different coins. Those pieces were then plated with gold, and polished to the semblance of real coins. Satisfied with the workmanship as commanded, he was quick to preserve these coins for posterity by ordering them stamped with his name. A monogram was also inscribed on these coins, depicting the date and the time, and duration of his reign as the emperor of Hindustan. Reflecting upon the honor of his promise and its absurdity in the face of reality, Humayun's thoughts were laughing all of a sudden, their first genuine peal of mirth after four months of grief suffered and mourned inside the silence of his soul.

"The voice of silence within and all around! It seems, if the emperor doesn't speak, the whole world crawls back into the shell of silence?" Humayun's feet came to a slow halt before the rigol of marble fountains, gurgling and splattering. "You must make the emperor talk and dispute, my love, or the world would go mute?" He stood facing Gunwar Bibi.

"Your Majesty!" Gunwar Begum was startled out of her reveries mute and painful. "I was thinking, Your Majesty. Don't know what I was thinking about? About so many things, I guess. About Prince Hindal, most of all. You know, since your return to Agra, he has shut himself up in Alwar. Since Prince Kamran is bringing him here today by your command, Your Majesty, Dildar Begum is sick with fright that you would be angry and would not forgive?"

108

"Is the emperor cursed to breed fear than love?" Humayun appeared to question his vacillating thoughts. "Against the wildfires of betrayals and intrigues, how many times did the emperor forgive his brothers? Love and forgiveness! Don't they breed rebellion and ingratitude? My empire is crumbling, and I still forgive my brothers, why?" He noticed her sudden pallor and claimed her hand gently. "Are you ignoring the counsel of our royal physicians, my love? You look pale. A bit feverish, are you not?" He felt her brow, his gaze tender and thoughtful.

"No, Your Majesty!" Gunwar Begum protested, her pallor suffused with a subtle flush. "I have but—" She was unable to voice her joy against the tender solicitation in the emperor's eyes.

"You too, then, fear the emperor! Is that it?" Humayun smiled.

"No, Your Majesty!" Another protest broke forth on Gunwar Begum's soft lips. "I am pregnant. Hoping to be the mother of a royal heir?"

"My lovely Gunwar!" Humayun caught her into one crushing embrace, kissing her eyes and lips. "The emperor would pray for a princess, just like our Aqiqa—" His thoughts were stung by the sudden shafts of loss and agony, but quickly as before he succeeded in forcing his grief back. "Time, we returned to our silken abode to share joys and intrigues alike." He linked his arm into hers, resuming his stroll back toward the sea of color and music in the garden.

The grand marquee with its ripples of silk and damask, was changing colors, and holding purple of the evening in abeyance. Humayun was seated on his jeweled throne, and contemplating the flickering flames in gold and silver candelabras. Though, his gaze would stray now and then up to the sky where a livid moon stood gathering clusters of stars around its waxen beauty. The leaves were turning silver under the flood of moonlight, and Humayun was fascinated by the tall, majestic poplars in the distance. To his right was seated Prince Askeri, and to his left Gunwar Begum, but he seemed to be courting the wine of solitude, in addition to the ruby-red wine in his goblet. Waves upon waves of gaiety and laughter from guests and courtiers alike were penetrating Humayun's awareness, and his gaze was straying over to the lawns and terraces, as if lit by the lamps of memories. Moveiid Beg, Terdi Beg, Ali Kuli and Haider Mirza were drowning the gurgle of fountains in their volleys of mirth and raillery. Down below, upon one gleaming terrace were gathered Dildar Begum, Bibi Mubaraka Begum and many more bright blooms from the harem of his late father. Amongst them, outshining all were Gulbadan Begum and Khazanda Begum. Humayun's solitude and quiet contemplations were splintering all of a sudden by the loud recollections of Prince Askeri. He was almost drunk and bloated with exhilaration, his voice sharp and mirthful.

"After his victory at Chausa, Sher Khan had hastened to the comfort of his camp, followed by his advisors and well-wishers." Prince Askeri was relating this tale to a couple of guards standing close to him. "Once inside, he had prostrated himself most dramatically, offering humble prayers to God. After displaying his gratitude in such fashion, he had conferred upon himself the title of Sher Shah Suri. Imagine that!" He looked past the guards with approval, where a few courtiers were gathering to catch his words, and he continued merrily. "With this grand title on his shoulders, he was happy to share his dream with the few assembled. In his dream, he and the emperor were standing near the throne of Prophet Muhammad, Sher Khan told them. Prophet Muhammed was talking to the emperor and telling him that God had favored Sher Shah Suri with the kingdoms of Hind. At the same time, Prophet Muhammad had taken the crown from emperor's head, and had placed it on the head of Sher Shah Suri, commanding him to practice justice and kindness. The king of the worms, I say, with a bagful of lies, concocting dreams!" Drunken mirth escaped Prince Askeri's lips, and he drowned it in a draught of wine from his gold goblet.

"The most hated of bigots! Cunning and vainglorious." Moveiid Beg murmured, casting an apprehensive look at Prince Askeri. "No grain of refinement in the character of that man. Vulgar in manners and vulgar in thoughts! His soul utterly deprived of song and poetry, which transform man into a human being—" His thoughts were plucked short by a sudden exclamation from Prince Askeri.

"No poetry? He spills couplets at each step, which lead him closer to the glory in power and deceit. Did you not hear what he recited at Chausa?" Prince Askeri laughed again. His inebriated look lit up with the poetry of exhilaration.

"O Lord, Thou hast power and pelf
And supporteth the poor Dervish
Thou hast chosen to bestow sovereignty on Farid, Hasan's son
And thrown Humayun's men to be devoured
By the fishes, alligator, crocodile, or tortoise."

110

"When men of low breeding take upon themselves to write poetry, they corrupt the very rivers of intellect with bad rhyme." Moveiid Beg opined aloud, catching and holding the stars of amusement in the emperor's gaze.

"As for you, my worthy Prince, your very brain is bloated with wine and you have lost all sense of propriety." Humayun shot a mild rebuke at his brother, softening it further with a volley of mirth.

Against this volley of mirth, Prince Askeri's comment was left unvoiced, as Prince Kamran's sudden appearance was noticed in the garden. He was approaching the throne in great haste, oblivious to the ripples of murmur and commotion as a result of his breezy appearance. Dildar Begum was quick to intercept Prince Kamran's approach, racing toward the throne after flashing a mute command at him, and he was stalled momentarily, indecisive and flustered.

"Your Majesty. In the memory of your late father, my loving husband, I plead for your love and compassion. Grant Prince Hindal forgiveness!" Dildar Begum's eyes were filling with tears, her voice faltering. "Do not summon him to your presence, Your Majesty, if you cannot forgive him. And yet, do forgive him. I would not be able to endure the exile or suffering of my son. He is not a traitor, only young and inexperienced—" She fell into one heap of a curtsy at the emperor's feet.

"My dear Mamma!" Was Humayun's anguished cry, as if his own mother had returned from the abode of death? "How could you ever doubt the love of the emperor for all his brothers?" He held out his hands, lifting her up to her feet, while he himself stood gazing into her eyes. "No harm will ever come to my brothers as long as I live. And the emperor has no intention of sending Prince Hindal to exile, or inflicting—" He ceased to speak, becoming aware of the other Begums at the foot of his throne, including Gulbadan Begum and Khazanda Begum.

This shining ocean of silks and brocades had eyes glittering with fear, and smoldering with appeals. Humayun's heart had begun to thunder with rage and despair at this sudden bolt of a revelation that all the ladies of his royal household feared him, expecting rage and punishment, not love and clemency. His gaze was sweeping beyond them toward the tides of courtiers in one hopeless attempt to dissolve all fear and to nurture love. Espying Mulla Nurreddin by the canopied pavilion, hugging his Quran to himself, another rude revelation was hitting Humayun on the head.

With one thunder of a command, Humayun could hear himself summoning Mulla Nurreddin to his presence. No sooner had the pious Mulla approached the throne, that Humayun had claimed the copy of the Quran from him, this time requesting, not commanding.

"With this holy book in my hand, I tell you all who disbelieve in the emperor's love for his brothers, that there is no anger in his heart for Prince Hindal. You have the emperor's solemn promise that—" Humayun's oath splintered with bitterness was cut short, as Gulbadan Begum snatched copy of the Quran from the emperor's hands without a dint of outrage or warning. Retreating back, she almost collided with Khazanda Begum.

Though a mingling of love and relief had replaced the glints of fear in the eyes of all Begums, their lips were trembling and murmuring protests. In a flash, all Begums had begun to speak. Babel of comments reaching the emperor's awareness.

"No need, Your Majesty. May what you do, be right. No need, no need to take oaths on the Holy Quran—" The voices of the Begums were dying.

"Your Majesty. Why do you say such things—" Khazanda Begum's lone protest was also dying on her lips, as she noticed Prince Hindal emerging from behind the poplars. Looking more like a mendicant than a royal prince, she was thinking.

All eyes were turning to that tragic scene, including the emperor's, his heart bleeding and churning the old wounds to foams of fresh grief and sorrow. Prince Hindal was dressed as a suppliant, with hangman's rope around his neck as a mark of complete submission. His head was lowered, and he curtsied low as he approached.

"Nay, brother, throw it away! Discard this mark of infamy!" Humayun exclaimed, a shadow of pain crossing his features. "Come, embrace the emperor. You are forgiven, absolutely and unconditionally." He held out his arms, into which fell the contrite prince, his eyes stinging with tears of shame and penance.

Humayun released his brother from his loving embrace, and stood gazing into his eyes, his own heart shedding tears of love and sorrow. With one imperious wave of his arm, he dismissed all, commanding only his brothers to stay. And of course, Moveiid Beg, who had the privilege of being the emperor's spiritual friend. The courtiers were leaving, and the Begums were anticipating a long stroll in the garden. Gunwar Begum too was granted

112

permission to join the other Begums, and the emperor had sought his jeweled throne, commanding his brothers to sit near his throne.

"It is very rare that we see each other, save alone be together and have time to talk." Humayun contemplated aloud, claiming his goblet of wine from Jouhar, and sipping thoughtfully. "What made you rebel against the emperor, my wretched Prince? Why did you murder my revered Sheikh?" He flashed Prince Hindal this abrupt query, though his look was tender.

"Your Majesty." Was Prince Hindal's choked response. He couldn't tell the emperor that he was more of a fool than a rebel. That he was ignorant of royal intrigues, yet influenced by the plotting, intriguing tongues of others. That he was willing to suffer the emperor's wrath, for he loved and admired the emperor with the innocence of a child who couldn't avoid getting into mischief. All these thoughts were surfacing in his eyes unvoiced, and not a word escaping his lips.

"Our traitor Prince is young and inexperienced, Your Majesty. That's all." Prince Kamran with all his Lucifer-charm appeared to mock and defend Prince Hindal in his utter misery. "He would gain wisdom if he could stay away from the den of scheming, ambitious friends." His eyes were lit up with the stars of merriment.

"The emperor could benefit from a few crumbs of wisdom too, my charming Prince, if he could learn to reward his brothers with punishments for their follies and intrigues?" Humayun smiled caustically, returning his gaze to Prince Hindal. "Speak, my innocent Prince. Let the emperor hear your defense for your revolt and cruelty, and treason?" He commanded.

"Your Majesty." Prince Hindal was able to loosen the knots of his thoughts. "I was led astray by the wickedness of Zahid Beg, Your Majesty. And of Haji Baba and Khusrau Beg. They all told me that Your Majesty would not ever return to Agra, and I believed in their false reports. I didn't murder Sheikh Bahlul, Your Majesty. Nurreddin Mirza did, he accused him of sending artillery and cannon to Sher Khan. I didn't even know. Now I know, Your Majesty, much to the chagrin of my shame and ignorance. I will not rebel, Your Majesty, not ever again, be assured—" Fever of remorse and gratitude was constricting his thoughts once again.

"Might as well forget all that!" Humayun commented, his look wearied and distraught. "What is past is past. We must now all join manfully to repel the common enemy." He pressed his temples, as if to check the flow of his grief.

"What a cluster of tragedies, Your Majesty, plunging us all in shock and disbelief!" Prince Kamran was quick to divine the rills of grief in the emperor's heart, and began with the gesture of commiseration. "Precious lives, all lost. Wives and loved ones, all gone. How bravely you have endured all, Your Majesty, I admire your strength and courage. Tragedies countless and kingdoms still smoldering in the flames of unrest and uprising?" He sighed, eliciting a mournful expression. Failing to notice that such affectation of his had lost its charm to deceive the emperor.

"Are we all not the victims of tragedies on the face of this earth? Some, the victims of greed and ambition and others the victims of grief and uncertainty! And all the victims of misfortunes, if fortunes happen to smile upon the privileged few, which others try to snatch with all their might, forgetting the wand of inevitability." The Sufi in Humayun was expounding, not his troubled soul. "Tragedies of the body and earth counted and witnessed. And tragedies inside the hearts and souls left unaccounted for." He smiled. "The emperor likes to believe that you love him, even if that love is no more than a drop in the ocean of hope and peace." His gaze appeared to dive deep into the very sea of corruption inside the heart of his brother.

"Your devoted subject, Your Majesty, and your most loving brother." Was Prince Kamran's affable response, a subtle flush pervading his features. "I love you more than my wives and children, though they are very dear to me." He was donning the mantle of love, his smile dazzling. "In the name of love and bewilderment, Your Majesty, may I be as bold as to ask, why did you let a lowly, witless fakir like Nizam defile the sanctity of your throne, even if it is for one day?"

"It is not for pleasure alone that the emperor has detained you, my prudent Prince. My prime concern is to discuss the issues of wars and rebellions. Are you trying to divert the emperor's attention from such worthy issues? Sher Khan, that bitter-gourd of a foe must be swallowed whole." Humayun began to laugh at the trickle of his dull wit. "As to that fakir sitting on the throne, the reason is quite ludicrous, he saved the emperor's life!" He could feel the weight of levity rising above the sea of his inner mysticism, but he continued heedlessly. "Caprice or madness, whichever guides most of us, is the

114

true prerogative of the emperors. No person is lowly, be he a fakir or a leper. If each one of us could sit on the *throne of power* for one fleeting moment, the whole world could be united with the chord of peace and harmony. Each one benefiting their friends and family and enriching their lives in return. With the result that poverty, discord and enmity could be reduced to dust by the hands of goodwill? To rule is the lifeblood of all living. Men must rule. Nature must rule. Each grain of sand in the desert, and every pebble on the beach, they too must rule. Each blade of grass and all things animate or inanimate, must rule, to benefit their own kind. That is the law of nature. Yet nature is both kind and harsh. Changing and changeless! And within its great soul, no form or distinction dare breathe dissent. One little reed is no different than the mighty oak, no man lowly or great, no faith inferior or superior, no judgment weak or strong, but peace and holiness in death and renewal. Life greeting darkness! Beauty cradling ugliness. Joy breeding pain! Peace cultivating chaos. Goodness befriending wickedness. Life welcoming death! All living, all breathing, all undying." He sighed. The Sufic stars in his eyes bright and feverish. "Yes, you have succeeded in diverting the emperor's attention from the marshlands of war and sedition." He shifted his gaze to Prince Hindal. "Agra is not to be your refuge for long, my young Prince. Nor it will be for the emperor, it seems. You are to come with me to fight Sher Khan. Or, is it Sher Shah Suri now, a worthy challenge?" One sliver of a smile lay chilled on his lips.

"I will wait upon you with all my heart and soul, Your Majesty!" Prince Hindal declared with great devotion. "Will always be with you, Your Majesty. All my life! Wars, victories or defeats, whatever our fate, we would share together."

"Victories, if God wills! And defeats, that's God's will too. Fates can't be averted. Greeks were wise to know and to surrender to their gods." Humayun's heart was missing a few beats, his gaze alighting on Prince Askeri. "May the emperor disrupt your intoxicated bliss, my fair Prince, to let you know that you would be accompanying the emperor too in our joint effort to crush our enemy?" His gaze was already returning to Prince Kamran, expecting no response from the inebriated prince.

"Your Majesty." Was Prince Askeri's only response, his eyes feverish.

"Your strength and loyalty are needed, my charming Prince, to defeat this most formidable of our foes. We must all join our forces and march against Sher Khan. If left unchecked, he would plunder and pillage all the kingdoms of our empire. Agra and Delhi, Sind and Hind. Our first move should be to march straight to Qunauj to check the treacherous advance of Sher Khan. His son, Kutb Khan, is posing another threat, though a minor one. He is planning to cross the river Doab, and launch an attack on Kalpi. And that happens to be your little kingdom." Humayun was thinking aloud, his look dreamy. "This long campaign has to be planned carefully. Enroute Belgram, we need to pass through Bijapur, then cross the Ganges to camp over the other side of Qunauj where Sher Khan's—" He stopped abruptly, noticing Prince Kamran's distress and his sudden pallor. "Are you ill, my Prince, or do you wish not to join the emperor in this campaign against our common foe?"

"Both, Your Majesty." Prince Kamran contrived a low moan, summoning regret and contrition in his eyes. "You already know, Your Majesty, I have recovered but recently from that illness, almost prolonged to four months. Still feel weak and disoriented at times. And if that is not enough to make one dejected, Lahore is brewing fresh threats of insurrections?" He paused, ensuring himself of the calm expression of the emperor, then continued bravely. "Besides, Your Majesty, Moghul troops don't need me, or the assistance of my army. Your imperial contingents are swollen in numbers since, well, now you have twenty thousand soldiers, I have been told. The best Chupatak horses and the warring elephants. Cannons, armaments, leaden bullets, all in great supply. Those seven hundred swivel carriages to be driven by healthy bullocks, I myself have checked. What need of seventeen thousand artisans though, Your Majesty, I wonder? Please, grant me the permission to return to Lahore. I will gladly die for you, Your Majesty, but—" The crumbs of his false devotion were scattered by an impatient wave of the emperor's arm.

"Yes, my valorous Prince, you would!" One bullet of a rebuke was shot from Humayun's lips. "You would die, not for me, but for the kingdoms lost and unconquered." He lifted his gaze up to the star-studded sky above.

The cold, livid moon up there seemed to be mourning, as Humayun gathered stars in his eyes. They were more like the pebbles on earth to his painful awareness, washed ashore, soft and

116

gleaming under the flood of moonlight. Within his heart the rills of pain was inhaling sorrow of the night air, absorbing its hush and silence. It was awakening like the splintering of the oceans, wild and terrible. An intolerable longing of the soul! An ache old and familiar! Gathering in its wake the reeds of a spiritual quest. This quest no other than finding the bride of his soul! The voice of silence inside him was listening to the sound of music from the lips of Sarvaqad. His soul was expanding, torn open by the spasms of agony. Agonized mists themselves were revealing one bloom of a face. A face, which he had forgotten amidst the hurricanes of deaths, betrayals and tragedies. It was that of Mah Chuchak, the bloom of Kabul! His heart was empty and inconsolable. Longing to sail high over the oceans and the mountains, to land into the pine-valleys of Kabul, to wed the bride of his soul. A sudden blight in seasons was alighting in his eyes, as his gaze turned to his brothers.

"Leave the emperor, my kind and loyal brothers." Humayun commanded, his gaze already shifting to Jouhar. "Request Gunwar Begum to join the emperor. All must retire to the palace while we explore the night beauty of this garden."

Suspended high above the face of the Venus was the gibbous moon, shining like one silver coin, smooth and polished. Humayun and Gunwar Begum were strolling once again, quiet and gulfs apart in mind and spirit. The emperor was chasing the moon-bride, his thoughts giddy and painful. *The cold, throbbing stars with their hearts bled white with pain*, Humayun was thinking, were longing to kiss the face of the Moon. *Never reaching close to the beloved, never knowing the bliss of nearness.* The scent from roses and lilacs, mingling with the overpowering perfume from Rat-Ki-Rani, was assailing Humayun's senses, his thoughts breaking into little dewdrops, bright and ephemeral. The whisper in the wind was kissing the cheeks of Mah Chuchak, agony and longing inside him wild and shattering. He could not reach the bride of his soul, his passion great and tragic was churning a tempest. One primal, savage need of the flesh and soul was effacing the dewdrops in his thoughts, and awakening him to the dream-reality of his lovely wife beside him. His feet were coming to an abrupt halt under the canopy of silvery poplars.

"Love! My lovely Gunwar." One groan of an endearment was dying on Humayun's lips against the shower of his kisses, hungry and insatiable.

The emperor had caught his own wife in one blind, savage embrace. Kissing her till her lips were bruised, the violence of his passion unslaked and mounting. He was ravishing his royal prey, unrobing her under the naked glee of the stars, and making one patch of grass his bed of lust and rape. Gunwar Begum was stunned and gasping for breath, her lotus of desire receiving the thrust of his violence with swoon and rapture. In Humayun's eyes, the bride of his soul was standing naked and aghast. His ears were ringing with songs divine. The night air was murmuring the name of Sarvaqad. The stars were laughing. The moon had veiled itself against the white shroud of a cloud.

Moon, Beloved! Where is she? The bride of my soul gone. Far, too far— Humayun's thoughts were afraid to look at the harlot of his desire. Lover closing his eyes. Beloved trying to cover her shame and nakedness.

Chapter Nine
Prophecy of Exile

The great palace at Lahore with its red sandstone façade was perched right on the banks of Ravi. Its waves small or great were flooding Humayun's dreams as he lay sleeping in this monstrous ugliness of an architect's nightmare, called a palace. Bega Begum was sleeping beside him on the four-poster bed rippling with lace and silk. Damask drapes and gilded paintings in wretched contrast to faded tapestries, were imposing their aura of gloom in this chamber furnished with chests and tables of all mahogany, carved and embellished. Humayun, drugged with the wine of his carnality, was mired deep into dreams savage and leering.

The emperor was dreaming, as if awakening to the nightmarish reality in living, then slumbering back into the peace-chaos of dreams within dreams. Dreams and reality were such a mingling of sorrow and disbelief, that he couldn't tell when dreams awakened, or when reality slumbered. Sher Khan had defeated him at Qunauj, and later he had conquered Delhi and Agra. The empire of Hind had slipped through his fingers, and had fallen into the hands of his tyrant foe, Sher Shah Suri. His dreams infested with tragedies were offering him no respite, but they were weakening in their resolve to torment him everlastingly. Astonishingly enough, they were commencing a slow retreat, leaving behind the ether of peace in void and silence. From this void and ether, was erupting forth one dream awesome. A tall man dressed in green from head to toe, and carrying a golden staff, was pouring words of comfort into his very heart.

Be of good cheer, O unhappy emperor. Do not grieve. In exile, you will find kingdoms richer than the ones you have lost. And yet Hind will await your return with longings pure and terrible. God will bless you with a son. You will name him Jalaluddin Muhammad Akbar. He will rule Hind under the canopy of justice and wisdom. This venerable man in Humayun's dream was offering him the golden staff.

What is your name, o revered sage? Humayun's dream-voice was asking.

119

I am the Ahmad of Jam, The Terrible Elephant. Your gentle mother, Mahim Begum was related to me. Your son will be of our lineage. He will be remembered as Akbar The Great. This vision was transfigured with light in Humayun's dream and then fading. Leaving behind silence and vacuity!

Humayun's eyes were opening slowly, blinking away all dreams, yet holding on to the vision of light and hope. One ribbon of sunshine was escaping through the chink of the drapes, and his heart went fluttering to catch the purity of gold in peace and renewal. Yet, peace was nowhere to be seen, but the horror in living and suffering. His gaze was turned to his wife, slipping over her smooth form, from the ivory in her neck down to the snow valley in her bosom with an opiate tenderness. The agony of his spirit was returning, holding out the naked sword of reality, and plunging it deep into the heart of his *memory*. Truth was lancing his awareness to smithereens, and his very soul was weeping and bleeding.

Sher Khan had sent Bega Begum to Agra under his personal escort. Proving his honor in this quarter and relinquishing the honor of loyalty and friendship which he could never fail to profess, into the hands of his greed, ambition and treachery. Humayun had then marched to Qunauj with the intention of defeating this inveterate foe, and mending the rags of his empire with the stitches of peace and order. But fate had decreed otherwise. Both the armies had confronted each other on the muddied banks of the Ganges, its waters swollen by monsoon rains and posing their challenge of flood and turbulence. The emperor's encampment was already flooded, affording respite to Sher Khan who had the advantage of being camped on the higher grounds.

Sher Khan had stayed on the defensive, and the imperialists themselves had launched an attack. Humayun was commanding the center with Haider Mirza riding close behind him. Prince Hindal was in charge of the infantry, Prince Askeri to his right and Yadgar Mirza to his left, commanding their separate contingents. The battle had begun favorably for the imperialists, for Sher Khan's son Jalal Khan was unhorsed while aiming a swift assault on the infantry commanded by Prince Hindal. Suddenly the sky was dark, lashing down its missiles of rain and wind. Not a single shot could be fired from the side of the imperialists, for artillery and cannon were rendered useless by pelting fury in the sky. Besides, the violence of the storm aiming straight at the faces of the imperialists was blinding their sight, and they were thrown into panic and confusion. The armies of Sher Khan were hemming in on them from all sides, and the imperialists were pushed further down into the churning waters of the Ganges.

The nightmarish reality of defeat and death by drowning had surfaced in the emperor's head this second time around, but once again he had kept fighting with the fury and valor of a madman. In a flash, Ganges itself had become a battleground of life and death for the imperialists. Men drowning in droves or being hurled ashore by the raging tides, which in turn were whipped by the bloated currents! Once again the emperor was saved, this time by his devoted eunuch by the name of Kafur. While still fighting and defending, the emperor and his horse were carried deep into the waters of the Ganges by one billowing current from behind. Kafur, witnessing this terrible mishap, had pleaded with one mahout close by to lend his elephant to the emperor, for he was in the danger of drowning. The mahout would not agree, so Kafur had slain him with one blow of his sword. Quick as lightning, then, he had lifted the swooning emperor from his steed, and had managed to transport him and his own self into the howdah. The emperor was not in swoon, but stricken numb with grief and shock. They had reached safely on the opposite bank of the Ganges. And one nobleman by the name of Shemseddin had assisted the emperor down from the howdah, Kafur plodding after them under the weight of his fatigue and trauma.

The few fortunate ones, who had escaped holy waters of the Ganges in this unholy war at Qunauj had joined the emperor. Then all of them had headed straight for Agra, knowing, that the armies of Sher Khan were following them at their heels. Agra was no safe refuge for the emperor anymore, though dazed and grief-stricken, he had known that even before reaching there. Prince Kamran had moved all the imperial troops to Lahore, and no one was left behind to defend this jewel of Hind. In paralysis of grief and hopelessness, Humayun had then sought the advice of his Sufi friend, Rafiaeddin, concerning the means of safety for him and his harem. Rafiaeddin had advised him to go to Lahore and seek help from Prince Kamran. With this advice as his talisman, Humayun had gone to Sikri to recover from his shock and to contemplate. At Sikri, Humayun was joined by his brothers, Prince Hindal and Prince Askeri. Soon, the emperor's cousin, Haider Mirza had arrived.

121

The advice of Rafiaeddin was discussed, and all had agreed that they should journey to Lahore. Humayun, in stupor of pain and indecision, before leaving Sikri, had straggled into the garden called Zar Afshan to contemplate the flower-wounds in his heart and soul. Pressed by his need for solitude, he had not told anyone, not even suspecting that Prince Askeri was not far behind. Seating himself on one white bench, he was plunged deep in thought, when an arrow had come whistling from nowhere and had pierced his arm. Prince Askeri, rushing to the scene, had found the emperor contemplating the blood oozing from his arm with utter calm, as if fascinated. Prince Askeri was not to know that the emperor was fascinated by beholding one invisible wound from within surfacing on his arm naked and unashamed.

The assassin-to-be was never found, and the verdict of the royal brothers was to move quickly to Delhi, and then to Lahore. At Delhi, Kasim Husein had joined the royal cavalcade now stripped naked of all pomp and glory. The threat of pursuit by Sher Khan's troops had proven quite true, for even before they had reached Lahore, Sher Khan had added Delhi to his sweeping conquests. Humayun was not to find any respite in Lahore either, for when the need for unification amongst the royal brothers was of utmost importance they had fallen into the cauldron of their greed and conflict. Prince Kamran was interested only in keeping firm his hold on the Punjab. Prince Hindal was concerned in safeguarding his little kingdom of Alwar. Prince Askeri was intent on saving his precious kingdom of Sambhal, trying to keep it out of the reach of Sher Khan. None of the brothers were willing to heed the emperor's advice in winning back Agra and Delhi, or even thinking of joining their forces for common cause. Pain and hopelessness were Humayun's little troopers, warning him that the conflicts and the betrayals of his brothers would lead them all to exile.

Banished from his thoughts by the quicksilver recollection of his dream, Humayun's eyes were shot open. His gaze was turning to his wife. She was awake, watching him sweetly and tenderly. *Sweet and adorable,* his own gaze was murmuring, and he pressed her closer to him, smiling.

"My love, I had the strangest of all dreams! Such a dream! I have not ever dreamt before." Humayun murmured.

"A dream of joy and peace, I hope, Your Majesty." Bega Begum murmured back. "Won't you share it with me?" She asked softly.

"A strange, beautiful dream." Humayun commenced dreamily. "A pious man all dressed in green. He had a golden staff in his hand. He spoke to me, saying, that he is Ahmed of Jam, The Terrible Elephant. Now I remember my father mentioning the tomb of one sage by this name, in Herat. He told me that that sage belonged to some illustrious line of saints, and that he and my mother had visited his tomb. Yes, the dream." He sighed without restraint. "That pious man handed me the staff, telling me that I would be blessed with a royal heir, and that I should name him Jalaluddin Muhammad Akbar. He would be the emperor of Hind, he said, a great emperor." His eyes were burning with the fever of pain and despair all of a sudden.

"A wonderful dream, Your Majesty!" Bega Begum declared with the fervor of joy and hope. "Since Gunwar Bibi is almost ready, we will have a royal heir with us soon. Akbar, how sweet the name sounds! That means you will conquer Agra and Delhi, and all the lost kingdoms. Yes, Your Majesty, you will."

"And you will be my empress." A volley of mirth, both painful and hysterical, escaped Humayun's lips.

His wounded spirit was unfolding like the petals of a red, red rose, but he could feel only the thorns of lust, all piercing, all stabbing. Against the violence of his passion he was kissing her feverishly until the dagger of his maleness was unsheathed and he lay there spent and exhilarated.

"Forgive me, my love. The emperor, in name alone, must take a bath to face another day of betrayals." Humayun got out of bed contrite and humbled.

With no empire in view, the legacy of intrigues and betrayals were left into the hands of Sher Khan. This was Humayun's first reed of a sane thought this bright afternoon, as he straggled out into the garden of this palace at Lahore. He was strolling alone, and yet his solitude was splintered by a flurry of sounds and footsteps from the red sandstone monument of ugliness in the distance. A horde of princes and princess', who dared not approach him, it was obvious, were appearing on the palace steps at frequent intervals, and then disappearing behind the closed doors. The emperor seemed oblivious to all, watching the clusters of summer flowers matching his blue silk robe, and the profusion of rubies on his cummerbund. Pansies, primula and impatience were edged on each side of the cobblestone path, upon which Humayun paced to and fro, cultivating solitude and entertaining neither grief, not despair. Paradoxically, the agony of his spirit had left him, only the pain of inner torments suffered and unsuffering, was swimming in his eyes, bright and shuddering. His gaze was feverish, and his mind quiet and empty.

This emptiness within Humayun was sloughing off its mask of peace with a slow, lingering stealth and caution. He was recalling the report of this early morning while he had breakfasted with his wives, Bega Begum and Gunwar Begum, and its contents were unfolding in his mind. Prince Kamran had long since been keeping an alliance with Sher Khan, and had been contriving to depose his brother, the emperor. Now, Prince Kamran had become the victim of his own deception, and was struggling to keep his hold on Lahore, with the hope of becoming the sole sovereign of the Punjab. This thought alone that his brother was the cause of all these tragedies past and present, was splitting the false peace of a vacuity in Humayun's head to smithereens. In fact, this vacuity was already a gaping rent in his mind, revealing follies and betrayals of all his brothers. A host of follies and betrayals he had neglected to see against the weight of his love for them, blind and tender. Even a couple of days ago, when his brothers had approached him with fear shining in their eyes that Sher Khan was intending to conquer Lahore, Humayun had written a harsh letter to the usurper, entrusting Mozeffer Turkoman for its delivery. Once again, the emperor had condoned the fresh knowledge of betrayals by his brothers, siding with them in their plight. Even before the letter could be sent, the three royal brothers had begun to dispute about the possession of jewels and the settlement of lands and kingdoms. The stealthy torment in Humayun's thoughts was yawning, shooting his own harsh words to Sher Khan, like the bullets dull and blunted.

Sher Shah Suri! Is that what you want now, Lahore, after usurping my throne? Your dung of lies and treacheries are scattered all over the kingdoms you have conquered. Do you not fear the anger of God? You are the breeder of cruelty, injustice and destruction. The emperor has left you the whole of Hind, now leave Lahore alone. And let Sirhind, which is the den of your pillage and plundering, be the boundary between the emperor and you.

The hide-and-seek of sun-gold on the rippling fountains and the gleaming terraces were attracting Humayun's attention, but he had not left the cobblestone path, feeling only an astonishing sense of peace and purity. His pacing accompanied by painless memories were only the mist-illusions in his head where the doors of reality were closed shut, admitting only the chinks of sadness', all mellow and harmless. His thoughts too were purged of all sorrow it seemed, aimless and wandering. They were entering kingdoms pure and nameless. These kingdoms were reflected in the purity of darkness, where chaos was the bride of peace, and discord wedded to conformity. Where the impenetrable truth was the only kingdom worth attaining! The only kingdom worth exploring and stripping naked before the sightless eyes of light!

Humayun's thoughts were taking a carefree stroll down the alley of illusion, yet gathering the dust of reality. The word *exile* was etched bright inside the book of his life, like some brand of inevitability, crimson and searing. He had been familiar with this word. It was a throb of prescience inside him, large and abscessed. He had known always that he would suffer exile, as if he had already suffered it, many times before, and would suffer it still, time and again, inside the wheel of timelessness. This prescience was leaving him, the divine edict of fate lost in mists spurious. The word exile was flowering into the bloom of a longing to renounce the pleasures of this world with all its needs and greeds. To find peace inside the fecundity of the woods or to seek the fruits of spirituality within the hearts of the mountains! In the memory-book of his thoughts, another word was surfacing, *King-Kalendar*, whirling out to sing songs of praise to his father who was known by this same name.

I will become a King-Kalendar, just like my father, giving away the wealth of the five kingdoms and— Humayun's thoughts were halting at the doors of reality, and knocking softly. *A dowerless emperor! What I have left to give away? A few chests of jewels, and my diamond Kohinoor! To give away even that, and become a hermit! A Sannayasi, perhaps! Nature as my palace and a saffron robe my sole possession.* He was becoming aware of the slanting shadows, peering in and out from behind the poplars, and burying their heads under the blades of grass.

The emperor was not alone. The shades and shadows were all around him. The shades of the dead and the shadows of the living! The mating of day with the night, Humayun was thinking. He could feel the breeze of a presence right behind him. The light, unobtrusive steps of a woman, his thoughts were trying to balance themselves on the pole of reality. He could hear one lone whisper in the wind. It was the sound of a prayer, as if the will to live was befriending the longing for death. Dreams were accosting reality.

Reality was defying the rills of pain, and challenging the mountains of agony. *The laughing lips of fate! Sanity gazing into the eyes of madness.* One small cry was curling up behind his back, and Humayun whirled on his feet, coming face-to-face with Gulbadan Begum holding a child in her arms.

"My Rose! You have a child of your own, I knew that? And yet, I can't help thinking that you yourself were a child a few seasons past, in Kabul." Humayun stood laughing as if he had not a care in the world. "What is the name of your lusty prince?"

"Saadat Yar, Your Majesty." Gulbadan Begum murmured apprehensively. "I know your pain, Your Majesty, yet have no words to offer solace. Instead, I am here, seeking your advice and protection. You must speak with Prince Kamran, Your Majesty. He is compelling us all, the Begums and the princess' to accompany him to Kabul. Bibi Mubaraka Begum stays firm on her resolve to stay in Hind though. She says she will not leave Hind until she is able to carry the remains of our father to Kabul, since he wished to be buried there, not in Hind." Her thoughts were choking with pain. "I don't want to go with Prince Kamran, Your Majesty. My mamma doesn't either. She wants to stay with Prince Hindal. All the Begums want to stay with you, wherever you decide to go. We went to Prince Kamran, pleading with him, but he started declaring on oaths that he would not let us stay with you— She could not continue, noticing a shadow of pain cross the emperor's brow.

"My lovely Rose!" One groan of an endearment escaped Humayun's lips, laughter gone from his eyes. "So dear you are to me that I can't think of parting from you." His look was kindling a fire of recollections. "And yet, this morning, I recall? Prince Kamran came to me, pleading, that I grant him the permission for leaving the ladies of the royal household with him. I denied him this request at first, but then he began a string of pleas, looking dejected and stricken and I consented. With the injunction, if the Begums and princess' are willing." His look was dazed, as if he didn't see her, but only the ocean of misery within him.

"I thought you loved me, Your Majesty, this insignificant one! How could you consent?" Gulbadan Begum's eyes were shining with bitter protests.

"My dear Rose!" Humayun exclaimed. "I love you as much as our father loved you. And he loved you the best. In Kabul, you will be safe. The emperor knows not his plans, still wading through the pools of uncertainties? I might go wandering into the jungles of Bengal? For years on end, much like Moses, seeking home for my people?" He resumed the ritual of his strolling, as if lumbering after the mirage of hopes and dreams. "Go back to the palace, my love, and find comfort in the thought that Kabul is your home, welcoming you always. Kabul is my sanctuary too, I have one *other* in Kabul whom I love the best, and I must see *her*."

Gulbadan Begum was a faded dream in Humayun's thoughts, already lost into the ribbons of sunshine, as he continued pacing. Dream-reality was banished, and dream-illusion was his companion. Mah Chuchak was with him, gazing into the rivers of his tragedies, and carrying the lamps of love and hope inside the blue lakes of her lovely eyes. His heart was one solid mirror of grief and agony, but reflected in there alongside such misery and hopelessness, were the wavelets of hopes and miracles. The magic-mystery in his reveries was shattering, collapsing at his feet in one heavy lump of awareness. More shadows were following him at his heels, this time the steps hard and uneven. There was only one shadow, Humayun's thoughts were confirming, lingering behind and then staggering onward, and then lagging behind once again. This shadow had caught up with him, and it was no other than Prince Askeri himself, delightfully and pugnaciously drunk.

"You know, Your Majesty, I have been meaning to talk with you, but never got the chance. Prince Kamran always comes up with his symphonies of tales, and never lets me say a word." Prince Askeri was now walking beside the emperor, feeling light and exhilarated. "One thing I never told you, Your Majesty, and I coined this phrase myself! Hind breeds nothing but nightmares. I will never dream of Hind again, but of Kabul and Kandahar and Badakhshan." His intoxicated thoughts were chasing the dreams of Sher Khan. "That evil genius, Your Majesty, that avaricious lout, how he boasts and boasts about his dreams and conquests! Have you heard about Sher Khan's latest dream? You are always in his dreams, it is obvious by now. This time you are riding together, and then challenge one another to wrestling. You, Your Majesty, fling him down on the ground, and he can't get up. And the idiot, how he interprets this dream? He says that he has fallen into the land of victories. Sure as hell, he—"

Humayun had ceased to heed, drifting into the inner sanctuary of his silence and vacuity. Prince Askeri was dwindling far behind his awareness, only a shadow under the sun, not the living, throbbing specimen of brotherhood and drunkenness. Actually, this shadow was staggering behind, deflated by his surge of levity and giddiness. Plodding back toward the palace, he could feel the misery and nausea of his wretched plans and dreams. The emperor was left alone, enveloped in his fogs of peace and chaos. Immersed in his reveries strange and peaceful, he didn't even notice that the haze in dusk had lowered a blanket of stillness over the garden. Now noticing this veil of tranquility, he was sighing relief that no one had disrupted his solitary ruminations after the drunken contemplations of Prince Askeri. Or, if someone did, he had no recollection. Sighing to himself deeply and blissfully, he was sloughing away the fetters of oblivion with the intention of returning to the palace. Retracing his steps, Humayun was half way to the palace when he espied Mozeffer Turkoman lumbering toward him with his head bent and shoulders sagging. Since the emperor kept walking without acknowledging his presence, Mozeffer Turkoman, upon approaching closer and keeping a respectful distance, began unloading his missile of a message.

"Your Majesty. After reading your message, Sher Khan entrusted me with one of his own which I dare not repeat. Brief as it is, it has the sound of a cannon. Tell the emperor, he says, *I have left you Kabul*." Mozeffer Turkoman intoned weakly. "Sher Khan is on his way to Lahore, Your Majesty—" This brief confession had the impact of a thunderstorm upon Humayun, his feet coming to one quick halt.

"Do the emperor's brothers know yet?" This query was torn out of Humayun's heart quite involuntarily.

"Yes, Your Majesty—" Before Mozeffer Turkoman could say more, Prince Kamran was seen blazing through the palace doors, down into the garden.

"Your Majesty, since Sher Khan is on his way to Lahore, we can't stay here any longer. Not enough troops to defend." Prince Kamran's Lucifer-charm was thrown to the winds, the fire of betrayals dancing naked in the hazel pools of his eyes. "I am abandoning this hated land of intrigues. No need to stay in this cauldron of plotters and cut-throats. Haider Mirza has decided to return to Kashmir. Prince Hindal will try his fortunes at Bheker on the strip of Indus. I am going to Kabul. Prince Askeri and ladies of our royal household are coming with me. Kabul, Kandahar,

Badakhshan. All my—" His claim to possessions was truncated by one thunder of a declaration from Humayun.

"Great wonder, that you have not planned anything for the emperor!" Humayun's eyes were smoldering with the fever of pain and bitterness. "The emperor will be left alone to fend for himself. Fighting Sher Khan? Without the troops! Or, perish in exile? Make Kabul his permanent abode, perhaps?" With one hopeless gesture of his arm, he appeared to be slicing his indecisions to pitiful rags.

"Not Kabul, Your Majesty." One bullet of a groan was shot right out of Prince Kamran's mouth. "Our father, in his lifetime, bestowed Kabul on my mamma. And I being her son, it belongs to me."

"You ingrate viper! You plotting, scheming wretch of a brother!" Humayun could not endure to look at the daggers of naked deceit and cruelty in the eyes of his half brother. "No greater sin is there than to distort the words of our late father, while he lies peacefully in his grave. I loved him, not for his kingdoms, but for his noble heart, which could entertain only love and compassion, not lies and hatred. How conveniently you have forgotten his words? *My Kabul, I will give to none. Far from it, let none of my sons covet it.*" He turned his back on his brother. Straggling away to continue the ritual of his pacing.

Prince Kamran had strutted back into the palace, carrying the burden of his fears, schemes and uncertainties. *The emperor was greeting mournful dusk as his* solitary *companion.* A succession of terraces polished to pale gleams by the evening haze was beckoning the emperor to take rest, but he was a prisoner to his world of misery and sorrow. The emerald sheen on the sprawling lawns was getting dull at the approach of sunset, and Humayun's gaze was turning to the heliotrope sky. His feet were coming to a stumbling halt, as if he had seen the colors of death so beautifully splashed on the canvas of life, his heart thundering with awe and humility. So smitten was he by this tragic, beautiful scene that he didn't notice Haider Mirza standing right beside him. One gasp of admiration and his spell of awe were shattered. Along with it, the shattering revelation that his cousin was doling out the rivers of pity form his eyes, which could be named love, if it was not mistaken as compassion.

"Your Majesty. Come with me to Kashmir. From there, you can keep a close watch over the warring factions, which are going to consume themselves in their own bloody feuds sooner or later. Much sooner! And you will re-conquer what you have lost." Haider

Mirza's soft tones were chanting solace and spilling comfort. "Prince Kamran is corrupt and heartless, as you know too well by now. For the past six months, he has been keeping secret correspondence with Sher Khan. In his ambition to rule, he has forfeited both Lahore and your whole empire, Your Majesty. Though Sher Khan had promised him Lahore, in addition to Delhi and Agra? *Paying deceit with deceit*, as he is boasting these days. If it was not for Prince Kamran, you would still be the master of the Punjab, Your Majesty. Too late now, and the traitor has yet not stopped plotting and deceiving. He is tireless in turning Moghuls and the Afghans against you, Your Majesty, even now. Do away with him, Your Majesty, he doesn't deserve to live!" Was his kind, yet cruel advice.

"No!" Humayun cried with all the agony inside heart. A heart gone mad with grief and bewilderment. "No. Never for the vanities of this perishable world, will I imbrue my hands in the blood of a brother. But will forever remember the words of my father on his dying lips. *Do naught against thy brothers, even if they may deserve it.*" He stood there like a man wearing the noose of death around his neck. "Command Abdul Ghafur, my kind cousin, to pack the emperor's jewels and treasures. Also, tell my wives to prepare for a long, long journey. My destination is Gujrat, the fates have decreed it, I am sure. Thank you for inviting me to Kashmir, just the same." He looked into his cousin's eyes wistfully before turning to his heels.

The emperor was floating on the floods of agony, it seemed. His only thought was to leave his scheming brothers behind, and seek the kingdom of truth, not the kingdoms lost and crumbling.

Chapter Ten
Emperor's Dream-Bride

A small library admitting ribbons of gold winnowed loose from the poplars were dancing on Humayun's shoulders. He was seated at one polished desk of solid cherry, trying to write his memoirs. His gaze would rest, now and then, on the neglected piece of paper, upon which he had scribbled a quatrain in some mad fit of joy and exhilaration. No joy had visited him during the travails of his flight and wanderings, but he had fallen in love at the last rung of his refuge and destination. Madly and utterly in love! Instead of his intended journey to Gujrat, he had found refuge in the fertile province of Pater. Forty miles north of Swistan, Pater was located twenty miles west of the river Indus. Shaikh Akbar Jami was the kind host who had already welcomed Prince Hindal and his mother Dildar Begum at his sumptuous palace, and now had offered same kindness to the dethroned emperor. And the emperor had fallen in love with the lovely daughter of his host, more intent on winning her love than his lost kingdoms.

Behind this *star of fate*, which was Humayun's love mad and love consuming, lay his kingdoms despoiled and pillaged. His journal was mottled with entries black and scalding, and yet he was tireless in recording each fact with the precision of a historian. Sher Khan had added Lahore to his great conquests without any opposition. Prince Askeri had found refuge in Kandahar. Prince Kamran, along with his retinue of royal household had retired to Kabul. Humayun had not left Lahore yet, when he had received an invitation from Khwaja Kilan to come to Bhira. The emperor had accepted. He was half way to Bhira when he had learned that Prince Kamran, who had commenced his journey to Kabul earlier, had stopped in Bhira, arresting Khwaja Kilan on the charges that he was plotting with the emperor to usurp his kingdom of Kabul. Humayun, upon learning of such news and choosing not to confront his wicked brother, had decided to go to Multan via Koushab. Barely had the emperor reached the narrow defile leading toward Koushab, when he had come face-to-face with Prince Kamran, who after arresting his vizier was on his way toward Kabul.

Throwing off his mask of devotion, Humayun was writing without bitterness, Prince Kamran had blocked the emperor's way in his act of crossing, demanding to be the first one to lead his entourage through the defile. The emperor as well as his vizier was outraged, the vizier suggesting the punishment of death, but the emperor would not agree to such violence against his brother. Prince Kamran's own vizier, Abul Baka, had then remonstrated with the Prince, reminding him of his due courtesy to his emperor brother. So, the emperor and his entourage had crossed the defile first, Prince Kamran following. Here, the royal brothers were parted. The emperor taking the road toward Multan and Prince Kamran heading toward Kabul. The emperor didn't know, but great hardships were in store for his small cavalcade during his journey through the desert between Sind and river Chenab. Their water supplies and provisions were cut off by the marauding Baluchis, who were laying waste the lands with their raids and pillaging. These marauders had also filled the wells with sand, and water was nowhere to be found in the desert of Sind.

After suffering the most intolerable of thirsts and hungers, the emperor's cavalcade had barely reached the valley of Gul-Baluch that one javelin of an ill-news had come racing after the emperor. Sher Khan's governor, Khwas Khan was following the trails of the emperor with the intention of making him captive. Stricken with despair, more than with hunger and fatigue, the emperor was compelled to continue his journey, choosing the route of Uch, and reaching Gara close to the banks of Chenab. The God-fearing chieftain of Gara by the name of Bakhusi Langa had treated the emperor and his small cavalcade with much respect and generosity. Providing them with boats, which he himself had furnished with grain and provisions, and wishing them safe journey toward Pater.

The jeweled pen in Humayun's hand was not obeying his thoughts, and he replaced it in the jade inkpot, sighing to himself. Paradoxically, the endless parade of tragedies following at his heels, had not blighted his soul, but had enhanced its appetite for hope and truth. Love alone was his bubble of truth inside the great bubble of Pater, shining with the light of hope and purity. Pater had become his sanctuary where his love for poetry and astronomy could breathe once again. Sufi at heart and mystic in temperament, he had yielded to his passion of spirituality with a carefree abandon. His pain and grief were silenced, and he had learned to compromise. Neither looking at the past with bitterness, nor thinking about future with dread, but living in the present. His former interest in the Zodiacal world was revived, and this particular morning, in conformity with his mood he was dressed in a robe the color of emeralds, the color for joy and pleasure. The green plume in his turban and the ropes of pearls around his neck were lending his gaunt features the glow of youth and vitality. His amber eyes were attaining the color of pale wine at the sudden recollection that he was the father of a beautiful princess. A daughter was born to Gunwar Begum in this humble palace at Pater, and the princess was named Bihar Banu. One more joy-bloom was alighting in his eyes, for his vizier Biram Khan, after contriving escape, had joined him in Pater. His eyes were turning to the neglected piece of paper before him, and he was leaning over to behold his poetic bloom.

Although one's image be shown in the mirror
It always remains apart from one's self
It is wonderful to see one's self in another form
This marvel will be the work of God.

The shutters on Humayun's eyes were closing, more so to resurrect the portrait of his love, than to shut out the gold in sunshine. With many a sigh and longing, his thoughts were arresting the reflection of his beloved, who had rejected him so far. Her name was Hamida Banu, the daughter of Shaikh Akbar Jami, who in turn could claim his lineage back to the Ahmad of Jam, The Terrible Elephant. The arrow of Cupid had hit Humayun even before he knew that the *rose of his love* which had pierced him with countless thorns, was linked to his prophetic dream. He had reached Pater, carrying the burden of his decision that he would renounce the world and become a hermit. But fate had conspired otherwise. Hamida Banu had emerged on the scene like his beloved lost, much like his unwedded child-bride, Mah Chuchak, who had espoused the valleys of Kabul as her bridegroom.

Hamida Banu, the prophecy of his dream!
Mah Chuchak, the prophecy of his soul!

The emperor had found one to lose another! Humayun's thoughts were bursting open one bubble of a mockery, and reaching for another one. The truth unattainable! The bride of his soul was forgotten, and the bride of his dream was a shimmering reality. Hamida Banu with ruby lips and diamond-blue eyes had stolen his heart. Her flowerlike face haloed by flaxen curls had become a source of bliss and agony to him, never leaving him alone, even amidst the moments of his mystical interludes and stark contemplations. He had courted Hamida Banu with the gallantry of a noble cavalier, serenading her with poems and entreaties, but she had not consented to marry him. His eyes were smoldering with sadness profound at the recollection that as a wooer with forty days in his reckoning, he had not reached an inch closer to his beloved. Tides upon tides of rejections had multiplied his longings more than he could endure. Suddenly, his thoughts were crying in revolt, the ache of desire and longing inside him one throbbing tempest.

How could I ever win her love? Without throne, without riches, without kingdoms? How, in the name of blessed truth, how? I will find a way. I must! Emperor just the same, I am, by birth, by title? In stature and demeanor! The revolt in Humayun's thoughts was catching the stars of revelations. But before he could pierce the hearts of these revelations, the unobtrusive voice of Biram Khan startled him out of his reveries.

"May I intrude upon your privacy, Your Majesty?" Biram Khan stood at the door, somber and uncertain.

"You are welcome, Biram." Humayun looked over his shoulders. Inviting him in and indicating a chair beside him. "You have yet to tell the emperor of your crafty escape? Your silence on this subject is unnecessary. Sad tales are the ones which bring me cheers these days." He smiled.

"Swistan is the font of cheers for you, Your Majesty, my tales long buried will be sad indeed!" Biram Khan bowed his head in a brief curtsy before lowering himself into the chair indicated. "I carry only the burden of wars, bringing no cheers, but the thorns of unrest and rebellion. Sher Khan, not content with his conquests, is inciting the Arghuns, the Afghans and the Baluchis to rebellion. They have taken to plundering all the way from Upper Sind to the deserts of Rajputana. Troubles will be coming our way soon. Shah Hussain is besieging the city of Schwan. Maladoe is claiming the territory of Bheker. We must move on, Your Majesty, to safety. In some place far from the horde of marauders and fortune-seekers. Amerkot may be the ideal place to—" His suggestion was swallowed by a loud protest from Humayun.

134

"Don't bring the clouds of wars into Pater, Biram!" Humayun's eyes were lit up with the fire of pain and longing. "The emperor is in love! Talk of bridal songs and bridal showers. When one is in love, Biram, the roar of guns and cannons can't reach him. I must be wedded to my dream, and love, before I leave Pater. Have you ever been in love, Biram?" His thoughts were drinking the wine of dreams.

"Love, Your Majesty, I lost it somewhere inside the dregs of my youth." Biram Khan's thoughts were suspended against the doors of poetry and romance inside his heart. "Pater is the land of love and magic, I agree. The valley of hope and renewal! Here, longings breed and find fulfillment, I am beginning to believe."

"What poetic melancholy sits on your brow, Biram? I have never heard you talk like this before? Are you in love? Is Pater really the land of love and magic?" The dream-sadness in Humayun's eyes was reflecting his inner sea of doubts.

"Not in love, Your Majesty, no!" Biram Khan denied with a sudden vehemence. "But Pater is sure a land of miracles, if not of love and magic. You becoming the father of a healthy princess, Your Majesty, despite all the hardships suffered by Gunwar Begum during that arduous journey. That is one lovely miracle! The other miracle is of Shemseddin falling in love with Jiji Anaga, your childhood nurse, Your Majesty. How swiftly things move here, can't believe, they are already married. And the greatest miracle of all, Your Majesty, your great love—" He stopped, recalling a string of rejections from the youthful princess.

"My great love, rejected many times over!" Humayun contemplated aloud. "Does she love another?" His gaze was sailing out of the window, as if seeking answers from the gold-warmth in sunshine.

"No, Your Majesty. She is only young, and heedless, if I may say so." Biram Khan followed the emperor's gaze, his look thoughtful. "If you could overwhelm her with commands, not entreaties, Your Majesty? Wed her tonight, if you would, and she would be humbled and devoted. The empress of Hind, someday, I hope!" He intoned with the passion of a diviner, not even knowing that he was prophesying.

"From wooing to commanding! And from serenading to croaking?" One spontaneous gale of laughter escaped Humayun's lips. "Your advice is priceless to the emperor in exile." Humayun eased himself up gracefully. "Let's take a stroll in the garden. I might find my beloved there? Will command her to marry me, and if she still persists in rejecting me, I will have to abduct her and seduce her?" His thoughts were grinning at the blooms of his levity.

"The emperor has the leisure to stroll, Your Majesty, I must confess." Biram Khan sprang to his feet exigently. "Our kind host has entrusted me with an urgent message. I am to go to the king of Maladoe, to secure alliance, if not his loyalty?" He curtsied with a flourish of his arm. "You will find company in the garden, Your Majesty. Prince Hindal is taking a stroll with his lovely wife, Sultanum Begum."

"The emperor desires only solitude, my prudent Vizier." Humayun demurred, his gaze searching. "Your obedience lies to the Shaikh. I myself would be his slave, serving him as Jacob for Laban, for seven years! For more than seven, if I can win the love of Hamida Banu. She will be my Rachel." He sprinted toward the door, overwhelmed by his emotions dark and painful.

"My loyalty and obedience are yours alone, Your Majesty." Biram Khan murmured after him.

With sadness as his lone companion, Humayun was promenading inside the grove of silvery elms and mighty poplars. The white scrolled balconies and the spires and cupolas embellished with gilt and mosaic were left behind, the palace looming in the distance like some hideous dream, Humayun had thought earlier. Now his thoughts were silent and aghast, shuffling back and forth from Kabul to Pater, as if going round and round on a pilgrimage, and attaining not the fruits of their *desire*. In Kabul, the bride of his soul was wearing the veil of holy snow, but his thoughts were returning to the bride of his dream in this unholy land of exile.

Can a man truly love, if ever? Am I really in love? Humayun's steps, as well as his thoughts were tracing their path back to the palace of dreams. *This ache and longing inside me, these knots of pain in the very pit of my stomach? Could this be love? Her beautiful eyes cutting my heart to lumps of agony! Cruel fates, teasing and grinning, yet holding one whip of a command to fall at the feet of my beloved. If this is not love, then it must be some sickness of the body and soul? Madness supreme! Deformity inviolate!* The fever in his thoughts was consuming him entirely.

The emperor didn't even know that he was back in the manicured garden, sprawling wide, and dissected by gleaming paths and terraces. The frolic and the gurgle of the fountains were reaching him, and his gaze was chasing the white butterflies. The star-like anemones and a blaze of calendulas were greeting him, but he appeared not to notice this dance of color and sparkle in the heart of nature. His own heart had begun to beat with the primal need of a beast, hungering for survival. He could see the lush contours of the Lakki hills in the distance, his gaze lost in the ether of horizons far and remote. His feet were his guide, leading him to the bower of roses in hope of finding his beloved. Instead, he was becoming witness to the flight of Sultanum Begum, pale and distraught. Prince Hindal standing there forlorn.

"Did you make your wife jealous of someone you wish to wed in this happy land of Pater?" Humayun's psyche itself demanded, struck by this mad revelation that his brother was suing for the hand of the same beloved he himself wished to wed.

"No, Your Majesty." Was Prince Hindal's sullen response.

"This sad and dreamy look! You certainly have the air of being in love?" Humayun prodded. "The other proof is that I couldn't help noticing the flight of Sultanum Begum, all flustered?"

"It only proves, Your Majesty, that she is pregnant." Prince Hindal smiled.

"Blessed stars! More blooms of joys." Humayun declared, his gaze still searching. "Deny as you may, you are in love." His thoughts were assiduous in following the trail of his psyche.

"Once again, no, Your Majesty." Was Prince Hindal's impudent response.

"Then why in the name of a whaling absurdity do you object to the emperor's love for Hamida Banu?" Humayun flashed him the daggers of rage and rebuke.

"Your Majesty. When you came, I thought you would cultivate brotherly love? Didn't know, you would seek a young bride?" Prince Hindal intoned bitterly.

"Ah, truth at last! One objection unveiled?" One snort of a laughter escaped Humayun's lips. "Brotherly love, you say! If even a little was lacking in my heart for my brothers, I would have impaled them alive for their follies and betrayals. And yet, true it is that I didn't come seeking for a bride, but became the victim of love. Just like you. Unfortunately with the same girl! Why don't you confess?"

"For the third time, Your Majesty, no!" Prince Hindal's eyes were blazing with unvoiced protests. "My love for her is like the love of a brother to his sister. She has become very dear to me. I am jealous and possessive, no doubt, much like an older brother would who must care for her future and happiness."

"She has to marry someone, someday? Why not the emperor? The emperor in exile, I should get accustomed to this fact." Humayun began to pace up and down, while Prince Hindal stood there ramrod and defiant.

"She is young, Your Majesty. Only fourteen. Nineteen years younger than you, Your Majesty." Prince Hindal's gaze was following the emperor, shooting arrows of disdain and mockery.

"The difference in age is not the issue for rejecting the emperor's love, she herself has told me so." Humayun demurred aloud. "If the emperor had riches and empire, her heart might yield to the wealth of his love." He was becoming aware of Subhan Quli under the tamarind tree, but breaking not the rhythm of his pacing.

"She doesn't love you, Your Majesty, isn't it obvious?" Prince Hindal was intent on emptying the quiver of his knowledge and objections. "I should have told you, Your Majesty, that when you summoned her to your presence, she sought the audience of my mamma instead. Declaring with the sarcasm of a born queen! *I already feel exalted by seeing the emperor several times a day, each day a week, every week in a month! Now I shall see His Majesty when my mood dictates, not when the emperor commands*!"

"Again and again, I will woo her forever—" Humayun was murmuring, his feet coming to a slow halt before Subhan Quli, who curtsied. "Go, seek Princess Hamida Banu, my devoted friend. And deliver this message that the emperor requests her to join him in the garden."

"Your Majesty—" Subhan Quli's lips were glued, unable to deliver his own message to the emperor.

"Begone, and dally not." Humayun waved impatiently, noticing his intention to say something. "The emperor will reward you for your service, if you succeed. "You may unload your burden of grievances, if you have any, when you get back." He waved dismissal, which didn't brook disobedience.

"How can you even think of marrying, Your Majesty, when the House of Babur has fallen to pieces? Our father would never have approved of such thoughts in times of peril and uncertainty." Prince Hindal was seeking the emperor's attention after Subhan Quli had stalked away. "Kingdoms lost, and royal treasuries plundered. Exile and homelessness! Fear and uncertainty! Poverty is staring us in the face, and we can't turn it around, ordering it to fetch us riches." His eyes were kindling the lamps of fright and confusion.

"You lack not riches but wisdom, my young Prince. Even the thought of poverty has made you harsh and bitter!" Humayun began to pace again. "Impoverished we are, yes, in spirit and spirituality. But you, my young colt, have grown most callous and skeptical, abandoning the virtues of manners and kindness. And yet, the emperor at times was ruled by his whims and caprice? Still does, perhaps? All kingdoms lost! Does anything ever belong to anyone, but God?"

"What reason is that, Your Majesty?" Was Prince Hindal's puzzled exclamation! "What justification is there in seeking a bride in times of exile?" His heart was one ominous thunder in his ears.

"Reason slays madness, and sanity kills love!" Humayun's thoughts were cradling the Sufi child within him. "And without love, life is not worth living. That should be the reason enough worthy of sane reasoning, if one chooses to get married." His eyes were gathering the dry wisps of lightning in mirth and ideation.

"Even when the world is crumbling around us and the enemy following us at our very heels?" Prince Hindal's eyes were glowing with the fever of rage and bitterness. "Prince Kamran is safe and secure in his kingdom of Kabul! Not even admitting you, Your Majesty, in his most cherished domain! You should have killed him, Your Majesty. Especially, at Bhira, when he defied your right to cross the defile first? He has caused much grief already, and would stop at nothing to cause more by the very nature of his plotting and intriguing mind." His heart was churning the butter of loyalty to the emperor, though he was wearing the mask of defiance.

"In the scale of brotherly love, the emperor's own stays heavy and cumbersome." Laughter was hovering over Humayun's shoulders in the ritual of his pacing and thinking. "Profoundest of my loves! Just for my brothers? One should learn wisdom form misfortunes, not cruelty and vengeance. I refused to condemn him to death at Lahore, and nothing could make me take his life at

Bhira. And not ever could I think of staining my hands with his blood, even if he plotted my death! Strange this love, and stranger yet the emperor's heart, suffered and unsuffering?"

"Is Kabul not home to us all brothers, Your Majesty?" Prince Hindal's fear from within was flaring into stormy rage. "And yet Prince Kamran has made it his own haven and sanctuary! Since Your Majesty has no wish to challenge the conceit and deceit of our wicked brother, while intent only in marrying Hamida Banu, I have no recourse left but to fly to Kandahar. Prince Askeri would offer me refuge, if not welcome." He concluded with one hopeless gesture.

"My dear, royal brothers! Now the emperor is deprived of all authority to guide them." Humayun ceased to pace and stood facing his brother. "Yes, you will find safety in Kandahar, and the emperor will wed his dream." He murmured.

"You would rather wed a dream, than reality, Your Majesty?" Prince Hindal exclaimed. His thoughts cut short by the breezy return of Subhan Quli, who curtsied, gasping for breath.

"Your Majesty—" Subhan Quli's voice was choking under the burden of his hateful errand. "The Princess says, Your Majesty. *In Pater, for all the princesses to see kings once in our garden is lawful. A second time, it is forbidden. I have had the pleasure of the emperor's company in our garden once, and I cannot come now. Not ever. Or, I will be transgressing the laws of my ancestors.*"

"You bold messenger of the divine law, lead me to the throne of the Princess!" Humayun thundered a command. "The emperor will break all the laws, except the law of courtesy." His feet were already leading him toward the kiosk, where he knew she would be sitting, shooting missiles of rejections.

Subhan Quli was following the emperor toward that jewel of a kiosk, glimmering gold and crimson at the farther end of the garden. Humayun was pressed by haste, and welcoming the jaws of oblivion. He was honing his will to conquer, to win the love of Hamida Banu with all the violence of his passion and recklessness. The brute, savage pain of longing and implacability was holding a whip over his shoulders, and he was trundling along. But his feet were coming to a sudden halt at the door of the kiosk, screened by silk hangings. The voices from within were clear, and brimming with arguments.

"After all, you have to marry someone? Someday? Better to marry an emperor, who is suing for your hand! Than to wait for

140

some king, who has yet to win kingdoms before he has the luxury to lose them?" Dildar Begum's bantering tones were escaping the silk hangings, out into the hearts of bougainvillea.

"Oh, yes, I will marry someone!" Was Hamida Banu's sing-song protest. "I will marry, but he will be a man whose collar my hand can touch, and not the one whose skirt it does not reach." A delicious peal of laughter was escaping her lips.

Humayun was standing there rapt, drunk by the sweetness of her voice and knowledge that she was referring to the difference in their height, not age. Her small, slight, porcelain-like figure was emerging in his head like a doll-princess, and his heart was melting in rivulets of pain and ecstasy. Uprooting his six feet tall frame from the blessed spot, Humayun had lost no time in hurling himself into the chamber of sweet intrigue. Both the Begum and the Princess were startled to their feet. Dildar Begum curtsied low, but Hamida Banu stood their regal, smoothing her gown of blue velvet absently. Diamonds in her hair and around her throat were cold and glittering, and the dazzling-blue in her eyes were flashing mockery and challenge. Humayun smiled at Dildar Begum, drifting toward Hamida Banu, his look dreamy and expectant.

"In Pater, Your Majesty, ladies do not offer curtsies to men, may they be kings or emperors, if they enter their chambers unannounced." Hamida Banu sang her displeasure, a deep flush pervading her cheeks all of a sudden.

"Moghul men, may they be lords or slaves, with the exception of the emperor, always bow before the ladies." Humayun laughed, offering curtsy with one flourish of his arm. "And right now, the emperor is your slave, my beautiful Princess. Do not abandon the emperor, dear mamma." He turned to Dildar Begum, stalling her in her act of fleeing. "You must witness this scene of prayer and rejection. The emperor praying and the Princess rejecting." He returned his attention to Hamida Banu, snatching her hand into his, mutely and reverently. "You would consent to marry the emperor, or he would die at your feet right here, worshipping you till his last breath. Is your silence my rosary of happiness?" He could not read her denial or consent, for she had closed her eyes. "May the emperor seal this joy with a kiss?"

"No!" Was Hamida Banu's flustered response. Her eyes were shot open, revealing rivers of love. "I mean, Your Majesty—

yes, to the—" Before she could confess, her lips were crushed by one passionate kiss from the emperor.

"This evening is the most propitious one for a royal wedding, my dear Mamma, don't you think?" Humayun turned to Dildar Begum, transfigured with joy. "We will have the ceremony in the garden, dining under the stars!"

"Not this evening, Your Majesty." Plea and disbelief were melting into the pools of laughter in Dildar Begum's eyes, and on her lips.

"This very evening, my dear Mamma!" The note of finality in Humayun's voice brooked no argument. "Monday is a lucky day for the emperor. Besides, has he not waited for forty long days, eons? One more day, and he will go stark mad." He stole a glance at the blushing Princess, and scurried out of this haven.

The evening had descended swiftly, carrying in its silvery wings the gold of joy and hope, visible only to the mystical sight of the emperor. He was donned in purple robes, the large amethyst in his turban, and ropes of pearls around his neck, lending his features the color of youth and vitality. Seated on his makeshift throne of gold and velvet under the canopy of stars, Humayun was sipping his wine, and talking with Khwaja Muazzam, the brother of his dream-bride. The garden was lit with colorful lamps, and strewn with garlands over the trees and around the fountains. Large tables in shimmering cloth of gold and laden with choicest of fruits and viands were attracting the wedding guests to their sumptuous display. The wine-bearers in gold turbans were fluttering from table to table, hugging the flagons of wine, and replenishing the quickly drained goblets. Humayun's gaze, now and then would turn to the dancing girls with gold studs in their noses and bright tilaks on their foreheads, but the center of his attraction was his lovely bride, perfumed and bejeweled.

Hamida Banu had her own throne of colorful velvets, hauled out into the garden from the palace parlor for this auspicious occasion of wedding celebrations. It was hosting not only her, but the Begums and princesses, who could be seen jesting and laughing, rather teasing the bride with the slings of their wit and humor. The bride, of course, was succumbing to the burden of her gold and jewels. Her wedding gown of pink satin, splashed with lace and pearls was billowing, more so at the sleeves than down below the waist, falling down in folds upon folds of shimmering

142

layers. Rubies and diamonds from her head down to her throat were lending her small white face the glow and sparkle of dewdrop morning. The radiant-blue in her eyes was bathed in its own purity of sunshine. To Humayun's poetic awareness, she was the moon-bride, wearing stars in her hair and moonbeams in her eyes.

Humayun's gaze, drunk with the wine of earthbound beauty as his bride, was turning to the blue lotus of a sky. The waxen moon riding on the carpet of stars appeared to be white and livid to Humayun's sight, as if mourning some loss and fleeing from pain. Paradoxically, the voice of psyche within him was reflecting the tombs of his loss and mourning inside the eyes of the moon, and he himself was sinking into his world of silence and introspection. Though apparently talking and laughing, his inner silence was leading him through the valleys of ruin and devastation, where pain and grief of the past years were chilled and buried. *He had visited these tombs earlier this afternoon. Unable to contain the joy of his success and the agony of his desires, he had tried to explore his slumbering pains with the intention of renewing his contact with the bliss in living.*

Humayun could see the barrenness in his soul, dark and savage, murmuring only one longing to possess something nameless and unattainable. Pain and nostalgia in there were only the dust of a yawning abyss within, drifting and shifting the storm-clouds of longings strange and wordless. Exile and tragedies were the children of illusions, and the babes of grief and despair were dead to the mother of reality. Truth was there too, black as the night and splintered with blackest of lies, yet emerging forth in mists white, all pure and magnificent. Inside the fabric of these mists were woven the deformed, mutilated puzzle of his existence. His sanity, his fortitude, his indifference, all the rags of his living, suffering *self* was torn and bleeding. He could see the tapestry of his life, tragic and beautiful, raising no cries, lamenting no loss. His inner self was swollen with the scent of mysticism. He alone could taste and inhale it, could feel and touch its essence. Chaos mating with peace! Ugliness sleeping with perfection. The fabric of his life was stained with the dye of wounds, but it was weaving the color of joy, fresh and soothing.

The sheer poetry of music in the night and from the ripples of tablas and harmonium, were awakening Humayun from his reveries. Bhangra tunes were beckoning all to whirl on their toes, and dance the dance of self-abandon and rejoicing. Humayun's gaze was returning to his pink rose of a dream-bride with ruby-red lips and diamond-blue eyes. He was getting to his feet, gathering light from the throbbing stars up there, and sailing toward his treasure of a bride under some spell of bliss and exhilaration. A colorful sea of dancers, with silks rustling and bright plumes bobbing up and down, were impeding the emperor's progress, but he was intent on reaching the *star of his desire*, even if the jewel-adornments of the ladies had fallen his way like the burning coals, much as they appeared to him this moment amidst this frenzy of dance and music. Though, his thoughts were unutterably sweet, hungering only for the fruits of consummation. Something inside him was snapping loose. His heart was unfolding, reaching out to embrace the moon, the stars and the heavens.

Delirium and madness were the emperor's demons of impropriety. He was abducting his own bride, not waiting for the formal leave of entering his bridal chamber. The hosts and the guests were stunned. The moon had concealed its face against one veil of a white cloud. The music was silent. The emperor with the silken bundle of a bride in his arms was mounting the carpeted steps of the palace. In a flash, the guests were cheering and applauding. The notes from tablas and harmonium were bursting forth afresh, wild and frenzied. The emperor and his bride had vanished behind the polished doors. The guests were lost in the renewal of dance and festivity. Even the moon had unveiled its face, bright and shining.

"Love, sweetness—" Humayun was unrobing his bride under the canopy of garlands in her bridal chamber. "My own Hamida! Lovelier than the starry heavens!" He was kissing her with the blind, savage lust of a man, pressed by his demons of madness and delirium.

The cry of agony was on the lips of the bride. His need and urgency violating the sanctity of her virgin womb! Smothering her cries with kisses scalding, he was entering the lotus of her pain and desire, the dagger of his maleness hurting and stabbing, again and again. The wedding sheets were stained with her virgin blood. And now that the emperor was sated with his need and desire, he was holding his bride to him most tenderly, murmuring endearments again. The ravished bride, swooning with pain was falling asleep in his loving embrace. His eyes were admitting no such comfort. His thoughts holding open the portals of their insanity.

Much like a book, life stays in abeyance. To the end! Beyond oblivion. Humayun's soul itself was silent and listening. The book, much like a tapestry with double knots! Each knot woven in its pattern of pain, sorrow and suffering. The weak chord of joy making its own small knots, cleaving to the string of love with all its torments and yearnings. Once the string of joy is caught and love arrested, life becomes dull and uninteresting. No stories to tell. No passions to feed. No words to describe the fruits of peace and fulfillment. Hope dies. Death endures. Mystery and renewal! Life suffers to live. Still! Suffering still the bittersweet memories of trials and tribulations! Suffering the pain in living! His thoughts drugged with the soma of love, were courting sleep with the wine of lullabies.

Chapter Eleven
The Birth of an Heir

The fates had brought the *emperor in exile* to Jun, the mingling of hopes and tragedies still trailing at his heels. Almost a year had trundled past since his wedding to Hamida Banu, granting him the hope of a royal heir, and bestowing upon him the burden of wars and defeats. Two months since he had departed from Amerkot where Hamida Banu was staying in the palace of Rana Parsad. Expecting the birth of her child at any moment now, Humayun was thinking as he stood at the parlor window with a goblet of wine in his hand and the taste of majun on his tongue. This palace at Jun was small, but boasting of a profusion of Crystal lakes in its large garden. Right now, Humayun was looking at those lakes, scattered in the garden like tiny mirrors, glazed with sunshine. This garden was called Mirror Garden, and Humayun could never fail to admire its aura of peace and beauty. At this particular moment, the weeping willows seemed to be dipping their arms into water in the ritual of ablution, as if making ready to pay homage to the noon sun.

Humayun stood gazing and gazing, even forgetting to sip his wine. Clusters upon clusters of gold daisies against the blazing red in roses were reflected in his eyes as miracles supreme, but his heart was gathering sadness'. His lean, tall figure swathed in pale silks and, a large diamond in his blue turban, were lending him the semblance of some lost prince out of the pages of the Arabian Nights. His eyes were dreamy and melancholy, and the journey in his head was commencing with the abruptness of a volcanic eruption. Three weeks after his nuptial bliss, the emperor had left Pater along with his harem, in the hope of winning back his lost kingdoms. Only the seeds of hope were his armor and bullets, for the men in his army were numbered few, and the supply of artillery and cannon was insignificant. Prince Hindal had left a few days after the emperor's wedding, taking along with him his mother, Dildar Begum, and a great portion of the soldiers and artillery. Yadgar Mirza, who was also with the emperor at that time, had decided to return to his estate at Rohri, unwilling to join the emperor in his plans of re-conquest.

Misfortunes were strewn on the way wherever the emperor decided to go, though he had erected pillars of hope at every step, not looking back to see them crumble to dust. Taking the route of Tatta, via Indus, Humayun had reached Schwan to gauge the efficacy of his first campaign in waging a war and winning. The fort of Schwan had proved impregnable. During the siege, much cannon and artillery were lost. Provisions had become scarce. The supply of corn for the horses was exhausted. Humayun had sent Abul Baka to Yadgar Mirza for provisions. But, while returning from Rohri, Abul Baka was murdered by the rebels of Bheker. They had pelted him with a shower of arrows, leaving him unattended in his throes of agony, while he had lain there, bleeding to death. Overwhelmed with grief at the death of his vizier, Humayun then, throwing cautions of defense to the winds, had launched a reckless assault, gaining only one small portion of the fort. While the rebels lay in ambush, retreating behind the fort, another calamity had arrived pounding at the doors of the emperor's tragedies. Shah Hussain in Tatta, unable to fight the temptation of war and booty, had hurried to Schwan with muskets and cannon. Seizing the flotilla of grain from Rohri, which Yadgar Mirza had sent for the emperor, he had descended upon the imperial troops without a warning. The emperor had suffered a grueling defeat.

The laughter of fates! Humayun could hear it in his head, and he began to pace in the parlor, unseeing the damask hangings and gilt furniture. Only his feet were pounding the Persian carpet with crimson rosettes without mercy, and his thoughts trooping back mercilessly. After this disastrous defeat, Humayun was faced with a pestilence of betrayals and desertions. Abandoning the tracks of Upper Sind, he had deemed the desert of Rajputana his sanctuary of rest and safety. On the way, granting permission to his soldiers to leave if they were unwilling to join him on further campaigns. His troops dwindling, and he and his harem suffering hunger and fatigue, Humayun had crossed the tracts of Auch and Bheker, and had reached the city of Maladoe. A ray of hope tainted with the soot of betrayal had confronted him once again. The Raja of Maladoe had extended his welcome to the emperor, promising him the comfort of his home and all the assistance he needed in arms and armament. Fortunately, the emperor's spy, Mulla Surkh, had discovered the treacherous plot disguised as warm welcome.

The Raja of Maladoe was hoping to capture the emperor, and deliver him to Shah Hussain, who had promised him the estates of Alwar and Nagor as his reward.

Mournful shadows burdened with the mists of shame and indignity was hovering over Humayun's shoulders in his incessant pacing. He had drained his goblet in one large gulp, and had abandoned it on the jade table by the hearth. *Laughter of fates still ringing loud in his ears.* From Maladoe to Jaselmir and on his way to Amerkot, the emperor was to suffer countless hardships and indignities. Raja Rao, in alliance with Shah Hussain, had ordered the wells to be filled with sand. Then a band of marauders had attempted looting the imperial treasures, wounding several soldiers, and killing more horses than men in their frenzy of confusion and desperation. A pack of soldiers left to the emperor had grown utterly savage, devoid of respect and becoming contentious. Each man had snatched one horse each for himself, and had become possessive of his mount. The emperor had no horse, for he had given his own to Hamida Banu, who was seven month pregnant, enveloped in her soft cloud of daze and disbelief, where such horrors could never exist. Humayun had asked his soldiers for a horse, but none of them were willing to relinquish their claim on their mounts. Jouhar, the emperor's cup-bearer, had offered him his camel, and the emperor had mounted it without saying a word. Shemseddin, upon noticing the emperor's plight, had offered him his own horse. Choosing to ride the camel along with his mother, since she was riding with him on the horse given to the emperor.

The last few days of journey to Amerkot were horrendous, like passing through the hellfires in Hades. The clouds of dust and the whirling gusts of wind! Fatigue and hunger and the searing tongues of heat! But reaching Amerkot was like entering the gardens of Babylon, and leaving behind the deserts of hell. The easterly winds, cool and soothing. A profusion of clear, bubbling streams! The verdure polished to emerald brilliance, and a succession of lush green meadows. And the hospitality of Rana Parsad! As soon as the beleaguered entourage of the emperor had grazed the borders of Amerkot, Raja Parsad had sent his son Ria to welcome them to his palace. Sending his regrets that according to his astrologers, it was an unlucky day for him to venture out. Next morning, the emperor and his entourage had received a great welcome at the palace of Rana Parsad. His generosity had extended as far as presenting the emperor two thousand horsemen from the tribe of Sodhas and five thousand Samicha horses. In return, Humayun had bestowed upon his kind host the bolts of silk, the choicest of rubies and pearls, and eighty thousand gold ashrafis. Adding to his gifts jeweled belts and swords, and richly ornamented daggers. The Rana moved more by the wit and beauty of Hamida Banu, than by the worth of gifts, had adopted her as his daughter.

The journey in Humayun's head was sloughing off the burdens of defeats and betrayals, his pacing light and measured. After three weeks of feasting and entertainment, Rana Parsad had requested the emperor to lead an expedition to Jun to settle an old score with Shah Hussain. A year ago, Shah Hussain had murdered the father of Rana Parsad in his fruitless attempt to conquer Amerkot, and the Rana was desirous of punishing this vile rebel and murderer. Humayun was too glad of the opportunity to serve his kind host, and had marched toward Jun at the head of a large force supplied by Rana Parsad.

Equipped grandly with armaments and provisions, Humayun had sprinted on through the north-west of Ran close to the borders of Chachkan. Crossing the eastern branch of Indus, he had then reached his destination, where the valley of Jun undulated high and low in breathtaking contours. Seven whole weeks of respite at Amerkot before he had commenced this campaign! *Glorious, glorious rest and reprieve,* Humayun's thoughts were sighing relief. Out of these glorious mists in his head was curling up a name in bold, slippery letters, Mah Chuchak. This name had not ceased to haunt him since he had wedded her exact twin with ruby-red lips and diamond-blue eyes, no other than his beloved Hamida Banu. Kabul was calling him at this very moment, the bride of his soul laughing, and the bride of his dream unveiling her charms with unutterable sweetness. Behind all this, Agra and Delhi were smoldering away, Humayun's feet were coming to an abrupt halt, noticing the quiet approach of Biram Khan.

"Your Majesty." Biram Khan curtsied. "From the look in your eyes, Your Majesty, it seems, you are still mourning the death of Abul Baka?" He smiled.

"No, my kind friend. The emperor has ceased to grieve for the dead." Humayun's eyes were lit up with Sufic light. "I have learned to court this thought that we bury not the dead, but release them into the arms of peace. Yet, this death, I do confess, has pierced the armor of my stoicism. Neither the ingratitude of my brothers, nor the treacheries of my adherents. Nor the calamities which had assailed me since my accession, had ever unmanned me so much as the loss of this faithful friend and vizier?" His look was reminiscent than melancholy. "No, I grieve no more. My heart is brimming with joy, rather. A royal heir is to be born this very day to reclaim my legacy of Hind. Any news from Amerkot?" He asked wistfully.

"None, Your Majesty. Except that Rana Parsad is so anxious and concerned about the health of the royal heir and the royal mother that he has driven everyone around him insane with his inquiries and commands." A thin, enigmatic smile curled upon Biram Khan's lips. "I have returned with the same request, Your Majesty, that that swarthy bandit as you call him, is still waiting outside, wanting to sell some precious gems to the emperor?"

"Where is your magic wand, Biram, to melt all bandits into puffs of smoke?" Humayun laughed. "Don't you remember the words of the emperor? Where was I at that time? Yes, At Filudi, when that merchant appeared from nowhere, trying to sell me a rare diamond. And what did I tell him? Such a diamond is fit for a prince to be won by sword, not to be purchased with money. Isn't that what I had said?" He trooped toward the window and stood looking out. "The emperor is not interested in the pebbles of the earth, as my father would have said, but in the jewels of the heavens. And heavens, right now, have deigned to visit earth in this Mirror Garden. Without the rivers of wine and houris, of course." He turned around, his eyes spilling wine of amusement. "Fill the emperor's cup with wine, my worthy magician. The emperor in name alone! Even Jouhar doesn't attend on me, that slippery sloth of a cup-bearer! We will take our wine with us and stroll in the garden. Our heaven, and you may tell me tales straight from hell— Hind? Yes, the emperor in name alone."

"Not in name alone, Your Majesty, but by birth and by the divine will of God." Biram Khan murmured, filling two goblets from the gold flagon on the ivory table.

"In name and riches alone!" Humayun claimed the goblet laughingly. "A treasure full of rubies, pearls and diamonds still in my possession. The pebbles rare and priceless to blind all the avaricious beasts who could be willing to lend asylum to the emperor in exile? Kohinoor alone has the worth of many kingdoms."

A shadow of pain crossed his gaunt features. He abandoned his goblet and reached for the door.

The Mirror Garden with gold daisies and scarlet roses, was welcoming the vizier and the emperor with bright smiles. They were both silent, humbled by the beauty and silence of this earthly Paradise. But the tall elms and the proud cedars behind them were boasting of their own grace and majesty. The weeping willows bending low over the crystal lakes were whispering their songs of praise and serenity. Along the way, on either side of the cobbled path, the gardeners could be seen pruning the bushes, and yet all were hush and quiet. Humayun, in appearance, was admiring the peace and glory of this garden, but his thoughts had pulled him back to Agra. He was with the Rani of Gwalior, young and ardent and his heart bleeding. *The dark, adorable beauty of the night, Rani of Gwalior*, Humayun's thoughts were murmuring. *Mah Chuchak, the white lily of the mountains*, he was trying to get away from the mists dark and shuddering. Biram Khan's voice, soft and gloomy, was lending him the opportunity to escape the gloomy mists in his own head.

"Prince Kamran is assuming the title of kingship." Biram Khan was not addressing the emperor, but voicing his thoughts aloud. "Prayers are being read in his name in all the mosques. Even the coins are struck in his name. He is planning to fight with Prince Suleiman in Badakhshan, knowing, that Prince Suleiman is devoted to the emperor. Prince Askeri has lost Kandahar to Prince Kamran, and now is in Ghazni, a virtual prisoner of his tyrant brother. Prince Kamran captured Prince Hindal also, kept him in Kabul for a while, and then dispatched him to Jalalabad, allotting him this little kingdom. A prisoner, just the same—" He was quiet suddenly.

"Are Kabul and Kandahar forever to remain the cause of contention between my unworthy brothers?" Humayun exclaimed. "I have no kingdoms to feed my ambition with conquests and subjugation. And yet, all ambition has left me. Only the quest for truth remains? Not a strip of land on this continent far and wide offers refuge to the emperor in exile? I have a mind to go to Mecca in the guise of a holy dervish, and turn my back on all worldly pursuits. Let my heir, when he is of age, fend for himself, and claim the legacy of his grandfather, if he wishes?" One hysterical peal of laughter from his lips was splintering the hush in this garden.

152

"Your Majesty." Biram Khan murmured apprehensively. "Mecca is not the sanctuary for you. "Your spiritual quest, as I understand, would find fulfillment in Din Panah after you reclaim your kingdoms. My advice if you permit me, at present, is to find your fortunes elsewhere. Persia is the right place to do so. Shah Tahmasp is an irresistible ally. With his support, you would be able to release Kabul from the yoke of Prince Kamran. Make it the foothold for further conquests. Agra and Delhi will melt like butter at your feet, after you have regained your power and might. One more advice, Your Majesty. You need to command your soldiers to the sense of duty and loyalty. The desertions are becoming so common, even here at Jun?"

"All these gadflies in the blistering cauldron of Hind!" Humayun's senses were gathering the blooms of mirth and caprice. "Their aim is to sting the valorous and to spare the cowards. And what blistering need is there to conquer and subjugate? Kingdoms gained in a lifetime and kingdoms lost in one day? As for the deserters, the emperor has no need for the maggots with craven hearts and souls corrupted!" His gaze as well as his feet was coming to one stumbling halt, as if some lovely mirage had made its home under the shade of elms and poplars.

"This garden is surely under the spell of magic and enchantment! Is that where the queen of the goblins and the fairies sits?" Humayun's gaze was arrested to the gilded throne under the canopy of gold and crimson.

"My apologies, Your Majesty. You were not supposed to see this, I forgot!" Biram Khan apologized. "Your devoted soldiers—we built this, a sort of court transported straight from Agra. To celebrate the birth of a royal heir! Or, to hold court, when needed? Rana Parsad himself sent us the orders, we built it last evening. A secret you were not supposed to know till—we got the news of royal birth."

"A royal heir! Prince, indeed." Humayun murmured to himself. "My son will be born this very day, I know somehow? The emperor can feel his little breath in the air, in sunshine." The large diamond in his turban caught a glint of sunshine and reflected its glow in his eyes, as he continued. "The moon and stars will dance this evening at the birth of my prince." One gleaming prophecy escaped his lips. "This very day the emperor will preside over his court, much like the ones in Agra and Delhi. Summon all the soldiers and the courtiers. Poets and astrologers too! We will gather here in the late afternoon. Since wars and campaigns take precedence, we will map out strategies for our next moves. Conclude our session with songs and poetry, hopefully." The amber pools in his eyes were warm and tender. "Your advice and friendship are precious, Biram, I hold them dear. And never hold your advice back, I might heed someday? Right now my heart is bloated with joy and hope. It's time for my siesta, and I will dream of Hind." He retraced his steps, sailing back toward the palace, and laughing to himself.

The stillness in the small bedroom with gilt and damask didn't suit the emperor's mood amidst this surge of joy and hope inside his heart. The air was stifling, and he lunged toward the window, flinging it open. The scent of tuberoses reached his nostrils, and something inside him lurched and swayed. A familiar ache! The pain of longing and sweetness! This sweet pain of a longing had nothing to do with possessing heirs, riches or kingdoms? It was the pain of love and despair. His soul parched and hungry! Famished for something, he dared not name. His thoughts were weak and shuddering, not daring to look into the silence and corruption within his soul, where Mah Chuchak sat enthroned as his soul bride.

My beautiful Hamida is about to deliver a princely heir to my lost legacy, and I am thinking about my beloved in Kabul? Humayun swung around, seeking the satiny comfort on his four-poster bed. *Is there something ignoble and mediocre about love? My love. Taking flight, as soon as it possesses the flower of its desire. Two weeks at the most. An eternity, I say. Much like the fates, which suffering no loss are always searching for next victims to practice their guile and tyranny.* His eyes were closing, as he lay sprawled on the bed fully dressed. *Love, where does it come from, and where does it go? Love is an essence, always there, until corrupted with need, lust and carnality. The animal hunger of the senses wild and savage! Can love be pure and eternal? Not ephemeral, or evanescent? Will my love for my soul bride sustain? Stay untarnished? Unutterably sweet! Ineffable! Everlasting! Love, truth, true love? Where, o, where—* He was entering the delicious voids of rest and sleep.

This bliss in sleep must have lasted for hours, for when Humayun opened his eyes the violet evening was already at the window, fanning his senses to awareness. Feeling light and refreshed, he sprang to his feet, aiming straight for the window under some spell of haste and anticipation. Smitten by the ochre in sunset, the crystal lakes down there had turned molten. The flaming torch of a sun dipping west rapidly, could be seen splashing the horizon with streaks in gold and scarlet. The same colors were throbbing further down under the thicket of elms and poplars, where the poets and courtiers had gathered. Rippling colors in silks and plumed turbans were painting their own canvas of awe and splendor. A lone note from sitar, carried on the strings of breeze was reaching Humayun, and he thought he could see the dancers whirling on their toes in shimmering circles. Turning away slowly and thoughtfully, he was thinking of wearing purple. The shadows of his former caprice were entering his wardrobe, goaded by the rod of astrology. Color purple for Sunday! Sunday, the day of the sun, favorable to the stars of the rulers and emperors!

The Mirror Garden was pulsating with the rhythm of song and music, as Humayun sat on his gilded throne under the crimson marquee. His poets, courtiers and astrologers were with him, re-enacting the scene of courts at Agra and Delhi. Dancers and musicians too, drunk with the wine of peace and beauty, were weaving their art to perfection. The night air scented by the perfume from Rat-Ki-Rani was drugging the emperor with its warmth of fever and nostalgia. He was issuing Farmans, as if his lost kingdoms had fallen under his sway miraculously. The strange miracle was *this* Mirror Garden itself, breathing the scent of home, and vivifying the sense of power. Wars and strategies were discussed, and Biram Khan was bent upon exposing the wickedness of the emperor's brothers. The large amethyst in Humayun's turban was changing colors against the blaze of colorful lamps, as he held out his goblet to Jouhar for replenishing. Jouhar was claiming the emperor's goblet most obediently, when a messenger appeared on the scene with a stormy haste. Prostrating himself at the foot of the throne, he began exigently.

"Your Majesty, Mir Dost has sent you one hundred quinces and three hundred pomegranates. He said he is hoping that the emperor would send him good news as soon as the royal heir is born."

"Any written message from the worthy Dost, my good man?" Humayun asked kindly.

"None, Your Majesty." The messenger dipped his head in another curtsy.

"We will share these fruits with Rana Parsad, since he is very fond of them. The emperor's wife too, she craved for pomegranate juice during our perilous journey through the desert of Sind." Humayun's look was tender and reminiscent. "Be as good to deliver half the quinces and pomegranates to Rana Parsad in Amerkot. And when you return to Mir Dost, tell him that the emperor sends him his thanks and greetings. Also tell him that the emperor's vizier Terdi Beg is in Amerkot, as soon as he returns with good news, Mir Dost would be the first one to know out of all the lords around Jun." He waved dismissal.

"Yes, Your Majesty." The messenger retreated after curtsying.

"Your Majesty." Keracha Beg stumbled close to the throne, even before the devoted messenger could weave his way out of the flood of the courtiers. "Have you heard the reports of our spies, Your Majesty? They just arrived this morning." He was half drunk, burning with the fever of a need to unload his bulletin of news. "Sher Khan is wreaking havoc in the Punjab. All his kingdoms are split and divided to satisfy the greed of his generals, all of whom want independent kingdoms of their own. The empire of Hind is no more. Though, he is consolidating all his conquests under the name, Sher Shah Sur Dynasty? Over your Din Panah, Your Majesty, he is building an edifice called, Sher Mandal." He paused in his attempt to wrest out the most important of news he wanted to tell first. "Our spies in Tatta and Bekher send ominous news, Your Majesty. Some of the Moghul soldiers have slaughtered the cows. If Rana Parsad finds out, he might withdraw his favors from you, Your Majesty. We all fear. Our kind host might turn into a cruel adversary." The rills of sobriety were alighting in his eyes, his fever and drunkenness disappearing.

"What is sacred to the Hindus must become sacred to the Moghuls!" Humayun's eyes were flashing rage and edicts. "In this time and age, glory and valor sit on the shoulders of the cut-throats who wreak vengeance on men? And the soldiers slaughtering cows for sustenance are condemned to perish without mercy? Why? Not, that they have killed the holy cows, but have violated the element of sanctity in men! Have desecrated the belief of the believers!" His rage was splintering, his heart heavy and troubled. "To pray five times a day doesn't make one a true Muslim, but the goodness to know and to find the essence of sanctity in oneself and in others." He paused, his gaze alighting on the sculpture of the dancing Shiva on the table

156

beside him as a centerpiece. "Look at this masterpiece. The dancing Shiva called Natraj! A great destroyer, isn't that what he is called? Dancing in a rigol of fire! One foot sailing in the wind! The other crushing the back of a small man. And that man doesn't even know that the Lord is dancing on his back?" He began to laugh.

"Your Majesty, may I?" Biram Khan edged closer. "Do you know, Your Majesty, why Mir Dost didn't send you a written message?" He asked enigmatically.

"No, my prudent Vizier." Humayun feigned ignorance, mirth and hysteria leaving him. "His secret message is concealed inside the hearts of the innocent fruits, boding misfortunes. Since you are expert in unveiling such secrets, pray, feed the emperor's gluttony for pain?" His eyes were kindling the lamps of mysticism.

"You do know, Your Majesty. But, how much? And how little?" Biram Khan stood contemplating.

"Little is all that we know of anything in this vast, vast world, rigged with conceit, avarice, betrayal." Humayun murmured, his gaze searching. "But, do edify the emperor of all the littleness of affairs, if you will, Biram.

"Mir Dost doesn't trust any written messages anymore, Your Majesty, since the deceitful plots of your brothers remain confirmed." Was Biram Khan's quick response. "The message is clear, as you well know, Your Majesty. By sending such fruits to the emperor, he is confirming his warnings that the emperor should not proceed, either to Kabul or to Kandahar. This fresh sprig of warning from him makes me bold to disclose the insidious schemes of Prince Kamran. His alliance with Shah Hussain is secured. He has already sent him gifts of precious robes and Chupatak horses, asking the hand of his daughter in marriage. Shah Hussain, in return has promised him to raise hurdles in your way if you decide to march to Kabul or Kandahar. Another plan of Prince Kamran in league with Prince Askeri is not so clear to me. *They want to gain your confidence, and make you captive,* I have heard. *Beware, a thousand times, beware.* Mir Dost warns." He paused, noticing the rills of amusement in the emperor's eyes. "Your life and the life of your harem are in danger, Your Majesty. It is of utmost importance, Your Majesty, to seek aid from Shah Tahmasp of Persia?"

"From Persia to Mecca then! From exile to pilgrimage?" Humayun's Sufic response was swallowed by an abrupt ripple of music in the distance.

This music was not from the sitarist seated at the foot of the throne, evoking gentle tunes from his sitar, but something wild and exploding. Soon, Terdi Beg was in view, followed by a procession of men sounding castanets and tambourines. This joyful procession was attracting the attention of all, and causing a stir of excitement. Terdi Beg was at the head of the procession, clapping with the beat and walking jauntily. Upon reaching the throne, he fell into a lengthy taslim.

"Your Majesty, a son is born to you." Terdi Beg could barely voice his joy, the name Miryam Makani trembling upon his lips. *Rana Parsad had given this name to Hamida Banu, and she was known to all by this name.* "Miryam Makani and the royal prince are in good health."

"Blessed be your tongue, Terdi Beg, and blessed be this day!" Humayun exclaimed beamishly. "You will be rewarded bounteously in Amerkot where my treasures lay hidden. For right now, the paucity of the emperor demands only celebration. Come, Jouhar, fill the cups of all." He commanded. "And Biram, fetch whatever little we have here to give and celebrate. Gold ashrafis on silver trays and even my musk-bag!"

Biram Khan, flushed with joy, was quick to fetch all those gifts, too poor for this great occasion in celebrating the birth of a royal heir. The musk-bag was broken on China plate by the emperor himself, and presented to his viziers as gifts. Besides gold ashrafis, Biram Khan had found silver wristlets, and they too were distributed amongst the viziers and courtiers. The night air was filled with music, and the dancers were whirling on their feet with a wild abandon. The flames from candles were performing their own flicker-dance, and Humayun's eyes were gathering the stars of happy omens.

"Jalaluddin Muhammad Akbar is the name of our royal prince. He is to be the next emperor of Hind, after I reclaim my lost kingdoms!" One sliver of a prophecy from his thoughts was recorded in the book of posterity. "The moon is in Leo. A propitious sign! It predicts wisdom and greatness for the newborn heir. And this celebration is not fit for my royal son, that's the emperor's only regret." His laughing eyes were showering gold on Terdi Beg.

"Your Majesty! At Amerkot, the celebrations are royal and worthy of a king." Terdi Beg boasted proudly. "Trumpets, castanets and tambourines singing the songs of felicitations! Dancing girls with platters of sweets balanced on their arms, sweetening the palates of everyone in the palace. Rana Parsad himself showering gold and silver coins on all the household servants. Khwaja Muazzam, the happy uncle, is busy arranging week-long festivities. Shemseddin was seen bestowing silver tankas on the peasants, while his wife, Jiji Anaga, was taken to her room, feeling the pains of child-birth. She too has given birth to a son. They have named him Aziz Koka."

"The emperor will choose Shemseddin as Prince Akbar's godfather, and Jiji Anaga, his godmother. A great godmother to suckle our prince to manhood." Humayun's eyes were unfolding more decisions than what he could voice.

"Prince Hindal needs godparents too, Your Majesty." Terdi Beg breathed one whiff of a concern. "Since the birth of his daughter, Princess Ruqueiqa, he is leading the life of a dervish. Disgusted with Prince Kamran's treatment of him, I guess?"

"Princes turn dervishes when they lose their kingdoms, and the emperors become hermits when they lose their empires?" Humayun murmured. His gaze was arrested to the astrologer, Totik Rai. "Come here, my learned star-gazer. Show the emperor the stars of your wisdom in divining the fortunes for our royal prince. Omens all good for our royal prince, though. Moon is in Leo. His Zodiac sign is Libra. Autumnal equinox. The constellations between Virgo and Scorpio. Librans are emotional, somewhat. Yet, they persevere against all adversities. The rest, you will discover in your precious scrolls. Get to work, and show me the results of your knowledge." He waved dismissal.

"Your Majesty." Totik Rai breathed punctiliously, unable to resist the temptation of flaunting his astrological savvy. "October fifteen happens to be the day of the revered Rajab, a most propitious one for the royal heir. The person born on this day, especially, when it falls on Sunday, has a firm character. Usually rational! Potential of great wealth. Nature, kind and forgiving." Bowing double, he retraced his steps.

A great sense of mystery was pervading the Mirror Garden, as Humayun sat talking with a few of his viziers. Totik Rai, joined by other astrologers, had unrolled the large scrolls with Zodiac signs on the Persian rugs, absorbed deep in divining the future of the royal heir. A soothing lull had descended upon all after the excitement of rejoicing and felicitations. The musicians were lolling against the satiny pillows in utter neglect to their instruments. One shimmering heap could be seen under the weeping willow, where the dancing girls sat huddled together, laughing and whispering. The white, throbbing stars in the sky, piercing the heart of this garden with silvery gleams, were drinking wine from the emperor's goblet and whispering white lies. *One minute, he was standing at* the *door of destiny like a lone pilgrim, and the next, hurled into the merry-go-round of the Safavid Dynasty.* His heart was sated with the wine of poetry and delirium, but his thoughts were catching the reeds of dark reason. Looking deep into Biram Khan's eyes, he exclaimed capriciously.

"The emperor has decided to heed your advice, Biram. For the sake of my son, I must reclaim my lost empire. Persia is the answer, my Mecca, where the prayers of the emperor in exile might receive the boon of possession? This jewel of Hind!" His thoughtful look was gathering rills amusement. "With a handful of chosen friends and my beasts of burden, I feel I am floating in the Ark of Noah. Beneath me are the storms and tempests of turbulence, and the waters of betrayals. Soon, I should write to the king of Persia, seeking asylum across the boundaries of Helmand?" His amber eyes were lit up with the stars of dreams and poetry.

"Your words alone will rain pearls of wisdom on the land of Persia, Your Majesty. And Shah Tahmasp would welcome the Noah's Ark with joy and reverence." Biram Khan's eyes were gathering stars of poetry.

"My pearls of wisdom, by the grace of your flattery, Biram, would be polished with the fire of loss and laments!" Humayun laughed, the gold-minted couplet in his head finding release.

"Perpetual kingdoms and eternity are not ours
It is to God to Whom belong perpetual kingdom and eternity.

If the emperor's intellect is reduced to such poverty of rhyme, he should retire to Mecca, and pray for inspiration?" He got to his feet, his gaze sweeping over the small groups of his courtiers who still sat talking and drinking. "The emperor needs rest, and so do you. Against the enchantment of this night and garden, fight not sleep, yet wage war against gluttony." He dismounted the throne, waving dismissal and goodnight.

The song-bird night with ardent stars was still reflected in his thoughts, as Humayun reached his bedroom of gilt and damask. Mehter Safai, the emperor's wardrobe keeper was waiting for him, but he dismissed him, accepting the night robe from him, and not willing to go through the ritual of changing in his presence. After Mehter Safai left, Humayun flung himself upon his bed fully dressed, as he had done this afternoon, his thoughts opiate and sinking.

A pilgrim in love! Is Kabul not my Mecca? I might find my altar of truth there? Love supreme and love sublime! One last bloom of love, sweet and exquisite. In Kabul, to find, to cherish till death. Humayun's thoughts had already abandoned the shrine of Persia, where peace and safety lay waiting.

Sweetness in dreams! Beloved standing at the portals of his eyes! The emperor was seduced by the lovely eyes of sleep. The tinkling of bells and the silvery lullabies inside the silence of his soul. Lovely songs from the honeyed lips of Sarvaqad. White mists were rising and shuddering. Effacing All! A pair of diamond-blue eyes was blinking away haze and mist. Hamida Banu! Mah Chuchak! One star, one love, one dream! One lie, one truth? One mirage! The dark, bleeding eyes of Hindustan! The emperor was exiled into the bliss-comfort of sleep.

Chapter Twelve
From Helmand to Persia

A spacious guestroom inside the palace of Shah Tahmasp was Humayun's abode of exile and leisure this particular afternoon. He was seated at a rosewood desk, copying an ode from his diwan. This ode he had construed at the border of Helmand, and had sent to Shah Tahmasp, seeking his permission to come to Persia. Humayun was seated by the window, feeling the softness of cool breeze on his face, while his back was warmed by the blaze of fire under the marble hearth. Behind him, the walls were painted in the patterns of acanthus, and the other two sides were adorned with gilt and mirrors. His robe of pale silk with a jeweled belt and turban hosting a large emerald in the middle, were lending his fair features the glow of ivory and sunshine. Sunshine was flooding in from the window too, though lending no warmth, but his jeweled pen was warming the page with this ode freshly alive.

O Thou whose mercy accepts the apology of all
The mind of everyone is exposed to Thy Majesty
The threshold of Thy gate is the Qiblagah of all people
Thy bounty with a glance supports everyone
A wanderer in the desert of destitution—

The jeweled pen was slipping through Humayun's fingers with the will of its own, his thoughts stealing into the adjacent bathroom. This bathroom was furnished with an oval tub which Hamida Banu found irresistible, and she was having a scented bath even at this time of the day.

Humayun pushed back his chair and swayed will-lessly toward the window, his thoughts staying with Hamida Banu. The blue and white tiles of this Persian Bath were reminding him that his dream bride was heavy with child. Their second child, a princess, was born one year after the birth of Prince Akbar, and was named Bakhshi Banu. Humayun's gaze was exploring the rich tapestry of the garden down below, but his mind with its usual tenacity of retreating into the past, was getting ready to unspool the knots of his journeys from Hind to Persia. Six weeks after the birth of Prince

Akbar, Hamida Banu had joined the emperor at Jun, and six month later all the ladies of his harem had arrived. Shah Hussain at Jun, feeling the brunt of the Moghul siege while still maintaining his defensive tactics, had resorted to the means of befriending Rana Parsad. Sending Rana Parsad the gifts of precious daggers and robes of honor, Shah Hussain had professed his loyalty and devotion to the Rana, requesting at the same time to withdraw his support to the emperor. Rana Parsad, as a proof of his contempt for this murderer, had dressed his dog in one of the precious robes sent by Shah Hussain. This was also his proof of support and friendship to the emperor. Alas, that this friendship was not to last long by the sheer stupidity of one Moghul soldier. One of the imperialists from the emperor's camp had the audacity to insult Rana Parsad. Then he had fled without apology or redress, and had joined Shah Hussain. Rana Parsad was incensed beyond measure, immediately withdrawing his support to the emperor, and exclaiming.

To please Moghuls is labor lost!

Recalling this tragedy, Humayun stood biting his lower lip, his thoughts running ragged in circles amidst journeys long and perilous. Without the support of Rana Parsad, Humayun was compelled to abandon his campaign at Jun. Deciding to find refuge in Fathehpur, the emperor along with his harem and small cavalcade, had barely journeyed a few miles when a host of ill news were unfolded before their path. Sher Khan, in connivance with the royal brothers, was intent on capturing the emperor, and planting hurdles all the way from desert lands to the rugged mountains. Different plans and routes were mapped out in a flurry of despair and confusion. An intolerable abyss of travails and hardships had gaped open its mouth at each step of the emperor's journey, no matter which direction he chose. Choosing the destination of Kandahar, they had to pass through Gandava, the land infested with Baluch banditti. Besides, the cold was so extreme that Humayun had ripped open the inner lining of his fur cloak to share it with Biram Khan, who seemed half dead with cold and fatigue. Months in succession, of hunger and misfortunes, and the food was getting scarce. Kandahar was still one hundred and fifty miles away when they had reached Baluchistan, the scarcity of food so extreme that they had to slaughter a horse. Its meat was boiled in helmets, since they had lost their utensils during the little skirmishes on the way, which could neither be avoided nor averted.

Ill-fortunes in droves were coming the emperor's way as soon as he had reached the Bolan Pass. Another treachery of Prince Kamran was unfolded. He had sent Prince Askeri just across the Bolan Pass with instructions to arrest the emperor and to bring him back to Kabul. Once more the emperor had to choose another destination, and he had favored the territory of Mastang. Braving the snow storms and icy winds, Humayun and his harem, along with a few followers had found refuge in Mastang. That's where Hamida Banu had given birth to a daughter, virtually imprisoned in a small palace surrounded by snow-capped hills and frozen trails. Princess Bakhshi Banu was barely three weeks old when another ill-fated news had reached the royal fugitives. Prince Askeri with a contingent of two hundred soldiers was on his way to capture the emperor by the orders of Prince Kamran, Chapi Behader was the messenger who had brought this news. He was the emperor's former soldier who had accepted the post of serving Prince Askeri a year ago. Since Prince Askeri was not familiar with the roads leading toward Mastang, Chapi Behader had succeeded in deceiving the prince that he would lead him to the emperor. And he had contrived a brilliant escape, thus becoming the emperor's confidant in warning him about the treacherous designs of Prince Askeri.

No sooner had Chapi Behader disclosed this news, that Biram Khan had pressed the emperor to flee to Persia. Another band of the emperor's devoted soldiers had joined Biram Khan in his urgent pleas to leave Mastang. No time was to be wasted in great preparations, so the emperor and Miryam Makani, along with Biram Khan and a group of devoted followers had commenced their flight without delay. Prince Akbar and Princess Bakhshi Banu were left behind in the care of Jiji Anaga and Shemseddin for fear that the journey on the icy highways would prove fatal to the royal babes. While the imperial fugitives were on their way to Sistan, Prince Askeri had arrived in Mastang, demanding, *where is the emperor*? Shemseddin had told him that the emperor had gone hunting, but the prince was not deceived this time, knowing, that the emperor had escaped. Donning the mask of innocence, he had affected disappointment in not seeing the emperor, and exclaiming. *I have come all the way from Kandahar to wait upon the emperor and he is not here*. Upon learning about the presence of the royal babes in the palace, he had ordered milk and fruit to be brought to them from his portion of supplies, and had treated them with tenderness. Within a few days, he had journeyed back to Kandahar, taking everyone along with him. So, Prince Akbar, barely a year old, had become a royal pawn into the hands of his devious uncles.

Though Humayun's thoughts were journeying far and wide, he was standing by the window in perfect immobility. In Sistan, the emperor's journey was interrupted by the sudden appearance of Baluch banditti who would not let his small cavalcade cross their territory until their Chief returned. So, the emperor, along with his ladies and followers were constrained to spend the night in the house of the Chief. In the morning, the Chief had returned quite distressed and crestfallen. Upon seeing the emperor already lodged in his house, he was overwhelmed by his sense of honor, from which no bandit would ever think of deviating, even at the ransom of his life.

Your Majesty! I was out there hunting for you to make you my prisoner and hand you over to Prince Askeri, as commanded by Prince Kamran? The Chief had been in dire haste to pour down a string of confessions. *But now that I see you as my guest, I could do no other but to offer you safety and protection, as the code of honor amongst our banditti requires. May Allah curse me if I as much as lay a hand upon you! My own sons would escort you as far as the borders of Sistan and you would leave unharmed.*

The fire of rubies and the smoothness of pearls were entering Humayun's head at this recollection. Those precious gems which he had bestowed on the Chief, moved by the character of his honor and nobility, were now throbbing alive in his mind's vision where journeys long and arduous were coming to an end. From Sistan to fort of Haji Baba and then along the banks of river Helmand, into Persia. Shah Tahmasp had offered great welcome, besides flaunting the treasures of the Safavid Dynasty, and responding graciously to the emperor's request of seeking asylum.

The Phoenix of the summit of auspiciousness will fall into our net

If you happen to come to our place

Was Shah Tahmasp's poetic response in the form of a couplet.

The emperor and his entourage were royally entertained from the city of Khorasan to the domain of Takht-e-Suleiman, where Shah Tahmasp was to receive them personally. Enroute Farra to Herat, and in all the cities through which the emperor was to pass, a great welcome was accorded the emperor and his entourage by the express orders of Shah Tahmasp. A thousand men on horseback, of Persian descent, were to attend upon the emperor, also arranging feasting and entertainment every evening, with no less than five hundred varieties in fruit and viand to be served to the royal guests. *The trumpets and kettledrums blaring before the procession of the emperor, and people streaming out on the streets and galleries to watch the grandeur and discipline of the Persian hosts and Moghul guests!* Reaching Herat, known as the Pearl City, Shah Tahmasp had sent his son Muhammed Mirza along with his viziers, Amir al Omra and Oghli Taklu, to welcome the emperor.

At Herat, Humayun had indulged himself in all sorts of pleasures, his heart brimming with the nostalgic memories of youth and grandeur. *Polo and archery, hawking and hunting and falconry, besides visiting the holy shrines and great palaces.* Then he had journeyed to Jam, visiting the Shrine of Hamida Banu's ancestor, Ahmad of Jam. She was, of course, with him always on his journeys splintered with hardships or pleasures. From Jam to Meshid, and then to Ardabil. At Ardabil was the tomb of the founder of the Safi Dynasty, where the emperor's father had inscribed his name, and now Humayun had added his own to Babur. Nishapur was the next stop, where he had gone to see the mines of turquoise. Damghan, Sebzawar, Bostan, seman, Sefiabad, all these cities were a jumble of black dots in Humayun's head, pointing toward his final destination, Takht-e-Suleiman.

A sad, thin smile was curling upon Humayun's lips at the memory of Takht-e-Suleiman. Shah Tahmasp, pressed by his curiosity about Biram Khan being a Turkoman and Shia by birth, had sent orders, summoning him to Takht-e-Suleiman, while Humayun was still touring and visiting other countries of the Persian Empire. The Persian king himself an orthodox Shia, after receiving Biram Khan, had ordered him to cut his hair and to don Taj. *Taj meaning, a Persian cap as the emblem of Shia doctrines, or a crown in Turkish.* Biram Khan had politely declined, stating, that since he was in the service of the emperor, his loyalty dictated to maintain the customs of the Moghul etiquette. Shah Tahmasp, though apparently forgiving, yet raging inwardly, had made his rage and authority known in a different manner. A couple of prisoners who were captured from Chiragh-kush were brought to his presence by the guards by his sudden command. And they were brutally executed while Biram Khan had stood waiting upon the king, mute and obedient.

The smile upon Humayun's lips was dying at the recollection of his own arrival at Takht-e-Suleiman. Shah Tahmasp after inquiring about the health of the emperor had requested him to wear Taj. Humayun, taking advantage of his wit and of his knowledge as to the double connotation of Taj, had accepted readily.

This Taj is a mark of greatness! Especially, for the emperor in exile. I will feel honored to wear it. The echo of his own response was loud in Humayun's thoughts, sending a quick shudder down his spine.

Shah Tahmasp had then secured the Taj on the emperor's head with his hands. All the men in his court, the Khans and the Sultans, the Mirzas and the Sayyids dipping their heads in reverence and exclaiming. *Allah, Allah. The most Great, the most Compassionate, the most Merciful!*

Mercy! One blister of an exclamation unfolded in Humayun's head as he noticed Shahzadi Sultanum down below on the terrace.

Shahzadi Sultanum was the sister of Shah Tahmasp, materializing on the terrace like some houri straight from the Paradise. Humayun stood there gazing, entranced, all thoughts of the past and present fleeing from his head. His heart was blooming into the splinters of longings nameless. But these longings had no life of their own. He could feel no love in his heart, only sadness and some spurious need to worship. So profoundly absorbed was he in admiring the object of his worship that he didn't notice Hamida Banu stealing behind him. She was following the emperor's gaze, her heart aching, and a singeing protest escaping her ruby-red lips.

"His Majesty is smitten with love, it seems?" Hamida Banu's eyes were sparkling like the diamonds she wore on her head and around her throat.

"My jealous Empress! And me without a throne and in exile too!" Humayun whirled around, his eyes gathering mirth. "The emperor loves only you, my love. And he will fall in love with his own Shahzadi." He bent forward, kissing the blue silks on her swollen stomach. "I know it's going to be a princess. I pray for a daughter, much like my sister Gulbadan! Princess Bakhshi Banu, does she resemble Gulbadan ? Our princely son, who does he look like? You have suffered, my love, suffered terribly. My Hamida, my Miryam Makani! Missing our children, rather grieving?" He murmured intensely.

"I do miss them, Your Majesty, that's true." Hamida Banu demurred without regret. "All those past sufferings are nothing as compared to these pangs of separation. And yet, I do not grieve, am only concerned." Her spirit of optimism was shining bright in her lovely eyes. Wish, they were still under the care and protection of Jiji Anaga and Shemseddin, instead of being hauled into the lap of Prince Hindal's wife, Sultanum Begum?" She breathed wistfully.

"Our royal charges are not missing the love of their godparents, I assure you! As long as Jiji Anaga and Shemseddin are in Kandahar, and they plan to stay there, they will not let any harm come to our prince and princess." Humayun began consolingly. "But they are in loving hands. Princess Bakhshi Banu has a lovely playmate, her cousin Princess Ruqueiqa. And Prince Akbar, I hear, is loved and cosseted by the horde of royalty, aunts and uncles, great-aunts and grandmothers, and by all the Begums in the harem. My only fear is that our lusty prince would be spoiled?" His look was ardent and mischievous.

"Our prince, Your Majesty, is born with the virtues of valor and wisdom. He would grow up to be a Moghul Solomon!" Hamida Banu's small, white face was lit up with the aura of a young prophetess.

"Solomon, indeed! With nine hundred and ninety-nine wives in his harem, and no heir to rule the kingdoms." Humayun laughed. "A missive came from Kandahar this morning, revealing a most tender scene." He kissed her hand, and then began pacing. "Our aunt Khazanda Begum has fallen in love with Prince Akbar. She never tires of kissing his little feet and hands and exclaiming, *these are the very feet and hands of my brother, the late emperor Babur. Prince Akbar is like him altogether.* Bibi Mubaraka Begum is in Kandahar too, now, and loves our prince to distraction. She has accomplished her mission in shifting the remains of my father from Agra to Aram bagh in Kabul. At the slope of one hill called Shahi-Kabul, Babur rests peacefully. A thousand pities that he could not—" His thoughts were truncated as he noticed a liveried page at the door, almost concealing the tall form of Biram Khan behind him.

"Come, Biram. You are welcome. No need to go through the formality of being announced." Humayun waved dismissal at the page, who fled with relief. "The empress misses her royal children, and the emperor is missing his Din Panah. Where did that luxury of poetry and mysticism go?"

"Your Majesty. Miryam Makani." Biram Khan bowed twice, a wide smile on his lips warm and beamish.

"Come, sit by the emperor." Humayun lowered himself in one gilt chair, as Hamida Banu returned to the window, gazing out.

"Good news, Your Majesty. We found your rubies. Or, to put it in a different prospective, we stole them back from Roushan Koka—" Biram Khan stopped, noticing a puzzled expression on the emperor's face.

"My rubies! Stolen?" Was Humayun's incredulous exclamation.

"My folly, Your Majesty. Didn't know?" One befuddled comment escaped Biram Khan's lips, as he noticed Hamida Banu turning abruptly, her eyes shining.

"Sorry, Your Majesty, I couldn't tell you." The lamps of contrition were kindled in the blue lakes of Hamida Banu's eyes. "That gold amulet-case which you gave me for safekeeping, Your Majesty, the one filled with rubies. One day when I was choosing to wear jewels, I forgot that amulet-case on the bed. Later, when I returned, the rubies were missing. I was afraid to tell you, Your Majesty, so I appealed to Muazzam to find the rubies."

"Afraid, my Moon! Afraid of me?" Humayun murmured disbelief. "Have I ever been harsh to any of my wives? Have I ever kept record of my jewels? The treasures of love in my heart are worth less than the pebbles of this earth, inspiring awe and fear?" He was smiling, ruefully and amusedly.

"I was only afraid, Your Majesty, that you trusted me with your favorite rubies, and I lost them!" Relief was now entering blue pools in Hamida Banu's eyes.

"My most precious of jewels is, *you*, Miryam Makani, and I am learning not to trust you to your own self. Come, join us." He indicated the chair beside him. "We must listen to this astonishing tale of rubies and jewel-sleuths by our master story-teller, Biram Khan himself." He turned to his vizier after Hamida Banu sank into her chair to the right side of the emperor. "This jewel-mystery, Biram, we must hear in detail. Might as well proceed?"

"The mystery, Your Majesty, in fact, was solved by Miryam Makani's brother, Khwaja Muazzam himself." Biram Khan began obediently. "He suspected Roushan Koka from the beginning and

170

kept a close watch on him. Getting in league with Khwaja Ghazi, he planned to sell them. Both these thieves had bought Chupatak horses and that confirmed Khwaja Muazzam's suspicion. He went to the horse-dealer, inquiring about the means of this purchase, and was told that they had promised him rubies. Then Khwaja Muazzam took in confidence the servant of Roushan Koka, who told him that his master keeps his valuables hidden in his cap which he never takes off, even while sleeping. A real sleuth became alive in Khwaja Muazzam yesterday when he pretending an accident, filched the cap off Roushan Koka's head, recovering the rubies, all five of them. He will be bringing them over soon, I am told." His look was thoughtful and apprehensive all of a sudden. "Actually, I came to warn you, Your Majesty. Both those thieves, intimidated by Khwaja Muazzam's discovery had gone to Shah Tahmasp, telling him all sorts of lies. What they told the king, I am not sure, but his zeal and antagonism are at their peak. He has ordered his scribes to write some sort of a religious contract, which he is planning to send it to you for your signature. What I have heard so far is that his pledge to give you assistance in conquering Kabul will depend upon your signing this contract?"

"Isn't *moderation* in religion the Law of Islam? Shias, as well as Sunnis, are Muslims, are they not? Where lies the contention, the emperor fails to understand the zeal of our kind host?" Humayun appeared to think aloud. "Miryam Makani is from the lineage of Jam. My own mamma belonged to the same lineage, both married to the Sunnis! Though the emperor in exile is in need of Persian support, he would not sign a contract, corrupted with the reek of zeal and bigotry. Have I not seen enough of that within these last two months? His imams trying to pound Shia doctrines into the heads of my soldiers! But, enough of that." He shifted his gaze to Hamida Banu. "Now that your jewels are recovered, my lovely Moon, you must learn to make the emperor your confidant in all matters, small or great?"

"Your Majesty, that page in crimson cap, waiting by the door? Isn't he the same one who delivers king's requests or Farmans to you at all hours of the day or night?" Hamida Banu murmured concern, her gaze disapproving.

"Yes, the devoted slave of our benevolent king!" Humayun's gaze sailed over to the servant, where he stood carrying a bundle of logs in his arms. "Come in, my good man." He intoned genially. "No need to feed the fire to another enormous blaze. As it is, the room is quite warm?"

"Your Majesty." The servant bowed double without relinquishing the bundle of logs. "Shah Tahmasp, the king of Persia, sends greetings to the emperor, along with this message. The king is hoping that the emperor would adopt Shia faith, granting him the favor of lending support and protection to His Majesty. But, if the emperor chooses otherwise, the emperor and his followers would be consumed in the fire like these logs of sandalwood." He delivered this message, his eyes lowered.

"Begone, you foul reptile." Humayun's eyes and voice were raining down the bolts of thunder and lightning. "My own vizier will carry the emperor's message to your king of Persia without the logs of rudeness." He leaped to his feet, scattering the logs to the floor with one violent blow of his fist. "Run, you Persian rag, before the emperor tears you to pieces with his bare hands." He began to pace.

The messenger, almost stunned with awe and shock, scrambled the logs into his arms and fled. Hamida Banu sat there mute and bewildered. Biram Khan was turned to the statue of ice, his head light and empty. The volcano of rage in Humayun's heart was boiling and churning. By the sheer act of his pacing, he was trying to master his rage and implacability. Another storm was brewing inside him, that of pain and anguish, and of honor and hopelessness. From the turbulent depths of his soul, were rising forth reason and quietude. Almost willing his rage to death and burial, he began to speak while still pacing.

"Tell the proud king of Persia, Biram, that in response to his insolent message, the emperor returns his greetings with many humble thanks. That the emperor would remain true to his Sunni faith to the end of his life. That he cares not for the kingdoms of this world, but for the kingdoms of love in everyone's heart. Whatever is in this world is by the will of the Almighty Whom I trust, and for Whose sole pleasure I obey and surrender. Also, inform the venerable Shah of Persia that the emperor has decided to proceed to Mecca, and that he requests his permission to leave Persia." He waved dismissal, his look distant and unseeing.

Biram Khan's lips were sealed. All speech had left him, it seemed, as he plodded out of the room. Hamida Banu sat counting the steps of her husband's pacing, her thoughts a maddening whirlwind which had no lips to voice their frenzy and bewilderment. Before she could summon enough courage to say something, Jehan Kazvini was announced by another page in livery of gold and crimson. Jehan Kazvini was Shah Tahmasp's minister, and endowed with the noble virtues of wisdom and compassion. He curtsied before the emperor most reverently, lifting his eyes up to him with a smile, both kind and tender. A roll of paper and a jade inkpot were held firmly in his right hand.

"Your Majesty." Jehan Kazvini held out the roll of papers to the emperor. "Shah Tahmasp requests the emperor to read this contract, and to validate it with his royal signature." He murmured.

"I trust you, O divine sage, as everyone knows you to be so!" Humayun claimed the roll in some fever of agitation. "Tell me, Jehan Kazvini, what venom lies concealed in these pages? On the flaming tongues of these words!" His look was getting wearied and thoughtful.

"No, venom, Your Majesty. Just a few dregs of pride and prejudice which one man in power can't help but present to others as a sweet elixir." Jehan Kazvini's tone was soft and comforting. "The king of Persia promises aid to the emperor in recompense to his consent to learn the Shia doctrine, and to let me preach such doctrines to his followers?"

"The emperor knows the Shia doctrines by heart, kind sage! And, are the emperor's followers already not subjected to the tyranny of such an instruction, without the emperor's consent?" Humayun could taste the dregs of his bitterness inside him and on his lips. "The emperor's belief is not on sale. Nor can it be bartered in the market of promises. It knows no greed, and covets no worldly wealth. Not even the soot of need or ambition can tarnish its purity." His eyes were turning to the papers in his hand, and he began to read aloud. "*The emperor has entered the domain of Persia voluntarily. The emperor has been received honorably by the king of Persia. Shah Tahmasp promises him aid on the condition that he and his followers observe the sanctity of Shia doctrines*—" He ceased to read. His gaze straying toward Hamida Banu, who sat there with her eyes closed, as if drifting into dreams.

"Your belief will suffer no dent, Your Majesty." Jehan Kazvini began speaking in soothing tones. "With one flick of this pen, you will gain liberty from the prison-like domain of Persia. Your royal signature would prove to be the magic wand of freedom. It's no secret, Your Majesty, that at times Shah Tahmasp is pressed by his need to play the role of an absolute tyrant. I must confess, Your Majesty, that if you decline, you will not only be endangering your own life, but the lives of your Sunni followers. All seven hundred of them, who are longing to return to Kabul and Hind!"

"Has Shah Tahmasp ever read Hadith? Didn't Prophet Muhammed say?" Humayun's voice was barely audible. "*Treat people with ease, and don't be hard on them. Give them glad tidings, and don't fill them with aversion. Love each other, and don't differ—*" His inaudible tones were further silenced by the abrupt entrance of Shah Tahmasp himself.

"Greetings, Your Majesty." Shah Tahmasp bristled forth ceremoniously. The large emerald in his Taj blazing. "You are still perusing the contract, I see? As to your request to leave for Mecca, it is absolute madness. The king of Persia has the right and the privilege to deny such a request." He waved his arms imperiously. "Please grace this contract with your royal signature, and let us stay on friendly terms. The king has neither the time, nor the leisure to indulge in your royal whims, or to engage in altercation concerning our agreement. I am getting ready to march to Iraq to exterminate the Sunni Osmanlis, and am pressed for time." His sharp features were flushed, the glint of pride and arrogance in his eyes glittering.

"My most kind and benevolent king." Humayun began suavely. "The emperor is in no mood to sign the contract, regardless of the fact, whether he stays prisoner in Persia, or departs as a pilgrim to Mecca!" The touch of finality in Humayun's tone had made Jehan Kazvini gasp and cower.

"Your Majesty, the king is not asking you to sign a death-warrant?" Shah Tahmasp thundered, anger flickering in his eyes with the quicksilver lightning of mirth and impatience. "The king of Persia is only requesting the emperor to abide by the customs and manners of Shia doctrines during his stay in Persia. In doing so, the emperor will have all the support and resources from the Persian army to chastise his brothers in Kabul and Kandahar, and to march toward Hind to reclaim his throne of Agra?" He smiled, rage still smoldering in his dark eyes.

"Allow me the privilege of quoting this snippet from Hadith, my king, before I sign." Humayun returned the smile, unable to force back the rivers of pain and anguish in his eyes. "*Do not dispute with one another, lest you become cowards and your kingdom and strength depart.*" He snatched the proffered pen from Jehan Kazvini, and signed the contract in blind haste.

"Your Majesty, the king has arranged a magnificent feast and a hunting party this evening in honor of the emperor, and the empress." Shah Tahmasp was bright and congenial all of a sudden, and laughing.

"The emperor is wearied of feasting and entertainment, my King. Please pardon his absence this evening." Humayun responded absently.

"Your Majesty's absence would rob us all of half the pleasure!" Shah Tahmasp exclaimed. The naked gleam of anger flaring in his eyes again. "Hoping, that the law and virtue of the Moghul etiquette won't permit the emperor to plead absence? I myself stand accused of violating the Persian etiquette at present, but would feel grateful to rectify such a breach of imposition this very evening, if you could accept the invitation?" A shadow of regret crossed his brow, his eyes attaining the gleam of warmth and tenderness.

"The emperor has no wish to be charged with ingratitude, my king." Humayun's eyes were lit up with the stars of poetry and caprice. "He would feel honored to join the king this evening for feasting and entertainment."

"Till this evening then, Your Majesty." Shah Tahmasp sang jubilantly. "No more intrusions this afternoon, Your Majesty, the king promises." He turned to his heels, commanding Jehan Kazvini to follow him.

Humayun drifted toward Hamida Banu like one flame to a moth. The taste of gall and bitterness were rising to his mouth once again, and his heart was a volcano of torments indescribable. Kneeling beside his dream bride, he abandoned his head into her lap. The beloved was licking away his pain and sorrow with kisses sweet and tender. The emperor was like a child into the arms of his blessed mother, seeking safety and protection in her loving arms. *Till evening, till evening*, his thoughts were drifting into the bliss-reprieve of oblivion and surrender.

This early evening, the garden in Takht-e-Suleiman was bathed in the gold and glitter of silks and brocades. Three hundred awnings in gleaming colors, hosting guests and royalty, were teeming with song and music. Twelve bands in separate groups were indulging the whims of the dancing girls in shimmering chiffons, their breasts and bellies adorned with jewels. Begums and Khanums and princes and princess', all were a sea of color, glittering with jewels. Poets, artists and courtiers too were radiating color and sparkle from their smiles and costumes. But the most splendid of all the blazing adornments was the red velvet throne, upon which the young king of Persia, Shah Tahmasp, sat entertaining and being entertained. Humayun was seated next to him, sipping his wine, and sated with viands and fruits on silver trays, which the pages in gold liveries were never tired of serving and parading. Hamida Banu and Shahzadi Sultanum had chosen their own gleaming terrace, brimming with gold daisies in brass pots and flanked by red roses from the climbers down below. The gurgle of fountains, mingled with music and laughter, were congenial to their spirit of youth and friendship, since they had become the closest of friends at the very rung of their first meeting. Both had decided to sit on this terrace, so that they could watch the king and the emperor, besides indulging in the pleasure of gossip and privacy.

Luxuriating in deep, velvety seat, Shahzadi Sultanum was bathed in the fire of emeralds in her ears and around her throat. Her Grecian features were soft and glowing and her green, laughing eyes absorbing the beauty of violet hills looming high in the distance. Hamida Banu, in contrast to this bubbling stream of sparkle and emerald, was hugging her blue silks, her belly swollen and protruding. She was a little jealous of the beautiful princess, but she knew her purity of heart and kindness, and her own heart was aching for the crumbs of love and friendship this evening. Besides, her thoughts were troubled by this recent rift between the king and the emperor, entertaining fears. Watching the Shahzadi nibble on sweets, she exclaimed.

"Is the emperor's life in danger, dear Shahzadi?" Hamida Banu's diamond-blue eyes were voicing their fright.

"Not as much as the king's own, my sweet Empress!" Shahzadi Sultanum laughed. "Cast away your fears, Miryam Makani. My kingly brother may seem to be a royal brute, but he has some noble qualities. He can be utterly cruel to his subjects, but he honors the code of hospitality. He will always be wary of the safety and comfort of the emperor. Besides, no harm will ever come to the emperor as long as I am alive. I am in love with him, if you didn't know?" She teased.

176

"Why is the king inimical all of a sudden?" Hamida Banu declared, condoning the levity of this young princess.

"The king is a slave of his moods, always vacillating between caprice and suspicion." Shahzadi Sultanum chuckled to herself. "A lot of canards are raining down on the Persian soil from Kabul, I guess. Those two louts who stole the rubies are holding those canards against the emperor, and corrupting the ears of my brother. And the king, mind you, is going to subject the emperor to inquisition this evening in view of those canards. If the king's mood drifts toward unkindness concerning the emperor, I have my plans to defeat his purpose." She retrieved the folded paper from her jeweled sash. The paper which she had snatched from Hamida Banu earlier, sprinkled with an ode to Shah Tahmasp written by the emperor himself. "My brother has the temperament of a poet, and in exchange for couplets, he is ready to barter his kingdoms." She tucked the note back in her gleaming sash. "Now, let us get close to the throne, in case, my brother is really planning to shoot the bullets of inquisition. I will be right there to ward off the blows. Besides, I am so much in love with the emperor that I want to watch him from close." She sprinted to her feet with the agility of a dancer.

"You will be stoned to death for hoarding such wanton thoughts, my lovely Shahzadi." Hamida Banu quipped brightly.

"For that honor, I must don my riding habit!" Shahzadi Sultanum squeezed her small waist, pouting deliciously.

"Before you taste the sweetness of death, my dear, could you please satisfy my curiosity as to why the king allows you the luxury of riding and hunting? While others, including myself, are imprisoned inside the gilded carriages, longing to ride and hunt?" She heaved herself up slowly and thoughtfully.

"Didn't I tell you, my brother is a bigot!" Shahzadi Sultanum chirped deliciously. "And yet, he loves me so much that he can't endure to deny me anything. This weakness of his serves me as a pawn against his rules and edicts. At times, I confess, I do make him wretched. His zeal is no match against the ammunition of my intellect and knowledge. I can quote from the Quran and Hadith with the wisdom of Solomon and all his arguments are rendered fruitless. Now! My sweet Empress, let's go." She sailed away, her step airy and graceful.

Not far from the throne, these two royal friends had settled themselves on the Persian carpet, lolling blissfully against the satiny pillows. The fire of jewels from the king's Taj was reaching Shahzadi Sultanum, from where she sat, apparently unseeing the glory and wealth of this garden and of the guests, giddy from drinking and feasting. What she wanted to see and what she had already arrested inside her heart was the portrait of the emperor, sad and beautiful. Donned in pale silks with smooth, glowing pearls around his neck and a large ruby in his turban, the emperor's aura of peace itself was portraying the saddest of portraits she had ever seen in her entire life, Shahzadi Sultanum was thinking. Behind this sadness were lurking wit and amusement, as she could not help noticing the king's own brother Behram Mirza passing ewer and basin for washing hands by king's edict, which brooked no challenge. Her eyes were flashing suddenly, as she became aware of that trio of louts, favored by her brother, and seated not too far from the king, drinking and playing backgammon. But her attention was diverted by the clear, smooth tones of the king who was addressing the emperor, and she was focusing all her attention to those words in order not to miss a single sound or connotation.

"Your Majesty, this inquiry might come as a surprise to you, but I must ask. Did you treat your brothers unfairly?" Shah Tahmasp coaxed a smile into his thick, mustachioed lips.

"If it was not for the wickedness of my dear brothers, my King, I would still have been the emperor of Hind!" Was Humayun's amused response, evoking memories bitter and unforgotten.

"This is the way you aught to have treated your brothers, Your Majesty." Shah Tahmasp indicated Behram Mirza holding out ewer and basin before one Begum in the ritual of washing her hands. "Then, you would never have lost your empire." He stroked his curly beard with his fingers.

"You possess the wisdom of the sages, my King. The wisdom which I lacked at that age!" Humayun took a big draught out of his gold goblet.

"Sages have no wisdom, Your Majesty, only faith?" Shah Tahmasp's gaze was shifting to the three louts, as earlier noticed by the Shahzadi. Roshan Koka and Khwaja Ghazi, the ruby thieves, and their consort, Sultan Mahmud. "Those impious colts over there tell me, Your Majesty, that in your court at Agra, you indulged in some sort of a fantastic game, divining fortunes by the use of arrows. The finest twelve arrows were inscribed with your name, and the thirteenth one of inferior quality, bore my name. Is that true?"

"Half true, my King, each one of the twelve was individually inscribed with the names of my viziers, one with my name." Humayun laughed. "The thirteenth one had your name inscribed. As confessed earlier, I lacked wisdom at that time. And yet, the empire of Hind at that time was twice the size of Persia." He added thoughtlessly.

"That sounds quite true, Your Majesty." Shah Tahmasp's eyes were lit up with the sudden shafts of anger. "Wisdom alone could have saved you from loss and grief, and you would not have been driven to exile by a horde of clowns and cut-throats, not to mention, by your own brothers, vile and wicked?" His deflated ego was seeking the breath of poetry, and he recited menacingly.

"What has passed over our head, has passed
Whether by river, or by hill or by forest."

"We are all in the hands of God, and all of us must submit to the decrees of the Almighty." Humayun murmured, noticing the breezy approach of Shahzadi Sultanum.

"My King." Shahzadi Sultanum curtsied, holding out the piece of paper to her brother. "Miryam Makani gave me this. It's an ode written by His Majesty, for you. Actually, she showed it to me, and I wouldn't give it back to her."

"For this stolen treasure, the king would bestow upon you the ruby necklace that you have been coveting." A trickle of mirth escaped Shah Tahmasp's eyes and lips. "Now, get back to your occupation of theft, and let the king read this ode in perfect peace." He waved dismissal.

"It's divinely written, my King, and it has stolen my heart." Shahzadi Sultanum sang mischievously, stealing a look at the emperor and then fleeing.

"To unfold such treasures is the privilege of the kings alone." Shah Tahmasp unfolded the paper without looking at Humayun. He began to read to himself.

"O King of the world
You are equal to the heaven in rank
Kindness and favor are always your capital
O King, in the world all seek Huma
See how Huma is under your shadow

Such supreme sentiments! Such exquisite depiction!" He turned to Humayun, his eyes flashing compliments. "Huma, the bird of the Paradise! The shadow of wealth and prosperity! All Muslims believe in that, don't they? And now Huma, you, Your Majesty, sits under my wings, in this exquisite piece of art woven with words priceless!"

"Generous compliments, Your Majesty." Humayun's eyes were shining with the stars of poetry. "That one was for my private collection. First, the empress stole it, and then? Well, I have another one, which I meant to recite. I still do, but it is morbid, rather full of woe?"

"I am longing to hear it, Your Majesty. Won't you recite it?" Shah Tahmasp pleaded with the fervor of a devotee.

"I might as well, my king, before I forget it." A profound and enigmatic smile was hugging Humayun's lips, and he began reciting.

"O King, it is a long time that the phoenix of my ambition
Has settled on the summit of the mountain of contentment
The deceitful world which sows wheat and sells barley
Has made the parrot of my genius content with millet
My enemy is Sher Khan, and for a long time has turned his
back on me
Now finding me unguarded, he has challenged me
My prayer to the king of Persia is this that he treat me
As Ali treated Salman in the desert of Arzan."

"Divine verse from the lips of divine inspiration!" Shah Tahmasp's eyes were brimming with tenderness. Overwhelmed with emotions dark and alien, he averted his gaze, shifting it to his vizier. "Oghli Taklu, seize these three rascals, Khwaja Ghazi, Roushan Koka and Sultan Mahmud, and lock them in the dungeon." He commanded.

All three men, stunned by this sudden edict, were being dragged away with the assistance of stiff guards. Such rude entertainment, as mandatory as music and dancing, Humayun was thinking. He had witnessed similar scenes before, and was becoming accustomed to such customs of the Persian court. The music and dancing were at their peak, and no one was concerned about the fate of the three condemned men, though some were following them with laughter in their eyes and on their lips. Humayun's eyes in his head were somersaulting down the rungs of time, and landing at the mouth of the hunting ground. A couple of weeks ago, at the great hunt, Behram Mirza, offended by his partner Abul Kasim, had shot an arrow through his heart right in the middle of the chase. Neither the king, nor the hunters had paid any attention to this brutal act of murder, and had continued hunting, as if nothing had happened. Humayun's thoughts were returning to the mystery of the present, *was theft of the rubies alone the cause of doom for these three men*? If the emperor could look into the mind of the king, he would have known. Shah Tahmasp was thinking that those idlers and thieves had hinted to him as much as to arrest the emperor and to hand him over to his brothers. *Those heathens*! Shah Tahmasp could not help but rage inwardly. Those heathens repeating foul lies that the emperor's father had betrayed the Persian king, Shah Ismael and now the emperor would betray Shah Tahmasp. *Vile, terrible lies*! Shah Tahmasp was returning his attention to the taciturn emperor.

"The keys to open the doors to your kingdoms are in my hands, Your Majesty, and I will hand them over to you." Shah Tahmasp began in all earnest, the shadow of Persian pride hovering over his Taj. "With my assistance, you will first insure the conquests of Kabul, Kandahar and Badakhshan. Then you will reclaim the empire of Hind. Be firm and relentless, Your Majesty. Trust no one, not even your brothers, certainly not them! They must be humbled, arrested—" He paused, noticing the rills of pain and sadness in Humayun's eyes. "I promised you feasting and entertainment, Your Majesty, not preaching? Let us shoot some birds before it gets dark, and then to great hunt." He clapped his hand, summoning his vizier.

Shah Tahmasp had announced to his viziers and grandees that he and the emperor were going to dove-cote for the pleasure of shooting the birds. Commanding them to proceed to the Lake Suleiman where he and the emperor would join them shortly. Even before the king could dismount the throne, Shahzadi Sultanum had come sailing by, declaring her wish that she and the empress would join them at the Great Hunt. Shah Tahmasp, much too exhilarated by the prospect of hunting, had merely waved a dismissal at his sister, dragging the emperor along with him toward the dove-cote. Shah Tahmasp, flaunting his skill in archery, was the first one to shoot, bringing down one dove, a hoopoe and a falcon with unerring precision. Challenging Humayun, he stood back to watch and criticize. Humayun, taking aim at the birds in flight, was quick to bring down sixteen without missing a single shot.

"Your Majesty! I wish you could liquidate your enemies with the same accuracy." Was Shah Tahmasp's bantering comment and applause.

"*Always shoot a bird in flight, never an enemy*! One Persian sage said that, my King." Humayun laughed. "As to my enemies, I am more prone to adopt Saadi's thoughts than to wander into the jungles of philosophy on my own. *Clemency to the wicked is tyranny to the good.* To the Great Hunt then, commands the emperor, not the king?" He stalked out of the dove-cote, his laughter loud and delirious.

The delirious time itself had transported the royal host and the guest to Lake Suleiman in a flash. Not that this was any act of magic, but all these pleasure-grounds were one giant conglomerate, against which the king's palace looked like a doll-house. The Lake Suleiman had turned molten, reflecting the haze in sunset and glinting like a mirror. Some princes of the royal blood had chosen to play polo, while motley of group was exercising their skills at horse-shanty called, Kebk-endazi. One bison was tied to a high pole, becoming the victim of men riding on their swift steeds and shooting mercilessly. Shah Tahmasp and Humayun were talking and laughing, while waiting for their special mounts. Not far from them were standing Hamida Banu and Shahzadi Sultanum. The princess was not clad in her riding habit, probably, had changed her mind at the last minute in deference to the empress, who could not join her in the hunt due to her pregnancy. Shahzadi Sultanum's gaze was restless, though she appeared to be listening to some tale pouring forth from the lips of Hamida Banu. Suddenly, she espied Behram Mirza presenting his Kermanian horse to the emperor.

Shahzadi Sultanum turned pale, knowing the intent of Behram Mirza. This Kermanian horse was a fiery steed, savage and untamed. It had hurled many skilled riders into the pit of death, if they dared harness its will and strength. Chilled with fear and shock, Shahzadi Khanum was drifting toward her brother, her heart thundering warnings, but no words escaping her lips. Her legs were weak and dragging, as she watched Humayun mount the horse. Hamida Banu was following her, not even suspecting that her husband's life was in danger, only bewildered by the dazed look of Shahzadi, and her sudden pallor. She was plying the princess with questions, but Shahzadi Khanum was not heeding. Humayun, as soon as he mounted this steed, was confronted with its wild antics. It had a savage will of its own, mad and terrible, whirling like a dervish and bobbing up and down to dislodge its royal intruder. But the emperor was endowed with the will and prowess of his own, coaxing him into the slavery of obedience much sooner than he had expected. By the time he rode back triumphantly toward the king, the lips of Shahzadi Sultanum were unsealed.

"God! Behram Mirza wishes the death of the emperor." Shahzadi Sultanum murmured, lifting her pale face to her brother.

"My dear Princess!" Humayun exclaimed, catching and holding this dear comment in his laughing eyes. "I have mounted chariots of fire in Hind, and have salved my wounds in the muddy water of the Ganges. The emperor knows how to tame horses as well as elephants." His gaze was turning to Hamida Banu. The diamond-blue in her eyes spilling love and pride. "To the Great Hunt." He commanded his fiery steed, flying on the wings of exhilaration toward the ring of animals, where other hunters had already gathered, waiting for the king's command.

Great God! The hunter and the hunted! Humayun's thoughts were giddy, as if he had drunk the soma of joy, love, hope. The hunter indeed! Slaughtered by longings? Slaughtering hopelessness. Haunted by truth, and murdering lies. To Kabul, to Kabul! Love and truth! The bride of my soul. This dream, how sweet, how intolerable? He was entering the ring of death, the laughter of the king trailing behind him. The chaos and madness in his thoughts were chewing the cud of hope, gluttonous and implacable.

Chapter Thirteen
Gift of Kohinoor to Persian King

The palace and the gardens in Takht-e-Suleiman once again were bathed in the colors of feasting and entertainment, this evening. But the feasting was to be provided by the cooks of the emperor, serving Hindustani cuisine as requested by Shah Tahmasp. The entertainments in the garden had commenced this late afternoon, but Hamida Banu assisted by Bega Begum and Gunwar Begum, had been supervising the preparation of the royal feast since morning. Longing for silence and solitude, Humayun had immured himself into the small library of a summer palace. His heart was light, and his head brimming with hopes, since Shah Tahmasp had promised him riches and soldiers to win back Kabul, Kandahar and Badakhshan. In fact, the king was to parade those gifts before him this very evening, while enjoying the Hindi Classical music and dancing. Humayun, this particular moment, filling his journal with entries sad and happy, was shifting his attention to his diamond Kohinoor, which he was to present to Shah Tahmasp as a token of his gratitude.

This rose-tinted diamond, cushioned on a bed of rubies, appeared to be rolling in mirth, and drawing emperor's attention to the ugly decor in this library. Two entire walls in blue tiles were smothered with the depiction of lotus flowers and palmetto leaves against the smudges of white islands called, Chinese clouds. The other two walls hosting stained glass windows were of Makrana marble, depicting stylized motifs in leaf, flower and tendril. His gaze was returning to his rosewood desk with koftgari design, where Kohinoor sat palpitating in its light of pulchritude.

Light of love, this Kohinoor! The gift of love from the Rani of Gwalior? Humayun's thoughts were stirring the dust of memories tender and youthful. *Love, truth, beauty, all illusion? Sarvaqad, Mah Chuchak, dream bride effacing all*—The dust of memories in his thoughts was reaching out to Kabul. Akbar, almost two year old, and Bakhshi Banu, the little flower! Will I ever see them? The *eye of hope* inside him was tearing open the veil of

185

golden dreams. His older princess Bihar Banu by Gunwar Begum was demanding his attention, but his thoughts were restless.

The hearts of candles in gold candelabras were casting their gleams on Kohinoor. Humayun could not tear his gaze away from this Mountain of Light. It had life of its own, radiant and palpitating. Concealing in its white bosom the secrets holy and ancient! He could almost feel its warmth, seething through his citron silks into the very throbs of his heart. The green plume in his turban was aflutter all of a sudden, as he reached out to retrieve his pen from the jade inkpot.

Hamida Banu is bursting with joy, her heart aching to hold her babes into her arms, and never to be parted from them again— One little thought was forcing entry into Humayun's head before he could spill even one word into his journal.

Soldiers and equipment are in readiness by the orders of Shah Tahmasp, to conquer Kabul, Kandahar and Badakhshan. Kandahar will be annexed to Persia under the nominal command of the three year old Prince Farid Shah, the youngest son of Shah Tahmasp. Emperor Humayun will retain Kabul and Badakhshan— Humayun's fingers were protesting against further journal entries.

Relinquishing his pen into the inkpot, Humayun's hands were reaching out to the fire of rubies beneath Kohinoor. Scooping the fiery gems into a velvet pouch, he pushed it aside. A sudden weariness was alighting in his eyes as he picked up the Kohinoor, wrapping it in red velvet with utter reverence. This act of reverence alone was pouring sadness into his heart that he was going to bestow this precious gem on a man, whose heart could never appreciate the worth of beauty, but in kingdoms large and prosperous. His sadness was splintered further into little wisps of aching tenderness at the thought of confronting his brothers. He could never be cruel or harsh to them, one pitiful murmur in his mind was seeking affirmation. Some sort of stunning revelation was pounding at the doors of his awareness. So chilling was this awful sound, that upon noticing Hamida Banu sail into this library, he thought the voice of illusion was manifesting itself in dreams and visions. This was a jewel-vision, her silk dress the color of night sky. The diamonds in her hair twinkling like the cold, throbbing stars. Only the sparkle of joy in her eyes and the roundness of life as her swollen belly, were the proofs of reality to Humayun. But he could not speak, as if entranced by the ether of illusion mixed with the perfume of reality.

186

"Your Majesty." Hamida Banu laughed. "If we were not in Persia, I would not doubt the look in your eyes which reminds me of Pater, when you saw me the very first time?" Her eyes were spilling mischief.

"And if you were not Hamida Banu, I would be happily mistaken that you were goddess Lakshami!" Humayun declared. "I wish we were in Pater! Those holy nights of bliss and rapture—" He folded her into his arms, kissing her eyes and lips.

"Your Majesty!" Hamida Banu contrived escape, her cheeks flushed and her eyes flashing. "Shah Tahmasp is waiting. Noticing your absence, rather! And getting impatient! Our own banquet, if you remember? Besides, he will not suffer delay."

"No love in your heart, my dream Bride." Humayun teased. "Be as kind to send Jouhar with a flagon of wine before the emperor ventures out into the garden. Also, your brother to guard these jewels until I am ready to present them to the king."

Blissfully content after draining the flagon of wine and entrusting jewels into the hands of Khwaja Muazzam, Humayun had joined Shah Tahmasp in the garden known as the jewel of Takht-e-Suleiman. The night air scented with the perfume from roses and Rat-Ki-Rani was making the Begums and princess' swoon with pleasure, the sparkle and glitter of silks and jewels on their royal persons wafting their own subtle scents. The poets and the scholars, and the Khans and the Sultans were charmed by the Hindustani dancers, forgetting even to applaud their Circassian girls whirling on their toes to please the royal guests. The Moghul night was awakening, it seemed, and the Persian night slumbering. Clusters upon clusters of lotuses swimming into the pools of marble fountains were attracting gasps of admiration from hosts and guests alike. Shah Tahmasp, seated on his jeweled throne, appeared drugged by the wine of music from sitar and tablas. He was catching the rhythm by tapping his hands on his knees. His head too was swaying with the beat, a pair of plumes in his Taj tracing four strings of pearls and a large ruby in the middle creating its own rhythm with dance and sparkle. He had unfastened the collar of his red robe, where rubies stitched with a pair of gold leaf on either side, were radiating their poetry of music and wealth. Each dish prepared Hindustani style had appealed to his taste, and he had devoured many with a relish on the verge of gluttony.

A succession of tables with gold cloths was now satisfying the appetites of the guests. Shami kabobs, nargasi koftas and curried mutton. Fish cutlets, roasted chicken and pheasants garnished with cashews. Sautéed venison, sprinkled with raisins and almonds. Stewed rabbit with mint sauce and many, many more varieties of viands surpassing all culinary delights! The main dishes of bread were chapattis, thin and soft, and nans baked with milk and butter. Mutton pilaf and chicken biryani were the rice dishes, spiced and scented. The Moghul cooks, watching the platters of rice disappear quickly, had feared that they would run short of this main dish. So, they had substituted it with a time-saving concoction of boiling rice with lentils, called *kitcheri*, and passing it as rice pilaf. Jouhar, while replenishing the cups of the guests, was shocked to hear the Persians complimenting the dish of kitcheri the most.

The food of the poor and the lowly. Jouhar was afraid to voice his derision. Saving this delicious piece of compliment for later to share with the emperor.

The emperor, right now, seated beside Shah Tahmasp was watching the parade of gifts bestowed upon him by the generosity of the Persian monarch. His gaunt features, absorbing pallor from the citron dusk and from his robe, were almost bronzed, like a Greek god sculpted in sunshine. There was no sunshine in his eyes though, his thoughts counting the burden of bounties, partially in view at this moment, but too heavy to carry on his weak shoulders in journeys long and arduous. A small batch of Kyzylbashes was marching in disciplined files to represent a battalion of twelve thousand soldiers, who were to accompany the emperor on his lengthy campaigns. The chosen few steeds, Arabian and Chupatak were cantering rhythmically in obedience to their riders, they too depicting the remainder of their breed, assigned to each soldier with rich saddles and Persian trappings. The Bactrian camels stately in gait were loaded with provisions for the journey. Bows and arrows and shining quivers! Guns and cannons and hosts of cavalry. Three hundred bodyguards called Korchi Khaseh from Shah Tahmasp's personal contingent of cuirassiers. Large caskets three thousand in number, filled with ornamented saddles and girdles in gold and silver. Luxurious tents and Persian carpets! Bolts of linen from Rum, Yezd and Iran, and from Europe and Astrakhan. Circassian slaves with ivory complexions and bright, dreamy eyes.

Humayun's attention was diverted by one creamy ripple of an ode from the lips of Shah Tahmasp. His gaze landing at the heaps of gifts at the king's feet, which he was yet to bestow on all present.

"The world is as desired, the sky is the slave and the angel is invoking blessing

Hope is fresh, State is strong and fortune is youthful

Victory is to the right and prosperity to the left

The sky—"

Shah Tahmasp paused, his eyes seeking applause. "Can't recall the rest."

"The gifts of poetry from bounties divine are yours to keep at least, my King!" Humayun complimented profoundly.

"And who gets the privilege of distributing all these gifts of the king to my guests, Your Majesty? Have you made your choice?" Shah Tahmasp asked whimsically. His face flushed and his eyes shining.

"No other than the brother of my empress, my gracious King." Humayun smiled graciously.

"Khwaja Muazzam it is, then." Shah Tahmasp clapped his hands, summoning the privileged man to his presence.

Khwaja Muazzam, at once, was transformed from a young cavalier to the master of ceremonies. Entrusted with bales of silks and velvets, and of damasks and brocades, he was gathering cheers of delights from the lips of the ladies. Robes of honor for poets and scholars! Ornamented swords for the princes. And daggers in hilts of jade and ivory! Gold dinars and precious gems, all were pouring from his hands like the showers of munificence. Humayun was overwhelmed, and Shah Tahmasp was smiling to himself, pouring forth one lone couplet.

"There came out a lapwing with the crown of greatness upon its head

And with the letter of glory and prosperity tied on its wings."

Shah Tahmasp's eyes were revealing the gift of his inspiration to the emperor alone. Catching and holding the gleam of praise and gratitude in Humayun's eyes, he continued hastily. "The laurels of victories await you at the end of your expeditions, Your Majesty. By the will and power of God, you will return to Hind much sooner than you anticipate!" There was a dance of prophecy in the gold-jingle of his eyes.

"May God bless you with blessings countless, my King." Humayun's lips were uttering the prayer of gratitude. "Your wealth is enormous, but the riches in your mind and heart I cannot even fathom to discover? My heart is heavy with the weight of joy and gratitude. So heavy, indeed, that it has ceased to throb altogether?"

"All bounties come from God!" Shah Tahmasp exclaimed with a rare sentiment of humility. *God, Who gives to whomsoever He wishes. And God is the possessor of great bounties.*" His lips were giving breath to a quatrain.

"No one is aware of the secrets behind this curtain
The door of divine grace is not open to all
One who knows the city well
Knows where our goods lie." He smiled.

"May the door of God's Grace remain open to us both!" Humayun sang this prayer aloud. "And your bounties, my King, wherever they are may remain safe. And may our friendship grow and prosper. Always trusting each other! Our thoughts filled with love and loyalty!"

"Amen to that, Your Majesty!" Shah Tahmasp declared beamishly. "To prove our friendship, I am going to condemn those base, wretched liars to eternal damnation. The ones who corrupted my ears against you, breathing vile and evil lies behind your back, Your Majesty." He clapped his hands, summoning Biram Khan to his presence. "Your loyalty to the emperor I admire, Biram, though you are a subject of Persia. Fetch those scheming rascals from the prison. Their fates, ill or deplorable, will be decided this very evening." He waved dismissal.

A great spell of love and amity had enveloped both the monarchs, after Biram Khan had departed on his mission, jauntily. Both sat talking and laughing. Humayun had thought he was transported into the garden of Irem, the Muslim Paradise where houris dwell amidst the rivers of milk, wine and honey. His houris were Hamida Banu and Shahzadi Sultanum, and one other Persian *nameless* he had not seen before. The violet hills down yonder were veiled in haze and mists. Moon was chasing the delirious stars, numbered few and scattered gleefully. The whisper of music in the wind, and the dancers floating so seductively, were attracting Humayun's attention. But before he could lose himself in that

190

scenic seduction, his gaze was arrested to the three prisoners attended by the Persian guards, Biram Khan trailing behind. Reaching closer to the throne, all three prostrated themselves before the king, their eyes glazed with fear and hopelessness.

"Rise, you groveling fools! Get to your feet!" Shah Tahmasp thundered. "How you tried to stain the character of the emperor with impious lies, and almost succeeded in convincing the king? You bags of offal and corruption, your reward for grand lies is the lowest pit of darkness." His flashing eyes were turning to the guards. "Cast these rapscallions into the dungeon of Mehter Suleiman, and let them perish there without food or drink."

"Your Majesty." Roushan Koka staggered to his feet, appealing to the emperor. His hands cupping his head, as if warding off the shafts of anger in the eyes of the king. "Your Majesty, have mercy on us. Intercede, please, in the name of your merciful father. He always forgave, the late emperor." He could not continue, doom written all over his face.

"My gracious King, pardon these crawling worms!" Humayun's eyes were lit up with the Sufic light of love and compassion. "Even a cankerous worm acts in obedience to the law and virtue of nature. Though making the fruit cankerous, it serves the mother earth in nurturing fresh fruits, more pure and bounteous than before." The amber stars in his eyes were gathering profundities. "Look at them, my King, how fear and doom sits mighty in their eyes! Show them the light of your mercy, my King. Pardon them." He appealed earnestly.

"Your Majesty!" A gasp of incredulity escaped Shah Tahmasp's lips. "How can an emperor wronged by foes and friends alike, ever think of granting pardon to the traitors who tried their utmost to destroy the emperor's life? Such vile, deceitful cut-throats, who, if succeeding in their plots, would have betrayed the emperor, into the hands of his brothers? If I was the emperor so maliciously wronged, I would not let these *worms* breathe another breath!" His gaze was searching the gentle pools in the emperor's eyes. "All those tragedies and misfortunes! So heavy, this weight of exile and uncertainty." His eyes were shining with the warmth of bewilderment.

"One must learn wisdom from misfortunes, my King, not gather the weeds of cruelty and bitterness." Humayun's lips were unfolding a thin, mystical smile. "Had I not forgiven myself for my follies, I would have never learnt to forgive the follies of others." The silent plea in his eyes for the fate of the prisoners was rising afresh.

"Take these vermin away, my good guards, and set them free." Shah Tahmasp commanded suddenly, his look dark and thoughtful.

"Thank you most profoundly, my beloved King." Humayun murmured warmly. "The emperor will remain devoted to you for life for this act of mercy!"

"My life, Your Majesty! Had you but asked, I would have given that to you, without a protest!" One strange quiver in Shah Tahmasp's heart let loose this sentimental arrow. "Such is the magic of this night? The enchantment of this music and dancing from lands alien and mysterious! The emperor has cast a spell over me!" The dark mists in his eyes were unfolding mirth and mischief.

"That spell, my King, if it could hold you under its charm for a few more moments, I would whip up a surprise for you with the skill of a magician?" Humayun laughed. Summoning Khwaja Muazzam, Humayun retrieved the jewel box concealed so adroitly under his robe. "To the king of Persia, my benevolent host." He held out the box most reverently. A gift of love from the emperor in exile."

"A gift most precious!" Shah Tahmasp intoned with a mingling of agog and wistfulness. "No emperor ever before, not even a soul in the entire world, have presented the king with the gift of love." He lifted the lid thoughtfully.

Suddenly, Shah Tahmasp's features were washed with the glow of awe and disbelief. His eyes were lowered and riveted to the jewels, as if he had seen the light of the heavens. Kohinoor was luminous and throbbing. Radiating sunsets and reflecting a million suns in its bosom. Beneath its mountain of light were the little hearts of the rubies, wild and bleeding. Dazed and speechless, Shah Tahmasp could not take his eyes off this miracle of light and beauty. Humayun, watching the king smitten blind by the dazzling light in his lap, began to speak softly.

"This is the diamond, Kohinoor, my King, the Mountain of Light. I have named it the *light of love*. Its worth is such that it can feed the whole world for two days and a half, I am told. And yet, nothing would have ever tempted me to barter it for food or kingdom, even if I myself was dying of hunger. A gift of love, indeed, and the emblem of my gratitude." Humayun smiled.

192

"Your gratitude outshines my hospitality, Your Majesty!" Shah Tahmasp cried with a sudden burst of passion. "My hospitality which boasts not of my sole pleasure, but the sum-total of Persian pride!" He dropped the lid shut on the Mountain of Light, his eyes kindling the light of joy and gratitude.

"This sea of love and gratitude inside me is not all that pure, my King, always throbbing with desires to seek favors, more favors? May I dare request another?" Humayun confessed brightly.

"Right this moment, Your Majesty, if you were to ask for the whole empire of Persia, I would not deny you that favor!" Shah Tahmasp sang under some spell of fever and delirium.

"What mad stars tempt fates of the kings and the emperors?" The stars of mirth in Humayun's eyes were leaping up to the heavens above. "No, my King, the emperor is fated to lose all kingdoms if he dares possess some? And he is not willing to satisfy the laughing fates with Persian wealth in land and sea. My heart longs to visit Tabriz and Ardabil before I commence long expeditions. If this request granted, I will go to those cities as a lone pilgrim, seeking all the holy shrines in quest for something I cannot name? If I could leave my harem at Sebzawar, especially for the sake of Miryam Makani whose time is near, and Sebzawar is an ideal place to bring new life into this world?"

"I will be doing myself a favor by granting you that favor, Your Majesty." Shah Tahmasp breathed happily. "Sebzawar itself will be graced with blessings at the birth of a royal child. Tabriz and Ardabil too, will taste the sweetness of pride and honor in welcoming the emperor." He slipped the gold ring off his finger, admiring the large opal with a great intensity. "Take this ring, Your Majesty, as the emblem of our true friendship. With this ring on your finger, you would be welcomed in Tabriz and Ardabil, not as a lone pilgrim, but as the king of Persia!"

It was Humayun's turn now, to be blinded by the light of love and generosity. Mute and stricken, all expression left him, as he slipped the ring on his finger, not daring to meet the gaze of the king. The king had already shifted his attention to his brother, Behram Mirza. Commanding him to present to the emperor the gold platter, Shah Tahmasp himself leaned back, his eyes dark and flashing. Two large apples, polished to brilliant red, were gleaming on the gold platter, accompanied with a gold knife. Behram Mirza was bowing before the emperor ceremoniously, before holding out the gold platter with all due courtesy. Claiming it eagerly, Humayun's gaze was shifting to Shah Tahmasp, his lips unable to shape the questions throbbing in his eyes.

"This is the gift of friendship and alliance, Your Majesty, to be shared equally, in order to put a final seal on the treasures of our promises and agreements." Shah Tahmasp expounded enigmatically. "You may share it with anyone deserving your trust and friendship."

"The fruits of temptation, which all men need to share with delight, not with guilt!" Humayun dealt a saber-cut with gold knife, splitting open one apple into equal halves. Holding one half out to the king, he murmured effusively. "We would share this for good health as well as for good fortunes." Chewing off a large chunk from his own half, he proceeded to split open the next one. "Dear Behram, this one is for you, since I have chosen you as my escort to the holy shrines at Tabriz and Ardabil." His thoughts were giddy, as if he was presiding over his court at Agra. He divested himself of his diamond ring and slipped it on Behram Mirza's finger swiftly. "In anticipation of all your devotion to become emperor's guide and friend!"

"You are very extravagant with diamonds this evening, Your Majesty!" Shah Tahmasp declared, watching the stunned expression of his brother with amusement. "Before you squander away all your diamonds, I must take you back into the gilded cage of my palace." Shah Tahmasp eased himself up gracefully, offering his hand as a gesture of friendship and brotherhood.

Behram Mirza was left there standing in utter stupefaction, while the king and the emperor waded through the sea of silks and brocades. They were talking and laughing amongst themselves, as if oblivious to the frolic and ripple of music all around. The colors of festivity were not left unnoticed by Humayun. Especially, the color of rose on the cheeks of the nameless princess, when they had passed the bevy of Begums! Shah Tahmasp seemed in no mood to halt and exchange amenities, as if totally intent upon reaching the steps of his palace without interruption. Humayun could feel the prick of diamond daggers on his back, straight from Hamida Banu's eyes, but his sense of propriety didn't afford him the luxury of talking with the ladies when the king himself didn't feel inclined toward this pleasure. The laughing bullets from Shahzadi Sultanum's eyes were dug deep in his back too, but he was keeping pace with the king with a stoic reserve. The king was hoarding a profusion of surprises, restless and unpredictable. The gleaming steps of the palace were barely in view, when Shah Tahmasp stopped, as if by the sheer force of his mirth and delirium.

"One last gift for you, Your Majesty! To keep and cherish. A precious link of love between our dynasties, Chaghtai and Safavid." Shah Tahmasp's eyes were brimming with the poetry in dreams. "A Persian princess, the daughter of my sister. Our jewel of alliance, if you are willing to marry?" He smiled, noticing Hamida Banu steal upon them. "This royal betrothal can be announced this very evening." He added, pounding his thoughts to order that the empress had been following them.

"A wedlock most precious than all the kingdoms in the world, my King!" Humayun declared. "The emperor feels honored. But he dare not possess such a rare gift, in fear of exposing it to the irreverent climes of wars and intrigues." He sighed, feeling the lameness of his excuse.

"To preserve the dignity of my dreams, I must beg leave of the Empress." A volley of mirth escaped Shah Tahmasp's lips, as he hastened to mount the gleaming steps, wishing rest and peace to the royal couple over his shoulders.

Overwhelmed by this sudden shock of his dream bride materializing before him out of the fabrics of ether, Humayun could not speak, his feet earthed to the ground. With tender coaxing and rippling mirth, Hamida Banu unearthed her husband, urging him along with her over the gleaming steps into vestibules of the palace. They were lost into the fogs of parlors and corridors before reaching the gilded staircase leading to their bedroom. No sooner had he stepped into his prison of gold and damask that Hamida Banu chanted merrily.

"The emperor is betrothed to—" Hamida Banu's merry comment was choked by Humayun's sudden violence in locking her into one crushing embrace.

"The emperor is betrothed to none, but to truth, my jealous Beauty." He was kissing her madly and feverishly.

The delirious moon, entering the cloister of stars, was daring a peek into the royal chamber. The emperor was kissing his dream bride, as if kissing the lips of truth. But inside his heart were dreams ravished and tarnished by the soot of tragedies.

Chapter Fourteen
Persian Nauroz

In celebration of the Persian New Year called Nauroz, the emperor and his entourage were being conducted into the palace garden of Ahmad Sultan at Sistan. Ahmad Sultan was the governor of Sistan, who had arranged a welcoming feast for the emperor, along with the festivities of Nauroz. Humayun had returned to Sistan a few days ago, after his much-coveted *pilgrimage*, and had found his host charming beyond expectation, since Ahmad Sultan was a Sufi by temperament and a scholar in the realms of theology. Right now, Ahmad Sultan was leading the emperor and his wives from palace to the garden with all the glamour of Persian pomp and glory. A shower of rose petals from the dancing girls was evoking gasps of admiration from the lips of Bega Begum and Gunwar Begum, and Hamida Banu was in absolute raptures. Hamida Banu's newly born princess, Sakina Banu, was now almost two month old, and she herself had recovered her girlish figure, along with her wit and vivacity. Walking gracefully beside the emperor, she was aware of one young poet and two artists following behind, also bathed in the shower of rose petals. Humayun had brought them along from Tabriz, a poet by the name of Bayazid and the artists were, Abus Samad and Saiyyid Ali, all favored by the emperor and the empress.

Suddenly, liveried men in gold tunics were unrolling a succession of Persian carpets leading to the grove of palms and spruces. A group of dancers were emerging forth too with castanets and tambourines. The Circassian slaves in shimmering costumes were holding out the garlands of roses and champa to greet the royal guests. At the end of this procession, a large colonnade was seen unfolding, decked with crimson marquee and colorful friezes. Tables laden with plates of gold and silver, and floral arrangements were wafting their scented greetings. This colonnade turned into a banquet hall was teeming with viziers and grandees, accompanied by their wives, all boasting of Persian wealth in jewels and brocades. The royal guests were heralded to the stage under the crimson marquee, lit by gilded candelabras, and the table before them holding jeweled goblets and fruit arrangements. Ahmad Sultan, seated opposite, was admiring the porcelain-like face of the empress, haloed by the fire of sapphires in her hair and around her throat. His gaze was turning to the emperor with equal admiration, arresting his melancholy features in his eyes with a sense of awe and wonder. The emperor's green turban with ropes of pearls and a large emerald in the middle was speaking to him volumes and he intoned rather wistfully.

"In Tabriz, Your Majesty, I have heard you witnessed the games of hockey and wolf-running, both of which incite my interest and admiration. And yet, Ardabil is the city of my heart. You stayed there only for one week. Did you get to visit all the shrines you wanted to?" Ahmad Sultan sipped his wine daintily.

"All the shrines of the Safavid kings and of the venerable saints, my kind host." Humayun smiled reminiscently. "The tombs of Safi and Shah Ismael are adorned most exquisitely. Shah Tahmasp is a dutiful son, forever vigilant in making the tomb of his father an emblem of perfection."

"I have heard about your beautiful offerings at the tomb of Shah Ismael, Your Majesty. Can't wait to go there, if time permits, to see it with my own eyes." Ahmad Sultan demurred aloud. "One ewer set with precious gems. The mosaic casement too, as I am told, all inlaid with ivory, turquoise and tortoise shell. And Suras from the Quran inscribed on it! Must be a piece of art and mystery?"

"Persia is seething with mysteries already!" Hamida Banu chirped happily. "There is one at Meshid, still unsolved." Her diamond-blue eyes were flashing. "Would you, Your Majesty, share that mystery with our kind host?" She coaxed.

"Yes, Your Majesty, we would be delighted to hear!" Ahmad Sultan urged hastily. "Didn't know, Meshid concealed any mysteries?"

"Since the empress is enchanted by that mysterious episode, she is well equipped to relate it." Humayun drank deep out of his goblet laughingly. "Yes, Miryam Makani, you will never tire of repeating it, as long as it stays a mystery, and it will! Remain a mystery, I mean. So, please share it with our kind host."

"If I don't die of curiosity while waiting!" Exclaimed Ahmad Sultan, his eyes pleading with the empress.

"There is the tomb of a saint called Imam Ali Reza in Meshid." Hamida Banu began promptly, a subtle flush pervading her cheeks. "His Majesty went to the tomb, but the gate was locked. It was evening, and the night gatekeeper didn't have the key. He tried to break the chain, so that he could let the emperor in, but couldn't do it. His Majesty, then, closed his eyes, praying silently. After offering that prayer, His Majesty tried the lock and it yielded to him, and he was able to see the tomb. Didn't have to wait for the morning gatekeeper to unlock the gate."

"A great mystery folded in the prayer-rug of the emperor's desire to see the tomb!" Ahmad Sultan's gaze was shifting to the emperor, but not before complimenting the beauty of the empress. "May I be as bold as to ask, Your Majesty, what kind of prayer was that which wrought such magic?"

"A simple prayer without the magic of supplications." Humayun offered genially. "With the lips of my heart, I had prayed most earnestly. O Imam, every person who has offered up his vows at your shrine, has obtained the object of his wishes. Your slave has come with similar hopes to your tomb, in expectation of succeeding in his request. Please let the slave enter and pray." He smiled. "From Jam to Tabas, to Qila-i-Kah, the emperor had grown quite expert in praying. Besides, in Baghdad, I met one poet-scholar by the name of Jalanju, who accompanied me as far as Meshid, reciting to me the poems and prayers of the Sufis."

"I wish, Your Majesty, Jalanju would have followed you to Sistan, not Masum Beg!" Hamida Banu's eyes were shooting daggers at one guest in the distance.

"He is an uninvited guest, Miryam Makani." Interceded Ahmad Sultan. "If his presence here is displeasing to you, I will ask him to leave?"

"No need, my kind Host." Humayun waved away this inhospitable suggestion, his gaze turning to his rebel of an empress. "Our empress is a little jealous, since she found out that Masum Beg offered me the hand of his daughter in marriage to strengthen our alliance."

"Following you, Your Majesty, all the way from Ardabil too!" Hamida Banu's eyes were lit up with the lightning of mirth and raillery. "No time for jealousy, Your Majesty." She stole a quick glance at Bega Begum and Gunwar Begum. "The prospect of seeing my son and daughter soon keeps me drugged with joy and longing. Prince Akbar, almost three! Will he remember me? Princess Bakhshi Banu won't, I know." She sighed deliciously.

"Our son and daughter, my dear Empress!" Humayun's eyes were beholding the reflection of Mah Chuchak in her eyes, his heart throbbing suddenly. "I will whisk them away to see the tomb of my father, before you can claim them as your own."

"Wish they had stayed at Kandahar with Prince Askeri, Your Majesty?" Hamida Banu murmured effusively. "Prince Kamran demanded that they be brought to Kabul, and I wonder how he is treating them?"

"Your wishes are many, my Empress, and your needs countless! Yet, none satisfied so far." Humayun consoled with a mingling of regret and tenderness. "Prince Kamran, though wicked and scheming, is endowed with that rare sense of Moghul honor so as not to let any harm befall the royal children. Kabul is more of a home to our son and daughter. Their godparents are with them, and their son, Aziz Koka, is Prince Akbar's playmate. Mahum Anaga, the wet-nurse to our Princess Bakhshi Banu, her son's Baqi and Adham are of the same age as our prince. Gulbadan's son, Saadat Yar and her daughter, Salima. Prince Kamran has sons and daughters of his own, so our prince and princess have a whole royal brood to keep them happy." He darted a quick glance at his host, but finding him entertaining the artists beside him, he demurred aloud. "I wish you could come to Kabul with us? A royal tutor to my prince! It is time he should learn to draw and paint. A privilege it would be, to learn from the master of Tabriz!"

"Command me, Your Majesty, and to teach Prince Akbar would be my supreme delight!" Abdus Samad exclaimed profusely.

"You would be imprisoned for life in the service of the emperor!" Humayun declared capriciously. "And that's a royal Farman."

"May I be honored with such a life sentence too, Your Majesty?" Nizami Khamash, the Persian artist, implored eagerly. "Abdus and I would turn our prison into a school of painting."

"For that kind of sentence, you must turn traitor, but the emperor would find an excuse." Humayun laughed indulgently.

"Kabul has no dearth of traitors, Your Majesty." Ahmad Sultan could not help but voice his concern. "Prince Kamran has erected a fortress for himself between Kishem and Qilah-zafar. He has a large number of forces at his command. The latest report is that he has sent Abdullah to the fort of Taligan, at the head of a large cavalry to check the advance of the emperor, Your Majesty."

"Almost ten years of exile, and the banquets of war and intrigue still chase the emperor down the valleys of pleasure and carefree abandon?" Humayun laughed. "I thought I was coming to a wedding feast, my kind Host? Did you not promise that? The wedlock of poetry with theology, or philosophy, or both, is that what you said? To honor Nauroz, under the guidance of Sufic priests!" The stars of poetry in his eyes were kindling to amber brilliance at the sight of the poets and the theologians who were joining them. "Nauroz, the day of vernal equinox when the Sun enters Aries. But I detect the presence of Sagittarius lurking behind the stately palms."

"Here comes the wedding procession, Your Majesty." Ahmad Sultan was laughing. "Bazmi, Hairati, Baqi Sadr, Hai Bokhari, Mulla Ilyas, Khwajah Hijri and many more." He was indicating them to the emperor. "They will stand there beating the drums of their arguments. A querulous lot that they are! Persia itself is their enemy, in their heated arguments, of course, and Safavid dynasty, their battleground. They make religion the harlot of theology, yet suffer not their zeal in ideation." His voice was drowned amidst the fluttering of couplets and arguments.

"Without trouble they have made good progress
The scribe, the painter, the Qazwini, the ass."

Hairati's rod of inspiration was whipping all to volleys of laughter.

"If you have not heard how Shah Tahmasp treated one English envoy in his court, you would never notice the waves of intolerance, already veiling the land of Persia in clouds of ignorance?" Mulla Ilyas was drowning the voices of the others with his bursts of fury and vehemence. "Anthony Jenkins is the name of that envoy, sent by Queen Elizabeth, on a mission of trade. Before receiving him, Shah Tahmasp sent him his own slippers to wear, so that his Christian feet don't pollute the holy carpet of our pious monarch. Then our venerable king asks the envoy. *Are you a Gaur, unbeliever, or a Mohammedan?* And he replies. *I am neither an unbeliever, nor a Mohammedan, but a Christian. Believing Christ to be the greatest of prophets.* At this, Shah Tahmasp got so incensed, that he dismissed him, saying, that he would not sign any trade agreement with the infidels. Commanding also, that the path upon which the envoy walked before coming to the court, should be sprinkled with sand in order to purge all uncleanness—"

"Say unto the Christians, their God and my God are one! Prophet Muhammad told his disciples." Bazmi was pouring down his own string of injunctions.

"I believe in God. I believe in God's angels. In Gabriel, Azrael, Israyel and Michael." Hai Bokhari's argument was curling up loud and vehement. "I believe in God's books! The Pentateuch of Moses. The Psalms of David. The gospel of Jesus. The Quran of Muhammed. In all the prophets too! Adam, Noah, Abraham, Moses, Jesus, Muhammed. Jesus, the sinless one! Muhammad, the seal of all Messengers! I believe in Resurrection and in the Last Day of Judgment!"

"*Verily, they who believe!*" Khwajah Hijri was reciting amidst the din of noise. "*The Jews and the Sabiens, and the Christians. Whoever of them believeth in God and the last day, and doth what is right, on them shall come no fear. Neither shall they be put to grief,* if you ponder upon the second Sura of the Quran?"

"By Him in whose hands my soul is, son of Mary will descend amongst you Muslims. And will judge mankind justly by the law of the Quran, as a just ruler. And will break the Cross and kill the pig and abolish jizya, the tax which non-Muslims pay to the Muslim ruler? There will be abundance of money, and nobody will accept charitable gifts. This is the prophecy of Hadith."

O people of the Scriptures, do not exceed the limits in your religion. And enough is Allah as the Disposer of Affairs
"I follow the religion of Love
Now I am sometimes called
A shepherd of gazelles—divine wisdom
And now a Christian monk
And now a Persian sage
My Beloved is Three
Three yet only One
Many things appear as three
Which are no more than One
Give Her no name
As if to limit one
At sight of Whom
All limitation is confounded."
Bani Sadr was drunk with the poetry of Ibn-El-Arabi.

More poets were rising to the occasion, quoting dead poets and keeping the sword of their inspiration sheathed inside their feverish heads. Rumi's verse was blossoming forth from the lips of Bazmi.

"If there is any lover in the world, O Muslims, 'this I

If there be any believer, or Christian hermit, 'tis I

The wine dregs, the cupbearer, the minstrel, the harp and the music

The beloved, the candle, the drink and the joy of drunken, 'tis I

The two-and-seventy creeds and sects in the world

Do not really exist, I swear by God that every creed and sect, 'tis I

Earth and air and water and fire, nay, body and soul too, 'tis I

Truth and falsehood, good and evil, ease and difficulty from first to last

Knowledge and learning and asceticism and piety and faith, 'tis I

The fire of Hell, be assured, with its flaming limbos

Yes, and Paradise and Eden and the Houris, 'tis I

This earth and heaven with all they hold

Angels, Peris, Genies and Mankind, 'tis I."

Hai Bokhari was singing the praises of the Sufi poet by the name of Shahabudin Suhrawardi, reciting one favorite out of the sea of his genius.

"The seed of Sufism

Was sown in the time of Adam

Germed in the time of Noah

Budded in the time of Abraham

Began to develop in the time of Moses

Reached maturity in the time of Jesus

Produced pure wine in the time of Mohammad."

Humayun sat there rapt and brooding. A few verses in his head were breathing dissent, and he was about to share them with Ahmad Sultan, when his attention was arrested to the words of Abdullah Ansari. Mulla Ilyas had begun to recite.

"Kindness to the young

Generosity to the poor

Good counsel to friends

Forbearance with enemies

Indifference to fools
Respect to the learned."

"Our young poets, Your Majesty, have made it a practice of paying homage to the dead poets, before airing their own inspirations." Ahmad Sultan expounded, feeling the warmth of the emperor's gaze fixed on him. "Maybe, you, Your Majesty, would honor us with a fresh couplet of yours?"

"All couplets are silenced in my heart under the weight of this exile." One splinter of a smile uncurled upon Humayun's lips. "This profusion of poetry reminds me of the happy times at Agra. My father who had no patience with the bigots and charlatans used to quote often this saying of Prophet Muhammad. *By pious fools my back hath been broken.*"

"Your late father, Your Majesty, was a great emperor, and a great conqueror." Ahmad Sultan reminisced aloud.

"And greatest in love and compassion." Humayun murmured tenderly.

"In Persia, Your Majesty, his acts of valor and benevolence are still repeated with awe and reverence. He had a noble character, and was a true devotee of Islam." Ahmad Sultan, absorbing sadness from the emperor's eyes, could not help but add.

"His first lesson of religion to me was this Sura from the Quran." The lamps of Sufic light were kindling Humayun's gaze to a sudden radiance. *"Allah is the light of the heavens and the earth. The similitude of His light is as a lustrous niche. Wherein is the lamp. The lamp is in a glass. The glass as it were a glittering Star. This lamp is lit from a blessed tree, an olive, neither of the East nor of the West. Whose oil will well-nigh glow forth. Though fire toucheth it not. Light upon Light. Allah guides to His light whomsoever He wills. Allah sets forth parables to men."* His gaze was shifting to Bayazid. "A poet-scholar from Tabriz! Are you from the line of that famous painter, Behzad?"

"No, Your Majesty. I have no claim to that illustrious patrimony." Bayazid sang cheerfully.

"You can claim to be the greatest of poets under the patronage of the emperor, and his historian, if you prefer the prison of Kabul! That is if you can leave Persia, and accompany us in our campaigns as far as Hind?" Humayun offered wistfully.

"A prison most suited to my temperament, Your Majesty!" Was Bayazid's ecstatic response. "From that prison, I will never seek release—" His voice was drowned against the tides of sudden chanting.

All the poets, mullahs and scholars had joined together, forming one Sufic Circle. With their feet tapping on the ground and their hands stretched sideways, they were chanting *Ya Hai, Ya Huk.* Ustad Qasim, the harpist, was teasing the strings of his harp to one dolorous tune. Suddenly, the trumpets were blaring, followed by the frenzied beat of the drums. The Sufic Circle was lifted off the ground in a whirlwind of ecstasy. The arms of the men creating the liquid pattern of *V*, their heads thrown back, their bodies limpid and swaying. *Ya Hai, Ya Huk* was now another violent beat in rhythm with the frenzy of dance, but this ethereal display was coming to a sudden halt. Crumbling and shattering, it seemed, for no one could mistake the orchestral sound announcing the arrival of the Persian King. All were plunged in utter silence at the unexpected approach of the king, only the sounds of the trumpets and tambourines from the king's band, loud and thundering. The Sufic Circle, the Circle of Unity was broken, while Shah Tahmasp himself emerged forth, wading through the sea of color and curtsies. Marching straight up to the royal guests, Shah Tahmasp fixed his gaze to the flustered host.

"Take these Nauroz festivities inside the palace, Ahmad Sultan. The king desires utmost privacy with the emperor." Shah Tahmasp commanded imperiously. "Pardon us, royal ladies, and of course, Miryam Makani." He offered one hasty apology to the ladies who had already risen to their feet, along with the emperor.

The stunned host, managing to herd his guests toward the palace, was escorting the ladies, mute and troubled. As soon as the guests were lost behind the gilded portals, Shah Tahmasp turned his attention to the emperor.

"Your Majesty, how mistaken I was in believing that you had left for Kandahar?" Shah Tahmasp lowered himself opposite Humayun, waving permission for him to be seated. "But you are still here, indulging in feasting and Nauroz celebrations. While Kyzylbashes, my faithful soldiers wait anxiously for the emperor's command to commence their march? The sole prerogative of the emperor, I guess?" He added sarcastically.

"And I thought I would not have this signal honor of seeing you before I left, my King?" Humayun quipped, succeeding in draining all bitterness out of his voice. "My idle pleasure in visiting the shrines, I admit, has caused this delay. Though, this pleasure stripped clean of idleness if one is to consider ones hungers of the soul. Those hungers now somewhat sated, I can devote my thoughts to conquests."

"Your soul, I fear, Your Majesty, is drained of all energy by doling out its treasures of love and generosity." Shah Tahmasp's gaze was feverish and restless, looking beyond Humayun into the grove of palms and spruces. "Wonder why you didn't pave the streets of Tabriz and Ardabil with rubies red and precious, which multiply in your treasury a thousand fold, it seems, every time you bestow a handful on saints and sinners alike?"

"The rubies in my heart, which I keep to myself, my King, are bled white with grief and losses." Humayun's eyes were gathering the stars of poetry. "And yet, I suffer no more. Only gather the treasures of art and architecture, while the art of suffering is lost to me. My heart has lost faith in everything." He murmured.

"In God too? I hope not, Your Majesty?" Shah Tahmasp's feverish eyes were searching Humayun's placid ones.

"Which God, my wise King? Of Sunnis, or of Shias?" Was Humayun's subtle challenge.

"Of both, I hope. The same One, as you would say, Your Majesty." Shah Tahmasp ruminated aloud.

"Your Persian scholar, Kuli Sultan, has summed up this issue most candidly, my King." Humayun murmured profoundly. "Shias maintain that to ban and curse the first Khalifas is an act of piety and agreeable to God. While Sunnis hold that such conduct is the mark of an infidel. In view of these statements, Kuli Sultan expounds. *If a man conscientiously believed that by doing a certain act, he was meriting the favor of God, this could never mark him out as an infidel.*"

"Your state, Your Majesty, such as it is at this moment, marks you as an infidel!" Shah Tahmasp laughed suddenly. "Infidel indeed, visiting all the holy shrines. No Persian sage will ever fathom this paradox? Tell me, O unsuffering emperor, which shrine made your soul suffer with awe, if any?"

"To be true, with shock and fright, my King!" A shudder of ecstasy was rolling in Humayun's head at this strange recollection. "The holy of holies, Qila-i-Kah! Have you ever been there, my King?"

"No, Your Majesty. But I have heard strange stories." Shah Tahmasp's eyes were lit up with the fire of curiosity.

206

"Qila-i-Kah itself is a volcano of sand-dunes and hurricanes, my King. But that's not what fascinated me the most. It was the Ziarat of Imam Zaid, up on the top of the hills, the winds and sands below them whirling, rather gurgling. I was standing at the tomb of Imam Zaid, half kneeling in prayer, when I felt the ground under my feet sucking me in. There was whistling of wind in my ears, voices serenading? Chanting of mantras? The dulcet notes of love and sadness from the strings of harp and sitar. Half dead with awe and fright, I thought I was going to swoon, when the earth under me wailed and groaned, jolting me to the awareness of my half kneeling posture. The songs were gone. The earth was baked solid. Even the wind was silent. I thought I had heard some sort of divine music from the very bowels of Hind? It was illusion, I think. Though, I had experienced something awful and unutterably sweet. The voice of my psyche, no doubt!"

"It was no delusion, Your Majesty!" Shah Tahmasp exclaimed with a sudden vehemence. "Whoever happens to visit that Ziarat claims to have heard sounds. Wild or awful, sweet or heartrending, they all hear something? Even the sonorous notes from Aeolian harp. I must visit that Ziarat too! Maybe, I will hear angels, singing the victory songs for Persia?" His look was dreamy and tender. "That music which you heard, Your Majesty, foretells of fortunes great and victories countless. The tales of your conquests will reach as far as Iran and Turan." Now zeal and prophecy were shining in his eyes. "By the grace of God, the black-faced enemy of His Majesty, and the hypocrites of Hind would be reduced to dust by the bright, flaming sword of Islam. Wickedness would be effaced. Infidelity would perish against the light of justice, from Kandahar to Badakhshan, from Kabul to Hind!"

"Hind, my King, where many a good deed remains slighted, and many a wrong stay unpunished?" Humayun's soothing tones were trying to melt the chill of fanaticism in the eyes of the king.

"If you don't destroy your enemies, Your Majesty, they would destroy you." A glint of tender solicitude was splintering the chill of fanaticism in Shah Tahmasp's eyes. "Spare neither a foe, nor a friend, that is the law of power and sovereignty. Love no kin or woman, if they stand in your path to glory and power." His heart was melting in tenderness at the thought of parting from the emperor.

"The law of nature, my King, proclaims three basic ingredients in good living." Was Humayun's Sufic response, condoning all advice. "Madness in love! Compassion in friendship. Rage in enmity! All illusions in sanity if one is sane enough to know that insanity must conquer!"

"Your parables, Your Majesty, are beyond the realms of my sane reasoning." Shah Tahmasp made an impatient gesture, his look sad and distant. "Strange, I have become extremely fond of you. But we must part. This will be our last farewell. I hope we remain friends. Not like brothers, I do not trust brothers!" He closed his eyes, the mingling of pain and sadness inside him one anguish indescribable. "O emperor Humayun, any defect that you may have found in my friendship or hospitality, let your generous nature excuse it." He opened his eyes, anguish reflected in there from inner turbulence. "May Allah be with you always." He sprang to his feet and stalked away. Summoning his guards with one thunderous clap of his hands.

Humayun could not offer any words of farewell, overwhelmed by his own sense of wonder and gratitude. Mute and ponderous, he stood chasing the naked, beautiful streaks of sentimentality in the king's eyes and words. Involuntarily, he held out his arms, as if to embrace the very ether to his aching heart. Shah Tahmasp whirled back on his feet, as if singed by the fire of love and warmth in Humayun's eyes, drifting toward him will-lessly. Both the king and the emperor were locked into each other's arms. Last farewell! Without a word! Only eyes brimming with the light of love and friendship.

The festivities of Nauroz, the surprise visit of the king and strange farewell, were all haze and illusion in Humayun's mind, as he lay awake beside Hamida Banu in the darkness of the guestroom. Ahmad Sultan had treated him and his family to another feast inside the palace, and then he had retired to bed with Hamida Banu. The taste of sadness was still in his mouth as he had made love to his dream bride, making this night the harlot of his agony and desire. Agony was of the soul, and desire of the flesh, both finding surfeit in the violence of his lust and passion. Hamida Banu had fallen asleep in utter bliss of fatigue and rapture, her young heart hugging the violence of love and pain most voluptuously. But sleep was continents away from Humayun's eyes, his thoughts teasing one cankerous wound inside him, which rested only within its own casket of dreams and nightmares.

That cankerous wound inside Humayun's heart was blinking away its pain and stupor. Growing larger and throbbing! All stars and galaxies were reflected in there. Kandahar was hurled out there into space like one shooting star, cold and fearless. Kabul was a bright constellation overhead, remote and unapproachable. Suddenly, there were chaos and confusion. Hot, searing flames! A conflagration wild and swirling. All galaxies molten, all continents swallowed whole. The wound alive and searing! His thoughts were shuddering, and closing shut all the shutters in his mind. Hush and darkness! Ether and silence. His heart was quiet, inhaling no pain, breathing no sorrow. The voice of psyche was entering his mind, but it was resting, contemplating.

What is self? Does the self know its own self? Is it the womb of truth? Is wisdom, knowledge, enlightenment its saplings? Is illusion the great tomb of love and pain, of quest and hunger, where the fruits of spirituality never mature into ripening? A blossom of unreality. Humayun's thoughts were beholding one flaming torch of truth, wedded to light.

The poet-emperor was sleeping. Sweet lullabies from the lips of Sarvaqad were rocking the wind. Mah Chuchak was blossoming in mists as the loveliest of flowers. Kandahar was greeting the bridegroom of Kabul. Kabul was holding the bride of Hind in one eager embrace. Dreams were somersaulting on the wings of moonbeams.

Chapter Fifteen
Kabul Conquered

The sole master of Kandahar now, Humayun was strolling in the palace garden under the spell of his usual need for solitude and solitary journeys in his head.

Clusters upon clusters of crocuses the color of his purple robe, were peering over the narrow paths. Upon which, his feet shod in gold shoes with pointed toes, were pounding the red brick dust into smooth ripples. The scent of home and fecundity was in the air, but his thoughts were wandering wild and homeless. Kabul was still unconquered, and the longing in his heart to see his soul bride was much more violent than the aching tenderness to be reunited with his son and daughter. Himalayan tulips in blazing profusion were waving him welcome, and the scent of hyacinth was wafting its own perfume of nostalgia.

Am I destined to forgive my brothers, to be trampled under their follies, and to never see the face of Hind? Have I not forgiven Askeri many times over? And do I need to forgive him once again? Where does this love come from, for my brothers? This canker of pain, slashed by betrayals again and again! Humayun's thoughts were throbbing, much like the large amethyst in his turban, reflecting one throb of a purple wound against the glint of sunshine.

From Sistan to Kandahar, the roads were rigged with spies and hurdles. Bidagh Khan, the Persian commander was bold and ruthless, winning territories with much ease in obedience to the emperor's commands. At some bordering territories, no battles were necessary, for the news of the emperor's advance, supported by rich contingents from Persia had already struck terror into the hearts of the petty lords. Abdal Hai, the governor of Germsir, had offered his submission in the manner of a suppliant, wearing a winding sheet from his waist down to his knees, and a quiver hanging down from his neck. A brief halt at the town of Laki, and the emperor had given command to Oghli Taklu to conquer the fort of Bist. Biram Khan was commanded to capture the fortress of Zemindawer, defended by Rafia under the patronage of Prince

Kamran. The fort of Bist was captured without much resistance, but the fortress of Zemindawer had withstood a siege almost one month before capitulating. After these conquests, the emperor had dispatched Biram Khan to Kabul with a letter commanding Prince Kamran to submit peacefully. And he himself had marched toward Kandahar, with the intention of offering Prince Askeri the same choice of peaceful submission.

Prince Kamran had received Biram Khan with all due courtesy, professing love and allegiance to the emperor. He had even gone as far as permitting him to see Prince Akbar and Princess Bakhshi Bunu. But Biram Khan was not deceived by this false show of Prince Kamran's fidelity to the emperor. He had returned confirming the report that the fort of Taligan was housing a garrison under the command of Abdullah and Keracha, supported by Prince Kamran. And Prince Kamran was professing to retire to the fort between Kishem and Qilah-zafar, posing the impression of peaceful retreat, but was all prepared to confront the imperialists and confident of winning. Meanwhile, he had sent a secret message to Prince Askeri, offering his full support and advising him to strengthen his defenses at Kandahar, and not to entertain even the thought of a peaceful submission to the emperor. To cover his tracks of deceit, Prince Kamran had then sent Khazanda Begum to Prince Askeri to plead with him on behalf of the emperor, concealing from her his embassy to the besotted prince.

Prince Askeri, encouraged by Prince Kamran's promises of support, was quick to strengthen his defenses with the intention of fighting and defeating the emperor. Humayun, upon reaching the borders of Kandahar, had sent his offer of peaceful submission, but Prince Askeri was defiant and heedless. So the imperialists had laid siege, still hoping for peaceful negotiations, so as to avoid war and bloodshed between the armies of two royal brothers. In all innocence, Khazanda Begum had pleaded with Prince Askeri, and the siege had lasted till five months, until the Kyzylbashes growing impatient of wait, had captured the fort. Prince Askeri had fled, but was captured and brought to the emperor's presence in the manner of a suppliant with the sword hanging from his neck. Humayun, unable to endure the shame and wretchedness of his brother had forgiven him. Kandahar was entrusted to Bidagh Khan to be ruled under the nominal command of Prince Farid Shah, as agreed by Shah Tahmasp.

Then the emperor had proceeded toward Kabul to chastise his other foe of a brother, Prince Kamran. Reaching close to the banks of Arghandab, where the imperialists had halted for rest, disturbing news from Kandahar were brought to the emperor. Bidagh Khan had turned tyrant, practicing cruelties, and making Prince Askeri a virtual prisoner in his own palace. Besides, he had received the news of Prince Farid Shah's death months before the conquest of Kandahar, but had concealed it from the emperor. After learning about such news, Humayun had abandoned the plan of conquering Kabul, and had returned to Kandahar, wresting this stronghold from the atrocious claws of Bidagh Khan. Bidagh Khan was packed off back to Persia with a message to Shah Tahmasp that Kandahar was to be ruled under the king's name by Biram Khan.

Kandahar! And Askeri turned traitor again? Humayun's heart was aching at the thought of Prince Askeri in chains and confined to his apartments.

Humayun was trying not to think, his pace dwindling. But his thoughts were a medley of rage and insurrection. While putting the affairs of Kandahar to order, Humayun had learned that Prince Askeri was keeping a secret correspondence with Prince Kamran, divulging the maneuvers of the imperialists to conquer Kabul. The emperor was left with no choice but to imprison his brother in order to devote all his energies in preparation of a war which could not be avoided. Though, Prince Kamran was still trying to absolve himself of all charges of plotting and scheming, and feigning innocence. His own followers had lost faith in him, and defections were becoming common in his household and amidst his troops. Nasir Mirza was the first one to desert Prince Kamran, and had joined the emperor six days ago, carrying a load of news from Kabul. Prince Hindal, who had been leading the life of a dervish since Prince Kamran had deprived him of his little wealth and small kingdoms, had devised this plan of escape. Prince Hindal, now expert in divining Prince Kamran's each little move and thought, had contrived the flight of Nasir Mirza. Prophesying that Prince Kamran would trust no one but Prince Hindal himself to bring the fugitive, Nasir Mirza back, so granting him the permission to journey to Kandahar.

An eternity! Six whole days since Nasir Mirza came? This fever and anxiety! Is Hindal ever going to come to Kandahar? Will

I always suffer the betrayals and intrigues of my brothers? Will I always forgive? Humayun's feet and thoughts were coming to an abrupt halt by the music of laughter behind him.

Hamida Banu in clouds of blue silks with diamonds glittering in her hair was making her presence known, still laughing. Khazanda Begum was following in spray of pale silks, a string of pearls around her neck her only adornment.

"I thought I heard the butterflies laugh! But, isn't it silly, butterflies don't laugh." Humayun's gaze was sweeping from one to the other.

"They do, Your Majesty, they do!" Hamida Banu sang happily. "I have heard them often. Especially, when they have had their fill of wine from the cups of the Himalayan tulips."

"This mountain air doesn't suit you, Miryam Makani! It's making you giddy to indulge in inanities." Humayun smiled. "I thought the company of our wise and noble aunt would check the riot of your wild imaginations?" He turned to Khazanda Begum, noticing her pallor, and dark circles under her eyes. "Are you ill, Dear Lady? How pale you look! You are not going to faint right here, are you?"

"No, Your Majesty!" Khazanda Begum's eyes were protesting denial, the periwinkle blue in them bright and vibrant. "Age, Your Majesty, is another name for illness. Soul longing for liberty, but body relinquishing not its claim on weak flesh."

"Your wisdom, dear Aunt, is quite baffling to the poor intellect of the emperor." Humayun breathed affectionately. "I can smell the scent of conspiracy? Some sweet, subtle fragrance from the souls of two beautiful ladies! Did the empress choose you as her escort, my beloved Aunt, with the intention of pleading pardon for some vile wretch who doesn't deserve any crumbs of mercy?"

"Your Majesty!" Hamida Banu's protest was left unvoiced by the sudden peal of laughter on Khazanda Begum's lips. "Your wit resurrects the dear, dear memories of my brother, Babur. Your father, of course, Your Majesty." Khazanda Begum was succeeding in concealing the daggers of conspiracy inside her heart. "If luring you to the feast of song and music is called conspiracy, then so be it. We have arranged a small court inside the palace, for your sole pleasure. Poets are planning mushaira, as you call it, that poetry competition."

214

"So fortunate that the emperor can't see beyond those alluring scenes, or he would be tempted to go wandering into the wilderness?" Humayun slipped one arm around Khazanda Begum's waist, holding out the other to Hamida Banu. "Song and poetry are temptations enough to lure emperor into the prison of any palace." He made them walk beside him, hurrying toward the palace.

The scent of spring and violets from outdoors was entering the palace where a makeshift court had been set for the pleasure of the emperor. Humayun, seated in his gilt chair, was drunk with the wine of poetry, astronomy and theology. Besides, there were the Begums all perfumed and bejeweled, and a group of poets and scholars with bright smiles and colorful plumes in their turbans. Hairata and Jahi Yatman were the poets from Persia. They were delighted by the company of the poets from Hind, Kabir and Said Ali. The emperor's poet-scholar from Tabriz, Bayazid, was enjoying discussions with the theologians. The artists too were present, Abdus Samad and Saiyyid Ali. Before the commencement of this happy court session, Biram Khan had informed the emperor confidentially that Nasir Mirza was not to be trusted. He had told the emperor about ill intentions of this fugitive in corrupting the minds of the royal princes, but the emperor had forgotten about that in this frolic and glitter of poetry and mysticism. The Begums were gloating at their success in drugging the emperor with the sense of peace and serendipity. And they were waiting for the right moment to shoot their pleas in gaining pardon for Prince Askeri. As soon the music had dwindled to insignificance and the dancers had retired to rest their aching limbs, Hamida Banu was the first one to pave the way for intended pleas from the Begums.

"Your Majesty, I have learned all about the courts at Kabul when you were a prince. How grand and opulent they were, Dear Lady told me!" Hamida Banu smiled winsomely. "Though we talked mostly about Prince Akbar and Princess Bakhshi Banu, both healthy and beautiful. Prince Akbar is taking lessons in archery. Didn't realize, he is five year old now, quite a soldier! Brave and reckless, Dear Lady says, *stealing out of the palace and exploring on his own the glens and the valleys*. Oh, how I wish to hold him in my arms! When can we go to Kabul, Your Majesty?"

"Young and naive you are, Miryam Makani!" Humayun smiled perceptively. "Kabul is not the home and sanctuary it used to be. We would not be blissfully stumbling into the welcoming arms of Kabul, but entering a hostile territory usurped by the wickedness of my dear brother. We have to win Kabul back, before the ladies can join us. And it won't be long, the emperor promises."

"Your Majesty!" Khazanda Begum, forgetting the cause of Prince Askeri, cried with a sudden apprehension. "I must come with you, Your Majesty. I must return to Kabul. I can't explain, but I must." She couldn't voice her premonition of dying in Kandahar, while longing to be buried in Kabul beside her brother.

My dear Aunt!" Humayun caught and held that wisp of a premonition in his own eyes. "I cannot permit you to be exposed to the perils of the journey long and arduous. You will follow us with the rest of the ladies of the harem after our conquest. No, dear Aunt, the emperor will not consent to this wish of yours. Any other wish which you might have, will find approval?"

"Anything, Your Majesty?" Khazanda Begum chortled with a sudden blithe, feeling the plea-daggers concealed inside her heart.

"Anything, my Dear Lady, with the exception of any plea in favor of Prince Askeri!" Humayun smiled to himself.

"Oh, how my heart bleeds, Your Majesty, to see the contrite Prince in chains!" Khazanda Begum began exigently. "All the royal princes, and you, Your Majesty, the sweet saplings of my dear brother. I played with you all, caring and loving always. And now, all these rifts and contentions! Prince Askeri, Prince Hindal, Prince Kamran, how I wish to see you all together, loving, not fighting. Babur must be turning and tossing in his grave with torments indescribable?" She added hopelessly.

"Do you think, dear Aunt, that the emperor doesn't feel the pincers of agony in his heart?" Humayun averted his gaze, focusing his attention to the gilded doors.

"Your Majesty, Prince Askeri says, he will be loyal to His Majesty for life." Hamida Banu interceded quickly. "Such misery and hopelessness in his pleas, he is really—" Her pleas were silenced by the sudden approach of Prince Hindal, followed by Biram Khan and Khwaja Khizr.

"Ah, the candle of my heart! You have come to light my way to Kabul, to Agra and Hind!" Humayun declared under the spell of euphoria and exultation.

Prince Hindal prostrated himself at the emperor's feet, but Humayun lifted the prince up to him and locked him in one warm embrace. Food and drink were ordered for the prince, and he had begun to disclose the schemes of Prince Kamran and of his own follies with the zest of a troubadour. Prince Kamran, not content with Kabul, had wrested Badakhshan out of the hands of Suleiman Mirza. Usurping his treasures, and throwing him into the prison at Kabul, along with his son, Ibrahim Mirza. Now that the emperor had come back, Prince Kamran, advised by his counselor Abdul Khalik, had released the Badakhshani prisoners. Restoring their kingdom and treasures after one whole year of imprisonment, with the hope that they would defend Badakhshan against any assault by the imperialists.

"Prince Kamran has sent a body of troops, Your Majesty, under the command of Kasim Birlas, intending to block the passage of the imperial troops through the Khimer Pass." Prince Hindal was starting afresh after a long pause, feeling giddy with drinks and excitement. "Most of his commanders are defecting though, and soon will be joining His Majesty, I have no doubt." He appeared to prophesy.

"This time, none of the defenses or treacheries could save my brother from an ignominious defeat!" Humayun's psyche was catching its own morsel of a prophecy. "The emperor would neither spare a foe, nor a brother, as advised by the king of Persia. The sting of my defeats and tragedies is my talisman to conquer and persevere. Our preparations for war would take a couple of weeks, and then we march to Kabul."

"In Kandahar it is spring, Your Majesty, but Kabul passes are still snowbound. Not wise to march just as yet?" Was Prince Hindal's inebriated advise.

"My sage Prince, the emperor's decision to march to Kabul, would brook no delay." Humayun intoned firmly. "This wise decision was made even before you ventured out into the world of the living from the hermitage of the dervish-hood. You are welcome to stay in Kandahar, while the emperor braves the snowstorms to reclaim his Kabul back." His look was thoughtful and searching.

"Pardon my indiscretion, Your Majesty." Prince Hindal murmured earnestly. "I will stay by your side wherever you go, Your Majesty, serving you always." His voice was choked by the lumps of remorse and gratitude.

"Right now, the emperor is going to retire for rest, and you cannot come with him." Humayun laughed suddenly. "At the hour of midnight feasting, I would welcome you back, my besotted Prince, we would talk of war and fidelity." He got to his feet wearily.

One night of feasting and a succession of wakeful nights after that in planning strategies and campaigns, had hurled the emperor into the arena of action and inevitability. All were order and discipline in Kandahar, before the emperor had started on his campaign toward Kabul. But Khazanda Begum with her incessant pleas had succeeded in winning the emperor's favor to let her accompany him, along with the troops. Prince Hindal too, winning the emperor's favor, was dispatched to Taligan to fight Abdullah and Keracha Beg who were laying claim on the fort as their stronghold, and to place hurdles against the emperor's march toward Kabul. Taking Prince Askeri along with him as his royal prisoner and leaving his harem behind, Humayun had then commenced his journey through the mountainous terrains of Koh-Baba. Along the way, Kasim Birlas, posted by Prince Kamran at Khimer pass, had tried to block the passage of the imperialists, but was routed and had fled. On the other front, Prince Hindal, reaching Arkendi via Pushteh, had sent an encouraging report to the emperor, before continuing his journey toward Taligan. The chief emir of Kabul by the name of Bapus, and his brother Jamil had deserted Prince Kamran, pledging their allegiance to the emperor.

Humayun had received this message three days ago just when he had crossed the basins of Helmand and Arghandab, halting at Tiri due to the sudden illness of Khazanda Begum. This very third day in a row of grief and uncertainty in Humayun's heart, and he was pacing outside his tent, his encampment concealed from view against the towering mountains, opalescent and snow-capped. Khazanda Begum was under the care of the Moghul physician, Sayed Rafiaeddin, but her fever and delirium were showing no signs of abating. This thought alone was burning like one blazing torch in Humayun's head, the mantle of chill and silence all around him penetrating not his awareness. The sun itself was sparkling with the eye of vengeance, it seemed, kindling the glaciers of snow to crystal palaces, all mysterious and unapproachable. Drawing his jeweled scimitar out of its Moroccan hilt, he held it before him for inspection. Sheathing it thoughtfully, he slung it at his waist, his broidered vest of lamb wool dyed purple, all stiff and groaning at this sudden act of thrust and violence. His features were calm though, gaunt and pallid, more so by the reflection of sunshine from under his gold helmet. Straggling farther from his opulent tent, he could see his soldiers in dun-colored palankeens. They were absorbed in the ritual of their morning drills, their kards and swords glittering, while the clashing of katars and khanjars were a ripple of dance and magic.

Stars of fate! Did I not steal them from the eyes of my dream bride, before the sky could claim them, so that they could stay there throbbing and mocking my hunger of the body and soul? Humayun's thoughts were dancing to the tunes of their memories of love and passion before he had embarked on this journey to win back Kabul. *His soul bride! Truth, beloved, sweetness, are they not one? Is love a delusion? Truth, one tainted pearl inside the heart of white lies? What do I see? The tear-streaked face of reality cradled into the bosom of the pine-valleys, in Kabul? The eyes of love, radiant. The soul bride! Truth! Do dreams come alive to the pain in living? Could the strings of reality escape the discordant noise of living, and cease to be? Is past not a lump of chaos, melting into the arms of present? And yet, awakening to the nightmare of future!* His thoughts were aghast all of a sudden.

Humayun's gaze was arrested to the swallows overhead, etched there like silvery arrows in their swift flight. Neat, little triangles, shooting for the heavens, the white emblems of trinity! *Past, present, future, the emperor has seen the face of reality.* Darkness in his psyche was wedded to the peace of silence within. His gaze was straying toward the red and yellow standards of the imperial army, sailing in wild abandon to the caprice of the winds. Reality was all around, alive with the pulse of nature. Horses grazing in the meadows. The ugliness of artillery and cannonade in stark contrast to the beauty of the emerald hills. The soldiers teeming close to the bonfires. The warring, throbbing, pulsating world in its entirety! Living and dying in the death and renewal of illusions. Holding on to the dreams of reality? Awe and bewilderment in Humayun's gaze and thoughts were espying the vision of reality in the form of his physician. Sayed Rafiaeddin was drifting toward him, clothed in the chill of woe and mourning.

"Your Majesty. The venerable Lady, your beloved aunt, is no more." Sayed Rafiaeddin murmured solemnly, his head lowered and his hands clasped to his chest. "Khazanda Begum, Your Majesty, breathed her last wish, to be buried in Kabul."

"The soul, Sayed, finds its own abode of rest and release, while earth claims only the perishable flesh." Humayun murmured back. "Her soul is already in Kabul, with my father, yet she must be buried here at Tirri. My father's remains were transferred from Agra to Kabul, and hers would be transferred from Tirri, when time affords us this luxury." His attention was shifting to the young rider, galloping toward him in breathless haste.

"Your Majesty." The rider jumped down from his mount, offering one flourish of a curtsy. "Prince Hindal sends his greetings from Taligan, Your Majesty. He says that Prince Kamran has come there in person with a large number of forces at his command. He has attacked once, succeeding in taking a few prisoners, while killing and injuring one fourth of a battalion. The prince adds that he is fighting defensively and holding up, but he needs reinforcements as soon as possible."

"What is the worth of Kabul and Kandahar that I should strive with my faithless brothers forever?" One hopeless exclamation escaped Humayun's lips, his eyes flashing commands at Sayed Rafiaeddin. "Summon Bayazid, my kind physician. He will be the emperor's noble messenger to his wicked brother."

Sayed Rafiaeddin had barely stirred, when Bayazid was seen strolling toward them, as if he had heard the emperor's command from the lips of the future, and was hurled back into the present to do his duty. Edging closer, he curtsied, waiting obediently to be addressed.

"Bayazid, you are to engrave these words in the book of your memory, and repeat them verbatim to my brother Kamran, the Prince of the Jinnis." Humayun's eyes were burning with the fever of rage and inspiration. "This is the message you are to deliver to him, and don't omit or forget a single word? O brother of wicked habits! O dear warrior! Desist from this act of rebellion which is the cause of war and the slaughter of our own brethren. The blood of men, who are slain today, will be on your head on the Day of Judgment. And their hands will be on the hem of your robe." He whirled on his feet, retracing his steps toward his tent of silk and damask.

Half way to his abode of tinsel comforts, he almost collided with Biram Khan, both jolted out of their blind ruminations.

"Here you are, my valorous Biram! We march to Taligan this very afternoon." Humayun snipped short the spool of his ruminations with the blade of a command. "Of course, the funeral first. You must have heard, how can I miss that look in your eyes? What a pity! The rite of burial takes but one brief hour amidst the clouds of tears and sorrows, while the ritual of birth nine agonized months, with the promise of joys and fortunes." He stalked past his vizier, forcing back the sting of tears and sorrows in his eyes.

Weeks in succession were buried deep in the ritual of life's needs and deeds in journeys long and arduous. Khazanda Begum was laid to rest at Tirri. One day of mourning, and the emperor had sent Biram Khan back to Kandahar to watch over his harem and that dearly-won kingdom, while he himself had marched toward Taligan. The reports were reaching him day after day of Prince Kamran's tyranny and madness as he was laying waste the lands and killing soldiers and civilians, indiscriminately. But upon learning that the emperor had crossed the Bangi River and was fifty miles away from Taligan, Prince Kamran had fled towards Kabul. After entrenching himself inside the citadel of Kabul, he had begun dispatching a string of messages to the emperor, seeking pardon and imploring him not to lay siege on the citadel of Kabul. His own commanders were defecting, and joining the imperialists on their way toward Kabul. The chief amongst them were, Mosahib and Amir Almora. No entreaties from the prince could now deter Humayun from his resolve to conquer Kabul. Though wearied with fatigue himself, he had urged his troops to keep marching till the citadel of Kabul was in view to afford them rest into the arms of victory.

Carrying the burden of victory on his shoulders, Humayun this particular evening, riding beside Prince Hindal, was entering into the dusk of Kabul. Actually, it was blue haze, all mist and gold, shuddering over the hills and suspended low over the citadel of Kabul, known as Bala Hissar. Seven hundred lancers were riding right behind the prince and the emperor, and the imperial cavalcade following them was a mighty sea of soldiers and commanders. A few lone clusters of stars were surfacing on the dark bowl of a sky, dancing and twinkling. All signs of fatigue from Humayun's eyes and limbs had vanished at the sight of his beloved Kabul. The star-spangled dance in his thoughts was a holy ritual, offering absolute surrender at the shrine of Kabul. His soul was expanding. Truth was a pulsating reality inside him. He was the bridegroom. *Has returned home to claim his soul bride.*

"Charge! We are going inside the citadel. Spare neither a foe, nor a friend, if they dare block our way." Humayun was already racing toward the gates of the citadel, seven hundred lancers behind him swift and vigilant.

The sudden blaring of drums and trumpets, accompanied with battle cries, were dissolved into the songs of victory. So swift was the violence of assault and so empty the threat of resistance that all were taken aback, plunged headlong into the horror of disbelief and bewilderment. No shot was fired, none there to slay or challenge. Humayun was literally swept into the welcoming arms of the emirs and viziers, all prostrating at his feet, uttering cries of fidelity and allegiance. Overwhelmed by this warm welcome and by the face of good fortune smiling at him in this sea of absurdity, Humayun could not even unleash the smoldering anger of his inquiry as to the state of Prince Kamran. A few small voices here and there had begun to chant this mantra.

"Prince Kamran has made his escape, Your Majesty, he has fled—"

With this little crumb of information penetrating his shock and disbelief, Humayun shifted his attention to Prince Hindal. The prince was hugging his wife, Sultanum Begum, their daughter Ruqueiqa squeezed between them, chortling glee. Smiling to himself, Humayun elicited one low command.

"Make haste, dear Hindal. Go after your traitor brother, and bring him back. Alive, if possible!" Humayun's heart was thundering all of a sudden, his gaze returning to the sea of emirs and viziers. "How did he escape? Which way is he headed?" He was afraid to ask about Akbar, this name dying on his lips like a wounded bird. Two more names were following this bird, and those were of Bakhshi Banu and Mah Chuchak.

"He escaped last night, Your Majesty. We noticed his absence this morning." Monaim Khan ventured an abridged account. "He had not been himself lately, sort of delirious and depressed. After learning about the desertions of his followers, we heard him murmur. *No one remains near me.* The back entrance of the citadel was locked. In the morning, we noticed the walls of the apartments where Bapus stayed, gouged and broken. That means, he must have made his way through the New Year's garden, and past the tomb of his mother, Gulrukh Begum. Planning to go to Tatta or Bhakkan, I have heard—"

Humayun had ceased to heed, his thoughts hanging a noose of prayer-beads around his neck, where the name of Akbar was choked, willing breath and release. So great was his will, and so inviolate his agony, that before he could utter the name Akbar, a bundle of miracles was seen racing toward him, his chubby arms outstretched, and his small mouth uttering the miracle of all miracles, *Your Majesty*. Humayun could only see his son, the procession of princess' and Begums behind him only a mirage, the lovely face of illusion.

"My son, my light!" Humayun whisked him into his arms in one crushing embrace. "Let me see! This small scimitar, a treasure indeed! A small soldier! A prince gallant!" He was holding him at arms length, gazing into his bright eyes.

"Your Majesty, your flower Princess." Gulbadan Begum, flushed by the presence of her husband Khwaja Khizr besides her, was relinquishing her hold on Princess Bakhshi Banu.

Humayun's face was transfigured with joy, pressing his daughter close to him, kissing her little mouth and pearly cheeks. He was becoming aware of the princess' and Begums. Gulnar Agacha, Nurgul Agacha, Dildar Begum, Bibi Mubaraka Begum. Humayun's eyes were searching the pearl of his soul. A spasm of ache in his heart was searching another face, and that was of Gulrukh Begum's. The gates of his memory were thrown open. He was remembering Monaim Khan's words about Kamran passing the grave of his mother? Dear soul, she died, and the emperor didn't even know? The great longing for beloved and nearness was overpowering all, and he murmured under his breath.

"Where is Mah Chuchak?" Humayun's look was ardent and searching.

"She is in Badakhshan, Your Majesty." Bibi Mubaraka offered sweetly.

"In Badakhshan." One sigh escaped Humayun's lips, his heart sinking under the weight of agony and despair.

The emirs and viziers were disappearing slowly amidst a flurry of curtsies and a chorus of well wishes. The princes and the Begums were leading the emperor into the parlor, dimly-lit and mournful. The whole palace was stirred to action, the servants fetching wine, and the Begums instructing the cooks what to prepare to be served to the emperor. Humayun, crushed under the weight of his misery and disappointment in not seeing his soul bride, had grown quiet and contemplative. Sipping his wine moodily, and oblivious even to his sense of relief and victory, he had not even noticed the absence of Prince Hindal. Prince Akbar and younger princesses were whisked away too, and he had watched them leave dreamily. The flight of Prince Kamran was forgotten for the moment, though Begums were profuse in relating each little detail of his rule and tyranny in Kabul. While Humayun was being fed with these stories, Prince Hindal had stolen into the kitchen, more so to escape the scrutiny of the emperor, than to inquire about the food to still the pangs of his hunger constricting his stomach.

Much to his shame and chagrin, Prince Hindal had discovered that the cooks were subsisting mainly on the grants from the Begums. Prince Kamran, feeling the dearth of his funds, had not paid the cooks since the last few months, and they were literally scrounging whatever they could. Supplying vegetables from their little farms, even slaughtering their own cattle at the risk of being deprived of milk and butter in the future. This very day, after noticing the flight of Prince Kamran, the entire household had been in utter chaos. The emirs and the viziers had convened meetings with prayers for the safe return of the emperor. They had met with the Begums, professing their fidelity to the emperor, and Begums were too proud to let them know of their impoverished means.

The meals, this particular day, had been more sparse than ever, only the younger princes and princess' getting substantial servings. Bibi Mubaraka Begum was in the kitchen too, talking with the cooks, and since there was nothing left to be served this evening, she had hastened to her own apartments to fetch what she had had prepared to supplement meals for the next day. Especially, for the older aunts, who were always famished! Prince Hindal, after absorbing these rueful details, had straggled out into the garden, disgusted. *At least, the army has their provisions great and bounteous, he was thinking.*

"After learning about your conquest of Kandahar, Your Majesty, Prince Kamran had gone insane, it seemed." Gulbadan Begum was saying. "Joking and laughing one minute, and raging and commanding the next."

"And what about those vile, terrible moods of his?" Dildar Begum appeared to contemplate aloud. "Imprisoning us all inside our rooms, and forbidding us to talk with each other?"

"Cutting our rations, and bullying the cooks if they didn't have anything to serve him and his followers?" Gulnar Agacha was whispering to Nurgul Agacha.

Prince Hindal had returned, seated close to his wife, quiet and humbled. Humayun's gaze was straying toward him, sad and wistful. He had forgotten about his former command, bidding him to go in pursuit of Prince Kamran. His gaze was returning to the Begums, seemingly avid and intense, as if he was catching each word which escaped their lips. But an overwhelming sense of pain and nostalgia was seething inside him in waves upon waves of loneliness. Something savage and mysterious were simmering inside the vacuum of his loneliness. Some sort of pain-elation, swollen by the waters of magic and mysticism. The tides of dreams and longings! The tempest of hope and hopelessness!

The mockery of truth! Bridegroom coming home! No beloved awaiting his return! No Bride entertaining her Bridegroom? Humayun's thoughts were drinking their own wine of pain and sweetness. *The joy of conquest defeated by the cowardly hands of truth? Hope demented! Truth cankerous! Illusion sane?* His mystic ruminations were splintered by the rustling procession of the female servants.

Bibi Mubaraka was at the head of this procession, graceful and smiling. The servants behind her were carrying silver platters, laden with hot, steaming dishes. They were quick to spread the gold cloth before the emperor, arranging plates of gold and jeweled goblets, but the feast was poor and unappetizing. Humayun sat watching, rather assessing the contents of these dishes, his delicate taste-buds revolting at the mere sight of these unsavory dishes. Curried beef and the sirwal of cow's tripe with rice pilaf as the main dish were lancing his senses with the whip of revulsion. He was remembering the recent reports of the Begums how miserly Prince Kamran had become and how insane? One stab of a memory was following this recollection, whirling his thoughts back into the royal court and royal kitchen in his father's time. Babur would have never allowed beef even to be cooked in his royal kitchens, Humayun's thoughts were inhaling the reek of nausea and retching.

"O Kamran, was this the mode of your existence?" One groan of an exclamation escaped Humayun's lips. "And did you feed the *asylum of chastity* on the flesh of cows?" His anguished gaze was turning to Bibi Mubaraka Begum, whom Babur had named, asylum of chastity. "Could you not keep a few goats for her subsistence? O,

225

wretched brother! O, wicked Kamran! Had you indeed come to such a length as to make fare of this dear Begum, to be only cow's flesh and cow's stomach? Could you not reserve one single sheep?" His voice was choked, rage and bitterness gnawing inside him. "The emperor is not hungry, take these away." He waved at the servants, his gaze sweeping over the Begums. "Tomorrow, we will have a grand feast. Mutton, venison, rabbits, pheasants, anything you desire, and much—" He could not continue, stung by the downpour of a song from the lips of some angel.

A voice so clear and sweet, like the murmur of a cataract, was trickling down into the parlor from some chamber above, plunging all into the spell of awe and hush. *Sarvaqad!* Humayun's heart was lurching and missing a few beats. He could not mistake this voice and yet he was not sure. A splinter of agony was cutting his soul. His heart was torn and bleeding. Memories stark and inviolate. Loneliness, a big rent, soul-bride missing. Sarvaqad present and hidden?

"Who is this nightingale? Where is she?" Humayun asked under the spell of swoon and languor, which was lulling his senses to reveries.

"Shaham Agacha, Your Majesty." Gulbadan Begum murmured low.

"Shaham Agacha?" Humayun was jolted out of his reveries, the vacuum of his loneliness shuddering and expanding.

"We call her the child of the mountains, Your Majesty. Though, she is an Afghani girl, quite mature and sensible." Dildar Begum expounded mysteriously. "We found her in our garden singing one night, and brought her in."

"She sings when she is lonely or troubled, Your Majesty. But our requests, no matter how warm and persistent, never reach her, if she is not in a mood to sing." Bibi Mubaraka Begum offered another morsel of information.

"The emperor wishes to see her." Humayun leaped to his feet under some spell of delirium and agitation.

The Begums, all excited and flustered, followed by the princes, were leading the emperor up the gilded staircase into the private apartments of the harem. The doors of one spacious chamber were thrown open, revealing the *nightingale* in pale robes, leaning against one crimson pillow. She was startled to her feet, her golden eyes wild and glittering. Dildar Begum clasped her hands

226

into her own, announcing to her the presence of the emperor. The emperor was struck by the arrow of the Cupid, his heart torn and bleeding. The golden bird fell at his feet in one sweeping curtsy, but he could not speak, gazing, gazing. Suddenly, the pain of silence and loneliness was ripping his soul to pitiful shreds, and his voice was one blister of a command.

"She will be the emperor's bride! The emperor has decided to feast after all." Humayun's gaze was shooting flames of fever and implacability. "Summon any Mulla and two witnesses." The flames of desire and longing in his gaze were splintering the veil of incredulity in the eyes of the princes and the Begums.

The bridal ceremony as impoverished as the meal untasted by the emperor, was affording a promise of riches beyond imagination. Ravishing his bride with kisses hungry and searing, he had soothed his fever and hunger of the body till passion and madness were dissolved into the blissful arms of sleep. The bliss in sleep though was slashed by the daggers of dreams mad and tortured. The fires of hell were scorching his flesh, his thoughts moaning and groaning. *Afghan rose! Mountain lily! Houri of Kabul! Child of the Himalayas! White truth? My golden illusion?*

Chapter Sixteen
Feast of Circumcision

The Audience Hall at Kabul overlooking the palace gardens was brimming with festivities. These festivities were in honor of Prince Akbar who was being circumcised this very day with all due rites and ceremonies. The prince was not present though to watch all these festive colors, adorning the halls and the palace grounds. He was far from the palace, taken to his favorite hill, and attended by the royal physicians. Under one crimson tent with sprays of gold silks, he was to be circumcised, and then brought back to the palace accompanied by royal orchestra. For the sole pleasure and diversion of the royal heir, Humayun had chosen forty girls, who were to sing and dance till the circumcision was done. Then they were to come dancing all the way down the hill into the palace garden for the sheer delight of the hosts and guests alike, their presence alone confirming the rite of circumcision fulfilled. And right this moment, they were seen sailing into the garden in shimmering skirts of green with white rose-buds in their hair. Humayun, seated on his gold throne in the Audience Hall, was watching the magicians unfurling their turbans and revealing treasures, when his attention was diverted to the clouds of dancers weaving their way into the garden. With a capricious nod of his head, he turned to Hamida Banu seated to his right.

"Now begins the Circumcision Feast, my Empress! And you didn't even know that our royal prince was being entertained by these beautiful dancers?" Humayun indicated the shimmering circle in green, ethereal and whirling. The large amethyst in his turban changing colors, while he sat twirling the ropes of pearls around his neck.

"You are getting into the habit of concealing everything from me, Your Majesty, including your moods and whims?" Hamida Banu laughed. "All that dancing and feasting on the streets for days, and I get to learn about that only today! And you commanding all the emirs and viziers to deck their palaces in friezes of gold and silver, and did I know about that? All houses in Kabul painted fresh and adorned with colorful banners, and I haven't even stepped outside of the palace in days?"

"Your own fits of jealousies, my love, which don't permit you the luxury of managing all these grand celebrations, which you should have done, not the emperor?" Humayun breathed enigmatically, stealing a look at the objects of her jealousies. His two new brides, Shaham Agacha and Khawish Agha, the latter wedded as quickly as the former one.

"You are acquiring brides as quickly as your conquests, Your Majesty. But I am learning not to be jealous anymore." Hamida Banu's eyes were flashing daggers at Mah Chuchak, seated not too far. "All these festivities! Wish, Dear Lady was here, she would have loved it so." She murmured, returning her gaze to the emperor.

"She is here! Resting peacefully beside her dear brother. All the way from Tirri to Kabul, just to be with my beloved father." Humayun murmured back wistfully. Though gazing into the eyes of his dream bride, his heart was longing to snatch his soul bride to his side, but the cruel beloved had rejected his love so far.

"Maybe, they are both watching us, Your Majesty? Sharing our joys and celebrations." Hamida Banu began cheerfully. "Your father would have been proud to see our prince *recognizing* me amongst all those ladies, when I reached here. Running right up to me and crying, *mamma*? How sweet!" Her gaze was arrested to the dancing girls, pirouetting closer to the throne.

"Yes." Humayun's gaze was sweeping over the arena of viziers and grandees, and returning to the flower of his soul bride.

The flower of jealousy was unfolding in Hamida Banu's heart once again, her gaze fluttering over the beds of primula and gentian to soothe the splinter of her jealousy. She could not endure to look at Mah Chuchak amidst the bevy of other ladies, their feet almost crushing the blooms of edelweiss and honeysuckle.

How dare she reject the emperor's love? Hamida Banu's heart in throes of jealous rage was eliciting this strange inquiry.

Paradoxically, Hamida Banu's memory of her own youthful defiance to the emperor's wooing had become her sole birthright alone! And no other woman could be permitted to claim that right, regardless of the fact that she didn't want the emperor to marry anyone. Upon her arrival in Kabul, she was fed with the story of the emperor's marriage to Shaham Agacha, but it had not disturbed her much, since she was fortunate to discover that the emperor was in love only with her voice. The other marriage of the emperor with Khawish Agha, she had dismissed as whimsical, since the emperor was no more in love with her than with the wives of his youth. She had befriended Bega Jan and Gunwar Bibi, even before consenting to marry the emperor, and she would get accustomed to the two new brides too, her optimistic thoughts had granted her this comfort and knowledge. *But Mah Chuchak,* her eyes and thoughts were gouging this pride of Kabul with the pincers of rage and jealousy.

Humayun's own heart was pierced, but by the pincers of longings alone, which he had stifled during all those years of his brief reign and long exile, in puddles of hopes and hopelessness. His gaze was dreamy and restless, returning too frequently to his soul bride, Mah Chuchak. But diversions were rich and colorful. Bowers of roses and gurgling fountains! Pines and cedars, dark and graceful under the night sky. The loveliest of scarlet blooms on palas tree. Shining like ruby-red tears against the flicker of candles, strewn so profusely over the lawns and around the fountains. The doves and the golden orioles, and the paradise flycatchers, all had gathered to invade this Circumcision Feast with their song and mirth. A succession of carpets from Persia, Tabriz, Kirman and Bokhara had stolen colors from dusk, it seemed. A few stars were appearing at random, teasing the heliotrope sky, and laughing. Humayun's own laughing eyes were turning to the Begums against the pillows of chintz and velvet. Some were sailing toward the tables laden with viands of all kinds and fruits piled high in exquisite arrangements. And some were enjoying the game of cards. Especially, Gulbadan Begum, since luck was in her favor and heaps of gold shahrukhis before her a shining witness to her success. Mah Chuchak opposite her was smiling at her losses, the glow of ivory on her small, white face spilling purity and passion. The shafts of her beauty were piercing Humayun's heart. It was aching and bleeding. He was abandoning his *Venus.*

Wish, she was Juno, not Venus? Humayun's thoughts were giddy with pain.

The renewal of pain and longing in Humayun's heart was seething into some sepulcher of silence where immediate past lay buried without the rites of burial and forgiveness. Prince Kamran had escaped, fleeing to Ghazni. He was denied asylum in Ghazni, and had sought the compassion of Khizer Khan from Hazara, who had offered him refuge in Tirri. Dissatisfied with living at Tirri and goaded by the whip of his ambition once again, he had repaired to Zemindawer with the intention of conquest, but was compelled to flee to Sind. Humayun's thoughts, right this moment, unwilling to follow the trail of his wicked brother were sulking and demurring, his gaze wandering over to the prominent guests, who sat laughing, sated with food and drink. Valad Beg was the Persian ambassador sent by Shah Tahmasp, and Humayun had affirmed his pledge as Kandahar belonging to the King, and ruled by Biram Khan in king's name. Another embassy was from Badakhshan sent by Suleiman Mirza of his loyalty and submission to the emperor, but the ambassador was not received favorably by Humayun since Suleiman Mirza had not come in person. Humayun's gaze was turning to Sayed Ali and Lawang Baluch, the lords of the Afghans, who had offered their submission most willingly, and were in return most favored by the emperor. Sayed Ali had received the kingdom of Duki from the emperor, and Lawang Baluch was made the ruler of Shal and Mastang. One sliver of a smile was curling on Humayun's lips, as his gaze fell on Biram Khan who had warned him against these lords of the Afghans, advising him not to lend them too much power. The smile was widening on Humayun's lips at the approach of Biram khan, curtsying impeccably.

"Glad tidings, Your Majesty, with all the condiments of love and ambition." Biram Khan's eyes were lit up with the stars of hope and mirth. "Sher Khan after laying waste Mandu, Raison, Multan and Gwalior, had marched onward to capture the fort of Kalinjar. This fort belonged to Raja Kirat Singh, who was well equipped to defend it till death. While laying siege, Sher Khan happened to see a beautiful girl in the camp of the Raja, and fell in love with her, delaying the attack as long as possible. Meanwhile, Raja Kirat Singh had further strengthened his defenses, and Sher Khan's attempts to lure the girl to his own camp had failed. So, he had decided to launch a sudden attack to capture the girl and the fort without any further delay. Unfortunately, one cannon-ball from his own cannon rebounding from the south wall of the fort, hit him, and he died instantly. Now, Your Majesty is the time to re-conquer Hind! This is the gist of my good news." He heaved a sigh of relief.

"How can you, Biram, with your cultured mind and compassionate heart, present the news of death, no matter of a foe, as glad tidings?" Humayun's eyes were gathering flames of disbelief and mysticism. "Death is sadness, Biram! Strange, how death which is the emblem of birth, really, makes us weep? And life which comes loaded with the gifts of pain and sorrow fills us with joy?" The Sufic light in his eyes was polished with profundities unvoiced. "And yet, tell me, Biram, how long did he rule, the emperor tends to forget? And who is his successor?"

"According to the messenger's report, Your Majesty, exactly five years, two months and thirteen days." Biram Khan's eyes were filling with regret and sadness. "His son, styled as Aslam Shah Suri is the successor. Another tyrant as the report goes. He is driven by his ambition, trying to quell all seditions with the rod of tyranny. The rebellions are rampant, Doab, Malwa, Bengal, and as far as the Punjab. There is utter chaos and confusion in Hind, Your Majesty, and the people would welcome the imperialists to restore peace."

"Peace in Kabul first, and in Badakhshan." Humayun's look was profound and reminiscent. "What does the absence of Suleiman Mirza portend, Biram? Isn't this an act of rebellion on his part to stay in Badakhshan, and not to come here to offer his submission to the emperor personally? Doesn't he consider himself the master of Doab, Khost and Kunduz also? Yes, he does. And we must march to Badakhshan to add it to our kingdoms of Kabul, Ghazni and Kandahar, before we think of re-conquering Hind." He was becoming aware of Hamida Banu stealing away. *Armed with royal secrets, to unveil before the Begums*, he was thinking.

"Yadgar Mirza, Your Majesty, must be beheaded before we march to Badakhshan, lest he contrive more intrigues in your absence to endanger the peace of Kabul." Biram Khan murmured under his breath, a shadow of fear crossing his brow.

"Isn't it punishment enough for the worthy traitor to be locked up in the prison of Bala Hissar?" Humayun demurred aloud. "While my traitor of a brother, Prince Askeri, is subjected only to house arrest under the vigilant eyes of Keracha Beg?"

"Prince Askeri is only the victim of Yadgar Mirza's scheming, conniving mind, Your Majesty." Biram Khan's thoughts were intent on Yadgar Mirza's punishment alone. "How many times you have forgiven Yadgar Mirza, Your Majesty? His follies outnumber your pardons. He has been the instrument of greatest harm to you, Your Majesty. The living, breathing cause of your exile and misfortunes! He doesn't deserve to live."

"I have forgiven him countless times, and would forgive him many more if it was not for the advice of my viziers, treating treason—and justly so, as the most unforgivable of crimes punishable by death!" Humayun's gaze was gathering edicts, which he didn't want to voice. "Bent double under the weight of thirty charges against him, and still professing loyalty and innocence, is he not? Yes, he is an inveterate liar, compelled by his nature to deceive and dissimulate, deserving death in conformity with the advice of my viziers and counselors. No point in delaying this worthy action?" His heart was a volcano of torment.

The scent of Damascus roses was wafting up to Humayun on the tunes of lutes and flutes, the ache of love and yearning inside him ripping and tearing his heart. Mah Chuchak was framed alive in his shuddering soul, but his gaze was too restless. Shooting up to the clusters of cold, bright stars and sailing back to the sea of color in turbans and robes adorning his viziers. Amongst them, he espied Ali Taghai, and summoned him to his presence with one blistering command. The astounded vizier stumbled closer to the throne, offering one hasty curtsy.

"Needless to remind you Ali Taghai that Yadgar Mirza is pronounced guilty of treason." Humayun, noticing his befuddled expression, commenced rather gently. "The jury has already condemned him to death, and what better occasion than this to relieve him out of his misery!" His eyes were kindling the fever of decision and impatience. "Since the emperor is planning to march to Badakhshan, you would be appointed governor to rule Kabul in his absence. And to root out all evil, if it dares surface once again. Beginning right now, with the task of relieving the soul of Yadgar Mirza, from this prison of existence! He is not to see the dawn of another day."

"How can I, Your Majesty?" One shuddering protest escaped the lips of Ali Taghai. "How can I kill him? I, who could never kill even a gnat?"

"You craven wretch!" Humayun exclaimed with the sudden smoldering of rage in his eyes and voice. "Are you fit to rule Kabul in the emperor's absence? Efface yourself from my sight, lest my anger consume you to ashes." He waved dismissal, his thoughts flashing profundities at Biram Khan. "Why are the virtues of duty and valor lacking in my men, Biram? Where can the emperor find them? Don't answer me, the emperor knows. All these maggots crawling on the face of this earth think that they deserve to live, though they have sucked breath out of the lives of the others with the weapons of their deceit and wickedness?"

"You don't have to look far, Your Majesty, to find the man of virtue and integrity." Biram Khan murmured soothingly. "Kasim Mochi is the man of action and courage. He is not afraid to kill traitors. Quite expert with his bowstring too. Many a foes he has strangled by this means, proclaiming this method a quick and painless one." Encouraged by the emperor's keen and attentive look, he was quick to shoot his own missile of news which he had been guarding so far. "Foes and traitors have been on my mind since this morning, Your Majesty. Prince Kamran is reported to be seeking the alliance of Shah Hussain. He has asked the hand of his daughter in marriage. Her name is Chuchak—" His thoughts were disrupted by the sudden blaze of agony in the eyes of the emperor.

"Chuchak! There is only one by that name, and that is Mah Chuchak, your own sister." Seething torment in Humayun's eyes was rigged with the shafts of longings and commands. "You must plead with your sister to accede to the wishes of the emperor, lest his anger and disfavor land on your shoulders, Biram?"

"Your Majesty!" Was Biram Khan's flustered response. His thoughts were exploring the liaison of his sister with the vizier of Badakhshan. One sting of a revelation was piercing his awareness that she was waiting for her monthly cycle to mask her loss of virginity, if she was to marry the emperor. "May I suggest patience, Your Majesty. Delicate as the subject is, but her moods change in relation with the moontides. Besides, her vanity and caprice are making her prolong this courtship as long as possible."

"The emperor's patience is running ragged, Biram." Humayun got to his feet, oblivious to the teeming of guests all around. "If our moods, mine and hers, don't match this evening, the emperor will shoot the stars blind, driving the moon insane by the sheer deluge of pain and longing in his eyes." He clapped his hands, announcing his wish to take a stroll in the garden with Mah Chuchak.

The night sky hosting the livid moon and radiant stars was murmuring its own dark secrets, as Humayun and Mah Chuchak strolled side-by-side. The garden of festivity was left behind and now only pines and cedars smitten silver by moonlight was their companions, as mute as their lips and hearts. Humayun was drugged by the scent of white rose of a beloved beside him, drinking the wine of poetry from his thoughts, and pouring Sufic bliss into his poetic spirit. White truth was his shadow. The pulse of beauty was throbbing right inside him. Yet, he was galaxies apart from his soul bride. Pain and elation were churning inside him like the rivers wild and swollen. He thought he was walking in the Garden of Bliss. *Eve, all clothed in light, was his beloved. The soul of his soul making him float in ether and guiding him toward the sacred altar of love, where truth and beloved were one.*

No such holy fires were kindled inside the heart of the beloved. Mah Chuchak was perfectly sane, not in love! She was in love with gold and jewels, with the promise of Moghul might and splendor, which would make her the envy of all queens. She knew her destiny, and was not ashamed to acknowledge to herself that she was destined to satisfy the needs of her body and soul, with whom she pleased and whenever she desired. Though her spirit was full of guile and courage, she had one little monster of a *fear* inside her, over whom she had no control. And this fear right now was invading her sense of invulnerability, spewing out warnings dark and grotesque. Fear transformed into brand of sin inside her body and soul was hot and searing, pleading with the moontides and cowering against a mountain of petty fears. The hours of her monthly cycle and the pincers of the emperor's impatience in courtship were cutting through her awareness with blood-thirsty vengeance. But her peace and poise were returning. She was to wed the emperor. Wedded to her ambition! When? At the first dewdrop of blood staining her desire with dreams grand and dreams fantastic?

Humayun was dreaming too, but dreams pure and innocent. Hush and silence, and the magic-mystery of the night had consumed him entirely, if not the sense of peace and nearness from within and without. He could see the face of truth etched alive on each leaf, on every sliver of moonbeam, and in the beauty and presence of his beloved. The dark mirror of a sky, reflecting cold moon and throbbing stars, were splintering his reveries. The pines and the cedars were whispering to him the sweet songs of bliss and rapture. His feet were obeying the command of the silent night and halting in reverence to kiss the very ground upon which his beloved walked. He stood gazing, rather lost into the blue pools of her eyes, a shimmering sea of light and sweetness! The glow of poppies on her lips and the blush of rose on her cheeks were lending her the semblance of some goddess wrought in ivory, with diamond-stars in her eyes and hair, sparkling and twinkling.

"A miracle sublime, your beauty, my love! I could stand and gaze at you till the end of time." Humayun's very eyes were murmuring endearments.

"Your Majesty!" A tinkling of mirth escaped Mah Chuchak's lips.

"A shower of rose petals from your lips, Beloved! May the emperor gather them in his hands?" Humayun cupped his hands, and poised them before his lips, as if drinking honey and perfume." He stood there prayer-like, gazing and worshipping. "Sweet soul, reject not the emperor's love, he cannot live without you."

"Your Majesty! Are you in love, with me, truly?" Mah Chuchak sang brightly, her heart facing the demon of fear once again.

"In love with you? Might as well ask the emperor if he breathes." The ache and hunger in Humayun's heart were uncurling their parched lips. "I could cut open my breast to show you the fire and tempest in there, Beloved, if you but command? The torch of my love burning eternally and pleading for the boon of your consent."

"I submit, Your Majesty." Mah Chuchak murmured, her heart pleading for the boon of moontides.

"That means, you consent. You will marry the emperor!" Was Humayun's awed, rather stunned response. He was smitten with joy at the very cores of his soul. "This Circumcision Feast will be turned into a wedding feast! The emperor can't endure another moment of separation." He could not move, only his gaze devouring.

"Not so soon, Your Majesty, no!" Mah Chuchak's cheeks were burning, and her eyes flashing. The demon of fear was constricting her heart into knots of pain. "Next week, perhaps? Friday, to be sure? A holy day—" She could not continue, longing to flee the very air of magic-torment in the night.

"So soon, Beloved! When each moment of separation from you is like a century to me?" Humayun managed one little step, edging closer, his heart embracing the heavens and the galaxies. "Friday, it is, since the emperor is the humblest of your slaves." He swept her into his arms in one violent embrace. "Just one kiss from your sweet lips, my love, and I can endure even the everlasting fires in hell, in wars and campaigns. Friday, holy as it is, will be the holiest of holy for me from now on." His kisses were drinking soma of life from her lips divine.

Chapter Seventeen
Emperor's Soul Bride

Humayun, lying unconscious on the four-poster bed, looked peaceful and resting. His features were as white as the satiny sheets pulled up to his waist. It had been four days since he had lost consciousness, and the royal physicians shifting from one remedy to the other were losing hope in reviving the emperor. This dismal abode inside the fortress of Shadan was by no means the emperor's choice, since he was oblivious to his state and surroundings. From Badakhshan to Kishem, he was on his way to Kila Zafar, when he was seized by this sudden illness. Fever and retching, followed by delirium, had resulted in a deep coma, and the tireless efforts of the physicians in reviving him were proving unsuccessful. In this state, he was brought to Shadan under the shadow of hopes and prayers for health and recovery. The only one not losing hope was Mah Chuchak, by the sheer power of her will and tenacity. Right now, seated by the emperor's bed, she was totally absorbed in feeding the emperor drops of pomegranate juice, slowly and religiously. This chamber smothered in green from Kirman rugs to velvety drapes and gilded paintings on the walls, was lending her pallor some angelic glow, so rarely seen on the faces of women with the passion for guile and ambition. A pair of royal physicians attended by a coterie of servants, watching Mah Chuchak feed the emperor, were awed and humbled, not only by the aura of her beauty, but by the virtue of her devotion and serenity. Not even guessing, that she was willing the emperor to return to this world of joys and sorrows.

Joys and sorrows were surely woven tight into the knots of two and a half years since her marriage to the emperor. The whimsical promise of her moontides had deceived her, and she was hurled into the vortex of her wedding night in a state of fear and shock. The emperor, though drugged with the ecstasy of consummation, was too experienced not to notice that the bride of his soul was not the virgin lily he had dreamed away all his life in hope of possessing. The knowledge that her hymen was already punctured by some *other* had struck him like a thunderbolt. And he

239

had felt devastated, loving her with the violence of a madman, and hating her with the passion of a man possessed. *Elatedly and pugnaciously drunk by his pain and madness,* Mah Chuchak had thought. And growing so possessive of her that he would not let her out of his sight at all hours of the day or night. Amidst this strange relationship of love and hatred, a daughter was born to Mah Chuchak, bringing a little peace and sunshine into the emperor's heart. Rather joy! Mah Chuchak had noticed joy and tenderness in the emperor's eyes, as he had named the princess, Bakhtunisa. Sharing with her—Mah Chuchak, the dream he had dreamed, out of which he had snatched this propitious name. Pale and serene, Mah Chuchak kept holding a silver spoon to the emperor's lips till each drop of ruby-red vintage from pomegranate juice could trickle down his throat. She had suffered terribly, and was suffering still the agonies of doubt. Her heart and soul, with wounds raw and throbbing, were pouring out all their plea-anguish into the silent soul of the emperor to come back to the miracle of life.

The Miracle of life had ceased to exist for Humayun since he had discovered that his soul bride was not a virgin. The bolts of agony and rapture which had pierced his heart on his wedding night had driven him to one insane impulse to disfigure the face of beauty in its entirety. Soul, nature, universe, all! To him, sacredness was corrupted by the tears of profanity. White truth was wedded to black lies. All bliss and purity had grown cankerous by the soot of time and knowledge. Inside the valleys of months slithering past painfully, he was rather possessed than possessing his soul bride. Possessed by hate and madness! Paradoxically, gloating in his pain and loving while hating. Jealous and possessive, he could not endure to be parted from her, searching for the balm of sanity in order to rule kingdoms, not to be ruled by love mad and muddied. The altar of love inside his soul was broken and neglected. He had finally succeeded in erecting a seal of silence over the indiscretion of his beloved.

The kingdom of Kabul itself was going through the labor-pains of change and renewal, as Humayun had marched forth to conquer Badakhshan, with the intention of annexing petty kingdoms on the way which were seething with rebellions. Hamida Banu was left behind with Prince Akbar as the nominal ruler of Kabul. Mah Chuchak, Khawish Agha and Shaham Agacha were accompanying the emperor on his campaigns long and unpredictable. Humayun had decided to take Prince Hindal and Prince Askeri along with him too, the latter for the reason of security against his propensity toward insurrection. Marching along the river Bangi, the emperor's cavalcade had reached Narin, without encountering any play at intrigue or rebellion. The onward journey from Ishkemish to Taliqan was swift and free of warring encounters. But after crossing the Shashen Pass into the valley of Khost, the ravages by the hands of Aimaks were visible on the very gates of the city. So Humayun had ordered repair of the city gates and new defenses to be added, before chastising the marauders. The leader of the Aimaks, Beg Birlas, had surrendered without much resistance, and his followers were taken prisoners. Badakhshan was conquered next, Suleiman Mirza fleeing. The vanquished prince had found refuge beyond the precincts of Amu in the city of Kulab, right across from the borders of Khutan.

Badakhshan was the place where Princess Bakhtunisa was born, and where Humayun had found a little reprieve from campaigns. There, he had indulged in his all-time love for astronomy, spruced with poetry readings. Taking solitary walks, and courting the seeds of mysticism inside the caves of his introspection. Even enjoying fishing and fowling. Sloughing off the burden of tragedies from his soul, he had even arranged a feast in celebration of his victory. Amidst those festivities, Kunduz and Badakhshan were assigned to Prince Hindal, and Khost was bestowed on Monaim Khan. Bapus was made the governor of Taliqan. Leaving Badakhshan under the rulership of Prince Hindal, Humayun had then returned to Khost, staying with Monaim Khan, who was ecstatic to be the emperor's host, entertaining splendidly befitting his post of governorship. Before returning to Kabul, Humayun's next stop was at Kishem, then Kila Zafar where he had wished to spend the entire winter to avoid icy roads and snowstorms. But fate had ordained otherwise. At Kishem, he had fallen ill, and was carried to the fortress in Shadan.

And now as he lay deep inside the caves of oblivion, Mah Chuchak's heart and soul were pouring tears of anguish into the silence of his soul, willing it to respond to her own mute sorrow. It was already dusk, and the candles were lit in gold candelabras. This green chamber with oppressive furnishings had attained a sepulchral hush, as if it was contemplating to unveil its cold secrets to the hearth of mysteries. The physicians were hovering over the emperor, their faces dark and anxious. One was checking his pulse while listening to the heartbeat and the other was forcing some awful concoction down his throat. The prayer-like attitude of Mah Chuchak was splintering, her hands trembling all of a sudden. Humayun's eyes were fluttering open, reflecting haze and bewilderment. His body was coming alive with one imperceptible shudder, his lips pressed tight.

"How are the affairs at Kabul?" A low inquiry was torn from Humayun's lips.

"Great God! Merciful God." Mah Chuchak covered her face in her hands.

"Why I am lying in this monstrous bed—and this hideous chamber?" There was some sort of uncanny echo in Humayun's voice, as if it was whistling the tunes of future where time had conquered all gulfs and voids. "Where am I? What in the name of sanity are you doing here in this prison of a chamber? Speak, you fools."

"Your Majesty! You were ill—unconscious—four days now." Sayed Rafiaeddin began incoherently. "Couldn't go to Kila Zafar, for you fell ill—brought you here in Shadan."

"Is that so? Is Shadan the city of the deaf and the dumb?" Humayun's eyes were lit up with the wisps of wonder and incredulity. He noticed his beloved, her lily-white hands shielding her face. "Let me see your beautiful eyes, my love. Did you really suffer?" One gurgle of laughter escaped his parched lips.

Mah Chuchak could not speak, her face ravished with pain and fatigue. Dewdrop mists in her eyes were shuddering, and so was her body, lurching over the bed, her head drooping right into the lap of the emperor. Humayun's arms were closing around her with the sudden kindling of torment in his eyes.

"Come here, you fools, the Begum has fainted." One agony of a command escaped Humayun's lips, his eyes flashing and startling the physicians to prompt obedience. "Revive her swiftly! Tortures of hell would be your reward if you allowed four days to lapse in bringing her back to consciousness, as you did to me? I have slept away centuries, and didn't even know that she suffered?"

The physicians had carried Mah Chuchak to the green davenport with the speed of lightning. Smelling salts were procured quickly, and the servant girls were fanning the Begum against the hurricanes of their fright. Sayed Rafiaeddin was concocting some strange potion, while cool compresses were applied on the brow of

242

Mah Chuchak. Humayun's eyes were closing, his burst of vigor fading as quickly as it had erupted forth. Four long eons of oblivion and surcease were a tremor-dance of illusions under the closed shutters of his eyelids. The sieve of his psyche was parading the past, present and future in rivulets clear and sparkling. He was reflected in there as the lover, the mystic and the avenger. Avenging the death of his soul and resurrecting truth out of its own white tomb.

The quest in life! Where was truth fleeing? Did he have a soul? Where do these wounds come from, all groaning, yet undying? Humayun's psyche was entering the realms forbidden and inconceivable. *Am I in love with my beloved? Can hatred be the womb, nurturing love sublime and love supreme? The only truth! The only virtue, inside the harlot of passions, holy and profane.* The light of love inside him was groaning and shuddering. *God is love, if one could see the light? If one could love one's God, truly love? Absolutely and spiritually, in love with one's God, soul? Love God in any form, Him, Her, the One and Only, with names as varied as moods and attributes? The Absolute Whole! The Essence Infinite! Do the faithful stop loving God when grief and misfortune visit? Is He not the God of perfection as well as of imperfection? Manifesting beauty as well as ugliness? Bestowing joy as well as grief? Hope in times of despair? Mercy and wrath intertwined so profoundly—* His thoughts were wading into the waters of love and hatred. *Can I stop loving my beloved just because she sinned? How can I absolve my own countless sins? Purity and perfection, the mingling of evil and good?* His eyes were half open, absorbing the entire scene where Mah Chuchak was sitting up, pale and spent. *God! Essence! Unknown and Unknowable! Inconceivable and Unapproachable! Living in each speck of dust, in each grain of evil, in each kernel of lust and greed? In each fruit of joy and compassion! God. With us, in riches and poverty? In famine and abundance? In pains and sorrows? In triumphs and failures? Does He not groan and suffer, when we do? Are we not in Him, and He in Us? Suffering and rejoicing with us? Perception blind! Eyes of ignorance! Horrors strange and nameless. Mortal men and immortal gods. God and Beloved! Holy and Divine! Forgive, forgive.* His prayer was left unvoiced, as the angel as Mah Chuchak returned to him.

The angels of cheers and health had adopted both Mah Chuchak and Humayun during their swift recovery within few weeks of rest and serendipity. And those angels were the God-given gifts of peace and tenderness. Loving tenderness between the lovers estranged, and this love breeding the fruit of passion inside the womb of Mah Chuchak once again before their journey toward Kila Zafar. Humayun's decision to spend the winters at Kila Zafar was being punctured by disturbing news from Kabul. Prince Kamran was brewing fresh plots to invade Kabul, and Humayun was left with no choice but to return to Kabul at the earliest possible. Two month of rest and recovery at Shadan, and one month of vacillating decisions at Kila Zafar were the shadows of danger and uncertainty, following at the emperor's heels as the avalanche of burdens rife and unpredictable. Badakhshan was smoldering in the flames of rebellion once more, ambushed by the Uzbeks. The Uzbeks were attacking the territories of Balkh and Kunduz with their ever-warring skill in raid and plundering.

A letter was sent to Suleiman Mirza, commanding him to rule the kingdom of Badakhshan, if he was willing to offer his submission to the emperor. Actually, this letter was addressed to his wife, Haram Begum, who was known to be the queen of defense, maintaining her own body of troops and horses. Pressed by the need of his dilemma and perception, Humayun had construed this letter himself, knowing, that Haram Begum was the wise one to snatch this generous offer of the emperor. Not her vanquished husband, who was still nursing the wounds of his defeat and humiliation, Humayun had thought. Another letter was dispatched to Prince Hindal in Kunduz, summoning him to Kila Zafar with all his troops, which might be needed if Prince Kamran was to succeed in laying siege over Kabul. One swift courier was sent to Keracha Beg in Shadan to escort Prince Askeri to Kila Zafar. Keracha Beg had imprisoned the prince during the emperor's illness, fearing, that he would plot and intrigue, and he was left behind as the emperor had journeyed toward Kila Zafar. Meanwhile, Shirefken Beg was sent to Kabul with the burden of fetching all rumors or reports about the plots and intrigues of Prince Kamran.

This particular evening, Kila Zafar was brimming with song and music, though the mood was somber rather than festive. Humayun seated on his gilded throne in one oval room was sipping wine, and discussing strategies with his viziers as how to safeguard his conquered domains amidst this wildfire of intrigues and rebellions. Not far from the throne were window-seats and davenports in blue velvets, where the Begums sat talking and playing backgammon. The royal servants in gold turbans, much like the gilded paintings on the walls were flaunting their gold flagons and serving sweets and fruits to all present. Wreaths of ivy with silver cones were gracing the mantle, and the candles in gold and silver candelabras were making the silks and jewels on the Begums sparkle and twinkle. Humayun's lean, waxen features, against the glow of large amethyst in his turban, were wreathed in smiles. Emanating no joy, but sadness. He was listening to the account of Fazil Beg, who was recounting avidly that Suleiman Mirza along with his wife Haram Begum, was on his way to offer his submission. In response to the emperor's offer, he had acknowledged emperor as the soul sovereign of Kabul and Kandahar, of Khost and Kunduz and of Badakhshan.

An ocean of mysteries, which tell no truth, reveal no secrets. Humayun's gaze straying toward the Begums was murmuring such inanities. It was arrested to the perfection of beauty in Mah Chuchak. Yet seeing nothing, but blue silks and blaze of diamonds. No lovely eyes, no lips divine. All were melting, dissolving. *Dream and illusion. Mysteries, indeed! Storm-clouds in hearts! Souls swollen with the gold-dust of ambition. Each dew-drop of existence famished for the light of purity and innocence. Each tear-drop of a thought crying why, when, where—* The rosary of his mysticism was broken, as he noticed Keracha Beg. He was leading Prince Askeri toward the throne.

"Your Majesty." Prince Askeri bowed low.

"Welcome, my Prince, welcome." Humayun got to his feet, as if carried by the waves of pain and elation.

Warmth and wistfulness were flooding in Humayun's eyes, as he locked his brother into his arms in one tight embrace. With his heart gathering rivers of regret, he seemed to be caught in his whirlpool of emotional intoxication. Holding his brother before him and gazing into his eyes, he was rewarded with the gift of rare sentiment in love and devotion. While arrested thus in his prison of pain and exhilaration, he didn't even notice the approach of Prince Hindal until he edged closer, falling into one sweeping curtsy.

"God be blessed!" Humayun scooped him into his arms, laughing and crushing. "How my heart sings and throbs at the sight of my dear, dear brothers! Go, sit with the Begums, they are longing to crush you into their arms too, since you are their favorite." His attention was returning to Prince Askeri. "You too,

245

my Prince! No more a prisoner to your ambition, the emperor can tell—" His joy was drained all of a sudden, as Shirefken Beg was announced. "A long, long night of woeful tales, my heart tells me." He mounted his throne, waving welcome at the messenger.

Even a thin layer of dust on Shirefken Beg's face could not conceal the tales of woe and tragedy engraved deep in his expression. Wine and food were brought to the wearied messenger by the orders of the emperor. Prince Hindal and Prince Askeri had joined the Begums, all agog and bright-eyed. Shirefken Beg was washing down each morsel of food with draughts of wine, as if he had been famished for days. Humayun sat brooding, his heart a thunder of omens and presage. He had waited patiently till the messenger had refreshed himself, and was framing his thoughts to a disciplined trot before questioning him. But the low murmur of voices from the lips of the viziers and grandees were attracting his attention. And then he was becoming aware of the charged silence of the Begums, fear and agog shining in their eyes. With a gentle wave of his arm, Humayun returned his attention to Shirefken Beg.

"You may begin now, Shirefken. Save the rumors for some other time, just relate the facts." Humayun commanded. "Be precise, yet neglect not one single detail concerning the acts and schemes of Prince Kamran."

"It all begins with rumors, Your Majesty, please pardon my lack of judgment." Shirefken began regretfully. "When you were recovering in Shadan, Your Majesty, the rumors were reaching Prince Kamran in Bekher that the emperor is dead. Securing the aid of troops from his father-in-law, he had hastened toward Kabul. Reaching Ghazni, he was opposed by Zahid Beg. But Prince Kamran killed him, while Zahid Beg kept repeating that the emperor is not dead. Then he entered Kabul in the guise of a common Afghan. First, he went to the college of Mulla Khaliq, who was not there. But he found Muhammad Ali in hot bath and murdered him. He has gone insane, people say. Right after this second murder, he went to the fortress of Bala Hissar, breaking open the doors and killing everyone who stood in his way. Your servant, Your Majesty, whom you had left as the guardian of the harem, tried to escape dressed as a woman. But was caught and murdered by Prince Kamran. Prince Akbar is in the custody of Prince Kamran. The ladies of the harem are arrested in the other palace, belonging to Prince Askeri. Every day, he tells them that the emperor is dead. They don't believe him, but know him to be insane. I personally told him that you are well and alive. He had me imprisoned too, but I escaped by bribing the guards." One bellow of a sigh escaped his throat.

"The prince is not insane, only wicked." Humayun managed one painless comment. "But for your devotion and hardships, Shirefken, the emperor bestows on you the jagirs of Zohak and Bamain. As for my imbecile brother, when he sees the ghost of the emperor in Kabul, his very soul will flee out of sheer terror." He turned his attention to Fazil Beg. "Fazil, you are to journey to Kabul post-haste. Assure the Begums that the emperor is on his way." His eyes were flashing now, arrested to Keracha Beg. "Inform the troops, my devoted vizier that we march tomorrow." His voice was splitting by the lump of agony in his throat.

Before he could swallow this lump of agony with a draught of wine, the arrival of Suleiman Mirza was announced. He was being conducted to the throne, accompanied by his wife Haram Begum and their daughter. The jeweled cup poised in his hand, Humayun's gaze was arrested to the rose-bud of a daughter in pink silks with ermine furs concealing her young bosom, and reaching up to her snowy cheeks. *All light and incandescence, as if plucked fresh out of the very mists from dawn*, Humayun's thoughts were murmuring with the sudden kindling of fever and delirium. He could not tear his gaze away from this celestial vision. The weight of tragedies in his soul was finding release inside the torment of his heart. *His heart, suffered by pain and betrayal for two and a half years in the love-hate relationship with his beloved!* Suleiman Mirza was bowing low, his wife and daughter curtsying gracefully.

"Your Majesty. Your most devoted slave offers his loyalty and submission to your sovereign rule. As long as I live, Your Majesty, I will remain devoted to your cause and authority."

"Welcome, Suleiman Mirza." Humayun intoned thickly, his heart somersaulting. "Your loyalty is ten times more precious than your submission, in these times of wars and betrayals." He was becoming aware of the hush all around and clapped his hands suddenly. "Wine and music for our guests." He commanded, turning his attention to Haram Begum. "And who is this rare bloom, Haram Begum that you are guarding so possessively?" His eyes were feverish and flashing.

"Our daughter, Shahzadi Banu, Your Majesty." Haram Begum murmured.

"Shahzadi Banu." Humayun murmured back under some spell of poetic exaltation. Fever and madness were constricting his heart, but his gaze was returning to Suleiman Mirza. "Kabul is in the hands of my wicked brother once again. Prince Kamran, the tyrant is back. We are leaving early in the morning, and marching straight to Kabul. Badakhshan, I leave to you, to protect and safeguard. Uzbeks are staying in ambush, planning raids, I have been informed." The churning of pain and violence inside him were surfacing in his eyes.

"I will guard Badakhshan with my life, Your Majesty!" Exclaimed Suleiman Mirza with unusual vehemence.

"Your life, my good cousin, is very precious to the emperor." Humayun's lips parted in one enigmatic smile. "Assured of your health and prosperity, my heart will gain some semblance of peace while I fight my brother to win back Kabul." An overwhelming sense of pain and weariness were constricting his heart, his gaze shifting back to Haram Begum. "Your daughter has stolen the emperor's heart, sweet Lady." He murmured deliriously. "May I seek her hand in marriage, in alliance?"

"At this point in time, Your Majesty, you are much in need of soldiers and ammunition than brides." The sun-gold eyes of Haram Begum were lit up with mirth. "When the emperor is wearied of wars and happily enthroned in Kabul, then, Your Majesty, I myself will come seeking this royal alliance." She added thoughtfully.

"A most prudent response from the lips of a war-goddess, my Lady." Humayun laughed. "The emperor needs rest." Pain and delirium in his eyes were courting madness, not rest. "Enjoy this music and feasting to your heart's content, and if you are awake in the morning before we leave, I will say fond farewell." He got to his feet, his eyes lingering on the *daughter of dawn*, her cheeks suffused with the blush of a rose.

The emperor was leaving this chamber of woe and happiness. Beauty and sadness in the form of Shaham Agacha was his companion of the night to lull him to sleep. She was his golden-bird, as he called her, not the bride of his lust and desire. Crossing the bridge of ice in Mah Chuchak's eyes, he had chosen his golden-bird, blinded by pain, his heart lacerated. The beloved was left behind as some reed of a white delusion. His heart was hugging the blisters of truth and torment, all molten, all cankerous. Delirium was his shadow, and he the shade of the past, entering the gates of reality through the dark tunnels of his own soul and psyche.

The jade and ivory bedroom with pale damask walls was cradling Humayun in its comforting arms. More so, the great bed with chintz covers and a ripple of pillows, where he had abandoned himself fully dressed, his hands locked under his head, his elbows sticking out. Shaham Agacha had found refuge on the velvety davenport, hoisting one crimson pillow behind her with utmost care so as not to disturb the emperor. Humayun's eyes were closed, only the large emerald in his turban blazing.

"The hour is late. Athena has retired long past into the folds of the centuries. Where are the songs? The voice of love." Humayun was murmuring with his eyes closed. "Sing, my love, sing. The emperor will not violate the sanctity of your soul with love vulgar and demanding, which always leaves you with the sense of aversion and loathing. How does the emperor know, don't ask? Yes, my golden-bird, sing."

Shaham Agacha was lost in the song-ecstasy of her voice and solitude. The wine of music gurgling in her throat, and the pearls of poetry trembling on her lips. Humayun was transported into the world of bliss and rapture. Floating in ether, riding on the clouds. Embracing the cheeks of sadness. Kissing the feet of surrender. Looking into the eyes of the ineffable one, stricken and dazzled. The angels and heavens above were caught in abeyance, drunk and swooning.

Awakening of the Soul! Fluttering and expanding. Where does this voice, sweetness come from? A symphony of music divine and celestial, from the throat of my golden-bird? Humayun was drifting into the bliss of sleep and oblivion. Songs never dying, knowing no surcease. Purity and holiness. The wine of joy. The bread of peace. Dream. Delusion. No pain? No betrayal?

Chapter Eighteen
Celebration of Riwaj

At the foot of the Eagle's Hill, Humayun astride his Chupatak steed was inspecting the disciplined files of his soldiers. Donned in chain mail and gold helmet, his only distinction from his troops was his jeweled scimitar, proclaiming him the emperor in command. Up on the hill were the cannons, booming and roaring, showering down muskets over the fortress of Bala Hissar, where Prince Kamran had entrenched himself under the cover of great defenses. He was holding on to the fort, rather defying the tenacious siege of the imperialists, while keeping the royal prisoners as his pawns in case of extremity. The imperialists could not bombard the citadel directly, lest they endanger the lives of the prisoners, so their intermittent assaults of cannon and artillery at the gates of the citadel were fiery reminders in forcing the prince to capitulation. Right now, the gold dusk was thick with clouds of smoke, hanging low over the ramparts of Bala Hissar. But the ruby-red sunset could be seen piercing through all, and donning the hills in mists pale and violet. Watching the sunset, Humayun's poetic soul was smitten with awe, all noise from cannon sounding distant and muffled. The only sound he could hear was of the wings of time, flapping overhead, marching backward in tune to the journeys long and arduous.

The journey from Kila Zafar to Taliqan was swift and uneventful. But at Taliqan, further progress was delayed for two whole months due to rains and snow-storms. When the imperial cavalcade could travel at last, their onward march was impeded by the unexpected raids of the Afghan banditti, as soon as they had reached the boundary of Deh-Afghanan. These marauders in fact, as the imperialists were to learn later, were posted by Prince Kamran to attack and plunder the royal encampment. Under the command of Keracha Beg and Haji Baba, those marauders were defeated. Fleeing as far as the town of Khiaban, and pursued by the imperialists, quite a few of them killed and some taken prisoners. Their chief, Sher Ali, had escaped, and had returned to Prince

251

Kamran. Without further disruptions, the imperialists had made entry into Kabul through the Iron Gate, choosing Eagle Hill as their site for battle and encampment.

While Bala Hissar was under siege, another daughter was born to Mah Chuchak, and the emperor had named her Farida Banu. Meanwhile, Prince Kamran, still employing defensive measures had dispatched Sher Ali to loot a rich caravan in Charikan. Humayun, informed of this fresh outrage, had sent a body of troops under the command of Bapus and Kasim Mochi, to lend protection to the caravan. But Sher Ali had succeeded in looting, and just as he was about to get away, Bapus had arrived with his soldiers, launching a sudden attack. The booty was recovered and restored to the injured party, but Sher Ali had escaped, fleeing toward Ghazni. Though, thirty of his followers were captured. Then Bapus advised by Kasim Mochi and without consulting the emperor, had brutally murdered all the prisoners. The grief-stricken relatives of the victims had gone to Prince Kamran, demanding vengeance, and threatening violence if their demands were not met.

Humayun's thoughts, at this juncture, were coming to a stalemate. Aghast and foundering inside the jungle of their revelations. Sedition-bound and whispering that his gentleness was making his generals cruel and arbitrary. That they were taking command into their own hands as far as redress and punishment was concerned. This sudden assault of revelations was jolting him to awareness, only to plunge him back deeper into the dark pit of his own soul. Mah Chuchak was there in each fabric of his soul, besmirched with the mud of his love and hate. Inside each crevice of that mud was entombed dark, slippery knowledge too that his beloved could not help but gloat over the emperor's self-inflicted torture of loving and hating. Out of the reed of this torture supreme, Humayun's thoughts were hurled back into the tether of reality. There was a mantel of silence lowered over the hills and the glens. The mists of hush and quiet so stark, as if boding a challenge and explosion. The cannons were silent as death. All eyes were riveted toward the citadel in the distance. Humayun swung his horse around, his gaze suspended over the citadel, chilled and glazed.

The citadel of Bala Hissar was a scene of absurdity. The pall of black horror and incongruity hanging low over the ramparts. Slung over the great wall of the citadel and dangling in mid-air was the body of a naked woman. Prince Kamran himself was leaning over the parapet, his loud guttural commands cutting the very heart of silence to bleeding lumps. Kasim Mochi, slumped low over his cannon had recognized his wife, inert and speechless, if not stunned with shock and grief. Breaking the seal of his inertia, he cried to Bapus beside him to let the cannon-balls land over the head of the mad prince. A fresh roar of cannons, and Kasim Mochi was heard appealing to stop, fearing, lest his wife be killed in this mad attempt to kill the prince. Prince Kamran's voice was booming high over the hills and glens.

"Cease your bombardment, you heathens, or I will hurl the dead bodies of your loved ones over your very heads." Prince Kamran was waving his arms like a man gone insane. "Bapus, I know you can hear me, and this bulletin of good news is for you alone. Your wife is given to the rabble in the bazaar, to be dishonored and murdered. And here, receive the offerings of my revenge." He signaled his guards.

The murdered sons of Bapus, ages three to five, were flung down from the walls down to the ground. Lost from view like the fleeting mists of a nightmare. Prince Kamran was laughing and swaying.

"And for you, Keracha Beg, your fate is sealed with Bapus. Your sons will be tied to the stakes, and suspended from ropes from this very wall of the citadel, if you don't intercede on my behalf with the emperor. I have decided to leave Kabul along with my harem. We want a promise of safety and—" His voice was truncated abruptly, as he noticed a bold rider flying closer to the very walls of the citadel.

"Your fate is sealed with mine, O tyrant Prince!" Keracha Beg emptied his lungs with the bellows of his rage, reining his horse to one violent halt. "Your wives, your children, your followers can't leave Kabul! Not until you pay the ransom of all these cruelties with your own blood? Your tyranny and evil threats frighten me no more. My children, they must meet death in the course of nature. But if such is their allotted fate, to embrace death now, they could not fare better in the path of duty to their emperor. My own life belongs to the emperor. From this allegiance, nothing could swerve me. But you, O vile Prince, if you pledge allegiance to the emperor, my own life, which at any time I will gladly give for that of my children, will be devoted to you as a mark of my loyalty toward the emperor."

"I will go to Mecca. Become a dervish. Do penance. Ask forgiveness of my sins. A pilgrim of love in the land of holiness—" Prince Kamran was raving.

The lamps of rage and agony were kindled bright in Humayun's eyes, but his senses—the victims of shock and revulsion, had clamped his mouth shut, locking his feet tight in the stirrups. Haze and blindness were in his thoughts, but they were resurrecting one horror of a memory out of the tomb of immediate past. Prince Kamran, after taking hold of the citadel of Kabul, had commanded his soldiers to tear the body of Hameddin Ali from limb to limb, as a lesson to all who dared profess loyalty to the emperor. This splinter of a memory alone was jolting Humayun to awareness, and he spurred his horse as if stung. Facing his matchlock-men, his eyes were flashing commands, but no words were issuing forth from his lips.

Why are the hands of the matchlock-men trembling? Humayun's thoughts were questioning the glazed look of wonder in his own eyes. *What evil fates have turned them to statues of ice? Why can't they raise their flints to the mouths of the cannons? Why are these men turned to craven fools all of a sudden?* His mind was tracing a circle of absurdities as he sat astride, unspeaking and wondering.

How long did the emperor stay prisoner inside this circle of silence and wonder, he himself had no recollection. But soon this enchantment was broken, as if by the very hands of the leering fates. Swerving his horse around, his eyes were leaping up to the citadel in the direction where the attention of his matchlock-men was riveted with a shuddering intensity. Humayun blinked away the fresh mists of shock and incredulity. He could see Prince Akbar standing their proud and dauntless, his own heart turning to glacier of ice. No trace of fear was to be detected on this eight year old prince, as he was held captive by the guards as a challenge to the imperialists if they dared shoot one more cannon ball at the citadel. Prince Akbar's calm demeanor was one of a challenge too, as if this small prince was not only challenging his wicked uncle, but the very fates themselves. The fates were meeting this challenge, it seemed, and coming to befriend him, if not to applaud his valor and composure. Mahum Anaga was seen storming on the scene, and flinging herself in front of Prince Akbar, her hands clasped tight on her bosom. A string of pleas and accusations were torn from her lips, lashing at Prince Kamran and his guards. She was being snatched away by the accursed hands of the guards. But some merciful hands had caught Prince Akbar also, whisking him away, Prince Kamran following.

"Fire and advance!" One loud command was torn loose from Humayun's lips. "Let no danger to the life of a prince weaken your resolve to conquer. "Are the lives of all those innocent victims not worth more than the life of one royal prince?" The bolts of lightning were escaping his eyes, his lips thundering commands.

Against the blaring of the trumpets and the thundering of the cannons, the imperialists were charging straight toward the citadel gates, the emperor leading. The imperialists had surrounded the citadel on all sides. Forcing open the iron gates, and meeting very little resistance. A few guards, who dared impede the entry of the emperor into the citadel, were put to sword. By the magic wand of time, this abrupt assault was turned into an easy victory. A small band of viziers who had sided with Prince Kamran, were prostrating at the emperor's feet, chanting their vows of loyalty and submission. The victory songs from outside were scaling the walls of the citadel with loud beats of drums and trumpets, and amidst this sea of cheers and rejoicing, Prince Akbar was brought to the emperor's presence. Humayun, snatching his son to his breast, could feel the glacier of ice inside him melting into rivulets of prayer and gratitude. In a blind haze of joy and relief, he was hugging all Begums, foremost amongst them, his dream bride, Hamida Banu. But before he could have his fill of love and greetings, the loud cries of his army were demanding the emperor's presence outside, as was customary, to announce the edicts of punishment for the vanquished.

Standing tall and wearied on the citadel steps, Humayun could sense the raucous mood of his soldiers, who would not be pacified, but with edicts harsh and exacting. By the virtue of his perception and introspection, he could not fail to notice their stormy needs, where their spirits savage and warring were famished for the morsels of riot and vengeance. In conformity with their needs, quick Farmans were pouring down his lips amidst cheers of applause and more demands. The mullahs and the governors, who had sided with Prince Kamran, were to be put to death. The whole city of Kabul was to be given to plunder for one night, as a concession to the soldiers who had been barred from their homes by the powerful lords of Kabul, favoring the tyranny of Prince Kamran. Still not satisfied with all these Farmans, the soldiers had begun to chant for the death of Prince Kamran. Humayun's heart was lurching, espying Keracha Beg emerging out of the citadel with his verdict of woe and disbelief.

"Your Majesty, Prince Kamran has escaped—along with his harem and children." Keracha Beg croaked painfully.

"How?" Humayun could barely hear his own feeble inquiry.

"We just discovered a breach in the north wall of the citadel, Your Majesty." Keracha Beg breathed pontifically. "Those cowering viziers of his say that Prince Kamran had been planning such escape since the past few weeks. They didn't believe him though, since he was planning different strategies, as how to defeat us."

"Prince Hindal, with a selected body of troops is to go in pursuit of his traitor brother." Humayun turned his back on all, plodding toward the front entrance.

Tides upon tides of days interspersed with joy and sorrow and with fatigue and reprieve had become his lifelong companions. Humayun was beginning to memorize this lesson after his victory at Kabul. But it had taken him one and a half year after that to realize its true meaning and that too this very day as he sat on his gilded throne with crimson canopy painted with Zodiac signs. Kabul had become Humayun's home and sanctuary both, and this particular day he had decided his throne to be erected in the middle of the garden to enjoy the beauty of the spring, while receiving embassies. In fact, this was his sentimental farewell to Kabul for awhile, since he was marching toward Balkh this very afternoon with the intention of chastising Pir Muhammed and a whole horde of Uzbeks, who were rising in sedition against his authority. His last embassy was from Rashid Khan of Kashgar, who had become his devoted ally since his victory over Kabul. Right now, he was dictating a letter to Bayazid, who was happy with this royal privilege of writing to Shah Tahmasp. The gist of this letter was the emperor's assurance that Kandahar was well guarded under the nominal command of the Persian monarch, but Humayun's gaze as well as his thoughts were straying toward the clusters of purple lilacs the color of his robe.

The large amethyst in Humayun's turban was reflecting its own light and sunshine, as his gaze rested on Prince Akbar. Prince Akbar was chasing golden orioles, his jeweled scimitar radiating colors much like the blaze of anemones and hyacinths in oval flowerbeds. Not far from him, against the profusion of jasmine and

256

honeysuckle, lending colorful borders to the arrays of pines and cedars, were the court painters, Abdus Samad and Saiyyid Ali, absorbed in arresting the glory of this garden on canvas. The mighty palas trees were hosting Begums, who were lolling against satiny pillows on Persian carpets. They were being entertained by the viziers, Haider Qasim and Abul Maali. Sarvaqad was there too, whispering blissfully to her husband, Monaim Khan. A flicker of jealousy was alighting in Humayun's gaze, as he noticed Abul Maali looking at Mah Chuchak much like a devotee at his patron goddess.

Isn't it fortunate that my moods of jealousy are rare? Humayun's thoughts were holding a flint to rage, but kindling no fires. *My jealousy, scattering pearls of laughter in delirium! Or, blazing with the fire of madness? Or, slithering down the pits of despair and sadness? Haider Qasim should be the one inciting my jealousy, by the sheer sin of his handsomeness, not Abul Maali? Should I invite these two cavaliers to this afternoon excursion, to test my own shafts of jealousy?* His thoughts were exploring the mists of his promise to the ladies.

The emperor had promised the ladies of his harem that their wish to see the lovely blooms of riwaj in Koh-daman would be granted, before his expedition to Balkh. And this wish was certainly to be fulfilled this very afternoon, a sort of brief siesta on the way to Balkh. The blooming of these flowers in spring was the most exquisite of nature's miracles in Kabul, which the emperor himself did not wish to miss. These lettuce-like shrubs with flowers changing from downy green to pale violet were appearing in Humayun's mind as the tenderest of blooms, which he wanted his artists to arrest in the book of eternity. His gaze sweeping over Abdus Samad and Saiyyid Ali was returning to Bayazid, who sat polishing his Persian script while copying the emperor's dictation.

The emperor wants to see riwaj, while Balkh is in danger of being consumed by the malefic designs of Pir Muhammed? A sudden sense of loneliness and bewilderment was visiting Humayun's thoughts.

The emperor was to commence his expedition to Balkh right after his indulgence to witness the miracle of riwaj in Koh-daman. Loneliness and bewilderment were making themselves visible, but his thoughts were looking into the eyes of future where the peace of Kunduz, Kandahar and Badakhshan was in danger, if Balkh was not protected by the assaults of the Uzbeks, incited by Pir Muhammed.

Paradoxically, right now, his thoughts were taking shelter under the cover of the past in order to uncover the future imponderables.

Prince Kamran, after his flight from Kabul, had turned to Suleiman Mirza, seeking asylum in Badakhshan. Since his request was denied, he had gone to Taliqan. Restless and conniving as ever, he had begun to gain fresh alliances in the hope of gaining fortunes and kingdoms. Learning about his brother's latest intrigues, Humayun had then marched forth in his pursuit, where Prince Hindal had left off, unable to catch his chameleon of a brother. Prince Kamran was caught in Kishem, and brought before the emperor in the pavilion of a public audience. Expert in donning a mask of humility, laced with histrionic gestures, he could not fail to adopt *one* suited to this particular occasion. While being led toward the throne, he had snatched a whip from the girdle of Monaim Khan, wrapping it around his neck in the manner of a lowly suppliant, offering submission.

Alas, alas! There is no need of it. Throw it away. What is past is past. Humayun was remembering this emotional outburst of his love and forgiveness.

Not only had the emperor forgiven Prince Kamran, but had embraced him with the spirit of love and generosity. Prince Hindal and Prince Askeri were there too, and a grand feast was arranged to celebrate the re-union of all four brothers at Kishem. After two days of feasting and entertainment, they had journeyed to Bend-Kusha in the vicinity of Ishkemish. This place was familiar to Humayun where his father had inscribed the names of his brothers on a flat slab of rock, after receiving submission from his younger brother, Jahangir Mirza. Flanked by gurgling fountains, Humayun had no trouble finding this rock, ordering his name and the names of his brothers to be inscribed right below the names of his uncles and father.

This pleasure trip was turned to warring expeditions, as soon as they had reached the city of Nurin. Across from Amu River, the northern states were plunged in the fever of unrest and rebellion. Marching toward these territories, they were able to conquer Muk and Karatigan. The districts of Kulab were subjugated without much resistance. Here, Humayun had bestowed Kulab to Prince Kamran. Prince Askeri was given the kingdom of Karatigan. The kingdoms of Nurin, Baklan, Kahmerd and Ishkemish were added to the kingdoms of Ghazni and Kunduz, already in the possession of Prince Hindal.

Suleiman Mirza and his son Ibrahim Mirza were to rule Taliqan and Kishem, in addition to Badakhshan. Leaving his kingdoms into the care of his cousin and brothers, Humayun had then journeyed to Penjeshir. A magnificent fort was the pride of this city built by Tamerlane as a monument of his victory over the *infidels* of Kittur. Finding this fort in utter neglect, Humayun had ordered repairs. Within ten days, the fort was restored to its former magnificence, and Humayun had changed the name from Penjeshir to Islamabad, meaning, *The city of true faith.*

That city of true faith was fading in Humayun's memory at the sudden recollection of his rift with Keracha Beg. Keracha Beg was assigned the post of Prime Minister with Khwaja Ghazi of Tabriz as his governor. Two weeks ago, Keracha Beg had come to the emperor, seething with rage. He had promised ten tumans to one of his officers as a gift, ordering Khwaja Ghazi to pay that sum from the royal treasury. Khwaja Ghazi was unwilling to obey his orders, dismissing this gift as some act of caprice on the part of Keracha Beg, which had no claim on the royal treasury. So Keracha Beg had rushed to the emperor, demanding that Khwaja Ghazi be dismissed from his post, replaced by Kasim Husein as the governor. Humayun, incensed by the audacity of Keracha Beg had dismissed him, commanding him to deal with this rift on his own and not to burden the emperor with such petty matters.

A subtle whisper in Humayun's psyche was issuing warnings, as if a host of misfortunes were in ambush to disrupt his veneer of peace and tranquility. *As if the sweet wine inside the heart of this spring was to turn into hot cider of summer, tainted by the poison of doom and calamity.* No such omens, dark and impending, could be seen in this garden brimming with colors wild and throbbing. Humayun's gaze, admiring the blaze of color in Himalayan tulips, was slipping over the musicians and dancers, before landing on Prince Akbar. Prince Akbar was brandishing his scimitar, as if slicing thin air into ribbons of sunshine.

"Are you bent on slaying the beauty of this spring, my Prince?" Humayun chided. "Come here, the emperor will assign you the task of a royal messenger."

"Your Majesty." Prince Akbar bounded closer, afraid to lose his cap while curtsying, so pressing it down with his right hand over his head.

"A charming way of curtsying with your right hand over your head and your left sweeping the floor. We would name this curtsy Kornish as a part of Moghul etiquettes." Humayun laughed. "Since the Begums have decided unanimously to show you the loveliness of riwaj, you might as well be their happy messenger! Go whispering into the ears of each one that the emperor is ready for this excursion, as if you are telling each one a different secret?" He commanded.

"Your Majesty!" Prince Akbar's gold-brown eyes were lit up with protests. "I would rather stay here, or go hunting. Riwaj, I have seen it so many times, Your Majesty." His merry eyes were pleading favors.

"Hunting, that's all you are interested in, it is obvious!" Humayun laughed. "I have a mind to take you with me to Balkh to fight the Uzbeks."

"Would you, Your Majesty, really? Could I?" Was Prince Akbar's exultant plea. "I would hunt Uzbeks down the wild steppes. Killing each one of them, Your Majesty, if they dared block my way?"

"While hunting is a pleasure, my little King of Kabul, wars offer no such luxury. Besides, you have to rule Kabul in my absence, as a nominal king, of course." Humayun heaved a mock sigh. "Balkh is no place for your fun-loving expeditions. But you have my permission to skip this ritual of riwaj-watching. The emperor will plead with the ladies on your behalf, so that you could explore the valleys of Kabul at your heart's content. And you will while we are gone, for sure. Not for long, hopefully. I will surely take you to Hind, winning my kingdoms back, and making you the king of Agra." One sliver of a prophecy escaped his lips. The fever of wistfulness in his eyes turning to Hamida Banu, as she sailed up to her son.

"You are not pleading with the emperor, my ungrateful Prince, are you?" Hamida Banu flashed an accusing look at her son before turning her eyes to the emperor. "Don't heed his crafty appeals, Your Majesty! He is known to run wild down the valleys, trying the patience of his guards who look for him desperately. Besides, all the Begums are looking forward to his company. We won't see him for a long, long time. Not for too long, I hope. A family excursion, Your Majesty, and he—" Her pleas were silenced by a sudden burst of mirth on the emperor's lips.

"Let our Prince stay imprisoned in Kabul, my sweet Empress." Humayun waved his arm, noticing the swift approach of Khwaja Khizr.

Humayun had missed noticing the flicker of fear in Hamida Banu's eyes, as if she had caught some dark prophecy folded inside the mists of his laughter. The word *imprisoned* alone was making her thoughts rush toward Prince Kamran who had made her son a prisoner twice already. Her heart was thundering, but her Nile-blue eyes were gathering warmth from diamonds in her hair. Her ruby-red lips were parted in expectation of some good news from Khwaja Khizr, her hands smoothing the blue silks at her waist absently. None had noticed Prince Akbar slipping away most cautiously. Khwaja Khizr, after offering a brief curtsy stood twirling his mustache.

"Your Majesty, a messenger from Kashmir brings glad tidings." Khwaja Khizr began slowly. "Haider Mirza has extended an invitation to the emperor to visit Kashmir. He says that spring is the most beautiful of seasons in Kashmir, and the emperor must enjoy it before commencing his expedition to Hind."

"A generous and tempting offer! Could the emperor abandon the cause of Balkh and march straight toward Hind?" The light of mysticism was shining in Humayun's eyes. "Wars are much like the plagues. Unexpected and uncontrollable! If one could shoot the bullets of sense into them, not the cannon-balls of destruction." He shifted his gaze to Hamida Banu. "How would you like to see riwaj in Kashmir, Miryam Makani?" The capricious glow in his eyes was banishing all profundities.

"If the snow doesn't march ahead of us to bury the riwaj in white graves, Your Majesty?" Was Hamida Banu's attempt at mirth and levity. All melting against the hasty approach of Biram Khan, wearing anxiety in the very plume of his turban.

"Your Majesty, pardon me for bringing sad news in happy times." Biram Khan breathed low half way through his taslim.

"The emperor is no stranger to sadness, my good vizier." Humayun's eyes were gathering profundities. "The facade of joy conceals sadness, both fighting to claim their rightful place, before or after. Proceed, Biram, this mirage of joy must empty its own quivers of deception." He commanded.

"Keracha Beg, Your Majesty, has defected." Biram Khan was prepared to unleash his bulletin of news without delay. "Bapus and Duldi are with him too, and so are Moshaib Beg and Ismael Beg, along with three hundred soldiers fully armed. Stealing herd and cattle at Pia Minar Pass, they were seen bivouacking in Koh-daman. They are on their way to Kulab now, as the messenger asserts. Keracha Beg was heard boasting. *I am the slave of the emperor in the guise of a Prime Minister, but I am headed toward Kulab to profess my allegiance to Prince Kamran.*"

"The splintering of a mirage! But joy must precede before sadness." Humayun's gaze was turning to Hamida Banu. "Tell the Begums, Miryam Makani, that we are leaving for our excursion shortly." He returned his attention to Biram Khan. "After commanding the grooms to saddle our horses, and getting ready the troops to meet us at Koh-daman, Biram, you are to summon a meeting of the generals. Choose Terdi Beg, Kuli Sultan and Monaim Khan, commanding them to select their body of troops to follow the traitors. They are to be brought back bound and shackled, if they are caught alive." He commanded, his gaze shifting to Jouhar. "Replenish the emperor's cup, Jouhar, and fetch my box of opium."

The magic of wine and opium had worked wonders on Humayun's spirit, even making his horse fly like the Pegasus, without noticing that Koh-daman was already there, its seductive contours arched and undulating. Actually, his spirits were not that high before the commencement of the journey, the affect of the narcotics taking its sweet time to bestow the gifts of lightness and exhilaration. He had rather been impatient. Prince Akbar had gone hunting without an escort, and he had sent the guards scurrying after the prince to make sure of his safety and protection before embarking on this journey. On the way to Koh-daman, Bibi Mubaraka had fallen off her horse, while crossing a stream and the emperor had lent her a hand to mount her steed, not-too-gently. Then the Arabian horse of Mah Chuchak was seized with one wild impulse to toss its royal rider into the ravine, but the brave beloved had brought it to obedience. A spasm of agony had crossed Humayun's features at this scene, his thoughts refreshing his memory that she was carrying his royal seed into her womb much too carelessly. All these sand-dunes of annoyance and inconvenience, and Koh-daman had materialized before the emperor's sight like a dream. Against the gold dusk of the evening, the wild terrains and lush valleys were almost violet, scattered with the clusters of riwaj, waving greetings at the riders from the bosom of the foothills.

The emperor was riding ahead, inhaling the scent of beauty and fecundity. Now, quiet and contemplative, since the affects of wine and opium had lifted their spells of giddy exhilaration. Gulbadan Begum had joined him, riding beside him silently, and luxuriating in the sense of nearness without feeling the need to break this link of solitude. Endowed with keen perception, she understood the emperor's moods with the precision of a psychic. *Almost all of his moods, of sadnesses and of jealousies, of raging, churning debates and inquisitions inside his heart and soul.* And right now, she was sure, he was suffering despair at the imponderables, along with the stings of jealousy for one woman whom he would love to hate, if he could. Mah Chuchak was coming to her mind, soiled with passions dark and unutterable, but she had certain tenderness for this woman, and would defend her with her own life if her guilt and indiscretion were known, one little voice within her mind was affirming.

Suddenly, the air was filled with music from the lips of the Begums. They were riding at a leisurely pace not far behind, and had begun to sing. Amidst these fluttering notes in songs, Shaham Agacha's voice was rising above clear and trilling, followed by Sarvaqad's. The guards in the rear were smitten to silence, rapt and intoxicated. Even the camels with book-loads of burden on their backs were craning their necks and matching their strides to the rhythm of the voices. Gulbadan's heart was singing along with the Begums, her gaze welcoming the valley of Laghman in shimmering shades of ruby and citron from the dusk. Humayun's soul was expanding and fluttering. The ache and tenderness in there, though moved by the ripple of song and beauty, were not relinquishing their hold on memories past and recent.

Do naught against thy brothers, even if they may deserve it. Humayun's thoughts were repeating this injunction of his father under some spell of pain and exhilaration. *They deserve to be strangled by the noose of their follies and wickedness', and yet they bask in the sunshine of my forgiveness? Is this a curse, this splinter of forgiveness? Especially, with Prince Kamran, whose cruelties sit not well on my throne of forgiveness. Alienating my devoted generals, whose families suffered terribly through the evil of my Lucifer brother.* His mind was closing shut the gates of memories, but a journey in his soul was commencing. Mah Chuchak, garlanded with the buds of sin and beauty was mocking and laughing.

A volley of painful mirth was choked inside Humayun's heart, where a giant puzzle lay throbbing with passions stark and insufferable. *Love and hate. Lust and purity.! Jealousy and tenderness. Cruelty and compassion! All dark and evil. All pure and vulgar. All sublime and profane. Ignorant of truth and wisdom. Obedient to the will and caprice of his mind.* His mind, right now, was molding the clay of his passions, into lumps of absurdities. The serpentine valleys before his sight were dipping and emerging much like the roller coaster giddiness in his thoughts.

"What a sentimental fool the emperor is?" Humayun exclaimed suddenly, flashing a quick look at Gulbadan Begum. "All those atrocities committed by Prince Kamran, and I make him the ruler of Kulab? And my faithless vizier, Keracha Beg, honored with the post of Prime Minister? Now turned traitor, he is seeking the alliance of Prince Kamran. Do you think, my sweet sister that my ever-intriguing brother would rise again to challenge the emperor's rule over Kabul?"

"He might, Your Majesty? He is wicked as you already know!" Gulbadan Begum laughed, more so to cheer the emperor than to still her own fears. "After you made him the ruler of Kulab, he rushed to Kuli Sultan, protesting. *What, have I not been the sovereign of Kabul and Badakhshan? And what is Kulab, a mere perghana?* Kuli Sultan didn't want to be the cause of a rift amongst the royal brothers again, since you had forgiven Prince Kamran, that's why he didn't tell you, Your Majesty." She demurred, her heart breathing warnings. "But Kuli Sultan's response to Prince Kamran is to my liking, of what he said. *With due respect, Prince Kamran, after all that has passed between you and the emperor, it is a wonder that you have even got Kulab! I have heard that you are wise. And I know you to be so. So, keep this perghana and be content.* Prince Kamran is jealous of you, Your Majesty. Jealous of your valor and power. And ambitious too. Yet jealousy, not ambition, would be his ultimate downfall." Her heart was a cauldron of dark omens.

"Jealousy, sweet manna for passions terrible and inviolate." Humayun laughed. "The emperor is jealous of all his wives, and they would be shut behind the walls of the harem after my conquest of Hind." His gaze was shifting to Hamida Banu and Mah Chuchak. "Riwaj and riding, are you enjoying it all?"

"Most beautiful than ever, this spring and these flowers, Your Majesty." Hamida Banu sang ecstatically.

"The sweetest, the prettiest! Never seen them bloom with such profusion before, Your Majesty?" Was Mah Chuchak's dreamy confession.

"Bled white clear down to their purple hearts, Your Majesty!" Shaham Agacha was singing her own poetic praise.

"Sated with all this beauty and sweetness, now I am famished for real feasting, Your Majesty." Was Khawish Agha's unpoetic appeal.

"To endure the gluttony of a feast, my love, you must taste riwaj first." Humayun teased. "Though astringent in taste, it is a panacea for stomach ailments."

"A collyrium of its juice, Your Majesty, strengthens the eye and prevents opacity, Your Majesty." Khwaja Khizr's horse whinnied, rather groaning over the fallen tree trunk, which he neglected to avoid.

"Your sight needs it the most, Khwaja!" Humayun laughed, watching him steady his horse to an even trot. "But if you fall from your horse and injure yourself, a poultice of riwaj mixed with barley might work, since it cures sores and boils."

"All this mirth and raillery is making me hungry too." Gulbadan Begum raised one protest, watching her husband Khwaja Khizr spurring his horse closer to her.

"This is an ideal spot to rest and feast, Your Majesty, since all of us are getting hungry." Prince Hindal appealed from behind.

"Men's appetites are larger than life! More urgent, more irrepressible. Thus to be satisfied accordingly." Humayun commented over his shoulders. "Yes, we will camp right here." He commanded. "Fetch my books, sweet Prince. The emperor might read couplets to camels while the feast is being prepared."

The preparations for night-long feasting were still under way, as Humayun sat luxuriating in his sumptuous tent. Besides the ladies of the harem, a few privileged guests were keeping the emperor company. Amongst them Abul Maali and Haider Kasim. A few younger princes sat huddled in one corner, listening intently to the stories told by Mir Falut, the royal storyteller. Against the dance and flicker of the candles in gold candelabras, Zarif could be seen squatted on the Persian rug, entertaining the ladies with couplets and anecdotes. Sarvaqad and Shaham Agacha, half lolling against the satiny pillows were singing a duet at the request of the emperor. For some strange reason, Humayun's soul was on fire, its fever and implacability not to be appeased even by the sweet serenade in Shaham Agacha's voice, or by the wine of poetry in Sarvaqad's eyes.

Humayun's gaze sweeping over all the Begums was dreamy and restless. While talking he appeared not to see, his laughter too dry and joyless. Some sort of mad violence was brewing inside him, which had nothing to do with love and hate, only lust and carnality. Each fiber in his soul was lit with desire to consume Mah Chuchak, and to be consumed by his own madness. The soul bride of his hate-love was shooting daggers at Sarvaqad with her eyes alone, and Humayun's heart was expanding with elation to watch this sea of jealousy in her eyes. But this bubble of elation was bursting with a sudden violence, as he became aware of Abul Maali, his eyes brimming with ardor and reaching out to Mah Chuchak. A bolt of serpentine rage was alighting in Humayun's eyes, whipped by the thunder of jealousy. He heaved himself up as if stung, commanding abruptly.

"Leave us, please." Humayun waved dismissal, claiming Mah Chuchak's hand savagely. "A great feast is waiting for you all. The emperor might join you later."

All were startled to their feet, mute and abashed. Especially, the Begums, unable to comprehend the light of fire and rage in the emperor's eyes. Mah Chuchak stood there smiling and flustered, but she deigned not speak even after all had left.

"Maybe, the cold sparkling stars out there would appease the pain and hunger in my soul?" Humayun murmured to himself, gazing into the midnight blue of her eyes under some spell of daze and delirium.

"Your Majesty, is the food to be served to us here?" Mah Chuchak Begum ventured an innocent plea. "I am hungry."

"Me too, love." Humayun put his arms around her waist and held her close to him. "But my hunger is not for food! I am hungry for love. It is the hunger of the soul, rather. When the emperor is done feasting on your beauty with the violence of a passion mad and insatiable, you would hunger no more for food. We would both hunger for love. Again and again! Making this night the harlot of our passions, for the journey to Balkh is long and arduous, and we must replenish our souls with the food of love." He crushed her to him in one tight embrace. Then he began kissing and unrobing her with the madness of a man possessed.

The journey to Balkh indeed had been long and arduous. Though, Humayun was thinking about that mad, passionate night of love and violence in the valley of Laghman. This afternoon, he was seated in his tent at Astanch, attended by a coterie of viziers and grandees. Amongst them was one Uzbek leader by the name of Khwaja Bagh, who had signed a peace treaty with the Moghuls, but his followers had attacked the royal encampment this very morning. A little skirmish and a great scuffle had resulted in the death of one Moghul soldier, and many were injured. More than half of the audacious Uzbeks were hacked to pieces, and the rest had fled. Khwaja Bagh was summoned, charged of spying, but was proven innocent. He was more embarrassed by the conduct of his followers, than fearing any edicts of reprisal from the emperor. He had even sent his general Behader Shah after the fleeing Uzbeks to be brought back bound and shackled before the emperor for violating his own oath of honor in this manner, since he had signed peace treaty with the emperor. The air in this pale damask tent was charged with silence for the moment, and Humayun's thoughts were journeying back in time, as if searching for answers in the rubbles of the past.

From the valley of Laghman to Yuret Chalak, and the emperor had to wait for two long months, since he was expecting reinforcements of three thousand horse and men from Haji Baba. Haji Baba was sent to an expedition to subdue the Aimaks, but the rumors were afloat that he had intentions of defecting and joining Prince Kamran. Finally, when he had returned to Yeret Chalak after subduing the Aimaks, all the canards had proven false. The emperor had bestowed upon him the title of Khan. The imperialists had then resumed their march along the Bangi River, passing through the cities of Anderab and Istalif to reach Taliqan. From Taliqan, they had to cross the Narin Pass to enter the valley of Niber, but this journey had suffered delay due to attacks from the marauders, resulting in several skirmishes. Besides these skirmishes, Humayun had enjoyed the beauty of Niber valley, feasting and hunting for two whole weeks before marching forth to Balkh. Pir Muhammed, learning of the advancing army of the imperialists had taken refuge in the strong fort of Eibek, strengthening his defenses. So, the imperialists had taken the route of Khulm to reach Balkh, choosing Astanch for their encampment to chastise Pir Muhammed in his stronghold of Eibek.

With such beehive of thoughts humming in his head, Humayun had begun to pace in his tent, while his viziers and grandees sat discussing the strategies to chastise not only Pir Muhammed but the whole horde of Uzbeks. The morale of the soldiers was high, and the Moghuls were certain of their sweeping victories, the viziers were murmuring. Humayun's thoughts were wearing the laurels of optimism too, but some shadow of primeval darkness could be seen shuddering in his psyche. Some canker of a presage? *The abyss of agony and grief, where death battles with life to end the chain of sufferings?* And yet, there was the *sun of hope*, peering through the clouds of darkness, and emitting the warmth of renewal. And yet again, this warmth was leaping out of his head and scorching his very sight.

"Since you have proven yourself to be brave and honest, Khwaja Bagh? Tell the emperor, what are the best means to vanquish the Uzbeks and to conquer Balkh?" Humayun's abrupt inquiry startled Khwaja Bagh to his feet, his look smoldering.

"The Uzbeks, Your Majesty, are a heedless, belligerent race." Was Khwaja Bagh's flustered response. "And this is the truth, not ever spoken before by one Uzbek against the other, Your Majesty." He murmured darkly. "Cut off their heads, Your Majesty. March to the capitol with all your troops in one quick assault, and Balkh will be yours." He laughed, as if mocking his own fate and challenging death.

A volley of laughter, loud and hysterical, escaped Humayun's lips. His gold helmet seemed to be laughing too, catching glints of lights from the flickering candles and emanating sparks of mirth. This laughter was truncated as abruptly as it had ensued by the breezy arrival of Khan Behader. He had a large gash in his left arm, where blood was caked dry, marking a purple wound.

"Who attacked you?" Humayun's eyes were kindling a fever of rage.

"Muhammed Sultan of Hissar, Your Majesty. He was sent by Pir Muhammed, I heard him boast." Khan Behader lowered his head.

"Has he gone mad?" Humayun's hand was reaching to his hilt, blood rushing to his cheeks.

"He has high spirit, Your Majesty." Khan Behader murmured painfully.

268

"The emperor is grateful for your advice, Khwaja Bagh." This comment tossed over his shoulders, Humayun was leaving his tent in blind rage.

In a flash, the emperor's commands were stirring the imperialists to action, granting them the permission of a swift assault. A flurry of commands was carried through the whole encampment in waves upon waves of fervor and excitement. The cannon and artillery were secured to appropriate places to storm the fort of Eibek. The red and yellow standards of the imperialists were unfurled, and the soldiers in shining armor gathering in disciplined files. At the blaring of the trumpets and the beating of the drums, Humayun was leading his army, as if driven by fate. The emperor's guard, Mehter Sagai was trying his best to catch up with the emperor's flying steed. Biram Khan had barely time to mount his Chupatak horse when he noticed the emperor flying full-speed into the enemy's territory, unguarded. A loud warning boomed through his lips with the bolt of a prophecy.

"Watch out, Your Majesty! Uzbeks might be lurking not too far. Don't rush into the pit of danger, Your Majesty. I see the face of death." Biram Khan was aghast at his own words, spilled out will-lessly.

"Better face death with courage, than succumb to it with a cowering heart." Was Humayun's delirious response, writ by the pen of destiny.

The pen of destiny was moving fast with the quicksilver urgency of a tyrant. One bold Uzbek was seen darting out of his ambush, his naked sword glittering under the Sun. Before anyone could check his advance, his swift mount was right beside the emperor's, who was unaware of this crafty assailant. Only after he had felt the violence of a sudden blow on his head that he could see the *face of destiny* grinning and disappearing. The unerring saber of Mehter Sagai had slit open the throat of the mad assailant in his act of raising his sword the second time. Humayun had received a deep gash on his forehead clear back to his left ear. A fountain of blood, streaming down his forehead into his eyes was as terrible as the blinding, excruciating pain in each fiber of his body and soul.

"Wretched rebel—" Was Humayun's groan of a comment, as he was caught into the loving embrace of Biram Khan, and whisked to safety.

The Messenger of life in the guise of Biram Khan was with the emperor. The Messenger of death as the headless foe was lying inert in his own pool of blood. The fountain of blood from the emperor's head had quenched the thirst of the nearby stream, where Biram Khan himself had washed and bandaged the royal wound. He had then carried the emperor with utmost haste to the safety and comfort of his own tent. Not even knowing that he had left the blood-soaked cuirass of the emperor, along with his quilted corset of gold, by the stream. He had wrapped the wounded emperor in the cloak of Mir Berken, oblivious to all else, only praying for the health of the emperor. The emperor was oblivious, even to the dance of evil, malign fates inside his head waging wars amongst themselves on the field of future.

Chapter Nineteen
Buddha's Blessings

The face of dawn with its dewdrop freshness was bathing the valley of Zahak Bamain into pearly whiteness. Especially the small palace at the foot of the hills where the royal occupants lay cradled in satiny sheets. Humayun, sleeping in one of the sumptuous chambers was restless and dreaming. His hands were reaching out to feel and absorb the warmth of his beloved beside him, but Mah Chuchak had stolen out of her bed to luxuriate in the comfort of a perfumed bath. This marble bathroom with tub the shape of a tulip, its petals tapering down in gleaming turquoise, had become Mah Chuchak's haven, tempting her at all hours of the day or night to seek its scented comfort. Her dreams were tainted with the soot of jealousy. She was jealous of Sarvaqad Begum, and her fits of jealousy had driven the emperor to the bed of Khawish Agha. And Mah Chuchak, upon learning that Khawish Agha was pregnant, had vowed to herself that she would curb her jealousies, not lending the emperor even one chance to sleep with his other wives. Right now, as she lay soaked in the bubbles of her reveries inside the bathtub, the emperor lay tossing and turning on his bed. His dreams were the phantoms of reality, escaping the prison of the past at night, and pounding on the door of the present till the dawn of another day.

Humayun could see himself wounded and swooning inside the ever-churning mists of his dreams, this very night. The imperialists, disheartened by the absence of the emperor, had suffered defeat by the hands of Pir Muhammed. The wounded emperor was brought to the palace of Zahak Bamain, where it had taken two whole months for his wound to heal. Mah Chuchak had given birth to a premature baby, and Humayun had named his son, Muhammed Hakim Mirza. The demons of jealousy were entering his dreams too, waging wars into the hearts of his wives, and revealing the seeds of his lust growing into the wombs of both Mah Chuchak and Khawish Agha. Pir Muhammed was emerging forth as the emperor's ally after he had been attacked by the Uzbeks of Bokhara. This proud Uzbek was quick to sign a peace treaty with the emperor, and the Uzbeks of Bokhara had retreated promptly after watching the imperialists come to the aid of Pir Muhammed. Another ghost of the past-present was invading the emperor's dream, no other than Prince Kamran himself. He had fallen in love with Haram Begum. Entrusting his devoted nurse, Tarkhan Bega with a love letter to be carried from Kulab to Badakhshan. Sending also a handkerchief embroidered in gold and silver to profess his love and madness.

Haram Begum, the chaste wife of Suleiman Mirza, was so incensed by this outrage, that she had shown the letter to her husband, raving and demanding redress. Suleiman Mirza, in return, in a fit of rage, had ordered Tarkhan Bega to be hewn to pieces, swearing a vow of vengeance to kill Prince Kamran, who had dared sully the honor of his wife. Haram Begum then, afraid of her husband's anger, had pleaded with him to spare the life of the prince. Prince Kamran, upon learning of these tragic events, has fled from Kulab, leaving Prince Askeri as the sole ruler and defender. Conflicting reports of Prince Kamran's flight had reached the emperor in Zahak Bamain, but the most recent one was that he had gone wandering somewhere in the manner of a dervish. And that he had left the ladies of his harem with the Uzbek Khans, either in Khost, or in Anderab.

Prince Kamran, in love? Could this sinful love purge the sea of corruption inside him— The dream-mists in Humayun's thoughts were murmuring. He could hear the echo of silence in his sleep, clear and confined. But out of this confinement was rising forth one reflection bright.

Humayun could see himself standing naked on the top of one hill in Kabul, called Gulkhaneh. The lower half of his body was on fire. The tongues of the crimson flames reaching clear down to the continent of Hind, as if tasting the sweetness of home and inhaling the scent of comfort and self-surrender. The upper part of his body was half chilled, swaying and shuddering. Carried on the wings of flames, it seemed, he was hurled against the very gates of Kabul.

Prince Akbar is my prisoner. Kabul is mine, mine. Prince Kamran's laughter was ringing loud and merry over the glens and the valleys.

Humayun was jolted out of this nightmare to the sting of awakening, the beads of perspiration trickling down his back in razor-sharp rivulets. The ribbons of gold from the pale disk of morning sun were peering through Venetian lace on the windows, their silk adornments in tassels of gold hanging limp, pleated and ruffled. The dream-laughter of Prince Kamran was still ringing in his ears, his gaze opiate and searching. Tossing down the satiny sheets with abrupt violence, he sprang to his feet, clad only in perspiration on his forehead and behind his back. Pressing his temples with both hands, he stood demurring by the bed, then dashed toward the adjacent bathroom, greeted by one ripple of a scented mirth from Mah Chuchak.

"You have seen me naked before, my morning bird, why this mirth and mockery?" Humayun demanded, thinking, that she was laughing at him.

"Your Majesty!" Was Mah Chuchak's startled cry, as she covered her breasts with her hands. "No mockery, only mirth, at my dream which I dreamt this very morning. Prince Kamran getting to his knees at the feet of Haram Begum and serenading! Such ludicrous scene, and he being so old." She was averting her gaze from the dagger of desire between the emperor's legs.

"Old? He is younger than me! Let me prove, how young I am!" Humayun landed on top of her, kissing her fiercely and deliriously. The tides of water in the bathtub a gurgling splash and splutter!

The afternoon sun spilling gold on the palace garden of Zahak Bamain, was painting its own scene of ripple and splash over the fountains and terraces. In the middle of the garden was erected a gold throne with a blue canopy, embellished with Zodiac signs. Humayun, robed in silks of blue and gold, was presiding over his makeshift court of viziers and grandees. His gaunt features with thin beard and mustache were suffused with a subtle glow as a result of his passionate surfeit in the morning. The large sapphire in his turban with ropes of pearls was lending his eyes the light of fire, which was actually raging inside him. Biram Khan seated next to him could not help voice one comment which he had been nursing inside his heart since they had come to Zahak Bamain.

"So glad, Your wound is completely healed, Your Majesty. But I have been wondering for quite awhile, why did you risk your life that fateful evening?"

"Life is one half of a great puzzle, Biram! The other half is death, and I was trying to explore its pieces to view living, if not existence, in its entirety?" Was Humayun's Sufic response. "Why should one not risk one's life, and why should one fear to lose it? Death is a worthy opponent and we must face it with courage, applauding its valor if we succumb? God have mercy on me for such levity and ingratitude!" He exclaimed with a dint of hilarity. "And yet, I cannot help thinking, where this greed for living comes from? And yet again, life is wonderful, if one were to see perfection inside the corruption of all evil and injustice?"

"You are right, Your Majesty! We should hail death as the mightiest of foes, admiring its blows with courage and gratitude?" Biram Khan quipped.

"You are utterly wicked, Biram." Humayun laughed. "Since this morning, I have noticed the downpour of poetry and wickedness from your lips, and nothing else. But the emperor is not deceived? You are trying to humor me with the feast of ideation. But even a few morsels of ideation don't lend any solution to my neglected problems. Some violent storm from within and without might help me tie the strings of my decisions together? If I am not contradicting myself, I must say that ideation suits my mood this afternoon. In my thoughts, life is pure and death sublime! Both loving, both breathing! Both radiating joy and light! Both seeking the lamp of truth inside the *valley of ignorance!*"

"Blinded by the *lamp of truth*, Your Majesty, I have decided to sleep in the valley of ignorance." Biram Khan breathed low.

"And yet, stupidity, not ignorance, is the cause of all evil in life." Humayun continued as if he had not heard Biram Khan. "Stupidity is the most abhorrent of all vices. Stupidity in thoughts, even without the bullets of action! Thinking that goodness prevails, and knowing that evil conquers. Thoughts alone carving wounds! Very deep, very painful. Mental wounds! Incurable and unhealing. Agonies of the souls? Tragedies vast and bewildering. Hopes and dreams. A mirage in the wilderness—" His self-ruminations were truncated by the sound of hoof beats.

A bold rider was seen galloping toward the garden, his horse almost trespassing the forbidden compound. The courtiers standing there laughing amongst themselves were startled to awareness. The air itself was charged with silence, it seemed, as the rider dismounted impatiently, expressing his wish to see the emperor. He was promptly assisted and brought before the emperor. All reeds of ideation had fled from the emperor's head, his heart a cauldron of black omens.

274

"Your Majesty." The young soldier gasped for breath, bowing double. "Nazeri Aleagi sent me, Your Majesty, the chief from Meshi tribe. He sends his greetings and professes his allegiance. He instructed me to tell you personally, Your Majesty, that Prince Kamran has captured the citadel of Kabul."

"That foul vermin, my own brother! That base insect, my everlasting foe!" The kindling of rage in Humayun's eyes was landing on the soldier. "Tell all, you Steppe Hawk, what evils are in store for the emperor? How did he manage that?"

"Your Majesty, Prince Kamran has been planning that since a long time, the chief told me. "Prince Kamran had been hiding in Taliqan when you got wounded, Your Majesty. One of his soldiers got hold of your quilted cuirass soaked with blood, and took it to the prince. Telling him that the emperor died in Balkh. Gathering all his troops, he started toward Kabul by the way of Gurbund and Istalif. On the way, killing the Hazaras, and plundering caravans which passed that way. Kuli Sultan was captured, and when brought before Prince Kamran, he struck him with his saber. Commanding his guards to tear his body to pieces. Takhti Beg received the same treatment when he was captured. Prince Askeri also left Kulab and joined Prince Kamran. Keracha Beg, with all his troops, is with Prince Kamran, acting as his chief vizier. Together, they besieged the citadel of Kabul, but when your devoted vizier Beg Birlas insisted on defending the citadel, Prince Kamran showed him the blood-stained cuirass. Telling him that the emperor is dead, so Beg Birlas surrendered."

"My son, a prisoner of his wicked uncle this third time." Humayun's voice was choking by the sea of agony and torment inside him. "Over the tomb of the emperor, what great offerings my princely brother is piling high in terms of cruelty and vengeance?" The shadows of pain in his gaze were rippling and flickering.

"None, Your Majesty." The young soldier lowered his gaze. "Only this, he has forbidden all to see Prince Akbar."

"Only God forbids! Men just command and hope to be obeyed?" Rage and mirth exploded on Humayun's lips in one hysterical thunder. "God Almighty, knowing the corruptions in our hearts, and letting us wallow in there till we perish." The shadows of sadness were alighting in his eyes. "Tell your chief, my kind, cruel messenger, that the emperor is grateful for such news. That the emperor would bestow upon him favors after raising the standards of victory over Kabul."

The messenger was plodding back to his horse under some spell of daze and bewilderment. A few of the courtiers, who stood whispering amongst themselves, had grown silent. The pines and cedars themselves had assumed the aura of hush and mystery. Even the sunshine was growing livid and lusterless, gathering the weight of hush in its pallid arms, and lowering its shafts of silence. Humayun's gaze, lifted up to the Zodiac signs on his blue canopy, was returning to the sea of silence. To his anguished awareness, all his courtiers seemed to be etched alive on the canvas of this garden, not a whiff of breeze to disturb their bright plumes or colorful robes. His gaze sweeping over all was arrested to Jouhar, a thin, capricious smile curling on his lips.

"Jouhar, let the ruby tongues of wine break this silence!" Humayun commanded, claiming his jeweled goblet from the jade table beside him, and holding it out. "From your gold flagon, pour merriment into the cups of all."

Jouhar leaped to his feet with the agility of a panther, too happy to serve the emperor. After filling the emperor's goblet, he was bouncing around jauntily, draining his gold flagon of all its flood of merriment into the cups of the viziers and courtiers.

"Let us drink to victory." Humayun poised his goblet before him in an act of proposing a toast. "We are going home! Drink to the health of Kabul, the laurels of victory await us. This time, Prince Kamran will be rewarded with punishment, not with forgiveness. He has tried the emperor's patience for much too long."

The tides of hope and laughter were splintering forth from the mantle of silence in cheers and applause. Humayun sat laughing and issuing Farmans, mirth and sadness playing hide-and-seek in his eyes. But rage and agony were constricting his heart to a ball of fire. This missile of torture inside him was rising to his head in a whirlwind of fears and doubts. A few scattered lumps of decisions were surfacing in his thoughts, his gaze turning to Biram Khan.

"To Kabul, to Kabul. To victory, to victory." Humayun repeated aloud, his gaze already straying toward Bayazid. "Come, my wise historian, test your skills in writing a letter to Haram Begum. Not to Suleiman Mirza, that besotted wretch. His wife owns more horses and troops than any king of the steppe, who might be able to supply the much-needed provisions of weapons to the emperor. Write to that venerable lady that the emperor needs reinforcements to thwart the designs of his wicked brother." He got to his feet, dismounting his throne thoughtfully.

"That letter, Your Majesty." Bayazid pleaded after the emperor, clutching his jade inkpot to himself.

"Biram Khan is best suited to this task, Bayazid, seek his assistance." Humayun murmured over his shoulders. "His noble thoughts would be worthy of a gentle request than the emperor's blistering commands." He was drifting toward the palace like the one drugged with pain and reveries.

The palace in the distance, shining like a jewel with its red brick facade and lofty columns, was luring Humayun toward its aura of silence and mystery. The chords of silence and mystery inside his psyche were snapping loose, and he could hear the trickle in his thoughts, murmuring, that the emperor needs more sunshine than the shining files of troops and armaments. He was not even aware that his right hand was feeling the healed wound behind his left ear. Suddenly, the awareness was dawning upon him at the touch of smooth silkiness at the back of his ear, where the scab had fallen off. His strides, pounding the red brick dust under his feet, were obeying their whimsical commands, abandoning the view of the palace and straggling toward the grove of Chenars. The bowers of Damascus roses, minted red-gold against the blaze of sunshine were attracting his attention. But his thoughts were clinging to the voice of his psyche, much like the whispering cedars edged with bridal ivy.

On the flimsy strings of hope, we dance to the sad tunes of our own pain and suffering. One little sigh of poetry in Humayun's thoughts was breathing dissent. *Softly, softly, very softly, we sing and dance. Battered hopes! Grieving melodies! Weeping willows! Shades and shadows in dreams. Dark and abysmal! Pain and surcease strumming their lovely tunes on the harp of existence. What dementia? I am going mad.* His mind was forcing his feet in the direction of the palace.

What I have achieved? What is it that I seek and hunger after? Where is Hind? Am I to wear this noose of Kabul around my neck till death? Humayun could see the gleaming jewel of a palace once again. *What mindless horror lies in this ocean of existence? War, deceit, wickedness? Is Prince Kamran destined to be the victim of his own Lucifer tricks? Am I possessed by this curse of forgiving again and again? What is this splinter of hope? Piercing always! Hurting and wounding. Does it ever die?* His thoughts were halting at the wind-blown steps under his feet, though he kept mounting to reach the gleaming facade. *My hunger, or is it a quest? My quest for truth. Have I found it? Is it hiding somewhere inside the tainted soul of my soul bride—* He was coming face-to-face with truth, beloved, *her*. As soon as he stumbled into the parlor, *truth* stood mocking him. Mah Chuchak was there, arrayed in the light of her beauty and diamonds, greeting him?

Truth was illusive and fleeting, much like the journeys in Humayun's head and on the roads. Truth had evaded him once again on his march from Zahak Bamain to Kabul. It was missing still, truth that is, as Humayun sat talking with his viziers under the shade of his open tent, embroidered with Zodiac signs, all bright and embellished. This imperial tent was pitched right in the middle of the encampment on the outskirts of Kabul. The encampment itself was flanked by a lovely garden called the Shuter garden. The emperor was not alone, a coterie of viziers around him were immersed deep in their pools of revelry and arguments. As was his wont, Humayun was crawling back into the shell of his solitude. But his thoughts were chasing the two camel-loads of books. Those camels had disappeared mysteriously down the Kipachak defile, during one skirmish on their journey toward Kabul. Wearied of lamenting the loss of those books, Humayun's thoughts were now commencing another chase. This chase was after Nesib, the emperor's trusted messenger to Prince Kamran. The emperor had sent a letter to his brother, offering him the choice of a peaceful surrender before waging a war. Nesib was instructed to bring back a message from Prince Kamran, and had not yet returned. Wearied of this wait too, Humayun's eyes were getting heavy and opiate.

The journey from Zahak Bamain toward Kabul had a propitious beginning. Some conjecturing, *blessed by the giant Buddhas carved on the rocks on the northwest of Kabul.* Haram Begum herself, in the manner of a Steppe Queen, had brought her army of ten thousand men and horse to join with the emperor's. Haram Begum had then returned to Badakhshan, and the imperial cavalcade had turned toward the Hindu Kush range, marching through Penjeshir into the valleys of Ashterkeram. Upon reaching Anderab, Prince Hindal from Kunduz had joined the emperor with his own contingent of troops. They had chosen Kipachak defile as their night encampment, and Humayun had ordered a sumptuous feast to welcome his brother. Sated with drink and feasting, the night guards had neglected to keep a watch, and the encampment was raided by a group of marauders. That's when the two camel-loads of books had disappeared, and Humayun had stayed inconsolable for weeks. Kipachak defile was also the place where Humayun had had his soldiers take the oaths of fidelity to the emperor. In return, he had taken an oath himself, that he would honor the wisdom and advice of his generals, with the intent of insuring their safety and comfort.

A just punishment would be meted out to Prince Kamran by the common vote and consent of the generals. Humayun had promised, and now this memory of a promise was raging inside him like wildfire. Some sort of fever was rising to his head under his gold helmet. He could feel it, as he sat there oblivious to the arguments of his viziers. The victory was within his reach since he had returned to Kabul, but he was delaying attack since his stoic resolve to punish his brother was shattering. He knew that his viziers would choose no other punishment but death-sentence for Prince Kamran, and he couldn't even endure the thought of such a tragedy. He was hoping and praying that his wicked brother would contrive escape, so that he himself could be spared from being the instrument of his brother's death. Overwhelmed by the deluge of agony within his soul, he had construed this last piece of warning to his brother.

O my unkind brother, what are you doing? For every murder that is committed on either side, you will have to answer on the Day of Judgment. Come, and make peace, that mankind may no longer be oppressed by our quarrels— Humayun's solitary thoughts had come to one lurching halt, as the shadow of reality and illusion met his gaze like a shuddering mirage.

The lost camels with loads of books had returned, too real to be dismissed as the phantoms of imagination. Humayun's eyes were kindling to starry brilliance, as if he had recovered his treasures from the very caskets of heavens. One young groom was materializing before the camels, whom the emperor had neglected to see. He was racing toward the Zodiac tent, bowing double as soon as he reached closer.

"Your Majesty, these camels just strayed into our camp? The same loads of books. How they got here, I don't know. Allah's will?" The groom's own joy was doubled by the beacons of light in the emperor's eyes.

"Thank God, the treasure which cannot be got again is safe! Other things are easy to obtain." Humayun sang exultantly. "Let every man take what booty he can find? These books are my share! Open one trunk, my worthy messenger, and fetch the emperor a few books. The eyes of my soul have longed for such treasures."

"Is this the time for books, Your Majesty?" Khwaja Khizr dared caution. "We should be making ready to conquer Kabul? To liberate Prince Akbar from the tyranny of his uncle! Enough time after the victory for such indulgence?"

"The emperor has yet to accustom himself to these cinders of bold advice and argument." Humayun murmured to himself, his gaze wistfully fixed to the groom.

"Your Majesty. The oath that we all took—" Another voice, slippery with complaint was sliding off Humayun's awareness.

"Your Majesty. Didn't you promise you would respect our advice—" More voices were escaping the beehive of complaints, but Humayun was hugging the books after he had claimed them from the groom.

"And you promised, Your Majesty, that rebels and traitors, even if they be your kin, would be punished accordingly." This fresh reminder was grazing Humayun's awareness.

"The emperor is waiting a response from his traitor brother, as you all know?" Humayun let his gaze sweep over all with a cutting intensity. "As soon as he—" He was spared the need to explain, as a sudden commotion in the garden was revealing the object of his thoughts.

Nesib was scaling the lengths of the garden in quick strides, his shoulders stooping, as if he was carrying the load of some grievous burden. Edging closer, he fell into one lengthy curtsy, and then held out one scrap of a paper, the only response from Prince Kamran. Humayun claimed it rather impatiently, his eyes absorbing the rude scrawl with rage and despair.

He who would obtain sovereignty for his bride
Must woo her across the edge of a sharp sword

Prince Kamran had written this couplet in bold, careless strokes.

"Is this the only response from my traitor brother?" Humayun crumpled that piece of paper into a ball, his eyes flashing bolts of lightning.

"Keracha Beg was with Prince Kamran when he wrote that couplet, Your Majesty." Nesib's eyes were lit with the anticipation of war and vengeance. "*I would rather die than leave Kabul into the hands of the emperor. Keracha Beg told Prince Kamran, raising a loud cry. My head or Kabul.*"

"Keracha's head! And the body and soul of Kabul? The emperor will claim all." Humayun thundered, as if the spirit of his father Babur was speaking through his lips. "Shatter the citadel to pieces if you have to, but enter you must! To war, to war." He stormed out into the open, the exultant viziers following him.

Humayun, at the head of his left wing, was shouting commands and fighting valiantly. The sun in its blaze of fury was lowering down the edicts of death and bloodshed, it seemed. The undisciplined horde of Prince Kamran's army was lost in a whirlwind of chaos and bewilderment. Being hacked to pieces by naked swords, or blown away much like the corn-husks amidst the clamor and clanging of sabers and scimitars. In the background the cannons were booming, raining down muskets and cannon-balls. The blaring of drums and trumpets were muffling the cries of the wounded and the dying. Prince Kamran's followers were fleeing pell-mell, but he himself was defending himself most splendidly. Prince Askeri could be seen charging right and left, madly and desperately. But soon he was seized by the imperialists and hauled on to one mount, chained and shackled. Prince Kamran, noticing his brother's capture, had taken flight. Galloping full-speed past his followers and disappearing down the wild terrains, as if swallowed by earth. Keracha Beg, left alone to fend for himself was charging headlong to challenge the emperor. But before he could reach closer, a musket-shot hit him in the chest, and he was unhorsed. Splattered with mud and blood, his curses and groans were the loudest amidst the throes of his death.

The war had ended! Much too swiftly than anticipated. The cannons were silent. *The standards of victory fluttering mournfully over the corpses of the slain and the dying*, Humayun was thinking. He was in some sort of daze, still astride, inert and pensive. The songs of victory not reaching his awareness, only the reek of death and devastation! The notes of jubilations from drums and trumpets were skirling high, as if to drown the groans of the dying and the vanquished. The infantry, not far from the palace gates, could be seen dancing their way to the citadel. Humayun was escaping his brief spell of daze and inertia, and espying Kambar Ali with a sudden jolt of awareness. Kambar Ali, while cradling a severed head in one arm, was spurring his horse madly to reach the emperor. Humayun blinked away his disgust as he recognized the head of Keracha Beg.

This trophy of war, ugly as doom! It could adorn Kambar Ali's head with the laurels of victory, while it is still on his shoulders. One giddy thought in Humayun's head was choked to silence, his eyes piercing the soul of his general.

Without a word, and smiling ruefully, Humayun spurred his horse, his very heart racing toward the palace gates. His heart was fluttering and expanding. Struggling to be free to embrace the earth and the heavens. But the ache and longing in it were to hold his son to his breast, and to never let him go. The palace gates were flung open, teeming with guards and soldiers, and even before Humayun could dismount, Prince Akbar was seen racing past the fountains and terraces to reach the emperor. This princely sprite, garbed carelessly in pale silks, was followed by Hasan Akhteh. Hasan Akhteh was pleading with the prince, shooting words of caution and warning, but the sprightful prince was not heeding. He was swept into the loving arms of the emperor, flushed and breathless.

"The emperor will never leave you behind, not ever!" Humayun released him from his tight embrace, gazing into his eyes. "The ripe spring of sixteen is dancing in your eyes, and you are only ten. Don't climb the rungs of seasons too fast, my Prince." He was becoming aware of the intrusion of one soldier.

"Your Majesty. Prince Kamran has escaped. We went after him, but he just vanished?" The soldier was suspended half way amidst his curtsy, as if bending double under the weight of mystery and disbelief.

"Maybe, the goblins of the valleys have swallowed him alive?" A sigh of relief and giddiness escaped Humayun's lips. "Leave the wretched prince alone, he can't go too far." He intoned evasively.

"Your Majesty." Kambar Ali materialized from behind, still holding the severed head most possessively. "Should we go searching for Prince Kamran?"

"The emperor has a better diversion for you, my valiant General." One snort of mirth escaped Humayun's lips. "Impale the head of Keracha Beg on the Iron Gate of Kabul. And don't forget to write the inscription under it, *my head and Kabul*, and his name of course."

Humayun's command was swallowed by a tide of billowing mirth from the lips of the soldiers assembled there. Some were there to demand the head of prince Kamran, but amidst this roaring sea of mirth, they had forgotten their demands. All were scuttling back jauntily to display the head of Keracha beg on the Iron Gate. Humayun, after spilling more commands as to escorting ladies from their encampment to palace halls, had linked his arm with Prince Akbar, making him walk beside him. Both were drifting closer to the gleaming facade in red sandstone, both quiet, both inhaling the scent of nearness.

"Your mamma will smother you with tears and kisses, my heedless Prince! Want to go hunting before she arrives?" Humayun teased. His laughter trailing behind as he was swept into the arms of his aunts at the very doors of his palace.

Chapter Twenty
Death of Prince Hindal

The scent of home and Kabul was wafting forth from Humayun's very thoughts as he sat at his desk copying memoirs from the entries in his journal. He had chosen this rose and ivory bedroom of his father as his solitary retreat, so that he could admire the glory of spring in the garden below, when tired of scanning and recording dull or happy events in succession. Seated by the window, he had succeeded in doing both this particular evening, accomplishing more than what he had anticipated. But he was still writing feverishly, aware of the tinkling of mirth and low whispers from the adjacent dressing-room, all screened with silk and damask. Behind this screen, Mah Chuchak was getting dressed, assisted by Mahum Anaga, in anticipation of the evening feast arranged solely by the emperor. It had almost been a year since the victory of Kabul, and the ladies of the harem had seen no feasting or entertainment inside the palace, since the emperor had been busy chasing his brother, or quelling rebellions. But a few weeks ago, Humayun had announced that he would arrange a grand feast in the Audience Hall, distributing rich and precious gifts to all the Begums, including guests and friends. In honor of this feasting, he himself was appareled in royal blue silks, the large sapphire in his turban glinting commands, and the jeweled cummerbund at his waist the envy of the kings.

These celebrations were also in honor of two royal princes, who were born in Kabul five months after the swift victory. One son was born to Khawish Agha, and Humayun had named him Ibrahim Sultan, meaning, a wise ruler. Farrukh Tal was the name given to the son of Mah Chuchak, meaning precisely, the harbinger of good news. Such news was recorded in Humayun's memoirs earlier, along with the news of seditions and rebellions. And now his pen was following the trails of his ambitious brothers. Prince Askeri was branded with a death sentence by the unanimous votes of the jurists and the generals. But Humayun had contrived to over-rule that sentence, banishing him from Kabul, and packing him off to a pilgrimage in Mecca. Prince Kamran fleeing to Deh-Afghanan was reported to have shaved his head and beard, living the life of a Kalendar. But that was only a disguise. He had escaped to Laghman, gaining support from the chief of Mandrawer. A flood of conflicting reports were reaching Kabul, one of them of dire consequences that he had collected a force of fifteen thousand men with the intention of attacking Kabul.

An expedition was led against Prince Kamran, but he had fled again. This time getting lost into the valleys of Alankar and Alishang! The imperialists, after returning to Kabul, had learnt that Prince Kamran was seen plundering the eastern territories of Kabul, after gaining support from two warring Afghans by the names of Dund Zai and Khalil Mehmend. Humayun himself had headed the next expedition, but Prince Kamran slippery as an eel had escaped, fleeing toward Peshawar. Before returning to Kabul, Humayun had visited Biram Khan in Kandahar, telling him that he would not go in pursuit of Prince Kamran until he appeared at the very gates of Kabul.

Paradoxically, Humayun's resolve to capture Prince Kamran was splintered with a sense of fear and despair. He was afraid that if he was captured, he would face the same fate as Prince Askeri's and this time the emperor would not be able to mitigate his sentence, or to send him on a pilgrimage to Mecca. After returning to Kabul, Humayun had bestowed the kingdoms of Gorduz, Lahger and Bangash on Prince Hindal, in addition to his kingdom of Ghazni. Mir Birkeh was made the ruler of Kunduz. And Khwaja Khizr was to rule the territories of Jui-Shahi.

Greed and ambition! Treason and disloyalty. Humayun's thoughts were bouncing off the page, and straggling into realms deeper than his psyche. They were loaded with rumors from Hind, of utter chaos and confusion, and seething with appeals to the emperor to reclaim his empire before it crumbles to dust. *Do I have the power to shake this horde of humanity out of utter chaos, and pound some sense of dignity into their heads, aiming to nurture some sort of civilization equipped with noble actions and inspirations?* He replaced his pen in the jeweled inkpot wearily. His thoughts were returning to Kabul.

In some mad moment of rage and jealousy, suspecting Mah Chuchak of indiscretions, Humayun had written to Haram Begum, suing once again for the hand of her daughter in marriage. She had consented, responding in most warming tones, and inviting him to

Badakhshan. Mah Chuchak had got hold of that letter, and her fits of jealousies along with his own vacillating thoughts splintered with the burdens of court intrigues, had made him abandon this idea of marriage and alliance. But Mah Chuchak had not forgotten, and he didn't know that she was keeping that letter concealed in her bosom at all hours of the day, each day in succession, to mock his confessions of love which were forever blistering even amidst his moods of rage and jealousy. Had he known that as he sat there brooding, he would have plucked the wound of jealousy out of his heart, hugging only the laceration of love inside his soul. Right now, his heart was longing for rest, in stark contrast to his thoughts restless and gallivanting. They were sedition-bound, mutilating the Zodiac signs on his tent and bellowing, *it was time that he plucked real stars from the sky, bringing heavens to earth to suit his needs and longings.*

Humayun's thoughts smitten gold with the glitter of pride, were bending low to scoop the dust of humility, but the rustle of silks behind him were distracting him from the privilege of this noble task. Tinkling of mirth, followed by the rustle of silks had made him swing his chair around, his gaze making both Mahum Anaga and Mah Chuchak captive. His heart was smitten afresh it seemed, by the dazzling apparition as his beloved. Arrayed in billowing silks the color of rubies, Mah Chuchak looked like the goddess of fire and light. Rubies and diamonds dripping from her hair down to her throat and around her tiny waist in bright sash were holding her in abeyance, ethereal and sparkling. The blue stars in her eyes and the fire of rubies on her lips were throbbing, yet she was arrested alive in the mold of ivory and sunset.

"Mah Chuchak Begum will be the envy of all the queens this evening, Your Majesty. Especially, Miryam Makani—" Maham Anaga was curtsying, murmuring, fleeing, all unnoticed by Humayun.

"Your Majesty, am I turned to Medusa, that you sit there mute and chilled?" Mah Chuchak dipped her head in curtsy, smiling to herself.

"Quite the contrary, my love." The flames of music and poetry in Humayun's soul were uncurling the tongues of fire. "You look like the goddess of lust, fire and light. A goddess who has the power to seduce all innocent men, robbing them of their wit and

sanity, their hearts slain by the diamond-daggers in her eyes alone."
He laughed, getting to his feet dreamily.

"Innocent men, Your Majesty! If I could only seduce you into believing in my innocence?" The stars of mockery in Mah Chuchak's eyes were vivid and sparkling. "And yet, I have failed to wound your heart."

"You have wounded it a thousand times more than you could ever recall, my Temptress." Humayun drifted towards her, crushing her in one violent embrace. "My heart, with tears of blood in its eyes, longing for you, always."

"I had hoped you would forgive me, as you do your brothers, Your Majesty?" Mah Chuchak's eyes were breathing fire and challenge. "Why do you hate me?"

"Hate you?" Humayun stood by the window, his hands knotted behind his back. "I love you more than my life! This pain, this agony! This accursed love. And yet, you are dearer to me than my pain and suffering, my dearest! You have blessed me with sons. Gentle boons amidst harsh climes. Lending me the power to conspire with fates, if not challenge them. Feeding me with the morsels of hope, to seek fortunes, to conquer Hind?"

"To seek a bride in Badakhshan, Your Majesty?" Mah Chuchak murmured.

"A bride?" Humayun whirled back on his feet as if stung.

"Yes, Your Majesty, a bride!" Mah Chuchak whipped out the letter from her bosom, holding it out to him. "Read it, Your Majesty, it will refresh your memory."

"A scented gift, I am sure." Humayun claimed it laughingly. "This is Haram Begum's handwriting, no doubt about it." His lips were uttering the words he had erased from his memory. "*Your Majesty, I am your slave and Mirza Suleiman is your slave. Thus my son and daughter are the offspring of your slaves. We happen to be near the Uzbeks and command some respect. You are a great king. If you want to marry my daughter, please come over from the hills of Hindu Kush, accompanied by the Begums and Emirs of Kabul. I will arrange to provide every one of them a good Badakhshani horse. Silks and jewels too as gifts. I will give my daughter in marriage to you, which will be a source of honor to us. And the enemies, who are near us, will know that you have done us this favor.*" He tore this letter into bits under the spell of sudden rage and violence. "Her progeny of slaves! One is in Kabul, isn't he? Her son, Ibrahim Mirza? The emperor might raise him to the rank of a king by making him the bridegroom of our Princess Bakhshi Banu. Am I getting old?"

"Your Majesty!" Mah Chuchak's protest was silenced, as Humayun dropped one little piece of the letter into the snow-valley of her bosom. "My token of love, my jealous beauty. If the Begums were not expecting us at the feasting this evening, I would prove my love by swallowing you whole, mockery and sweetness all." He held her by the waist rather savagely. "And yet, if the emperor could wear his heart in his head long enough, he would succeed in conquering Hind and the heart of the heavens." He whirled her out toward the gleaming staircase.

"Your Majesty, I am feeling giddy." Mah Chuchak protested.

"You should be feeling guilty, not giddy!" Humayun declared heedlessly. "When did you steal that letter? No, don't answer me, my raging Queen. Next time I lose something, I would be longing to search it inside the deep valleys of your body and soul." He released her laughingly, marching straight toward the Audience Hall.

Mirth and music were filling Audience Hall with the scent and color of festivity. The scent of joy was in the eyes of the Begums, the wealth of jewels on their royal persons adding their glee and sparkle. And the color was a profusion of wealth in gold friezes and crimson awnings. Gold and silver candelabras and Persian carpets in arabesque glory were lending warmth and welcome to guests and friends, who could be seen drinking and gormandizing without restraint. Humayun, seated amongst his courtiers, was indulging in his all-time love for philosophy and astronomy, but his gaze as well as his thoughts now and then, were shifting to his wives and children.

The entire brood of royal household had gathered here this evening inside the Audience Hall, with the addition of viziers and courtiers. Hamida Banu, the reigning queen, had gathered all the wives of the emperor under her shining wings. Bega Jan, Khawish Agha, Shaham Agacha, even Mah Chuchak, seemed to be subjected under her bright rule. The widows of the emperor's father, Dildar Begum and Bibi Mubaraka Begum, along with the late emperor's concubines, Gulnar Agacha and Nurgul Agacha, had formed their own circle close to the great pillars decked with ivy and pine cones, all painted gold and silver. Sarvaqad with her husband Monaim Khan were seated next to Prince Hindal and his wife Sultanum Begum. Princess Ruqeiqa, the daughter of Prince Hindal, was playing cards with Princess Bakhshi Banu and Princess Bihar Banu. Prince Akbar, restless as ever, could be seen sampling food from the tables laden with mounds of delicacies fit for a wedding feast. Fish and venison cutlets, shami kabobs, mutton korma, nargasi koftas, curried salmon, and the steaming platters of chicken biryani, just to name a few, were enough to tempt even a saint to gluttony. More than fifty varieties of desserts embellished with beaten-thin layers of gold and silver, had been the favorite of the younger princes and princess'.

Betrothals must join hands with festivities this evening, to invite happy fates to this sumptuous feast. Humayun's gaze and palate, sated with all food, were concocting fresh delicacies to whet the appetite of his decisions. *Yes, Prince Akbar should be betrothed to Princess Ruqeiqa! And the handsome son of Haram Begum, is he worthy to be the husband of my Princess, Bakhshi Banu?* His gaze was sweeping over all in search of Ibrahim Mirza. But, it was greeting Biram Khan, who was weaving his way toward him.

"Your Majesty. I was thinking we should take Prince Akbar with us on our march to Hind. He is—" Biram Khan's happy thoughts were swallowed by an abrupt volley of mirth on Humayun's lips.

"He is ready to be wedded to war, if that's what you mean?" Humayun declared poetically. "Old enough to take war as his bride. And young enough to be wedded to a princess of royal beauty? How happily you presume, Biram, have I voiced my decision to march to Hind?"

"Your royal brow is witness to such a decision, Your Majesty." Was Biram Khan's blithering response.

"The more a fool the emperor then to wear such decision on his brow!" Humayun quipped. "Before the emperor's decision falls into the scale of indecisions, Biram, feed him with the gist of insurrections clawing at the heart of Hind?"

"Such a gist may attain the length of a large book, Your Majesty? Yet, I can abridge the bare facts to suit the emperor's taste." Biram Khan smiled enigmatically. "Sher Shah Suri, as he styled himself to be, is remembered as a tyrant. His reign lasted, Your Majesty, only five years, two months and thirteen days. He died in the year fifteen hundred and forty-five, just to refresh my own memory."

"Your brevity kills my agog, Biram." Humayun flashed him a quizzical look, brimming with sarcasm. "I would rather that you roll those nine years from the time of my exile *then* into a cannon-ball, and shoot it right into the eyes of *now*, which of course brings us to the present time of the year of fifteen hundred and fifty-four."

"I could skip, jump and leap over the years, Your Majesty, but I would stumble for sure." Biram Khan began with a dint of hilarity. "Pleading for your patience most humbly." He added, noticing the smoldering of impatience in the emperor's eyes. "After Sher Khan's death, his son Jalal Khan came into power, adopting the title of Aslam Shah. He died in the year fifteen hundred and fifty-three, but his tyrannies had resulted in a wildfire of rebellions from the borders of Doab to Punjab, reaching as far as Malwa and Bengal. Now Sher Khan's nephew is trying his luck in ruling and subjugating. His name is Mubraiz Khan and he has assumed the title of Adil Shah. Surrounded by rebellions, he is holding on to only a few provinces east of the Ganges. Amongst the warring factions of the Rajas and the Afghans, Sultan Ibrahim Sur has taken Doab and Delhi. Sikander Shah has claimed Punjab. Mahmud Shah Sur has declared Bengal as an independent state, belonging to him alone. Daulat Khan's hold over Malwa is weak and precarious—" He paused. "Now is the time to march, Your Majesty, to dissolve all those factions into one united whole."

"A great task for the astrologers to boost my decision with the seal of a noble prophecy." Humayun demurred cheerfully. "For right now, my good vizier, summon the gift-bearers. The emperor is in a generous mood this evening." He commanded.

In a flash, the servants in liveries of gold, carrying silver trays laden with jewels, were flooding into the Audience Hall. Eleven plates in all, each gleaming with its heap of selected gems in jade, opal, topaz, pearl, ruby, diamond, emerald, sapphire, carnelian, lapis lazuli, mother-of-pearl, were presented to Mah Chuchak alone. The other wives of the emperor were receiving equal share of gold and jewels amidst gasps of wonder and admiration, while Mah Chuchak could barely tear her gaze away from her gifts, seated there rapt and stunned. Gulbadan Begum, admiring her necklace of gold with dewdrop rubies and diamonds, was drifting toward the emperor, dreamlike.

"Your Majesty. This gift is much too precious. Words are too meager to offer thanks. Have never seen anything so beautiful as this before! So exquisite, so precious—" Gulbadan Begum could not continue, overwhelmed by gratitude.

"My dear Sister, you *are* precious!" Humayun intoned wistfully. "More precious to me than all the jewels on this earth or in the heavens! But the ones you are holding, I ordered from Persia, especially for you." He paused, noticing her pallor and dark circles under her eyes. "You are not ill, are you?"

"No, Your Majesty." Gulbadan Begum's eyes were lit up with a radiant smile. "Haven't slept for two nights, it seems. Saadat Yar, how I have spoiled him since he is my one and only son! A little fever and he doesn't want me to leave his side?"

"My brave, little Sister." Humayun teased brightly. "Bibi Fatima is good in tackling the selfish vein of the spoiled princes. She should be his night watch? Our good physician, Sayed Rafiaeddin, was he not appointed to watch over both Prince Farrukh Tal and Prince Saadat Yar?" His gaze wandered away searchingly. Finding the good physician rolling in a fit of drunken mirth. "The *master of healing* is drinking himself to death." He commanded him to his presence.

"Your Majesty." Sayed Rafiaeddin curtsied, flushed with drink and merriment.

"Are you taking good care of Prince Farrukh Tal?" Humayun asked not-too gently.

"The prince is improving, little by little, Your Majesty." Was Sayed Rafiaddin's flustered response against the piercing intensity in the emperor's gaze.

"Is that all you have to say?" Humayun prodded harshly. "Have you been tending to the needs of Prince Saadat Yar as instructed? He needs devotion and company more than the bitter taste of medicines."

"Yes, Your Majesty. Three times a day, I check on him religiously." Was Sayed Rafiaddin's discomfited response.

"That's not enough. Look to his needs at all hours of the day or night, whenever he needs you. Especially, at night, if you can't concoct any potion to help him sleep." He waved dismissal, noticing the abrupt arrival of Khwaja Muazzam.

Gulbadan Begum was slipping away most discreetly, and Sayed Rafiaeddin was relieved to escape into the refuge of checking on his royal charges. Humayun had grown oblivious to all, his gaze riveted to this intruder who happened to be his brother-in-law, and whom he had not seen for months. His heart was thundering all of a sudden, spewing forth dark omens, as Khwaja Muazzam prostrated himself at his feet, unable to breathe even a greeting.

"What demons have been following you, Muazzam? Robbing you of voice and courage." Humayun asked kindly, in wild contrast to the violence inside his heart.

"Your Majesty." Khwaja Muazzam's eyes were lit up with fear and devotion. "Prince Kamran is in Jui-Shahi again. A large number of troops at his command, he is marching toward Khyber Pass, boasting to attack the citadel of Kabul."

"Oh, this vile fool of a brother!" One groan of an exclamation escaped Humayun's lips. "This serpent of evil and wickedness! This will be the last time my Lucifer brother dares challenge the emperor. Our soldiers who are ready to settle the dust of chaos and rebellion in Hind, will confront first the seed of wickedness and corruption in my brother, and this time he will not escape." He espied Biram Khan edging closer. "Command the battalions to prepare for a small skirmish, Biram, we march at dawn." He got to his feet wearily. "The emperor needs sleep in anticipation of a sumptuous feast at Delhi, someday?" He threaded his way out of the feasting hall into the cool comfort of silence and darkness all around.

"Your Majesty." Sayed Rafiaeddin followed the emperor on the terrace. "I went to check on the princes, Your Majesty. Prince Saadat Yar's fever is breaking. But, Prince Farrukh Tal—his breathing sounds dangerous."

"Danger will land right on your head, Sayed, if you don't find a medicine to ease his breathing." Humayun murmured than commanded.

Another dawn and Humayun could still smell the reek of evil and darkness, but it lasted for a moment. Now the morning was fresh and ominous as he rode ahead of his troops to chastise his wicked brother. The imperialists were riding through the wild steppes to enter into the valley of Surkhab where Prince Kamran and his troops were reported to be hiding in ambush. Prince Akbar, barely the sapling of twelve summers, was riding beside the emperor, a little soldier in golden cuirass and gold helmet. Prince Hindal was leading the right wing, and the left wing was entrusted to the command of Khwaja Khizr. Khwaja Muazzam was commanding the rear guard, while Biram Khan was at the head of the front battalion.

The red and yellow standards of the imperialists, fluttering in the wind, were lending no clue as to the whereabouts of Prince Kamran and his troops. The valleys of Surkhab and Jui-Shahi were left behind, but no trace of any encampment was to be detected anywhere. The ribbons of sunshine warming the hearts of the valleys were pouring no warmth into the hearts of the imperialists. They were feeling dejected, rather disappointed in not finding Prince Kamran. And suspecting that rumors concerning his ambush and intended assault had been false! Humayun himself was losing hope, his resolve to capture his brother, turning to dreams in conquering Hind. A small voice in his psyche was not letting him reach close to that dream. It was murmuring warnings. Swollen with the waters of tragedy and misfortune? Concealing and revealing the black face of fate, pregnant with torments stark and terrible. Yet, he was forcing his thoughts to the beauty of spring.

A blue bowl of sky lowering confetti of gold through the scintillating splendor of pines and cedars! The heart of the emperor was moved to awe and silence.

The mating of joy with nature! These newlyweds breeding abundance in life and love! The promise of peace and prosperity. Perfume and fecundity. Renewal and vivification. The awakening of hopes? Humayun's thoughts were heeding not the voice of his psyche, but he could feel the wealth of beauty and nature reflected inside his soul. *The soul of the world was within him, tinsel-awakening and mirrored vicissitudes. Voids and tragedies too. All remote, all fathomless. The light of clairvoyance dancing on the moonlit vistas of ether and nothingness. Life coiling inside the womb of death, and death uncoiling itself into a rainbow of seasons. The arms of fate were stretched out, lowering down the laurels of victory over the heart of Hind.* So profoundly immersed was Humayun inside the river of his visions that he had not even noticed that they had crossed the borders of Behshud and were entering the valley of Ningnahar. Suddenly, this valley was alive and throbbing before his sight, not by the virtue of its sheer beauty, but by the blaring of drums and trumpets.

The imperialists had espied the troops of Prince Kamran, weaving their way cautiously through the rugged terrains, and were galloping fast in that direction with cries of war and jubilation. Biram Khan had ordered the beating of drums and trumpets, and the imperialists were charging headlong to cut the enemy to pieces. The Judgment Day had arrived, it seemed. The clanging of swords and daggers! The booming of cannon and musketry. Prince Kamran's soldiers were falling like flies, wounded and groaning. Trampling over the rubble of the slain and the dying, the imperialists were racing after the cowardly and the fleeing. Prince Akbar, beside Humayun, could be seen fighting valiantly, rather blindly and fiercely. His jeweled sword so fast and unerring that it could barely be seen, but by the blaze of jewels in its acrobatic magnificence. This scene on the field of combat was rolling like an ocean of vengeance. Vast and crimson! Deep and awful. Awesome and mysterious. But there was no mystery in the fact that the imperialists had won. The enemy was fleeing, and Prince Kamran was nowhere to be seen. This Judgment Day had lasted but a few minutes short of one hour. A selected body of the imperialists were sent racing after the fugitives, while Humayun had decided to camp at Orange Garden, awaiting the arrest of his brother who had escaped once again.

The silk city as Moghul encampment was gathering a ripple of colors from the dusk, overshadowing the dusk-gloom of Orange Garden. The red hot disk of the Sun was already dipping in the west, but none of the parties in pursuit of Prince Kamran had returned, making each throb of time dissolve into anguished silence for the ones longing for the edicts of death and vengeance. But Humayun seated in his tent of Zodiac signs was gilding these hours of wait with gifts and compliments to his viziers and generals, whose valor and prowess had crowned this day with the laurels of victory. His joy and gratitude were genuine, and pride too, for Prince Akbar, whose very first battle in life had rewarded him with the boon of victory. While the emperor sat bestowing gifts and divining fates from the Zodiac signs above him, the clusters of stars out there were creating their own divinations, of which he had no knowledge. One reed of knowledge itself, as if erupting forth from the yawning abyss in his psyche, was making Humayun aware of something he had neglected to notice amidst the sea of victory in waves upon waves of cheers and jubilations.

"Where is Prince Hindal?" Was Humayun's abrupt inquiry, his gaze sweeping over all with a searching intensity. "I have not seen him since—did he come with us to Orange Garden?"

One moment of charged silence, and then the voices of the viziers were spluttering forth in half recollections, without the anchor of any solid information.

"Your Majesty. He was seen fighting side-by-side with the front battalion. I am sure I saw him."

"I watched him dealing a severe blow to one impudent soldier with his saber, Your Majesty. Then galloping away to deal with the other one."

"Many a foe was slain and unhorsed by him, Your Majesty, just before the enemy started to flee and dissemble."

"Your Majesty." Prince Akbar requested. "May I go and look for my uncle?"

"Keep your peace, my valorous Prince. You will not be permitted to ride out at night, no matter how much you wish or plead?" Humayun commanded him, his gaze turning to Abdal Wahab. "Go, look for Prince Hindal, Abdal, and bring him back with you if he is not sleeping?" His heart was carving omens dark and abysmal.

After Abdal Wahab had left, Humayun had grown silent and simmering. His heart was quiet now, rather heavy like a slab of ice, as if he had felt some stab of unvoiced sorrow, deep and nameless. The viziers sat murmuring amongst themselves, while Humayun had begun to pace in utter oblivion of his surroundings. Something inside him were sundering and expanding. Like the distant sound of a storm, approaching slowly, its lips tight and swollen, muffling the sounds of ruin and devastation. This inner storm was ebbing closer and closer, almost touching his heart, cracking open its slab of ice and entering its silence. The splitting and crackling of oceans deep in his psyche were churning foam and tempest. How long did he listen to that fathomless fury amidst his pacing, he had no recollection. *Only now when his thoughts had seen the face of Prince Hindal emerging forth white as foam from those volcanic deeps that he halted in his act of pacing.*

"I must go and fetch Prince Hindal myself." Humayun's voice sounded distant, as he stood demurring.

An abrupt flurry of noise, followed by racing footsteps, and Abdal Hai was stumbling into the tent, his wind-blown features dusted with sorrow.

"Your Majesty. Abdal Wahab—well—" Abdal Hai could not utter the words of doom and tragedy, his tongue stuck between his teeth.

"Where is Prince Hindal, and what about Abdal Wahab?" Humayun's sightless eyes were peering beyond Abdal Hai.

"Prince, I knew, Your Majesty. I was there when—" Abdal Hai began to weep silently and unashamedly.

"Where is Prince Hindal? O wretched man, why can't you speak?" Humayun demanded. Fire and recollection dissolving the veil of glaze before his eyes.

"Prince Hindal, Your Majesty. Slain. Prince Kamran's soldier, one Afghan, Tirenda—" Abdal Hai sucked in his tears, his thoughts still dazed and incoherent. "His body, Khwaja Ibrahim found. Covered it. He sent me. Now, Abdal Wahab—" He could not continue, as if scorched by the light of agony in the emperor's eyes.

That light was veiled behind the closed shutters of the emperor's eyes. The whirlwind of grief and sorrow was hovering above him like the cloud of nemesis. He was slumping down on the floor in one solid heap, no word escaping the sea of his agony. His features were washed by the glow of white suffering. Much like a man, crushed by misfortunes countless. A man robbed of all hope! A man, wearing a brand of defeat inside the *hall of victory!*

Another dawn, another day! Fresh and innocent! Bloated with the flesh of grief and tragedies this day of sorrow and hunting once again the viands in misfortunes with the shafts of sunshine, Humayun had thought. But Humayun, riding back to Kabul this sepulchral afternoon, was unaware of the silence and mourning in his heart and inside the hearts of his soldiers. The emperor had died last night, and had risen this morning from the Underworld of grief and torture. More like a living corpse, he was mounted ramrod on his Arabian steed, only his gaze feverish. Biram Khan was riding behind the emperor, as if guarding the dead body of Prince Hindal on the mount beside his, driven by a young rider. This royal cavalcade slithering back to Kabul was a mournful procession, and the veil of mourning in Humayun's heart was fluttering all of a sudden to reveal the horror of last night's tragedy.

Prince Hindal's body was brought to Orange Garden, wrapped in the shroud of many a woeful tales, which had scorched the emperor's heart with the brand of inevitability. After the victory while the emperor had decided to spend the night in Orange Garden, Prince Hindal had stayed close to the battleground in the valley of Ningnahar. He had had his tent pitched there not too far, telling his generals that he was anxious to wait for the return of his men who had gone in pursuit of Prince Kamran. Prince Kamran, it was discovered later, had not left the battlefield, but had concealed himself under the heap of corpses. At night, when all were quiet, he was able to heave himself out of this rubble of death and doom, more dead than alive. Noticing with sudden horror against the brightness of full moon that more corpses were getting to their feet, no other than his own soldiers. Probably, pretending death to save their lives during the maddening assault of the imperialists. He was quick to grab hold of this chilling, stunning revelation, standing there numb and speechless. One of his soldiers by the name of Afghan Tirenda recognizing his master was seized with mad elation akin to dementia.

"Let's go and slay the imperialists in their sleep!" One gurgle of a war cry with all its demented mirth from the lips of Afghan Tirenda had pierced the heart of the silence. He was racing toward the nearest encampment, followed by others.

The nearest encampment was of Prince Hindal's, the mood over there of joy and merriment, his soldiers drunk with the wine of victory and from the gold flagons. Prince Hindal was seated in his tent, along with a few of his chosen friends, amongst them his devoted friend Khwaja Ibrahim. Suddenly, he had heard the voice of his servant crying for help outside his tent, and had rushed out bare-headed. In a flash, one heavy blow had landed on Prince Hindal's head, leaving a deep cleft there from ear to ear, and he had died without even uttering a sound. The blow was from the sword of Afghan Tirenda. He had quickly snatched Prince Hindal's ornamental quiver bulging with arrows, and had fled, accompanied by his mad followers. By the time Khwaja Ibrahim and the other soldiers had emerged forth, the assailants had disappeared like the phantoms of the night. Khwaja Ibrahim and the rest of the soldiers were so stunned that they could not even speak, save alone ride after the murderers. Later, when the veil of shock had been torn asunder by the pincers of grief that the soldiers were dispatched after the assassins, returning only with the rags of reports with no clue as to the hideout of the fugitives. Afghan Tirenda, it was reported, had taken the quiver of Prince Hindal to Prince Kamran, boasting of killing, though knowing not whom he had killed. Prince Kamran had recognized the royal insignia on the ornamental quiver of his brother, and had burst out lamenting.

You have killed my brother! My gentle lamb, my sweet Hindal— Prince Kamran had dashed his gold helmet on the ground with the fury of a madman.

The parade of such raw, tragic events in Humayun's head was jolting his grief to awakening. His heart itself was voicing its vow of vengeance that it would make Prince Kamran pay the price of Prince Hindal's life with his own blood. The glacier of ice inside him was breaking, gliding down the very pit of his stomach in the manner of one terrible avalanche. Crackling shut the pores of his mute agony, and whirling his black despair into the fires of hell and damnation.

I will kill Prince Kamran! The mindless fury in Humayun's head was hugging the flames of hatred. *But, he is your brother?*

Humayun was becoming aware of the familiar palace grounds leading toward his palace, his gaze shooting accusations at the cold, bright stars so defiantly alive and twinkling. Inside the frozen sea of his black ruminations, he had not even noticed that it was evening and that they had arrived in Kabul. Along with this awareness, was unleashed a murmur of threats voiced by his generals after Prince Hindal's body was brought to Orange Garden.

We will impale Prince Kamran alive on the very gates of Kabul. We will throw him into the pit of fire, bound and shackled. We will tear his body from limb to limb and feed it to the dogs. An imperceptible shudder was passing through Humayun's stiff frame at this recollection, his thoughts cowering behind the shroud of his love.

Hindal! The dearest, the most beloved. The soul of my soul. The most handsome. The most adorable! Humayun was galloping toward the palace, as if goaded by the very whip of agony and torment.

The mournful pines and mysterious cedars were plunged in utter darkness. No lamps were lit to greet the victorious army, and no trumpets sounding to announce the emperor's arrival. The entire palace seemed to be plunged deep in mourning, as if it had received the brand of tragedy. But how could anyone know about Prince Hindal's death since no messenger was sent to Kabul, Humayun's grief was murmuring as he stormed into the dimly-lit parlor, startling the Begums to their feet.

"All Kabul in mourning? How did you know?" Humayun murmured.

"Your Majesty. This morning, Prince Farrukh Tal died—" Gulbadan Begum offered distractedly, not even catching the drift of the emperor.

Another spear of agony was piercing Humayun's heart, his gaze searching the faces of the Begums, ravaged with grief and weeping. He had not even noticed that Biram Khan had brought the body of Prince Hindal, lowering it gently on the davenport. The Begums were drifting toward it under some spell of daze.

"So, sweet Hindal will comfort my son in his cold, small grave—" Humayun stood murmuring to himself, while Gulbadan Begum raised a heart-rending cry.

"What pitiless oppressor slew my harmless brother? Would to heaven that merciless sword had touched my eyes and heart, or Saadat Yar's or Khwaja Khizr's?" Gulbadan Begum was wringing her hands and pacing in circles, as if gone mad with grief. "Alas, a hundred regrets! Alas, a thousand times, alas. O well-a-day! O well-a-day! O well-a-day! My sun is sunk behind a cloud." A cry of nightingale was choked in Gulbadan Begum's throat, her head falling over the corpse of her brother.

Chapter Twenty-one
Back to Delhi of the Moghuls

One terrace of a balcony at the citadel of Kabul was holding Humayun captive in its welcoming embrace. He was watching his troops gather beyond the palace gates in neat files. The cerulean sky above with its pewter gleam was lowering shafts of warmth and sunshine, as if pouring strength into the hearts of the imperialists in their long campaign toward the warring cauldron of Hind. Six whole months of grief and mourning since Prince Hindal's death and this very day the emperor was all in readiness to march to Hind without any further delay. He had suffered terribly and was suffering still, his features attaining the gloss and transparency of molten wax. There were taut ridges around his lips, his beard and mustache half gray, and his nose jutting out prominently due to his lean, gaunt features. He had aged within these past few months, wearing the burden of half a century over his shoulders, though he was four years short of that noble mark in age and time. Time had weighed heavy on him, killing the passionate man within him, buried inside the vault of ice and silence. The lover in him was slain. The mystic assassinated. The husband exiled. And yet the veil of black despair over his soul had carved tiny slits in its fabric, lending a few chinks of light, through which he could see hope fraying into a scuff of hopelessness. And yet again, that light of hope inside him, no matter how small and suffering a million deaths could never die. Admiring the discipline of his soldiers this bright morning, he was slashing the soot of despair with the sharp-edged sword of memories.

Prince Hindal was buried beside his father in Aram Bagh at Shahi-Kabul, the little grave of Prince Farrukh Tal cradled in between them. Prince Kamran had fled as far as Indus, seeking help from Aslam Shah. Aslam Shah had given the fugitive prince asylum, granting him the gift of one thousand rupees. But this act of his generosity was tainted with contempt, as Aslam Shah had whispered to his vizier, *how can a man be helped who killed his own brother.* Prince Kamran, overhearing this remark, had left his

301

safe refuge, fearing evil and treachery. Wandering through the territories of Bhira and Koushab, he had reached Ghakker, finding asylum under the protection of Ahmed Sultan. Ahmed Sultan had received Prince Kamran courteously, granting comfort and protection to the harem of the prince inside his palace. But he had designs of handing him over to the emperor. Ahmed Sultan being the enemy of Aslam Shah craved the support of the emperor. He had sent the emperor a secret missive that Prince Kamran was his guest and prisoner, to be delivered into the emperor's hands as soon as the emperor came that way to reclaim his throne of Hind.

So, my wicked brother is enjoying life, while Hindal— A stab of pain pierced Humayun's icy indifference at such recollections, but he smothered it before it could flare into a conflagration of more pain. He was steering his thoughts toward those few moments in life which offer hope and sunshine amidst the seasons of despair and hopelessness. Prince Akbar was betrothed to Princess Ruqueiqa, and Princess Bakhshi Banu to Ibrahim Mirza, Humayun was thinking. His gaze was wandering aimlessly, fluttering over the silk standards in red and yellow, and then settling on the caparisoned horses. The soldiers in gleaming armor could be seen parading their graceful mounts, hugging their polished shields, the velvety quivers at their waists bulging with arrows. Suddenly, Humayun was feeling a *presence* beside him, that of his father, as if Babur was standing next to him, but his gaze was espying Prince Akbar amongst the disciplined flanks of his regiments. Prince Akbar was galloping around carefree, his laughter ringing loud and clear.

This is the laughter of my father? My son is laughing with Babur. A quick shudder shook Humayun's lean frame, his senses inhaling the scent of nostalgia.

The *presence* was gone, yet leaving behind a subtle perfume of hope and sunshine. Humayun could see the fall colors bleeding through the thin veins of leaves in shades citron and crimson, his heart aching all of a sudden. So, his spirit was not totally dead, one thought in his head was kindling the lamp of perceptions. It was bloated with the abscess of rage and hatred, smeared black with the dregs of ambition to conquer and subjugate. And yet this familiar ache inside him had nothing to do with conquests, it was looking into the eyes of death and tragedy. The colors of death were painted fresh on the face of fall. Ruin and devastation were etched bright in nature, and the pulse of time was humming the songs of decay and renewal. But his spirit was fluttering open its wings to life, soaring toward the light of love, and falling face down blinded and stricken. Now he knew the source of that sudden and familiar ache? He was marching to Hind, leaving behind his harem, his love and beloved. Was this truth? Yet truth was blackened, and he had no flint to kindle his lamp of perception. Sadness and blackness! This hopeless, helpless pain. The emperor was turning his back on the colors of fall and death, his feet guiding him down the steps, and his thoughts urging him to bid a quick farewell to his wives.

A spacious chamber dripping with lace and silks was the luxuriant abode, where the Begums had gathered to exchange a few farewell words with the emperor. Hamida Banu was distraught with fear and apprehension, rolling a rosary of prayers in her head for the safety of her son and the emperor. She had wept almost the entire night, but was now lolling against the crimson pillows in a state of inertia and self-surrender. Khawish Agha and Shaham Agacha were feeling sad, rather lonely, their eyes gathering tears at the mere thought of the emperor's march to Hind. The entire household was plunged in tears and sadness, it was obvious, but Mah Chuchak was the only one whose eyes had remained dry, gathering no mists of fear or sadness. This goddess of ice was seated on the davenport, talking with Bega Jan, her head seething with plans to reign over Kabul in the absence of the emperor.

"Only a small chunk of time to gather you all in one loving embrace, and then seek the rugged terrains as my bedfellows." Humayun held out his arms as he straggled into this room unannounced.

The Begums were leaping to their feet with cries of protests and warnings. All were sailing toward the emperor, while he stood there hugging and kissing, and murmuring endearments. The false notes of mirth and cheers were frolicking around, but this veil of deception was shattering. One bellow of a sob escaped Hamida Banu's lips, tears falling from her eyes in a torrent, as if her heart was breaking.

"Don't grieve, my Empress, the emperor is still alive." Humayun hugged her tightly, his gaze alighting on Mah Chuchak.

Humayun could feel his heart crackling into splinters of pain and grief, and he turned his back on all, lest he be thrown into the sea of his own agony and torment, wallowing in its deeps forever without any hope of release. But he could not leave, his heart churning and throbbing with volcanic hunger to absorb his beloved into the very corruption of his soul. Swinging back, as if pressed by madness, he snatched Mah Chuchak to himself. Crushing her lips with the violence of one lingering kiss, he held her captive. Tearing himself away, the emperor was fleeing, a convulsion of agony inside him scorching his very eyes before retreating to oblivion.

This sense of oblivion and journey in the emperor's head, in reality in time too, had lasted several weeks. This particular morning, the imperial cavalcade was entering the precincts of Pirhala, not far from Ghakker. Prince Akbar was riding beside the emperor, behind them the contingents of ten thousand horse and men, followed by camel- loads of artillery and cannonade. The first streaks of dawn, ruby-red and dappled with gold, were arresting the emperor's gaze, his heart a mirror of awe and silence. Reflected before his gaze was light and beauty, but his sight was piercing beyond this visible glory trembling on the verge of extinction. He had caught a glimpse of light in all its essence of truth and purity. A light which was not born out of the womb of lust in the night, but from the ether of mysteries unfolding inside the soul of the morning! But this glimpse of light and its essence, illusive and fleeting as always, were leaving his mind and heart, rendering them stunned and speechless. *How could darkness breed such light day after day*, one little flint of inquiry in Humayun's head was igniting wonder.

"You are more drawn toward nature than books, my warrior Prince!" Humayun demurred aloud. "Rather, you shun books, your tutors inform the emperor? And yet, nature itself is a book of knowledge. The literature of the seers and the mystics. Nature is the holy book of wisdom, but few benefit from it." He flashed him another quick glance, his heart tender and aching. "You must wear the noose of discipline, my Prince. No more running away from reading and writing. Without such skills, how would you rule, if the emperor was to—" He couldn't voice the prophecy of death throbbing inside his psyche like a canker old and familiar.

"A long and healthy life to you, Your Majesty, as mamma says!" Prince Akbar protested, divining the emperor's thoughts with his honed perspicacity, which he himself didn't know he possessed. "Pardon me for disobeying my tutors, Your Majesty, but they read to me anyway since I don't like to read. I don't forget a word once I hear it, and that is better than reading without remembering. All the words which they read to me, I still remember. The valleys and the mountain talk to me. I can even hear the wind telling me so many things. Can you hear it, Your Majesty?"

"A poet, for sure!" Humayun laughed. "Let me test your memory, my little diviner. You were not that little when we came to Kabul. Five year old and a prisoner of your wicked uncle. Do you remember that scene, and the words?"

"Yes, Your Majesty." Prince Akbar demurred. *"See, if he recognizes his mamma.* I could hear the Begums, but I ran straight to her? I remember Khazanda Begum, the Dear Lady, how she bathed and kissed me. *These are the very feet and hands of my dear brother, Babur.* She used to make me laugh, tickling my toes."

"You would not forget your betroth, my wise Prince, would you, on this journey long and arduous?" Humayun teased.

"No, Your Majesty." Was Prince Akbar's murmur of a response.

"You don't seem pleased with this engagement? Don't you like her?" Humayun prodded.

"She is very pretty, Your Majesty. Beautiful." Prince Akbar murmured again.

"Beauty is an illusion, my son, something worthy to be remembered." Humayun murmured back.

"Truth and purity too, Your Majesty—" Prince Akbar could feel the surge of his intellect racing past time and knowledge, but he seemed flustered.

"What wisdom escapes the lips of innocence and inexperience, my wise Prince, I wonder?" Humayun flashed him a searching look. "Yes, illusions all! Even the stars on the sky and the tongues of astronomy?" He seemed to be carried away by the flood of mysticism in his thoughts. "Such giddy fools we all are, deeming ourselves wise? This noble delusion, cherishing ignorance as the pearl of wisdom." He brought his horse to a sudden halt. "From here on, my poet Prince, we fly to Ghakker. And don't you lag behind." He spurred his horse abruptly.

The emperor had literally flown to Ghakker. Neither noticing his speed, nor any scenery on the way, only the racing of his heart inside the currents of pain and excitement. Precisely, at noon the little palace of Ahmed Sultan was in view and Humayun was greeted by the host in all manner of pomp and courtesy. Ahmed Sultan had prepared a great repast, but the emperor wished for bath and a siesta.

What he really wished for was solitude, and granted this luxury, he had immersed himself in scented bath, his thoughts still walking on hot coals to explore the depths of his love and hatred for this brother who had been the cause of many misfortunes. The most terrible of them all the death of Prince Hindal! While cooling his body of fever, his thoughts were vacillating. He could not even endure the thought of staining his hands with the blood of his brother, though Prince Kamran was condemned to die by the unanimous consent of his viziers. No siesta was possible as soon as he had dressed, for Prince Kamran had begun to send appeals of mercy to the emperor through the hands of his personal page, seeking audience and forgiveness.

No such appeals of Prince Kamran were granted fulfillment, for Humayun besieged by these missives had sent a note to Ahmed Sultan, commanding him to forbid Prince Kamran in sending any more requests. Amidst the ritual of his pacing in that guest-room, Humayun had felt like a prisoner himself, the victim of his own agony and madness. A man condemned to isolation by the vices of his pity and compassion? By the virtue of his need to forgive! By the burden of his obsession to love all his brothers, no matter how many heinous crimes they had committed, or were destined to commit. Against the hurricane of such tyranny and torment in thoughts, Humayun had joined Ahmed Sultan in his sumptuous dining room to do justice to his hospitality. Appareled in turquoise silks with ocher turban, his pallor was accentuated by such contrast in colors. Revealing surface calm and concealing the raging, churning fury of a tempest within, which could not be dispersed? The large opal in his turban was changing colors in conformity with the tides of storm and turbulence inside him, these colors sparkling in his gaze too as he sat conversing with his gracious host.

Humayun, seated by Ahmed Sultan, appeared to be sipping his wine tranquilly. His gaze was lingering over the plates of gold and silver, which the kind host had purchased in honor of this great feast to the emperor, as Ahmed Sultan had boasted, parading his newly acquired possessions with the pride of a rich lord. The feast was over, the air inside the dining room still heavy with the aroma of curried lamb and roasted mutton, besides many more exotic scents from other foods and incense. Now the cups of the guests and the viziers were sparkling with wine, as they sat drinking and laughing. Prince Akbar amongst them content in admiring the exquisite arrangements of fruits piled high on silver platters. Biram Khan seated by the window was drinking abstemiously, bathed in a flood of sunshine streaming through the Venetian lace on the rectangular windows. The friezes of silk adorning the walls and windows were reflecting their own colors on the lace-patterns of sunshine on the marble floor. Humayun was becoming aware of each tremor of shade and design in this room, sensing the presence of his father beside him once again. This feeling similar to the one he had experienced on the citadel of Kabul, while watching his troops. This Presence was speaking to him, repeating the words which Babur had uttered on his death-bed. *Do naught against thy brothers, even if they may deserve it.* Humayun's heart was thundering, but he was seeking the attention of Ahmed Sultan.

"How would you like to join the emperor in his campaign against the warring lords of Hind, my kind Host?" Humayun asked abruptly.

"I would feel honored to be a part of this worthy campaign, Your Majesty, but I have lost the privilege of accepting this generous offer." Ahmed Sultan smiled winsomely. "Recently, I signed a treaty with the Afghans that I would not meddle with their warfare amongst themselves or with the emperor, if I were to be left in peace, ruling my small kingdom of Ghakker?"

"Honesty and politics go not hand-in-hand, my gracious Host!" A volley of dry mirth escaped Humayun's lips. "If you had already not done this great service to the emperor of keeping his brother to be delivered into his hands, he would not have forgiven this indiscretion of yours in signing that treaty?"

"Your Majesty. Before we march to Hind, the fate of Prince Kamran needs to be decided." Biram Khan ventured forth, abandoning his seat at the window. "The viziers and generals are anxious to see the results of a just punishment?"

"A weighty decision, Biram, needs time and patience." Another volley of mirth escaped Humayun's pain and delirium.

"Prince Kamran is to die a wretched death!" Khwaja Khizr, taking advantage of the emperor's mirth, stabbed this comment at no one in particular. "The generals are ready to flay him alive as an offering to the conquest of Hind."

"He is to be sent on a pilgrimage, to Mecca, banished forever from Hind." Humayun's gaze was shooting a blaze of reproof at Khwaja Khizr, before turning to Biram Khan. "Make sure, Biram, that none of the punishments devised by the generals land on Prince Kamran, until the emperor commands."

"Before we started from Kabul, Your Majesty, and in your presence too, the mullahs and the viziers had issued a verdict of death for Prince Kamran." Haji Muhammed stumbled to his feet, his eyes lit up with the fire of vengeance. "The Law of Sharia itself pronouncing this judgment."

"Divine justice of God alone, my venerable Vizier, bestows life, or seals it with the edict of death!" One thunder of a parable from Humayun's psyche itself trembled upon his lips. "A royal brother, though evil and wicked, will not be subjected to death until the emperor commands, or if it is the Will of God?"

"This royal brother, Your Majesty, is more dangerous than an army equipped with muskets and cannonade." Abdal Hai murmured a challenge under his breath.

Humayun could smell the reek of hatred and defiance in this room. Of malevolence too, not against him, but against his wicked brother who had wrought countless tragedies from the fabric of his own tyrannies. More voices were humming the tunes of vengeance, and the emperor sat listening with a stoic resignation.

"Who was the author of that misfortune, Your Majesty, when you were wounded most treacherously?"

"Children murdered. Women dishonored. Men slaughtered like cattle. Our brave Chaghtai soldiers perishing by the deceit of Prince Kamran."

"Isn't he the murderer of Prince Hindal, conspiring with the Afghans and killing his own brother?"

"If left alive, he would contrive means to lay hurdles in our way, and our dream of conquering Hind would be lost?"

"Death is the only answer, Prince Kamran must die."

"Death to the traitor, death to the eternal foe of the emperor!"

"How can I stain my hands with the blood of my own brother?" Humayun silenced all protests with one thunder of an appeal. "Carrying the burden of this sin on my shoulders to conquer Hind? Though the emperor's mind inclines to your judgment, his heart does not. What punishment would appease your sense of right and vengeance?" His eyes were burning with the fever of a revelation. "Yes, blind him, but do not kill. Once robbed of his sight, he would pose no threat to our dreams or conquests. Blind Prince Kamran, that is the emperor's edict and decision, not to be questioned or revoked." The touch of finality in his voice was one agonized cry.

"If it pleases you, Your Majesty, permit me to lance the eyes of Prince Kamran right away, so that we could continue our march to Hind without delay?" Gholan Ali emerged forth from behind, pressed by his zeal to get done with this act of vengeance.

"Go, brave Fool!" Humayun waved consent. "Deliver this foul sentence to the unfortunate Prince, while his eyes are still blessed with the light of pain in living?"

Gholan Ali aimed for the door, as if carried by the breeze of exhilaration, leaving behind an ocean of gloom and silence. A little regret was creeping into Gholan Ali's head though that he was permitted only to draw blood from the eyes of the prince, not from his heart. Humayun's heart was bleeding, as if it was lanced by a myriad of arrows from the quivers of his own stealthy wounds, awakening with vengeful cries. Ahmed Sultan was watching the emperor under some spell of awe and wonder. The hush was splintering with low murmurs. These ripples of voices were dwindling again, as Gholan Ali returned, giddy with pride and excitement.

"I told Prince Kamran, Your Majesty, that the emperor has commanded me to lance his eyes." Gholan Ali gasped for breath, his voice choking with elation. "But the prince says, *kill me*? I told him, that none dare so far overpass His Majesty's orders to kill you." He bowed his head most humbly.

"Blind him this instant!" Humayun commanded under some spell of pain and delirium. "The emperor will witness this sad deed with his ears alone, next to the chamber of his unfortunate brother." He plodded away, his sight blinded by grief.

The emperor was pacing in this cage of a chamber next to Prince Kamran's room, like a wounded lion caught unawares in his jungle of freedom and madness. His senses stricken numb with pity and grief were straining to catch a sound from the torture-chamber of his brother. But no sounds were breaking the barriers of his agony, not even the sound of his mad, rhythmic pacing. So thick and deep were the mists of oblivion hovering over him, that he could not even hear the ecstatic cries of Gholan Ali who had struck lancet into the eyes of Prince Kamran more than fifty times, counting each stroke with gloating. But Prince Kamran had taken all with the valor worthy of a knight, neither cringing, not uttering a groan. That was when Gholan Ali had devised another means of torture, pouring lemon juice mixed with salt into the wounded eyes of the brave victim. And that was when Humayun was earthed to one spot in his act of pacing by one song of a prayer from the lips of Prince Kamran.

O, Lord, for the offenses which I have committed in this world! Surely, I have suffered retribution. I may now entertain hopes of my salvation.

Then, there was a hurricane of sobbing and lamentation, not from the lips of Prince Kamran, but from the lips of a Begum. *Probably, the wife of my suffered brother,* one cry of agony in Humayun's own soul was silenced.

Though a veil is drawn over the eye of my body
I see thee still with that inward eye
That so oft has pictured thy countenance

Prince Kamran's voice was ebbing forth, drugged with mystic ecstasy.

Clothed in the light of sorrow profound, Humayun had no recollection as to how and when he had arrived into the room of his brother. His first awareness was of noticing the wife of Prince Kamran, Chuchak Begum, her tear-streaked face ravaged with misery and hopelessness. But upon seeing his brother, a bloodied handkerchief over the eyes of the prince concealing his blindness, Humayun's veil of oblivion was torn to shreds. A deluge of tears breaking loose from the ocean of his suffering was stinging his eyes, as he stood there weeping and sobbing shamelessly. Prince Kamran was moved to mystic exaltation once again after catching this subtle whiff of awareness that the emperor was shedding tears of pain and regret.

The cowl of the solitary hermit is exalted to the skies
When the shadow of a monarch like thee falls upon it

Prince Kamran sang painfully, his mystical exaltation unfolding on the wings of another couplet, enhanced by the emperor's silence and sobbing.

Whatever falls on my soul from thee is subject of thanksgiving
Be it a shaft of ruin, or the dagger of tyranny

Prince Kamran's sightless eyes were peering into the abyss of his agony.

The emperor was sobbing uncontrollably now, numb and speechless with pity and grief. Prince Kamran struggled to his feet, letting loose a flood of bitter pleas.

"Your Majesty, you had granted me a million pardons before, I ask forgiveness once more. You were always too kind, granting me the choice of a pilgrimage to Mecca, for my sins countless, but I always evaded that privilege. Now permit me that kindness, to this lowly pilgrim on the dusty road to Mecca? Allow me to take my wife with me, if you could grant me that boon."

"Oh, Kamran, Kamran!" Humayun groaned aloud. "My dear, dear rebel of a brother." He folded his brother into one crushing embrace, anguish flooding through his eyes in a fresh torrent of grief.

Humayun had succeeded in banishing that grief, or he thought he did, before journeying from Ghakker on the road to conquest, where Hind lay smoldering in the fires of wars and intrigues. Prince Kamran was sent on a pilgrimage to Mecca, accompanied by his wife and two escorts, Beg Muluk and Chilmeh Koka. On his own campaign-pilgrimage to Hind, Humayun was possessed by the demons of his inner will, fashioning cannon-balls out of his silent torment, and shooting them at the enemy whoever dared block his advance. Three whole months of hardships and victories since their journey from Kabul, and the imperialists had become the masters of territories vast and fertile. Marching north of the Jud hills, clear across the Salt Range, they had crossed Indus unopposed. After crossing the rivers of Jehlum and Chenab, they had held the northern parts of the Punjab under their sway without even striking a single blow, overwhelming the enemy by the number of their troops and cannonade.

The victory in Punjab had resulted in gaining followers and alliances on the way, the number of soldiers in the imperial army almost swelling to double. Tartar Khan, upon learning about the advance of the imperialists had abandoned his fortress of the Rhotas, fleeing to Lahore. The imperialists had then taken the route of Kalinjar, its fertile lands fed by two rivers, Ravi and Beas. They had followed the terrains toward a junction where the road was forked into two different directions, one leading toward Delhi, and the other meandering its way toward Lahore. That was where the emperor had divided his troops, sending a contingent of troops to Delhi under the command of Biram Khan, and advising him to subjugate Jalandar and Sirhind on the way before marching to Delhi. He himself had headed toward Lahore with a formidable array of troops. Prince Akbar and Abul Maali were the emperor's inseparable companions, entering Lahore in a manner quite contrary to their expectations. Tartar Khan had fled, taking refuge in Machiwarah. And the denizens of Lahore had come out on the streets to welcome the emperor and his army with cheers of joy and applause. Humayun was overwhelmed with gratitude, though feeling lonely amidst this sea of cheers and jubilations. Not knowing that he was coming down with a fever. His plan to follow Biram Khan toward further conquests was postponed, for he was afflicted with fever and dyspepsia.

This particular afternoon, half recovered from his illness, Humayun had ventured out to inspect the royal encampment cradled inside the very heart of the city of Lahore. After taking a few rounds, he had installed himself on his throne under his Zodiac canopy, to receive his viziers and courtiers. Seven days of fever and delirium, followed by indigestion, had molded his features into such waxen pallor that he barely seemed to breathe. And yet the sparkle of gold in his eyes and the fire of rubies on his lips were lending his features the expression of victories gained and of tragedies suffered. The rivers of peace and vacuity were frozen solid within him, as if he was imprisoned alive inside the glacier of his loneliness. His heart was yearning for bliss and love, for truth and beloved. *The white mists in illusions swallowing both, dream bride and the soul bride.* He was sipping his wine, its taste dry and bitter, much like his thoughts, voicing one abrupt lament over the fates of his brothers. Prince Askeri, exiled to Mecca. Prince Kamran, a lone pilgrim on his way to Mecca. Prince Hindal, the blessed pilgrim to heavens. Sloughing off the burden of such wearied thoughts, Humayun's gaze was turning to Prince Akbar. Prince Akbar was absorbed in practicing archery with one young soldier, the circle of admirers around him laughing and applauding. Beyond the ripples of this mirth and applause was seen a lone rider, galloping full-speed toward the encampment. Humayun had recognized him even before he came into view. Khwaja Ibrahim had alighted from his horse with utmost haste, sprinting toward the throne with the speed of lightning.

"Your Majesty, Biram Khan sends a host of news and urgent messages." Khwaja Ibrahim curtsied jauntily, gasping for breath.

"Good news, the emperor hopes?" Humayun flashed him a searching look.

"All good news, Your Majesty, all happy news! But the urgent message—" Khwaja Ibrahim could not continue against the flood of impatience in emperor's eyes.

"Spill the good news first, my good soldier, urgent message can wait its own turn!" Humayun commanded with one imperious gesture of his arm.

"Nesib Khan has suffered ignominious defeat through the hands of Biram Khan, Your Majesty. Though Biram Khan sent the prisoners, including women and children, back to the vanquished foe, escorted by imperial guards. Jalandar is also under the rule of the imperialists, since the warring Afghans left after learning about our advancing troops under the command of Biram Khan. Then he marched to Machiwarah, where Tartar Khan opposed him with thirty thousand troops of his own, but the imperialists gained victory once again. Then Biram Khan marched straight toward Delhi, thinking that the road was clear. But as soon as he reached south-east of Sirhind, he learned that Sikander Shah with his army of eighty thousand is advancing their way to challenge the imperialists. Now Biram Khan is in Sirhind, Your Majesty. He has strengthened all the defenses, but implores reinforcements, for he says he cannot win this battle with Sikander Shah until more supplies of armaments and contingents of troops come to his assistance."

"If this illness had not drained the emperor's strength, he would fly to Biram's side right this moment." Humayun wiped the beads of sweat off his brow with a silk handkerchief, his gaze alighting on Prince Akbar who had edged closer along with other viziers. "You are the commander of ten thousand troops this very moment, my valorous Prince. Commence your march toward Sirhind this very evening, the emperor will send a letter with you to Biram." He waved dismissal.

Humayun had closed his eyes for one brief moment, feeling a wave of nausea and weakness in the very pit of his stomach. Not even noticing the sparkle of joy in Prince Akbar's eyes and his gallant curtsy, before he fled to obey the orders of the emperor. Bayazid, as commanded by the emperor, had settled down with his papers and feathered quill, waiting to catch the emperor's words in neat, bold strokes of his penmanship. The emperor, without opening his eyes, began in low, measured tones.

"Dear Biram—" Bayazid caught the first words of the missive, straining his ears not to miss a single expression escaping the emperor's lips. "Your stoutness of heart is as great, if not greater, than that of the Saiyed. The Great God is with us. Fear not the result of any encounter with the Afghans. An attack of colic compels me to rest in order to gain my strength back. I will join you as soon as I am fit to travel. May God give you victory. My faith in you is complete."

"Give this missive to Prince Akbar, Bayazid." Humayun opened his eyes, his look wearied and distraught. "And now, dear friends, leave the emperor. I intend to rest right here." He swept his gaze over the assembly of his viziers and courtiers, and closed his eyes again. "We might follow Prince Akbar tomorrow, depending upon the renewal of my health and resolve."

Two whole, grueling days of rest and preparation until Humayun had felt confident of his strength to march toward Sirhind. A few more days on the dusty roads, and the imperialists were already on the borders of Sirhind, planning a swift assault as soon as they espied the troops of Sikander Shah. On the way, a courier had brought a message from Biram Khan that Prince Akbar had arrived safe, and that they were engaging in a few skirmishes to keep the enemy at bay till the entire troops of the emperor could join them. The emperor, though pale and gaunt, was equipped with the daggers of resolve and strength to win back his lost empire, even if he was to perish in this struggle, welcoming death, not exile. He was flying like the king of nemesis, oblivious to the rent of loneliness inside him. This rent was swollen and abscessed, expanding and throbbing.

Joy in life! Pain in living? This life of joy and sorrow! What is the secret of one's greed to keep loving life in all these castles of sand, fashioned with the grains of hopes battered and dreams shattered? The fever of mysticism was coursing in Humayun's veins, even on this journey toward Hind, simmering in the wildfires of insurrections. *Why do I live? Or, did live, for the quest of truth? For the glitter of love and beauty? Still living, without truth? Without joy? For what? For the conquest of Hind alone? Would that mark the end of living, or would it breed a string of quests strange and mysterious?* He was becoming aware of the shadows of dusk, chasing the gold and crimson clouds over the very heads of his marching soldiers.

These little clouds painted bright with the streaks of sunset, were gathering larger clouds, dark and billowing. Under the galloping strides of the war horses, the pale, shimmering rays of dusk were being trampled, appealing to the impotent clouds above to come to their rescue. The whip of inevitability was goading Humayun to come to the rescue of his son and vizier who were exposed to the danger of annihilation by the mighty forces of Sikander Shah. So overwhelming was this need to shield and protect his son from all danger, that he was urging his horse to fly. And yet he had no need, not now at this precise moment, for he had espied the encampment of Sikander Shah. All his warring instincts, blunted by years of misfortunes, were now coming alive, sharp and inviolate.

Against the roar of the drums and trumpets, the imperialists were charging headlong into the files of the enemy. Humayun had commanded the right and left wing to surround the enemy on both sides before launching a full assault. The battle had barely commenced, when the rain in torrents came pouring down, followed by gusts of wind and storm. The rumbles of thunder so loud that it could swallow the fury of the cannon. The arrows of the imperialists were raining their fury over the heads of the enemy, their whistling flight checked here and there by the clanking of swords amidst this sea of the wounded and the unhorsed. The war elephants of Sikander Shah were frantic and raging, trampling to death their own friends and masters in this flood of chaos and confusion. The wind and the storm too were adding more confusion to the ranks of the enemy, their spirits heavy with despair.

It seemed like the blink of an eye, but this fierce fighting has lasted for more than two hours. Sikander Shah's troops were scattered pell-mell and fleeing amidst the stampede of their own rider-less horses and elephants. Humayun astride his horse and no foe to challenge was shuddering under some brief spell of disbelief and bewilderment. In the distance, he could see Prince Akbar unhorsing a rude assailant with one violent blow of his flashing sword. Biram Khan beside him was dealing severe injuries to another youth intent on fighting. Abul Maali was racing after someone in wild chase. Humayun, by the flash of gold cuirass on this fugitive could divine that this was no callow soldier but the proud foe himself, Sikander Shah.

The drums and trumpets of the imperialists were sounding victory tunes under the downpour of rain and storm. The slain and the wounded were left behind under the watch of one Moghul contingent, while the rest under the command of Humayun were marching on the road of victory toward the gates of Delhi. Prince Akbar and Biram Khan were riding beside the emperor. The sky had cleared, the face of livid moon peering from behind the lace of stars, cold and shivering. Higher and higher, the moon was waxing, much like a florescent lamp to light the way on homeward journey to the beloved gates of Delhi.

Another surprise on the streets of Delhi to welcome the emperor was melting Humayun's heart to tears of joy and gratitude. Rapture and bewilderment were there too, hovering over his shoulders, as he watched the tides of people streaming out on the streets to cheer him and his troops, much in the manner of reception he had received at Lahore. His fifteen years of exile were dissolved like tiny dewdrops against the warmth and sunshine in his eyes, his soul waxing up to the very chariot of stars, which was following the haughty moon with twinkling glee. Humayun's soul had torn its veil of hopelessness, it was fluttering and expanding. The emperor had come home! To stay! His destiny had mapped his destination on the soil of Hind.

Chapter Twenty-two
Exiled from the World

The essence of truth sinking deep down the marshland of lies! Could one see the face of light if the soul of darkness was missing? How could one know impurity, if purity did not exist? How could one distinguish one without the other? Evil from good, joy from grief, love from hate, peace from chaos, beauty from ugliness? How, in this cauldron of duality, one could separate the nectar of wisdom from the poison of ignorance? Humayun was thinking while enjoying the solitude of his palace gardens.

The red sandstone palace at Delhi with its gold domes and spiraling columns was looming in the distance like a forgotten dream, as Humayun kept sauntering in utter seclusion to his own reveries and ruminations. He was oblivious to the gold in sunshine and to the profusion of scent and humanity in the form of flowers and gardeners, who could be seen greeting him with mute reverence without splintering the peace and serenity of this glorious morning. The emperor himself was attired gloriously, the ochre silks on his royal person and a large diamond in his turban radiating gold and glitter to match the glowing colors in this garden, from the heart of the fountains to the hearth of the terraces. But the emperor's heart was sad and lonesome. The sense of time itself was moving at such a giddy speed since his swift victory at Sirhind that Humayun's senses were drunk with the sense of magic and mystery in this *cosmic whole* of living and striving. This was the first day after a string of many, many ambitious months that he was able to court this luxury of solitude. And sadness was the result of his sudden awareness that Prince Akbar was not with him to share his mental quests in the peace-loving capital of Delhi. The young prince was sent on a campaign to fight Sikander Shah, who had emerged once again as a belligerent foe to challenge the Moghuls. The emperor was missing his son, and yet his heart was longing for the nearness of Mah Chuchak.

Mah Chuchak is! Yes, the truth? The bride and the beloved! A revelation of truth, both holy and unholy. The flower of beauty and imperfection! Humayun's heart was aching all of a sudden, reaching out to the valleys in Kabul, than hugging the valleys of conquests in Hind. *Can one learn to love both evil and good, to acknowledge and understand one's faults, and to forgive the faults of the others?* His psyche was buzzing with the songs of revelations he had not ever heard before. *Light and truth! Am I blinded by it? Oh, this lamp of darkness! Where is my soul? Fleeing, fleeing. Why is it counting each breath of life outside the body and inside the ether of nonbeing? Measuring the pulse of time and timelessness?* The songs in his psyche were silent, looking down the rungs of time at the material gains.

A mound of victories and celebrations was unfolding its treasures inside the casket of Humayun's mind, though his gaze was chasing the white butterflies over the beds of ranunculus. The song and frolic of the fountains was fading in the distance, as he promenaded close to the palace gates, aware only of the solitary rhythm in his thoughts and ruminations. The victorious emperor, returning after fifteen years of exile, had become overnight, the idol of worship by the populace of Agra and Delhi. Prince Akbar was proclaimed the royal heir, invested with a robe of honor and a jeweled crown. Khutba was read in the emperor's name in all the mosques at Delhi and Agra, followed by a succession of feasts and celebrations. Alms were distributed to the poor, and gifts to the soldiers and generals. Though, the laurels of victory were heaped on Prince Akbar alone, since rift and jealousy between Biram Khan and Abul Maali as to the claim of victory had begun to sprout forth, tainting the mood of the festivities, both contending for the title of great valor for this great victory. So, Humayun had ended the dispute between these valorous viziers by choosing Prince Akbar as the neutral claimant of valor and victory. At the royal banquet, Biram Khan was appointed the guardian of Prince Akbar, and Abul Maali was favored to sit by the emperor as a mark of honor and friendship.

Abul Maali was sent in pursuit of Sikander Shah, who was reported to have taken refuge somewhere beyond the mountains of Sewalik. He was also made the governor of Hisar Firuza. A courier was dispatched to Kabul to announce the victory of Hind, and to arrange for the journey of the emperor's harem to the land of victory. Biram Khan was to retain the governorship of Kandahar, and Terdi Beg was to rule Mewat. The kingdom of Shambal was entrusted to the care of Kuli Sultan. A great number of ruling lords and Afghans,

318

upon learning of the emperor's victorious return, had flocked to Delhi to pledge their support and allegiance. The emperor had recovered most of the territories of his empire through voluntary alliances and pledges of fidelity and friendship. Amidst this flurry of goodwill and good fortune, Humayun had turned his attention to his cherished abode at Agra, Din Panah. During the emperor's exile, Sher Khan had added one octagonal chamber to Din Panah, naming it Sher Mandal to be used as a House of Worship. Within a few months after his victory as peace and discipline were restored in the empire, Humayun had ordered Sher Mandal to be converted into a vast library. This work was completed within a few weeks short of two months, and Humayun had arranged a great feast, inviting poets and scholars and pundits and mullahs to share their beliefs and talents. Din Panah had become a center of learning once again, hosting great discussions each week, and welcoming theologians regardless of their creed or religion.

The scent from champa and Chambeli was teasing Humayun's senses, as if breathing its rhythm into his solitary walk, but his thoughts were following Sikander Shah. Abul Maali had remained unsuccessful in his pursuit of Sikander Shah, declaring, that the chameleon-foe was swallowed by the mountains of Sewalik. But Sikander Shah was in hiding, gathering arms and alliances covertly, with the intention of challenging the rule and authority of the emperor. Recently, he had come out in the open, marching straight to the borders of the Punjab and inciting rebellion amongst the peaceful lords who had pledged allegiance to the emperor. So, Humayun had dispatched a considerable number of forces at the command of Prince Akbar to chastise the inveterate foe, and to prove himself worthy of throne and empire. Biram Khan, invested with the title of Khan-Khanan was accompanying the prince, and Abul Maali was to join them since the emperor had granted him this permission at his own request . At this recollection Humayun's sadness was carving a gulf of rifts and dissentions within his soul and psyche. He was also becoming aware of the red berries crushed under his shoes with gold pointed toes, leaving purple stains on the red dust. His feet were coming to a standstill. For a moment, he stood inert, contemplating the army of ants, intent on gathering nectar from the crushed berries, before retracing his steps toward his palace, listening to the silence in his soul.

Even rotten fruits are fit to offer a royal feast to the ants! Nothing goes waste in this house of nature? Earth itself a royal kitchen to feed and nourish all, from lowly insects to the mighty kings blessed with riches and power. All feeding on each other and all fed to the furnace of death? Ants eating the fruits of this earth and birds feeding on ants. Animals killing the birds, men slaughtering the animals? All succumbing to death in this symphony of survival and surcease. Where does this life come from? What makes this life a living, breathing cauldron of needs and greeds? Breath! The mysterious, throbbing pulse of time, pouring breath into the tiniest of insects with as subtle a passion as into the lungs of the thinking, aspiring animals called men-beasts. His quiet ruminations were breathing dissent at the sudden approach of Khwaja Khizr, as if he had materialized from the fabric of very sunshine.

"Your Majesty." Khwaja Khizr curtsied low, the red plume in his turban a blaze of fire. "The courtiers are waiting for the emperor to preside over the court."

"No courts are to be in session this glorious day. Can't you sense this throb of riot and glee in the very eyes of nature?" Humayun declared with a sudden animation. "How feeble is the memory of our courtiers? Didn't the emperor announce in the morning that we are to watch the rising of Venus this evening at Din Panah? And to honor Venus, the emperor has canceled all engagements, didn't he?" He strode past him, resuming his leisurely stroll.

"We all remember your earlier commands, Your Majesty, but this is no real court session." Khwaja Khizr followed the emperor at a respectable distance. "Just this morning, several pilgrims returned from Mecca, and a few emissaries from Kabul also arrived. A messenger from Prince Akbar too. All suing for your audience, Your Majesty, and courtiers are anxious to gather all news in one court session."

"To catch even a whiff of news from the lips of his son, the emperor would revoke all his earlier commands!" Humayun's pace was accelerating, his laughter trailing behind him.

The Audience Hall with its gilt pillars and decked with gold umbrellas from Gujrat, was hosting a motley of viziers, courtiers and emissaries. Humayun seated on his jeweled throne under the canopy, dripping with European brocade and Portuguese silk, was listening to Hasan Akhteh, the messenger from Prince Akbar.

"Prince Akbar, Your Majesty, doesn't trust Abul Maali." Hasan Akhteh was recounting rather reluctantly. "He trusts Biram Khan though, who suggested that they march to Sultanpur. From there, they plan to journey to Kalinjar through the city of Hariana. Sikander Shah is in Kalinjar, inciting all our allies to sedition against the imperial rule, and Prince Akbar is intent on defeating and capturing this enemy."

"May God grant my son this victory and victory over all for the peace and glory of Hind." Humayun smiled, his look profound and thoughtful. "I have had disturbing news concerning Abul Maali, but didn't know Prince Akbar distrusted him? What has Abul Maali gained during this past one and a half year, besides vain judgments and perpetual failures?" He appeared to question his own convictions.

"Nothing, Your Majesty. Distrust and disesteem from all, I hear. He has earned the reputation of a tyrant, that's all." Hasan Akhteh began cautiously. "When he was returning from his unsuccessful mission in not finding Sikander Shah, he arrested several men, subjecting them to torture and humiliation for any scrap of information about the fugitive enemy. They are still in his captivity, locked up somewhere, I have heard."

"Captives!" One thunder of an exclamation escaped Humayun's lips. "He was here when I issued a Farman that the emperor would allow no man, who are servants of God, to be made captives of men?" The bolts of disbelief were alighting in his eyes. "And is this man of captives now in Sultanpur?"

"Yes, Your Majesty." Hasan Akhteh smiled enigmatically.

"And why are you smiling, you Heathen?" Humayun demanded.

"Pardon me, Your Majesty. I was remembering—well. Prince Akbar showed his disfavor to Abul Maali in a subtle way, and the tyrant was humbled, if not incensed." Hasan Akhteh breathed mysteriously, his look contrite.

"Tell us all, you master of Brevity! Are you trying the emperor's patience?" Humayun commanded.

"Abul Maali, Your Majesty, after his unsuccessful attempt to capture Sikander Shah had returned to Sultanpur." Hasan Akhteh obeyed promptly, all the light of mystery and reluctance fading from his eyes. "Prince Akbar received him courteously, but didn't offer him the seat of honor at the dinner table. After dinner, Abul Maali retired to his home since he owns one on the outskirts of Sultanpur. He must have felt slighted, for he sent a long letter to Prince Akbar in the morning. *Your Highness, I am hurt beyond words. Your Highness is well aware of the esteem in which I am held by His Majesty the emperor. At the banquet held in my honor at Lahore, the emperor did me the honor of seating me by his side. The humiliation inflicted upon me last night in the presence of the viziers much junior to my rank saddened my heart. My services to you and your respected father have been marked by devotion and selflessness. His Majesty, I am sure, will bear me out in this contention. I would, therefore, request Your Highness to let me know the indiscretions I may have unwittingly committed to deserve a fall from your grace. I take this opportunity to assure Your Highness of my loyalty till eternity.* Prince Akbar sent him this brief reply. *Your representation has been considered. I find little substance therein. You will agree that a line has to be drawn between the laws of the state and personal equations. Anyway, my relations with you stand on a footing different from that of the emperor. The rules of protocol were strictly observed at the banquet. You should have no cause for offense. This view is fully shared by my Khan-Khanan.*"

"The wisdom of Babur speaks through the lips of my son! He will be a wise and just emperor when the time comes." One sprig of a prophecy escaped Humayun's lips. He dismissed Hasan Akhteh laughingly, his gaze turning to Khwaja Ibrahim. "What do you think, Khwaja, isn't my son scattering the pearls of wisdom, while the emperor is merely gathering the pebbles in laws designed by prudent Sher Khan himself? No doubt, his methods of provincial government and revenue collection were superb! No need to discuss that now, since I am most anxious to hear about the journey of my harem. Have they left Kabul yet? Are they close to the very gates of Delhi?" His gaze was lit up with the stars of mockery.

"Not quite, Your Majesty." Khwaja Ibrahim protested happily.

"The emperor may not live to welcome them to Hind?" Another sprig of a prophecy escaped Humayun's lips, his eyes lit up with Sufic light. "We are celebrating the rising of Venus this evening, as you all know, but before we journey to Agra, the emperor wishes to share his dream with you all." He let his gaze sweep over all with a burning intensity. "To think of it now, it was not a dream, but a vision. I was wide awake. After my morning prayers, while still kneeling, I felt a presence. A strong, throbbing presence behind me! Yet, I could see the play of light and shadow all around me. That presence whispering in a most tender voice.

O Lord, of thine infinite goodness make me thine own
Make me a partaker of the knowledge of Thy attributes
I am broken-hearted from the cares of sorrows of life
O call thee Thy poor madman
O grant my release.

Strange words and strange presence." He got to his feet, his gaze searching. "The Turkish Admiral, Sayed Ali is not here yet, I can see. We must prepare for our journey to Din Panah. When Sayed Ali gets here, conduct him to Din Panah with all due respect and ceremony. He must meet all the lovers of arts and sciences in our asylum of faith, besides the madmen as philosophers and theologians." He smiled, floating past the sea of courtiers as if sleep-walking.

Sher Mandal, inside the heart of Din Panah, was already brimming with the wine of music and poetry even before the emperor could arrive in Agra to indulge in his all-time love for theology and astronomy. It was almost dusk when Humayun arrived at Din Panah. Mounting the narrow staircase up to Sher Mandal, he could see yellow finches and pigeons circling above the ornamental parapet. At the last step, Humayun paused, admiring the white domes and slender minarets of the grand mosque across from Din Panah. In a flash, he was inside the octagonal hall, aiming for his gilded seat amidst the din of laughter and arguments. At Din Panah, the fetters of etiquette were removed by the express command of the emperor, so anyone were at liberty to do or say whatever they pleased, even ignoring the emperor if that was their pleasure. Amidst the sea of color with turbans bobbing up and down, Humayun wended his way to his seat without any interruption. Heaving a sigh of relief, he abandoned himself on his chair, catching snippets of recitation and versification.

"Hurt not others in ways that you yourself would find hurtful." One Buddhist monk in saffron robes was quoting from the book of Udanavarga.

"This is the sum of duty: Do not unto others which would cause you pain if done to you." A Brahman with shaved head was reciting from the holy book of Mahabharata.

"What is hateful to you, do not to your fellow man. That is the entire Law; all the rest is commentary." One Jewish scholar was reciting.

"Do unto others as you would have them do unto you." Someone was quoting from the Bible.

"No one of you is a believer until he desires for his brethren that which he desires for himself." Sayed Ali, the Turkish Admiral, was singing passionately, as if he was the author of the Sunnah and Quran both.

"That nature alone is good which refrains from doing unto another whatsoever is not good for itself." The voice of one Parsi was booming loud and clear.

As the grains of truth and wisdom were being whirled around in a hurricane of words, Humayun's thoughts were blocking out the voices, and losing themselves into the silence of introspection. His mind was plucking out stars from the heavens and affixing them on the pages inside his book of astronomy. He could feel the light of love and peace within him, as if his heart was unfolding its wings to sail beyond the clouds of ether and nothingness. His soul was light as a feather, white and luminescent. Why was he feeling so giddy and at peace, his thoughts were standing aghast, murmuring disbelief and demanding answers.

What answers? Have you not drunk deep of nothingness out of everything? Humayun's psyche itself was assuming the role of an arbiter. *Are wisdom and knowledge not illusions? Only the spool of uncertainty one continual string of reality! What is truth, you ask? It is love. My heart knows it. It's in me, in you, in everyone. What happened to your quest for God? It is over, God is love. Love opens the doors to understanding, can't you see. Mah Chuchak is truth. She is love and beauty, revealing the essence of God in each and every one of us, do you see it? Why do you look appalled? Can't you feel the pulse of God in every throb of life? Listen, be silent.* His features were bathed in sunlight, voices penetrating his inner sanctuary.

Truth with all its lies and ugliness, is still the virgin lily of Knowledge, growing inside the mud of Wisdom— The profile of the speaker was dark and passionate.

Truth is Wisdom! If we could notice the roses sleeping on the bed of thorns, perfumed and peaceful, revealing love and beauty? Only the arrows of vulgarity in our minds uproot the bed of wisdom, hurling truth against the face of ignorance—

Truth is the wine of enlightenment! We are forbidden to drink this nectar. The pure, white light of the soul concealed from the unholy sight of the mortals. With our limited intellect, how could we reach the Throne of God? This blinding, dazzling light if one was to see, still courting ignorance and mistaking the glitter of gold in wisdom as reality—

What a strange world it is? A potpourri of beliefs, all sprinkled with parables, all knowing only One? If you stumble upon this verse from the Quran, don't just get nailed to the floor, fly on the wings of your heart and explore.

How disbelieve ye in Allah when ye were dead and He gave life to you. Then He will give you death, then life again, and then unto Him you will return.

Oh, Venus! Venus, the blue-eyed goddess of Libra and Taurus. Come to our assistance. Solve these riddles of—

Venus! Your goddess of love and beauty has green eyes. Her locks are coppery and her face bronzed.

Why not invoke Al Hamal? The first constellation, Aries? The scent of anemone, hawthorn, sweet peas?

Humayun's own mind was whirling like an astronomical globe, shooting stars of fate into the very abyss of dreams. His eyes were lit up with the fire of dreams, yet his heart was plunged in utter darkness. His soul was singing, but this was the song of a swan. Her last song of life, reaching up to the heavens in throes of agony and rapture. Humayun could feel his soul expanding. The fluttering of heart and the flapping of wings inside him were making him giddy, and before they could overwhelm him, his gaze itself was making Terdi Beg captive.

"Now that the Sher Mandal is converted into a great library, the emperor is dissatisfied. We would convert it into a great observatory. What do you say, Terdi Beg? Would you like to be the architect of this great observatory?" Humayun's eyes were flashing commands than suggestions.

"Yes, Your Majesty." Terdi Beg murmured. The vision of glory in future reflected in his eyes.

"Sher Mandal will match the glory of Ulugh Beg's observatory in Samarkand, yes! And you will be its architect."

Humayun demurred aloud, his thoughts communing with the spirit of his father.

"The plan of such an observatory is twinkling in my head, Your Majesty!" Was Terdi Beg's ecstatic response. "I would fly to the heavens and fetch all stars to light Sher Mandal with the lamps of astronomy!"

"Flying against time, and saving the pitcher from falling." Humayun laughed.

"Pardon my ignorance, Your Majesty, but I don't know what that means?" Terdi Beg's vision of glory was fading in his eyes.

"Legends and miracles, my besotted vizier! How come you never heard about the Prophet's mythical journey to the heavens on a horse called Buraq? Though, it was no Buraq, but the angel Gabriel, as many believe?" Humayun's eyes were lit up with amusement.

"Don't know, Your Majesty. Many war stories in my head though." Terdi Beg murmured regretfully.

"If you were not afflicted with the fever of ignorance, my brave warrior, you could hear the reeds whispering the songs of magic and mystery. Even envision the Night Journey of the Prophet, perhaps?" Humayun chided, reciting this Quranic verse with a sudden wistfulness.

"The Night Journey
Glory be to Him
Who carried His servant by Night
From the sacred temple of Mecca
To the temple that is Remote
Whose precinct We have blessed
That We might show him of Our signs
For He is the Hearer and the Seer."

"If you could save me from this pit of ignorance, Your Majesty, I would become the humblest of your slaves! The Prophet and the Pitcher, the words are familiar, but I don't know the story?" Terdi Beg's eyes were appealing devotedly.

"No pit of ignorance is that deep that one can't come to the surface once awhile to have a peek at the ocean of wisdom. And yet, it is not deep enough to accommodate all the fools in this world, stumbling along dark paths to find the lamp of enlightenment?" Humayun contemplated to himself. "And yet the emperor is in a mood to refresh his own memory, as well as to whet your appetite for myth and beauty. That mythical journey starts with the archangel,

Gabriel, being the messenger of love and prophecy. One of the Gabriel's wings had landed on the pitcher of water by the bedside of the Prophet. The pitcher was tilted to one side, making a gurgling sound and awakening the Prophet from his sleep. Then the Prophet was lifted upon the wings of Gabriel, making a swift journey to the heavens, communing with all the other prophets and talking with God Almighty Himself. The Throne of God was left behind, and the Prophet had returned home to catch the pitcher from falling. Not a drop of water was spilt, as if this journey sublime to the heavens and back was completed in one fraction of a moment."

"Such a beautiful journey, Your Majesty! Are there no more prophets to guide us in this age and time, Your Majesty? My heart is moved to—"

Terdi Beg was spilling a string of emotions, but the emperor had ceased to heed. His senses were absorbing the beauty of a verse, recited by Said Ali.

"On the flimsy strings
Of hope we dance
Listening
Softly, softly
Very softly
Battered hopes
Weeping willows
Melodies grieving
In dreams
Dark, abysmal
Songs and shadows
Singing and lowering
Moonbeams of gold
Death and renewal
Lullabies profound."

Said Ali was swaying under some spell of swoon and inspiration.

"God! How exquisite is the tongue of poetry and inspiration, snatched out of my very own soul? Blessed is Said Ali." Humayun applauded passionately.

All eyes were turning to Said Ali, the flames of envy and admiration in them leaping toward the poet. Cheers and applause were exploding forth in one thunderous fury, and Sher Mandal was swollen with the echo of mirth. So great was this ocean of fervor

327

and excitement that no one had noticed the emperor slipping out on to the small balcony with the staircase winding down in contours soft and seductive.

Humayun, standing there alone, appeared to be seduced by the beauty of the peace-loving heavens above. His gaze was kissing the white, luminous face of Venus, his heart aching for the light of love and beauty. He could hear his soul expanding and shuddering, blinded by its own radiance of purity and innocence. Venus was holding out her arms, as if longing to crush his soul in one everlasting embrace.

"Allah-hu-Akbar. Allah-hu-Akbar." The muezzin's call to prayer was escaping the white minarets of the mosque, and entering the stark purity of Humayun's soul.

Startled out of his grand reveries, Humayun's knees and thoughts were bending low to pay homage to the God of love and beauty. He was making this staircase the prayer-rug of his devotion, bending before his own soul against the dazzling downpour of light from the eyes of his beloved. His heart was empty and luminous, drinking light upon light and so profound was the agony of his spiritual thirst that he didn't even know that his foot had slipped and he was tumbling down into the vortex of death and surcease.

The emperor was lying in one saffron heap on the marble floor, his head crushed between his knees, and blood spluttering from his left ear with the fury of a volcano. The cries of fear and alarm were silenced, as the emperor was being carried back into the sanctuary of Din Panah. Humayun's soul was hovering above, rapt and sightless, awaiting the rites of bliss and union.

The beloved son was united with his beloved father. Humayun had breathed his last at the feet of Babur, the viziers were murmuring and sobbing. They had heard the emperor whisper Babur's name twice before his lips were sealed with the balm of surcease. Prince Akbar, another whisper was the echo of fear from the hearts of all present, who could see the prince waging war with fates at the ransom of his own life. *Another beloved son?*

Bibliography

- The History and Culture of Indian People by R. C. Majumdar. Bhaharatiya Vidya Bhavan 1994
- The Lives and Times of the Great Mughals by Abrahm Early. Viking 199 Humayun Nama translated by Annette Beveridge. Sang-E-Meel publications 1987
- India and the Mughal Dynasty. Discoveries Series. Harry N. Abrams Inc. 1976
- The Koh-i-noor Diamond by Iradj Amini. Roli Books 1994
- Mediaeval India under Mohammedan Rule by Stanley Lane-Poole. Low Price Publications 1903
- History of India from the Earliest Times to the Present Day by Sir George Dunbar. Low Price Publications 1936
- The Moughal Empire by A. L. Srivastava. Shiva Lal Agarwala & Company 1952
- The Mughul Empire by R.C. Majumdar; J. N. Chaudhuri; S. Chaudhuri. Bhaharatiya Vidya
- Bhavan 1994
- India and the Mughal Dynasty. Discoveries Series. Harry N. Abrams Inc. 1976
- The History and Culture of Indian People by R. C. Majumdar. Bhaharatiya Vidya Bhavan 1994
- The Lives and Times of the Great Mughals by Abrahm Early. Viking 1997

www.ingramcontent.com/pod-product-compliance
Lightning Source LLC
Chambersburg PA
CBHW060945030726
47503CB00003B/734